Augustina

ALSO BY REBECCA BELLISTON

Sadie

Heart of Red, Blood of Blue

The Citizens of Logan Pond Trilogy

SEQUEL TO SADIE

Augustina

a novel by

REBECCA BELLISTON

Gated Publishing

To Michael, Laura, Andrew,

Katelynn, and Jacob

You will always be my favorite characters

Gated Publishing
rebeccabelliston.com

ISBN: 978-1490453958

This work is a work of fiction. The characters, names, incidents, and dialogue are
products of the author's imagination and are not to be construed as real,
and any resemblance to real people and events is unintentional.

CHAPTER 1

The funeral of Sarah Augustina Dawson was held on a Thursday in the church her mother attended for thirty-five years.

Every pew was filled with friends, coworkers, and tear-stained loved ones overcome with grief. Sadie's brother, Damien, was there from California, plus an aunt and uncle from Minnesota. Even Sadie's long-forgotten father came with his wife.

The ceremony was supposed to be short, and maybe it was, but it felt like the longest hour of Josh Young's life. Thankfully the pastor never used the word suicide, nor did the obituary in Kalispell's newspaper. Instead, the pastor focused on the happy things in Sadie's life: her love of music, her love of laughter, and most especially her devotion to her family.

As Josh listened, he kept his eyes on the large portrait of Sadie up front. It was a gorgeous picture of her—as if she was capable of anything less—showing off her captivating smile, her dark curly hair, smooth olive skin, and a set of eyes surrounded by the most beguiling lashes known to man. No one questioned why her beautiful portrait replaced a coffin. Ironically, the fire in Sam's cabin simplified many things. No casket or body meant no viewing or grave. It was a blessing to have things turn out so easily on this end. Everything else would be hard enough. Especially for Sadie's mom.

Ten rows up Marcela Dawson blew her nose.

Josh glanced sideways, wondering what his new bodyguard would do if he tried to move up there. Between Deputy Harrison's U.S. Marshal training and his linebacker body, Josh wouldn't get far. Besides, the last thing Marcela needed was a scene.

Frustrated, Josh sat back. The pastor was stuck somewhere in the Gospels, seemingly content to drag out the mock funeral all day.

Marcela's crying picked up volume. Though Sadie's mom was supposed to put on a show today, Josh had no doubt those tears were real. Saying goodbye to a daughter—even if temporarily—was never easy, but Sadie and her mom were especially close, talking on the phone every day. Yet until Sadie's ex-boyfriend, Guillermo, was found, caught, and brought to justice, the Dawson women would have absolutely no contact. No phone calls or texts. No online chats. Nothing. Josh admired Marcela's resolve. She was more than willing to endure pain and loneliness if it meant she could keep her only daughter safe.

Safe.

Josh's skin crawled.

He scanned the sea of mourners. Special Agent Bruce Madsen, the FBI agent running the show, expected Guillermo to have men in the church to verify Sadie's death. Guillermo Vasquez had eyes and ears in every corner of Montana these days. As a precaution, Agent Madsen flooded the church with several of his agents plus a fleet of U.S. Marshals like the one next to Josh. No one in the congregation stood out to Josh, but knowing Guillermo's men could be checking on things was a disturbing reminder of how close they'd come to a real funeral for Sadie today.

Too close.

Too many times.

Josh's mind began filling with dark images: burnt-down cabins, Sadie's ashen face in the snow, and Guillermo's raging fist. He blinked hard and focused on her smiling portrait, silently praying the 'death' of Sarah Augustina Dawson was the death of Guillermo's revenge. At least on the Dawson family.

Josh was supposedly a walking target.

However, Josh didn't think Guillermo would carry through with those threats. Josh was a nobody. Plus with the FBI hot on Guillermo's tail, the sleek Venezuelan had plenty to worry about. He wasn't even in the country for all they knew. Josh was the last thing on Guillermo's mind.

He hoped.

He scratched his week-old beard and his knee started bouncing.

A redhead on the other side of him shot him a look as if to say, *Who are you, and what is your problem?*

She was one of Sadie's many friends Josh sat with. Deputy Harrison placed him there on purpose hoping Josh would blend in with the twenty-something group. While Josh might blend in, Deputy Harrison had to be pushing forty.

Josh forced his bouncing knee to go slack and wondered if he'd ever get to meet Sadie's friends and family under normal circumstances—or if they'd recognize him when he did. He barely recognized himself. Thankfully his bleached-blond hair was only temporary. As was the matching itchy beard, brown contacts, and linebacker-sized bodyguard. And with any luck...all the lies.

He glanced down. The ring on his left hand felt more foreign than the rest of his disguise, but that would last long after his hair was dyed dark again. Though Josh and Sadie had never talked marriage—technically they'd never been on a date before—there were parts of this new identity he wouldn't mind too much.

Mr. and Mrs. Josh Peterson.

Josh twisted the ring around and around as Marcela's crying picked up volume. So much for a short funeral.

Kevin, Trevor, and Sam got the better deal today. They were with Sadie in the nursing home, entertaining her and hopefully keeping her mind off the funeral. Between night boarding, roasting marshmallows, and making fun of Trevor's hair over Christmas break, Sadie had become part of their group. It was awesome. Josh smiled, momentarily forgetting his morbid surroundings. It was very awesome. But only he and Sadie were heading to Mississippi, and his buddies wanted to spend their last few hours with her instead of enduring a pointlessly-long funeral.

Even better, Josh's parents were with Sadie, too. Not only did they want to get to know Josh's new girlfriend, but they brought Josh's stuff from Spokane since he hadn't been home since the fire at Sam's cabin—and wouldn't be returning home for who knew how long. If only the pastor would quit talking, Josh could get a decent goodbye with his parents and buddies.

Ironically the only goodbye he wouldn't get was with Sadie's mom. He'd been finalizing plans with Agent Madsen when Marcela left last night. Josh craned his neck to see her. Her hands covered her face as the tears continued to flow. Josh was sorely tempted to sneak up there.

"Don't even think about it," Deputy Harrison whispered without looking away from the pastor. "You have orders."

Josh nearly rolled his eyes, but Agent Madsen's lecture from this morning filled his mind.

"Don't speak to anyone at the funeral," Madsen had said. *"Marcela most of all."*

To which Sadie had quickly jumped in. *"It's the only way I'm letting you go, Josh. Guillermo can't know you're there. Seriously. Don't look at or talk to anyone—especially my family. Otherwise, the deal's off."*

Whatever Guillermo said to Sadie in the back of that Mercedes had her paranoid.

"Why do you have to go to the funeral anyway?" Sadie said. *"Your parents and the guys want time to say goodbye to us."*

Josh couldn't explain why other than he needed to see, he needed to hear, and he needed to make sure this funeral was as real as real could be. All he told Sadie was that he wanted to make sure her mom was okay. Marcela didn't sound okay. Her sobs echoed through the church.

Frustrated, he shifted in his seat. That earned him another strange look from Sadie's redheaded friend.

The one bright spot in everything was Damien who sat with an arm around Marcela. Sadie's brother was one of the few people in the church who knew the truth about Sadie and how carefully the FBI was guarding their key witness in the murder of FBI Agent Dubois. The original plan was to pack up Marcela and let her disappear with Josh and Sadie in the backwoods of Mississippi and the Witness Security Program. But Guillermo would have grown suspicious if Sadie's mom disappeared. He'd go searching. That meant leaving Marcela behind, which didn't sit well with anyone. But then Damien not only quit his job in San Diego, but volunteered to move into Marcela's apartment in Kalispell. Twenty-four hour surveillance that wouldn't arouse suspicion from Guillermo. Just a concerned son coming home to console his grieving mother. Damien was a godsend.

Miracle of miracles, the pastor finally announced the closing hymn, "Be Thou My Vision."

Josh bit back another smile, remembering how Sadie fretted over her own funeral.

"The music has to be perfect," she had said. *"Especially the last song. It tells people how to feel going forward."*

Josh still couldn't believe he found someone who loved music as much as he did. But when she showed him the closing song, he'd never heard of it. She smiled her radiant smile then—the one that made Josh wonder how a girl like her ever looked at a guy like him.

"It's gorgeous," she said. *"It's been one of my favorites since I was a little girl. I know you'll love it—if I let you go."*

He was already determined to go but he had said, *"I think you better sing it for me in case I don't. Otherwise, I'll never get to hear it."*

Though it took a little coaxing, he was grateful he pressed because as the congregation started singing, Sadie's beautiful voice filled his mind instead, quickly making it his new favorite hymn as well.

Be Thou my vision, O Lord of my heart;
Naught be all else to me, save that Thou art.
Thou my best thought, by day or by night,
Waking or sleeping, Thy presence my light.

Be Thou my battle shield, sword for the fight;
Be Thou my dignity, Thou my delight;
Thou my soul's shelter, Thou my high tower:
Raise Thou me heavenward, O Power of my power.

High King of Heaven, my victory won,
May I reach heaven's joys, O bright Heaven's Sun!
Heart of my own heart, whatever befall,
Still be my vision, O Ruler of all.

As Josh finished singing with the congregation, the lyrics became his silent prayer. *Be Thou my vision, Thy presence my light.* Joshua David Young, a man who planned out his entire life out at the age of five, was suddenly leaving his last semester of undergrad, his family, his three best friends, and the entire Pacific Northwest for the unknown. Had he not been absolutely certain it was the right path, he might be overwhelmed. As it was, he prayed for God's watch and guidance over him and Sadie in leaving and for those left behind.

Whatever befall, he repeated silently, *Still be my vision, O Ruler of all.*

And then it was done.

Damien helped Marcela to her feet as row by row was dismissed. People dressed in black stopped just shy of the door to offer their final condolences. Damien shook their hands first, and then person after person fell into Marcela's arms.

Josh filed out of the pew behind the redhead, realizing he might get that goodbye with Marcela after all. He just had to be discreet.

As they neared the front, Deputy Harrison leaned close and whispered, "Don't linger."

Josh nodded. He shook Damien's hand first and tried to communicate with his eyes what he couldn't say. Josh only met Damien a few days earlier but already liked him. Damien reminded him of his quirky friends, a mix of Kevin and Sam.

Then Josh turned.

From the looks of it, Marcela hadn't stopped crying since she left last night. She shook Josh's hand as ritual demanded before she looked up. Her swollen eyes widened in sudden recognition.

"You came?" she whispered.

Josh couldn't think of a single thing to say—or at least that he was allowed to say—so instead he opened his arms. Marcela fell into them as more tears erupted.

Deputy Harrison shot Josh a dark look which he ignored. A hug was well within the realm of acceptable funeral behavior. Agent Madsen could have no complaints.

Josh whispered in her ear, "You hanging in there?"

"Barely," Marcela squeaked. "How is she?"

Deputy Harrison grunted a warning so Josh shortened his answer. "Strong. Like you." Then he released Marcela and cleared his throat. "I'm sorry for your loss, Mrs. Dawson," he added more formally.

"Thank you...uh..." Her brows furrowed, too distraught to remember his temporary name.

"David," Josh said. "I know it's hard, but you'll get through this. And I'm sure"—he closed his eyes, willing the words to be true—"I'll see you soon."

He squeezed her hand one last time and moved toward the doors. It wasn't a perfect goodbye, but it was more than he hoped.

"Wait!" She grabbed his suit coat. "You can't go. Not yet. Please! Just another minute. I'm not ready."

Josh stopped. Marcela wore the same expression she had a week ago—the same expression *he'd* worn a week ago—as they waited for news of Sadie's whereabouts. Josh and Marcela had been through the war and back, and he couldn't leave her like that. Not now.

Shrugging at his bodyguard, he stepped behind Marcela and Damien, staying in the shadows while the church cleared out.

The look Harrison shot him could have split hairs. Josh knew he was going to hear about this later from the U.S. Marshal, Agent Madsen, *and* Sadie, but Deputy Harrison couldn't make a scene. He was forced to step beside Josh, hand discreetly on the gun inside his suit jacket as he scanned each person coming through the line.

Even though Josh stood to the side, a few people still stopped to shake his hand. He couldn't exactly ignore them. People wanted to talk to anyone, even a stranger, to make sense of Sadie's sudden "death." Names she mentioned in passing became real people overcome with grief. All of them dismissed him without a thought, too overwhelmed to realize he was introducing himself as his long-deceased grandfather.

"Hi, I'm David Peterson," he said to the next person.

The man could barely tear his eyes away from his wife falling apart on Marcela's shoulder. "I'm Martin. Sadie's uncle."

Josh's eyes widened. *Uncle Martin?* Martin was the BYU football fan and member of Josh's Mormon religion. Josh was desperate to pull Martin aside and ask about his and his wife's conversion—and Sadie's unfettered willingness to join as well—but Josh was forced to offer a simple, "I'm sorry for your loss, Martin."

Deputy Harrison caught Josh's eye and motioned to the door. The U.S. Marshal looked like a caged animal. Part of Josh was eager to leave as well, feeling his time with his parents and friends slipping away. He and Sadie had a four o'clock flight out of Missoula. But then he heard what Sadie's aunt said to Marcela, and suddenly he couldn't move.

"Where is Guillermo?" her aunt asked, dabbing her eyes with a tissue. "Augustina spoke so highly of him. I've been waiting to meet the man that captured my niece's heart. He must be so *angustiado.*"

Josh's blood boiled. It wasn't Aunt Silvina's fault, but having anyone mention Guillermo at a time like this was nauseating. Guillermo was the reason Sadie disappeared after Christmas, the reason she disappeared again a week ago, and the reason she was disappearing for a third time. Guillermo and Guillermo alone was the sole reason Marcela's olive cheeks had been tear-stained since Christmas, yet without missing a beat, Marcela gave the reply Agent Madsen suggested.

"I am afraid Guillermo wasn't able to attend today. He and Augustina broke up recently, but he is aware of"—Marcela cleared her throat—"what happened. He was even kind enough to send his sympathies."

And Guillermo had.

Just yesterday, Marcela received a bouquet of white roses with a card saying he'd *"heard about Augustina's untimely death."* That he felt a *"deep sadness at losing such a wonderful creature."* The ease of his words and quickness of his response showed his utter confidence in his plan. Not only had he silenced the only witness to Agent Dubois' murder, but he'd made Sadie's death look like a suicide. However, Guillermo mentioned he was out of the country and unable to attend her funeral. *"But I shall be there in spirit."*

"Or, in other words," Agent Madsen had explained, *"he'll have spirits there for him, so make it convincing."*

The note didn't mention his multi-million dollar cabin, or the fires that destroyed it and Sam's, but Agent Madsen warned Marcela she might hear from his lawyers soon since Sadie was the supposed arson of both fires before her "suicide." As if Josh needed another reason to loathe that man.

But the card was a stark reminder. Wherever Guillermo ran, whatever hole he found to hide in, he was keeping tabs on things—on Marcela.

It was another minute before Josh cooled down enough to focus on his surroundings. By then, Sadie's aunt and uncle were gone and only a few stragglers remained.

Another woman approached him, hand outstretched. He shook her hand. "Hi. I'm David Peterso…"

His voice trailed off. It was the redhead he'd sat next to during the funeral, only Josh had already followed her through the line. For some reason, she was back, looking up at him in an eerie, hair-raising way.

"Hi Da-vid," she said, drawing his temporary name out a little too long. "I'm sorry for your loss, but I, um…" She looked around and moved in close. "I like your new beard."

Josh felt the blood drain from his face. "What?"

"The color is perfect," she whispered. "Sadie would have loved it."

Josh stared at the redhead, heart thrumming.

"I'm supposed to give you something," she said, digging through her purse. "It's from some guy outside that—Wait," she interrupted herself. "What is this?"

Time slowed as Josh watched her pull an object from her purse. It was small, black, and looked an awful lot like a—

Deputy Harrison leaped forward. "Gun!"

He shoved Josh aside. Josh flew into Marcela, sending them both sprawling as a dozen agents jumped the girl.

CHAPTER 2

Sadie glanced up at the clock. The funeral should be over by now. She was anxious to get Josh's report on how her mom did, plus Damien and everyone who ever meant anything to her. It seemed cruel to drag them through a fake funeral. If she wasn't convinced it would protect her mom, she would have never agreed.

Agent Madsen sat in a dark corner of her nursing home room that served as her recovery place. He was going over a stack of paperwork with Deputy Croff, Sadie's new bodyguard. Madsen didn't seem bothered by the time. Sadie took a deep breath and tried to relax.

"Hold still, girl," Trevor said.

"Sorry." Sadie straightened her leg, struggling to hold up her heavily casted foot. "What are you writing anyway? A novel?"

Grinning, Trevor swirled the permanent marker as he finished. Sadie bent her leg to read his message on her cast.

Don't think this gets you out of snowboarding—Stud Man

She laughed. Not hard, but it stabbed her three broken ribs. Rookie move. Laughing was for lying flat in bed. She knew that. But between the neon green cast—Josh's idea—and Trevor's message, she was stuck thinking about a frigid night and a bright green snow beast.

Night boarding with the boys.

She pushed herself up in the chair to find a comfortable position. "I don't think there's any snowboarding in Mississippi, Trevor. Or snow, thankfully."

"No snow?" Kevin said. "What are you gonna do, Ice Woman?"

After two days of freezing—literally—in the Montana snow, that was the best part of going south. "Sip lemonade and work on my tan. How did you get that nickname anyway, Trevor? Stud man? Really?"

Trevor jerked back. "What else would you call me?"

Sadie was more careful when she laughed the second time. It still killed. Stupid ribs.

With a roll of the eyes, Kevin grabbed the marker from Trevor. She held up her foot again. Though it might have been a little juvenile to have them sign her neon green cast, she was thrilled to have a piece of her friends to take with her to Mississippi, personality included.

"How am I supposed to sign your cast?" Sam asked from the small screen in her hand. He wanted to come back and say goodbye as well, but he was in over his head in medical school in California. He'd already missed the first few days of the semester when Sadie went missing and his family's cabin burned to the ground. She refused to let him miss any more school.

Her foot grew heavy while she tried to think of something. The video chat was nice, but she wouldn't be taking the phone with her either.

"No worries," Kevin said. "I just signed it for you."

For a second time, Sadie strained to see what was written. And for a second time she forgot she was sitting up. She laughed and had to grab her ribs. "Ow!"

"What?" Sam asked. "What did Kevin write?"

Sadie read the message again with a shake of her head.

Even though you broke my heart and you're running off with my best friend, I'll never ~~forgive~~ forget you—Sam

Not only was it untrue, Sadie refused to read it aloud.

Kevin flashed her a conspiratorial grin. "I just signed your name, good buddy."

"Kevin!" she mouthed. Sam was going to kill him if he ever saw it. Not that he would. The cast would be off long before she saw Sam again. Still.

Trevor leaned over, read Kevin's message, and burst out laughing. Sam's face turned red on the small screen. "What? What does it say? Kevin!!!"

Kevin ignored him to sign the bright green cast for himself.

To Ice Woman, the perfect woman for my man, Josh.
Take care of him for me—Kev

By the time he finished, Sadie's voice clogged with tears. She wanted to ask how in the world she could take care of anyone, but she couldn't. Nobody knew anyway. Besides, they all promised to keep things light today. Enough heavies.

"You wanna sign it, babe?" Kevin asked over his shoulder.

Kevin's wife, Amy, shook her head. "No. That's okay. It looks like you guys took all the room."

They hadn't, but Sadie wasn't surprised. Though she'd only spent a few hours with Amy, Kevin's wife hadn't exactly been friendly. She laughed and joked with the guys, even with Josh's parents, but she barely spoke to Sadie. Sadie didn't blame her. Her naiveté endangered more than herself and Josh. Guillermo burnt down Sam's cabin without a second thought. He could have easily gone after Kevin and the others.

Josh's mom scooted closer to her. "Are you alright?"

Sadie smiled. Where Amy had been distant, Josh's mom, Kathy, was the complete opposite, asking Sadie every question imaginable: where she'd grown up, what types of music she wrote, and if she liked southern cooking.

Josh's mom was easy to talk to, like an old friend. Technically she was Josh's stepmom, but Sadie wouldn't have guessed that on her own, not with the way she and Josh teased each other. When Kathy mentioned she was the one who "knocked some sense into Josh's thick skull" she completely won over Sadie's heart. If Kathy hadn't convinced Josh to come back to Montana, he might be in school and Sadie would be…

Dead.

She shivered. It was cold outside of her heated blankets, but she was thrilled to be in her own clothes again. No more hospital gowns. No more nursing home beds. No more pink walls and old-lady curtains. No more doctors and nurses. Maybe. Hopefully.

Possibly.

Josh's mom looked even more concerned.

"I'm fine," Sadie said, realizing she hadn't answered. "I'm just ready for it to be over."

"I am, too. Although"—Kathy's smile faded—"I'm not ready to say goodbye yet."

"Me, neither." Sadie barely met Josh's parents. How long before she saw them again? Before Josh saw them again?

With a sigh, she twisted her leg around. "Do you want to sign my crazy neon cast?"

Kathy's smile returned. "I'd love to."

"Hey, Sadie," Trevor said. "I got this buddy in Spokane who can rig up some internet thing where we can chat without being tracked by Guillermo or any of his—"

Deputy Croff whirled around. "Exactly what part of 'no contact' don't you understand, Mr. Fillion?"

Trevor scowled but didn't answer. Though Deputy Croff was an elegant black woman, the kind Trevor might hit on under different circumstances, she had a commanding personality—plus she was six feet tall, towering over Trevor's obnoxiously curly head. It was amusing to watch him squirm under her steady gaze. Sadie was glad Josh picked out Deputy Croff for her.

Once Deputy Croff went back to her paperwork, Trevor leaned toward Sadie. "I'm telling you," he whispered, "it can be done. Nobody would be able to trace a daaa—rn thing." He glanced up at Josh's dad as he corrected himself mid-curse.

Sadie smiled. She was going to miss Trevor's wild hair and wild ideas. Most especially she would miss watching him try to curb his language around a bunch of Mormons. Josh's dad didn't even notice.

"Sadly," Peter said, "this setup is for the best. If you or Josh need anything, Sadie, you can always contact us through the U.S. Marshals' office."

"Or myself," Agent Madsen added from the corner.

Yes, but only in an emergency, which there better not be any.

She looked at Josh's dad. "What about you? What if"—she swallowed— "Guillermo goes looking for Josh in Spokane? Or at your house?"

Peter Young ran a hand through his peppered gray hair the way Josh always did when he was stressed. Even his face was Josh's, minus twenty-five years of law-enforcement-induced wrinkles.

"It's possible," he said, "but unlikely. Young is a popular last name, and with my police job, we've kept our phone and address unlisted for thirty years. You wrote little about Josh's hometown in your journal other than to say he was from the Spokane area. We should be fine."

Sadie winced as she remembered her little blue journal, the one Guillermo used to convict her; the same journal the whole world seemed to have memorized of late.

"All things considered," Peter said, "I think it would be impossible to track us down."

Kathy patted Sadie's arm. "Guillermo won't take his revenge on Josh that far, if at all. There's been no sign of him since he left. Really, sending Josh with you is just a precaution, not that he gave us much choice," she added with a wink. "Don't worry about us. We'll be fine."

They sounded confident enough, but Josh had five younger siblings. Could Sadie ever forgive herself if something happened to them? Could Peter and Kathy?

Could Josh?

A deep ache filled her chest, not from her broken ribs, not from holding up her neon green cast for so long, but from how many people she dragged into her nightmare life.

Guillermo dragged. Josh was always quick to insist everything that happened was because of Sadie's ex and not her. Even though she dated Guillermo in the first place. Even though she ignored the FBI's warnings about him. And even though she went back to Guillermo when Josh told her not to. Twice.

And now the number caught in the middle kept climbing. Josh's parents. His siblings. Her mom and Damien. Kevin and Amy. Trevor. Sam. Sam's parents. All twenty-five members of Sam's family for that matter, since it was their beautiful cabin Guillermo burned to the ground.

And what about Special Agent Stephen Dubois?

A lump lodged itself in her throat. A week ago Agent Madsen's former partner followed Sadie to Guillermo's cabin. That was the night of the four shots. What would Dubois' wife and two kids say if they knew Sadie stayed on the couch when she heard the gunshots, trying to save herself instead of finding a phone to call for help? Still Guillermo's fault?

Josh's mom squeezed her hand. "Are you sure you're okay, sweetie?"

Sadie's lungs began to constrict. She closed her eyes and took a slow breath. "Why don't you come with us? All of you."

"We'll be fine. I promise."

Everyone else around the room echoed Kathy's sentiments, but none of them had been in the back of Guillermo's dark Mercedes and looked into his black, murderous eyes. None of them heard his dark laugh when he promised to hunt Josh down like it was a game. No one felt Guillermo's fist in their face or his gun to their forehead. They didn't know. They didn't.

But she did.

If Guillermo knew every word and every step she took from Christmas until the fire, who was to say he didn't know theirs?

She looked at the tiled floor as hot tears pool behind her eyes. The only one who looked as scared as Sadie felt was Amy. That's when Sadie understood. Amy wasn't mad about the past. She was terrified of the future, the future Sadie created the second she stumbled into Sam's truck.

Her fault again.

Sadie rubbed her eyes, feeling a migraine coming back. The headaches never went away for long. She didn't reach for the nurse's button, though. She was done with the pain medication and accompanying fog. Instead she checked the clock again, wondering what was taking Josh so long. They had to leave for their flight soon. Josh's family and friends were waiting to say goodbye. Time was slipping away.

Kathy patted her hand. "Stop worrying about us and just take care of yourself and that son of mine. I'm worried Josh will be so wrapped up in making sure you're safe, he'll forget to eat and—"

Agent Madsen leaped to his feet. "When? Where? How?!" he shouted into his phone. He listened a second and then swore over and over again.

Before Sadie could think, Deputy Croff whipped out her phone and punched several numbers.

Madsen shook his head as he received more of the report. Then he whirled and glared at Sadie across the room.

"The funeral," Sadie breathed.

Her pulse pounded. Something happened at the funeral.

"And Mr. Young?" Madsen asked. "Was he hurt?"

Sadie's heart stopped.

Kathy grabbed her hand.

"Josh," they whispered together.

Madsen slammed the phone down. "Everybody out. Now!"

CHAPTER 3

"Go! Get up!" Harrison yelled at Josh.

Agents and deputies sprang out of the woodwork, shouting orders at Josh and the others. Damien scrambled to get Marcela to her feet. Yet Josh couldn't move.

Two men in suits had the redhead on the ground. Her face was smashed against the floor as they cuffed her ten feet from Josh. Her wide, frightened eyes locked on him. He had to look away. Past her another five feet laid a small gun on the church floor.

"Get up! Go!" Harrison shouted, kicking Josh to get him to move.

Josh finally came to his senses. He went to push himself up, but pain shot up his right arm. Wincing, he stumbled to his feet.

"What about Marcela?" he huffed. "Where is she being taken?"

"GO!" Harrison yelled.

Josh's feet obeyed. He trotted outside the church in the direction he was ordered.

A black SUV screeched up to the curb. Harrison opened the back door and shoved Josh in. Josh landed on the same bad arm. He yelped in pain and barely righted himself when the driver tore out of the church parking lot.

As they sped down the highway, Josh cradled his arm, trying to make sense of what happened. What had the redhead said? Something about the color of his beard? A guy outside?

Josh froze. *Guillermo?*

No. It couldn't be. Guillermo was too smart to show up to Sadie's funeral. He sent someone else. The redhead? But she sat quietly beside Josh the whole service. If she was working for Guillermo, why wait until the end to…to… He didn't even know what she intended to do.

"Was the gun loaded?" Josh asked, breathing heavily.

Harrison answered without turning. "Yes."

Josh felt sick. Marcela. Damien. Everyone. *What have I done?* His heart pounded as the adrenaline coursed through his veins. His arm was pulsing, too. Ignoring both, he rubbed his bleach-blond beard that hadn't done a thing to hide him.

Not good. Not good!

Harrison glared at him. "Just so you understand, Mr. Young, no Witness Security Program participant who followed guidelines—strictly followed guidelines—has ever been harmed while under the active protection of the U.S. Marshals."

"I know." Josh was counting on that. With the FBI's mounting case against Guillermo, Josh wasn't the only one anxious to keep Sadie alive. Two government agencies were protecting them now. He just wasn't sure which one did what moving forward—or who jumped that girl at the church. FBI or Marshals. Probably both.

"Then I expect you to trust my judgment!" Harrison snapped. "I have a job to do, so let me do it!"

"Right. Sorry." Josh forced himself to breathe slowly. "I'll do exactly as you say from now on."

"You better believe you will!"

The SUV grew chilly and silent. Snow and sleet whizzed past.

Josh was a rules guy. He always had been. What possessed him to stay behind with Marcela? He knew better. He knew better!

He almost took off his suit coat to examine his throbbing arm but then thought better of it. Burning or not, broken or not, his arm didn't matter. Nothing mattered except keeping Sadie and her family safe.

Harrison shot him another dark look. "What's wrong with your arm?"

Josh stopped massaging it. "Nothing."

"You better believe it's nothing, not compared to what could have happened. Let that little *nothing* of yours become your new reminder. No more mistakes."

He got it now. He didn't need a reminder. His knee was bouncing again, only he didn't stop it.

"What were you thinking?" Harrison raged. "Why not just draw a target on your forehead?"

Josh didn't answer. Sadie was going to kill him—so were his parents. Madsen, too. He wasn't sure how much protection a boyfriend of a key witness normally received, but he was more than grateful Agent Madsen acted like Josh was as important to the case as Sadie was. He wasn't. But without Harrison back there…

Not good!

It was another minute before his mind slowed enough to register the green sign above. He jerked up. "Where are we going? We just passed the exit."

"To the airport," Harrison said. "We're getting you out of Montana right now."

"But…" Josh watched Kalispell fade from view. His parents. Kevin, Trevor, Sam. No contact, and he wasn't going to get any goodbyes.

He rubbed his right arm and focused on the pain. It was time to stop thinking of himself and start playing by the rules. No more mistakes.

"Okay," he said.

With a last glance out the window, he said a silent goodbye.

Breathe.

That's what people were supposed to do in extreme situations. Just breathe. Keep calm. Keep the brain oxygenated. Sadie's cracked ribs wouldn't allow it. So she stared at Agent Madsen who cleared her room to break the news.

"We have the woman in custody now," Madsen explained, "but she's claiming to be a friend of yours. I need you to identify her before you get on the plane. It won't take long. With any luck, you'll still make the four o'clock flight."

"Josh?" Sadie asked, blinking slower and slower.

"He's fine. The deputies intercepted before anything happened. Can you walk, or do you need a wheelchair?"

Her body forced a first real breath. It exploded against her lungs painfully. Almost as painful as knowing Josh had been attacked by a woman with a gun. Almost as painful as knowing Guillermo found Josh.

"I wish I had known then what I know now," Guillermo sneered from her memories. *"I would have finished your new boyfriend off then. Although"*— Sadie remembered the second his dark smile turned evil—*"I shall truly enjoy the game of hunting him down."*

"And if they hadn't intercepted?" she whispered.

"Mr. Young is fine. He's headed for the airport, and everything will go as planned. But you won't make it unless—"

"What?" Sadie looked up. "Is he being followed? If Guillermo knew he was at the funeral, then he knows what Josh looks like now…that he was there, and, and… He knows everything! And he tried to…to…" Her breaths came in short bursts, punching against each and every rib. Guillermo was back. Back and hunting Josh.

"They've switched cars and changed routes twice," Madsen said. "He's completely safe and will make your scheduled flight, but unless we get moving, you won't. So…" Madsen scanned her empty room, stopping on the only other person left. "Deputy Croff, get Miss Dawson a wheelchair."

Sadie picked up her crutches and hoisted herself to standing. She couldn't breathe, but she could walk. Sort of. After all the cast signing, her leg ached like the rest of her body. She'd come to terms with her injuries, figuring her stupidity brought every one of them on herself. But Josh...

She pushed herself down the long hallway behind Deputy Croff and Agent Madsen. If identifying that woman meant helping Josh or stopping Guillermo, then so be it.

That's all she and Madsen did lately. Identify people in Guillermo's inner circle. Though she'd known Guillermo for two years, they only dated the last three months. Yet she had twenty-two names and counting already. People from his dinner parties, people he introduced her to at the New Year's Eve party. Judges. Attorneys. A few mayors. All suspected to be on his payroll. The most important ones she identified were the two men with Guillermo the night she heard the four shots. FBI Agent Dubois' murderers.

This woman is just another face, she told herself. *Number twenty-three.* Only this time it was personal. This one had gone after Josh.

Madsen drove them down the icy streets of Kalispell to a standard-looking office building. They drove behind a solid fence and past three security guards. Deputy Croff helped Sadie out of the car and into the two-story building.

Only then did Sadie realize she wouldn't be identifying this woman from a picture like the others. She was being taken to the actual person. To Josh's attacker.

The three moved in silence down a long white hallway and into a dark room. The only light in the room shone through a large window. On the other side of the window was a man in a dark suit and a redhead. They sat at a small, white table, as white as the rest of the room.

Sadie took in the size of the redhead and shuddered. Unlike huge Mr. Ugly that Guillermo left with Sadie in the cabin, this woman was tiny, almost Sadie's size, looking smaller as she hunched over.

"I swear it!" the redhead said, half sobbing, half yelling at the officer. "I don't know anything!"

Sadie stayed in the furthest corner of the dark room, away from the window and out of sight. Though the redhead had her back to them, Sadie couldn't risk anyone knowing she was alive. *Especially* someone working for Guillermo.

"Do you want to sit?" Deputy Croff asked her. "There's a chair by Agent Madsen." When Sadie shook her head, Croff added softly, "It's a one-way mirror. She can't see or hear us."

"Oh." Sadie still wasn't thrilled to approach the glass. But if she was going to identify the redhead, she needed a better view. Still not proficient with crutches, she pushed her way up to Agent Madsen and eased herself into the chair.

"Look," the redhead said, "this man just came up to me in the parking lot and asked me to give that David guy a card from his mom. That's it, I swear. You have to believe me. I didn't do anything wrong!"

"Do you recognize her?" Madsen asked Sadie softly.

Though the redhead was mostly faced away, Sadie didn't recognize her. She would have remembered that bright shade of hair anywhere. The red was very distinct. Almost orange. Like the fire in Sam's cabin.

"No. I've never seen her before," Sadie said. "Not even at the ski lodge."

Madsen nodded. "Another of Guillermo's pawns. Seems he has an endless supply these days."

Sadie thought about a different pawn of Guillermo's, a different FBI agent from Madsen's own group. When Sadie went missing a week ago, Agent Griffin supposedly checked out Sam's cabin inside and out at Josh's request. Griffin reported nothing amiss. Like this woman, he also claimed innocence when questioned. Guillermo trained them well.

She hugged herself and tried to focus on what was being said.

"And what did this man outside of the church tell you to do?" the interrogator asked.

The redhead wiped her nose. "He told me to give a note to that David guy, the one I sat next to at the funeral."

"Why didn't he do it himself?"

"I don't know!" she cried. "The guy was wearing a mechanic's uniform. He was all dirty and oily like he just left work. He wasn't dressed for a funeral. He said his mom was sick and asked me if I could go back and give the note to David. That's it!"

Sadie looked at Agent Madsen. The redhead sounded convincing enough. The fake mechanic was Guillermo's employee, not the redhead. It was easy to believe her. Madsen was stone-faced. Croff, too. Both looked unsure. Then Sadie remembered the loaded gun and shook her head. The redhead was just a great actor. Like Guillermo.

Madsen leaned forward and spoke into a small microphone. The interrogator received the message in his ear and repeated it. "Why did you comment on David's beard?"

The redhead grabbed a handful of tissues and blew her nose. "The guy said it was important because Sadie always wanted him to grow a beard or something. The guy wanted David to know she would have liked it."

The interrogator shot her look of disbelief.

"Look," she said defensively, "I know it sounds crazy, but I just came from my friend's funeral for crying out loud! I wasn't thinking straight!"

Friend? Sadie shuddered at the word. She'd never seen the girl.

"What about the gun?" Madsen asked into the microphone.

When the officer asked, the redhead shot to her feet. "I didn't know it was in my purse, I swear! I've never even held a gun before. Check for fingerprints or whatever and you'll know I'm telling the truth. Except"—she swore loudly—"I pulled it out when I reached for the note, but that's the only time I touched it. And that's only because I was surprised to see it in there. Wait!" Her head jerked up. "Oh, no! Wait! You don't think I was going to…No! I wouldn't hurt that David guy. I don't even know him. Please! You have to believe me. I was just trying to help out that mechanic. That's all. I loved Sadie. I didn't mean to do anything." She buried her face in her hands. "I loved Sadie."

Sadie's skin crawled with the familiarity of her words. "I've never seen her before," she insisted, reminding herself as much as Croff and Madsen.

Deputy Croff looked at Agent Madsen. "What do you think?" she asked.

Madsen sighed. "I think it's time to get Miss Dawson on a plane."

Croff nodded. "Are you ready, Sadie?"

Sadie's eyes stayed on the redhead. The anger started to bleed through the shock. She'd never seen that woman before. How dare she say otherwise? How dare she add more pain to Sadie's family? To Josh's?

Sadie ran through the information, trying to find anything to convict her. A woman with a note. A mechanic. A gun. Nothing made sense. Of course, nothing ever did these days.

"What did the card say?" she asked Madsen.

"Yours is next," Madsen quoted. *"Better start planning."*

Sadie repeated the words, coming up blank. "What does it mean?"

"The redhead insists she doesn't know," Madsen said, "but with a little pressure she might remember. She might also agree to identify the man who gave her that note if she thinks it will save her hide, although I can already guess it will be another dead end."

"Do you have a lawyer?" the officer asked the redhead.

She grabbed more tissues. "No. Do I need one?"

"Yes. You're definitely going to need one. Let's go."

The woman stood and turned, giving them their first clear look at her face.

Sadie's hands flew to her mouth. "Chalyce?"

Agent Madsen whipped around. "You know her?"

"High school," Sadie choked.

Agent Madsen grabbed the microphone. "Bring her forward!" he yelled loud enough the redhead turned to see where his voice came from. The officer pushed the woman in front of the mirror where she froze, realizing for the first time she was being watched.

"Miss Dawson," Madsen said clear and slow, "do you know this woman?"

Sadie squeezed her eyes shut, summoning the courage to identify one more face, just one. This one was flushed and tear-stained, but she already knew. Though she hadn't seen her in eight years and though her bright red hair was nothing like the dark shade it once had been, she had no doubt.

"That's Chalyce Krauss," she said. "My senior-year locker partner."

The world spun out of control. Guillermo was using her high school friends now—people he'd never met—to hunt the enemy. To kill Josh.

Who else? When?

Suddenly Guillermo's note hit her.

Yours is next. Josh's funeral.

Better start planning.

"I can't do this anymore," she whispered. She grabbed her crutches and stumbled out the door.

CHAPTER 4

The winding roads from Kalispell to Missoula were icy and slow, elongating the already long two-hour drive. At the last car switch, they dropped off the other agent, leaving Josh and Deputy Harrison alone in a small sedan. Every few minutes Josh glanced at the map. In another fifteen minutes they'd be to the airport and Sadie.

"Have you ever been to Mississippi?" Josh asked.

Deputy Harrison scowled. The two-hour ride hadn't improved his mood. "Yes."

"I haven't." Nor did Josh know much about the state. In fact, he'd never been anywhere down south and neither had Sadie. Hopefully, neither had Guillermo. The town they chose—Olive Branch, Mississippi—was small, but not so small they'd attract attention. Plus, a town named Olive Branch sounded like a safe place to hide. More importantly, it was twenty minutes from the Memphis Airport should any problems arise and they had to relocate quickly. As far as Josh knew, Deputies Harrison and Croff would escort them to Mississippi, but Agent Madsen never specified how long the Marshals would stick around after that.

Josh glanced down at Harrison's left hand. He didn't wear a wedding ring, but that didn't mean the deputy wasn't leaving a family behind.

Josh twisted his own ring, thinking of the warning his dad gave him before handing it over.

"Don't forget who you are and what you stand for." Very cliché but also very Peter Young. *"Just because you're pretending to be married doesn't mean that you are. At all. Not even a little bit. I'm trusting you. So is Sadie—and so is her mother."*

Harrison pulled off at the next exit. Josh looked up in surprise. This wasn't the airport exit, not that Josh dared mention it. But even more surprising, Harrison turned into the first parking lot. A plane flew overhead letting Josh know they weren't far, but for some reason, Harrison was pulling into a King's Motel.

The deputy drove alongside the old run-down motel and parked in the last stall. Mid-afternoon on a cold Thursday in January, their car was the only one in the parking lot.

The curiosity won out. "What are we doing here?" Josh asked.

"Change of plans," Deputy Harrison said. "Follow me."

Josh pulled up his suit coat collar and reached for the handle. Pain shot up his right arm. Even with the ACE bandage an earlier agent had provided—or maybe because of the tight wrap—his fingers couldn't grasp the handle. Harrison glared from the sidewalk. Reaching across with his left hand, Josh yanked on the handle and left the heated car.

The bitter winter wind ripped past as he followed Harrison up the snowy stairs to the second floor.

The last door opened before they reached it, and Special Agent Bruce Madsen stepped outside. That's when Josh knew something was definitely wrong, even beyond the obvious. Agent Madsen was the only person Josh said goodbye to.

Agent Madsen held the door wide with an expression more frigid than the weather. He looked ten years older than when Josh met him two weeks ago. Even his goatee was more salt than pepper now. In a lot of ways, Guillermo had humiliated the FBI, specifically Agent Madsen. While they carefully tracked Guillermo's every move, he invited them to the New

Year's Eve party to let them know he couldn't care less. When Madsen put more people on the case, Guillermo added more people to his payroll—including Agent Griffin, one of Madsen's own. The FBI got a search warrant for Guillermo's cabin, and Guillermo burned it down, taking out any clues into Sadie or Dubois' disappearances. And it was taking its toll on Madsen.

"Come in, Mr. Young," Madsen said coolly.

Josh finally realized why he was here. He was headed for a hefty lecture before departure. Though he dreaded it, he knew he deserved it.

He entered the queen-sized room and stopped in surprise. There were two other agents with Madsen—or deputies; Josh couldn't tell them apart. One sat at a small table. But the other had Josh panicked. A tall, black woman. Sadie's bodyguard, Deputy Croff.

"Where is Sadie?" Josh asked.

Madsen sat at the table. "We have some things to discuss."

Josh's pulse picked up. He scanned every inch of that tiny motel room. Like Harrison, Deputy Croff wasn't supposed to leave Sadie's side for the next forty-eight hours, at least, and yet every key player was in that run-down motel except the most important one.

The second time, Josh asked Deputy Croff directly. "Where is Sadie?"

"Having second thoughts," Croff said evenly.

"About what? Why? What happened?"

"What happened?" Agent Madsen snapped. "Why don't *you* tell us what happened, Mr. Young? Did I not give you specific enough instructions?"

Josh felt an inch tall. "Yes, but Marcela..." He stopped himself. It didn't matter what Marcela wanted or needed. He almost got them both killed. His actions were unacceptable. He straightened. "Sorry. It won't happen again."

"It better not!" Madsen yelled. "This whole thing has Miss Dawson so shaken up she's second guessing the entire plan."

"What plan? Mississippi?" Josh felt his own voice rising. "Where is Sadie?"

Madsen pointed to the last open chair at the small table. "Sit. Down."

Josh wanted to dig in his heels, but he was playing by their rules now. He pulled out the chair and sat rigidly.

Madsen brought his hands together. "Miss Dawson wanted you and me to meet alone. She hoped if she wasn't here, you'd have a chance to reconsider your options."

"My options?" Josh said. "Don't you mean *our* options?"

Madsen looked at him for a long, hard minute. "No."

Things started falling into place. The change of plans. Sadie gone. "So," Josh said, "by second thoughts you don't mean about Mississippi. You mean about me. Because of the funeral. Because of what I did."

Madsen's eyes narrowed. "Miss Dawson won't sign the papers."

"What?" Josh cried.

"She refuses. She says she's not ready to commit to WITSEC."

"Why? She was ready to sign them this morning."

Madsen's face went red. "Yes, before a protected witness was nearly killed! Now she doesn't trust the FBI, the U.S. Marshals, or anyone."

"But that was my fault," Josh said. "Not Deputy Harrison's. If I'd just listened to Deputy Harrison—"

"The damage is done!" Madsen yelled. "She's backing out faster than I can keep up."

Josh looked at Deputy Croff. His muscles clenched as he realized why Deputy Croff was in the room and Sadie wasn't. Sadie hadn't signed the papers authorizing the U.S. Marshals to protect her. Croff wasn't her bodyguard anymore.

"Oh, no," Josh said, blood pressure rising. "Tell me Sadie's not alone somewhere. Tell me you're not stupid enough to let some signature keep her from a 24/7 bodyguard when Guillermo is out there trying to kill people. If he knows she's alive—"

Madsen cut him off again. "Miss Dawson is still under Marshal protection. The temporary permit has not yet expired, allowing us to keep her in protection until I can get her to calm down."

Josh looked at Croff.

"She's safe," the female deputy said. "Don't worry."

Everything had fallen apart in the last two hours, and he wasn't supposed to worry?

"Right now," Madsen said, "I'm here to deliver Miss Dawson's message to you." He leaned forward. "She doesn't think Mississippi is the best place for you at this time."

It was like someone knocked the air from Josh's lungs. He was losing Mississippi. He was losing Sadie.

"What's really going on?" he asked. "Where's Sadie? I need to talk to her."

"She's gone," Madsen said. "Her flight left an hour ago."

Josh shot to his feet, knocking over his chair. "What?" The betrayal sliced to the core. The plan he and Sadie discussed involved the *two* of them leaving. Not one! He checked his watch. Maybe there was time.

"Look," Josh said, "I don't know what happened, but I deserve the right to talk to Sadie face to face, to explain what happened at the funeral. If she doesn't want me to go with her to Mississippi"—the words knotted his stomach—"then I'll have to respect that. But I promised Marcela I'd keep an eye on her. I have to keep that promise!" He whirled around to Deputy Harrison. "I have to get to the airport!"

Madsen glared at Josh. "Sit down!"

He couldn't. He started pacing around the queen-sized bed, good hand running through his fake blond hair as he tried to figure out what else might have set off Sadie. Their relationship had been a whirlwind of events, under strained and horrible circumstances. But now that she was free from Guillermo and he was free from Megan, he was determined to find some normalcy with her—or at least as close as they could given the circumstances. If that meant Mississippi as a 'newly married couple' then so be it.

Married...

His gaze dropped to his dad's wedding ring on his left hand. Maybe that was it. Maybe Sadie really needed breathing room. Maybe she wasn't ready to be Mrs. Josh Peterson, or whatever name they were supposed to go by now.

He slumped on the bed. "Where does she want me to go?"

"She said she needs a few months to recuperate from her injuries," Madsen said. "She wants some time to decide if the Witness Security Program is something she can commit to. During that time, she hoped you could focus on your studies and finish your degree. She says you have one semester left. Then you could join her in Mississippi, assuming that's what you still want."

Josh looked up in disbelief. "She wants me to go back to school? Now?"

Deputy Harrison grunted next to him, echoing his sentiments, but Madsen's eyes narrowed to angry slits. "Believe me, this isn't my idea, Mr. Young. I have a crime boss murderer on the loose, and I have to worry about you finishing some stupid degree?"

"Why do you care?" Josh asked, suddenly curious. "About me, I mean." Sadie needed a bodyguard. Josh understood their need to protect her, but Josh was nothing. He was just the boyfriend.

Madsen looked at the three federal agents in the room a moment before answering. "I'd like to use your testimony against Guillermo Vasquez as well."

"Really?" That was news to Josh. "How? I barely know him."

"You saw Miss Dawson's injuries after Christmas, you saw the man who came to the Jackson cabin posing as a federally-employed park ranger. Guillermo threatened you on New Year's Eve, and you found Miss Dawson after the fire. You can testify to her physical and emotional state afterward. That's plenty."

"Okay. I'll do it," Josh said without hesitation. Anything to get Sadie's ex locked away forever.

Madsen leaned forward and lowered his voice. "There's another reason. I have a fear—I've seen it happen too many times—that Miss Dawson will refuse to testify altogether. Testifying means bringing her back from the dead, bringing her face to face with Vasquez again, and frankly, he won't be happy when he finds out she's alive. Given the size of his organization, threats will come in strong against her, her mom, and anyone else he thinks will sway her. After seeing what happened to you, she's really shaken up. There's a good chance she'll refuse to testify at all."

From the corner of his eye, Josh saw Deputy Croff nodding. "It happens all the time," she whispered.

"Trials against men like Guillermo Vasquez are long and arduous," Madsen continued. "My hope is having you testify with her will convince her that WITSEC can keep both of you safe. You'll be going through the process together. Plus—and maybe I should have mentioned this first—I'd rather not see you killed, Mr. Young."

Josh thought of the crazed redhead and nodded somberly. "Me, too."

"So…" Madsen leaned back. "Where do you want to go?"

Just like that, they were back where they started. His mind raced, coming up blank. There wasn't a single acceptable scenario that didn't involve Sadie.

He twisted the ring on his finger that suddenly felt invalid. No Sadie. No fake marriage. No Mississippi. He tried to pull off the ring but struggled since his right hand wouldn't close properly. Somehow he managed to get it off. He slid it in his suit coat next to the one he planned to give to Sadie. Both would be mailed back to his parents as soon as possible.

"Sadie mentioned in her journal that you attend Washington State," Madsen went on. "However, Guillermo read her journal, so going back there is out of the question. But what about the University of Washington? According to my file"—Madsen motioned to the agent with the laptop—"your engineering credits would transfer easily."

Seattle? With Sadie 2500 miles away? That wasn't just a little breathing room, it was a virtual goodbye.

"Why is she doing this?" Josh asked. "What's the real reason? No more games. Just give it to me straight."

"Because I'm tired of ruining your life," Sadie answered softly.

Josh whirled around. Sadie stood in the bathroom door, cast, crutches, and all.

He crossed the room in two giant strides. Every instinct begged to sweep her up and twirl her around in a crushing hug that could possibly further her injuries—and his—but he forced his arms to stay at his sides as he drank in the sight of her. Here. Two tiny feet away.

"What's all this about, Sadie?" he asked. "You have my poor heart panicked."

She looked him over head to toe. "Are you really okay?"

"How can I be okay when I thought—"

Her dark eyes lifted to his. They were filled with tears, and with a blink, the first ones escaped down her olive cheeks. "Madsen told me about the funeral…and I thought…I thought you were…"

As gently as he could, Josh pulled her into his arms.

CHAPTER 5

Josh stroked Sadie's short, dark curls with his good hand. She folded herself into him, her tiny body fitting against his chest. His chin rested on her head, and just that fast, chaos dissipated into order. His heart resumed its normal pace.

It was another minute before she sniffed back the tears and straightened. "When I heard what—"

Her elbow went back and jabbed his right arm. Pain shot up his fingers to his shoulder. A low groan escaped before he could stop it.

"What's wrong?" she said suddenly.

He tried to erase the pain from his face. "Nothing." His arm throbbed like mad.

Her eyes grazed over him and zeroed in on the bulk under his suit coat. She reached out and felt the hidden bandage. Her eyes shot up to his. "What happened?"

"Just a little sprain. It's fine."

"A sprain?" She spun around and glared at Madsen. "You said nothing happened to him. You promised me he was fine!"

Madsen waved a hand in dismissal. "It wasn't the redhead. Harrison shoved him out of the way, and he twisted his arm. It's nothing."

"It's nothing," Josh echoed. "It will be better in a day or two."

Sadie's jaw tightened. "Let me see it."

Josh didn't fight her. He shrugged out of his suit coat, careful to free the left arm first. Then he rolled up his white sleeve to where the wrap ended.

"See," he said, rotating his arm with minimal pain. "It's fine. I just fell, that's all."

She backed away and slumped on the bed, quiet for a time. Josh sat next to her and noticed her studying her wrists. She softly traced the red lines that refused to fade. The duct tape that bound her for two days left a mark that scarred her thoughts as much as her skin.

"If only..." she said.

Josh knew this conversation before she even finished. If only she'd helped Agents Madsen and Dubois on Christmas Day, maybe Guillermo would be locked up right now. If only she pressed charges the first time Guillermo hit her, maybe he would be locked up right now. If only she never dated the abusive crime lord in the first place, her life wouldn't be in danger now. Yet all that mattered was she was alive *and* dead. Alive to Josh and dead to Guillermo.

"If only we'd never met," she started again. "You'd be safe and—"

"Whoa!" His fingers flew to her lips, cutting her off. "That one's not allowed."

She brushed his hand aside. "It's true, though. You went from a healthy, happy, marshmallow-roasting engineering major to *this*." She looked from his bad arm to his bleached hair. Her eyes started to water. "Your mom wanted to say goodbye to you so badly."

Her words reminded him they were in an old motel instead of the airport. "What's all this about me going one place and you another?" he asked, working to keep his voice light. "Are you trying to get rid of me already?"

She didn't answer. She didn't even meet his gaze. And that's when he realized he still might lose her.

Ignoring the other four people in the room, he scooted closer to her on the bed. He and Sadie hadn't been alone much in the last week. With two round-the-clock bodyguards, it would be awhile before they would be alone again. Still, he longed for privacy and lowered his voice.

"I know this is a lot to take in when you already don't feel well. Especially"—he took a quick breath, grateful he'd taken off the ring—"the whole Mrs. Josh Peterson thing. I mean, I know it's just a show or a cover, but if you don't want to be married, it's fine. Because really, I just want what's best for you. I'll be your friend or your neighbor or…or your older brother even. Whatever you want." *Just don't leave me.*

One of her dark brows rose. "*Older* brother?"

He smiled briefly. She had him by fourteen months and wasn't letting him forget it. "Younger, much less mature brother," he relented. "I just don't want you to be worried about being a 'Mrs.' on top of everything else."

The tiniest light shone in her eyes. "I kind of like that part." And then the light faded. "It's the ruining your life part that I don't."

"Sadie…you're not ruining my life."

"Really? When's the last time you looked in a mirror?"

She turned him toward the bathroom so he could catch a glimpse of himself. He grimaced, but that was more from the itchy beard than the bleached hair and brown contacts. He hated beards. Always had. The experience with the redhead only solidified that.

"What?" he teased. "You don't like the mountain man look?"

"No. You're as bad as Trevor."

"Trevor? Ouch!"

She didn't smile at all. Instead, she went back to staring at his wrapped arm.

"Come on. With a little dye and a razor, I'll be back to normal in no time."

"Normal?" Her eyes narrowed. "Is that what you call this? Is that what you call almost getting killed today? Is this normal for you now?" She swallowed. "Just that fast, you've adapted to having your name on some…some hit list?"

He couldn't come up with a response fast enough.

"I've spent weeks convincing myself that my dreams where you get killed aren't real. And now…" Her eyes filled. "My life has become my nightmares, only I've dragged you in."

"Everything that happened today was my fault, Sadie. No one else's."

She blinked slowly. "Not Guillermo's?"

He stared at her, caught. For the first time, he understood how she must feel knowing—in theory—that the events weren't your fault, yet feeling responsible all the same. He was a fool for walking into Guillermo's trap today, especially when he'd been warned. He knew better.

For several long moments, the only sound in the dark room was the heater starting up. Josh appreciated the others giving them time to work it out, but he could feel their eyes on the back of his head, waiting for a decision to be reached.

"Madsen said you won't sign the WITSEC papers," he said.

She shrugged.

Josh decided not to press. That could be resolved later. He had a bigger concern at hand. "So is it true? You want to go to Mississippi without me?"

Sadie shot a dark look over her shoulder. "Agent Madsen was supposed to give you time to think about what's best for you without me interfering by throwing guilt on your shoulders. He was supposed to give you a chance to choose *you* for once, but he messed it all up."

"So it is true?" Josh asked, pain lacing his voice.

"I don't know."

Seattle. Mississippi. Already he could feel the distance growing between them.

He could only manage one word. "Why?"

She traced the lines on her wrists again. "Everything I do hurts someone I love and I can't take any more, Josh. I don't know how to stop hurting people, but I have to try somehow."

He tried to grab her hand, but she moved it away from him.

"Sadie…" he whispered, feeling his future—*their* future—literally slipping through his fingers.

Her shoulders lifted. "What if you finish school while I figure out how to get rid of these stupid crutches? What if you graduate while I put myself back together? Then you'll be happy, and I'll be happier knowing I did something for you for once."

"For me?"

"Yes."

"All this"—he wanted to say 'nonsense' but instead waved his good hand around the room—"is for me?"

She looked confused. "Yes."

"If you want to do something for *me*, then let me come with you. You think I'll be able to think straight enough to graduate when you're 2,000 miles away?"

"2,343 miles," she corrected quietly.

"Sadie! There's no way!"

"Why? I'll be in physical therapy all the time, and you can't sit around doing nothing while we wait for them to find…him. There aren't any universities in Olive Branch."

"I'll get a job," he said.

She cocked her head to the side. "You're one semester away from graduation. *One!* Please let me do this for you."

"Just do something!" Madsen cut in. The FBI agent looked like he was ready to pull out what was left of his hair.

Deputy Croff approached them. "Josh, Sadie's right. This could be a long-term situation. You'll need something to occupy your time, but—" she continued quickly when Josh tried to cut in, "I don't think Sadie should be alone in Mississippi either. What about a compromise? Take Sadie to Seattle with you."

Josh shook his head. "No way. Seattle is way too close to Montana."

"What about somewhere else then?" Sadie said, perking up. "Somewhere far away but where you could still finish school?"

"And you would come with me?" Josh asked.

Her dark eyes lit up. "If you let me. Or are you trying to get rid of me already?"

He wanted to smile, but he'd been too close to despair. The wounds were too fresh. "You mean it? You and me? Together wherever they send us?"

"Mrs. Josh…"

"Peterson," he supplied. "My dad's name is Peter, so I'm Peter's son."

She smiled. "Mrs. Josh Peterson. I can get used to that."

Josh's stomach did a little flip. Sadie was smiling. A true, honest smile. It was crazy what they were planning, yet logical. Logical always won out with him, only logic usually didn't get him the most beautiful woman as his 'wife.' He was tempted to ask her how she felt about becoming Mrs. Josh Young someday, but he didn't dare press his luck. A fake wife was better than 2,343 miles. *Anything* was better than 2,343 miles.

"Alright," Josh said to Madsen. "I guess we decided."

Madsen growled something under his breath, but he and the other agent began pouring over the laptop. It was their problem now.

Josh's heart, nerves, and mind heaved a huge sigh of relief. He slid his hand into Sadie's again, bringing him warmth he hadn't realized he craved. Her warm hand reminded him of one last thing.

"Oh," he said over his shoulder, "and it has to be some place warm." After Sadie had nearly frozen to death—twice—Josh promised to take her somewhere without snow.

"UT," Madsen said.

"Utah?" Josh shook his head adamantly. "No way. It's not warm enough *and* not far enough away from here."

Sadie sat up. "Wait. But you were just accepted into BYU's MBA program. What if you finish your undergrad there and go right into your MBA. That would be perfect. BYU it is!"

Sadie in Utah. With a bunch of Mormons. That brought up a whole host of new thoughts, but Madsen spoke before Josh could.

"BYU is out of the question, Miss Dawson. You mentioned it in your journal. Besides, we're using it as a decoy. All of Mr. Young's records will say he transferred to BYU, which means he needs to be far from it."

"Oh." Her countenance fell. She could barely look at Josh. "I...I'm sorry."

Her hand started to pull away again, but he held tight, refusing to let her beat herself up anymore. "I would have never gone there anyway," he said. "It's too close."

"That's not what I meant by UT anyway," Madsen continued. "Have either of you been to Tennessee?"

"Tennessee? No." Then Josh understood. "You mean University of Tennessee?"

"UT—Knoxville," Madsen read off the screen. "The climate is mild, the engineering program is highly recommended, as is the medical center with accompanying physical therapy clinic. Is that acceptable?"

Josh ignored the edge in Madsen's tone and nudged Sadie. "What do you think of Tennessee?"

"What do *you* think?" she shot back.

"I think it sounds perfect."

She smiled. "Then so do I."

While Madsen and the laptop agent worked out the details, Josh filled Sadie in on the funeral. Though the subject was heavy, she sat taller than before. Then she filled him in on her time with his parents, friends, and the green cast. As Josh read Kevin's cruel message from Sam they both laughed.

"Sam's going to kill Kevin," Josh said. "He's mortified enough."

The color drained from Sadie's face. "Wait. It's not true. Sam doesn't like me, does he?"

Josh shook his head. *Sadie, Sadie, Sadie.* At one point, three of the four guys at the cabin were interested in her. The only reason it wasn't four was because Kevin was happily married. Sam was smitten the second Sadie spoke Spanish, his mission language. But Josh wasn't about to throw his best friend under the bus. "Let's just say it's not completely true. What did my mom write?"

"I forgot to check. She signed it before everything got all crazy." Sadie leaned sideways to read the short message.

Don't think you're not worth all this because you are — Kathy

Sadie sighed. "Why does it feel like your mom knows me already? I only met her Tuesday."

"She has a gift of reading people within seconds of meeting them. What did my dad say?"

Sadie twisted her neon green cast around.

Take care–Pete

Sadie smiled. "Short and sweet. I like him already."

"Typical for my dad. Big heart. Small words." Then Josh noticed something. "Pete?" He looked at Sadie. "Pete?"

"What? Doesn't he go by that?"

"I've never heard him go by anything but Peter. Just how strong is that charm spell of yours, Miss Dawson?"

She elbowed him. "Strong enough to charm you. Let's hope it doesn't wear off," she added softly.

Before Josh could answer, Madsen stood with a stack of papers. "Alright. Here are your new IDs, tickets, and passports. Guard these like your lives depend on it, since they do. Your flight leaves in exactly seventy-three minutes." He tapped his watch. "Seventy-three. Here are new cell phones. You each get your own. Keep these on you at all times, day or night. They're only for emergency, and they only call me. Any other information should be routed through your deputies. Understood?"

"How will we know when it's safe to come back?" Sadie asked. "Or what's going on with finding…"

"Guillermo," Josh said for her. Ever since the fire, Sadie struggled to say Guillermo's name.

"I'll contact you when we find him," Madsen said. "Anything else?"

Josh knew there was one last question, but it wasn't for Madsen. He turned and stared into Sadie's magnificent, dark eyes. He procrastinated another moment, imagining his future with her, both the immediate and long term. Even though he and Sadie talked about this and everyone, including his parents, agreed it was the best way to keep a low profile, suddenly Josh was floundering.

He reached into his suit pocket. This moment was nothing like he imagined it would be. Especially with four government employees watching him struggle to pull out the two wedding rings.

He wondered if he should drop to a knee, but that didn't seem right. Someday—with luck—he'd do it right, velvet box and all. For now, he clutched the rings.

"It's not, well, it's not like we originally planned," he said. "I know we said we could get some cheap rings somewhere along the way, but this morning my parents thought maybe…I don't know…we could use these until we decide—or you decide…" His mouth felt full of cotton. "…that you want…or think…" He groaned. This is what he got for not practicing.

"Seventy-one minutes," Madsen said.

Josh finally looked up. Instead of grimacing at what a loser she was stuck with, Sadie bit back a smile. That released his tensed muscles. He was taking this too seriously as usual. This was just part of the plan. He liked plans, and Sadie happened to like this one. So he turned over his hand and opened his fingers.

"Oh!" she cried softly. Her fingers reached up but stopped just short of the two rings. "They're real."

"Yeah. My parents said we could borrow theirs until"—Josh almost said *we get our own,* but thankfully caught himself—"for now. They thought these would be more convincing."

"Oh, they're convincing alright."

43

He nearly grabbed his mom's first, but since everything else in this situation was backward he bypassed it for his father's simple gold band. It was harder to get the wedding ring on his finger than it had that morning, even without the bad hand.

"It looks good on you," Sadie whispered.

"Yeah," he agreed, pleased by the thought. "Kevin would be happy."

She laughed, a beautiful sound. "Yes, he would."

With dark eyes dancing, she held up her left hand.

Working in the police department, on top of raising six kids, never amounted to much wealth for Josh's dad. His mom's diamond ring was nothing magnificent by the world's standards, yet it was beautiful and elegant in its own way—and undeniable: Mrs.

Josh slid the ring on Sadie's finger. The simple gesture sent electricity through him. That is…until he realized it was too big. It hung loosely on her tiny finger, something he hadn't anticipated.

He looked up, panicked. "It doesn't fit."

In an instant, he was backpedaling. The plan, the 'marriage', Tennessee, giving Sadie more time. They'd known each other three weeks and they were married?

Her gaze stayed on the ill-fitting ring with an unreadable expression.

"Maybe this is a bad idea," he said.

Madsen grunted in frustration. "No, it's not. Married couples attract less attention. Less attention means fewer questions. Fewer questions mean fewer mistakes. Joshua Young is single. Joshua Peterson is not. Joshua Young is transferring to BYU, but Joshua Peterson will never make it to Tennessee if he doesn't leave in the next two minutes. Stop waffling. Get the ring sized for all I care. Just do something! It's time to go!"

"Okay," Josh said. "We'll figure something out later."

"No, this is perfect." Sadie flashed him the tiniest smile. "For now."

For the life of him, Josh couldn't figure out why she ever picked him. He wasn't about to sit around and wait for her to change her mind. He slid his fingers into hers. "Alright. We're ready."

CHAPTER 6

"Things are going well, Mr. Vasquez. The markets are turning around."

Guillermo nodded. "Good. Thank you, my friend."

As his financial adviser gathered his things, Guillermo looked down on the Magnificent Mile, thinking more about his personal life than the Chicago Stock Exchange. It had been a rough couple of weeks, one horrible moment after another, but maybe his adviser was right. Things were finally turning around.

Augustina's funeral went well. The note was delivered with no traceable ties to him. And he found out what he suspected. The FBI was protecting that little punk of a college student. Why or how they knew Joshua Young needed protection, Guillermo wasn't sure. But if he ignored that side of things—it would be taken care of soon enough—everything else was settling down. Turning.

The city of Chicago was hidden in the dense winter fog as was Lake Michigan. As was the truth behind Sarah Augustina Dawson's death. It was hard to believe she was truly gone. In the heat of the moment, Guillermo had been rushed and strained. He'd been whisked away from Montana before he could even process her death. But now he had all the time in the world to process, and it hurt like hell. He'd loved Augustina like he'd loved no other.

A few of his contacts backed out after hearing of her death, cowards who weren't sure what to make of the drama. The rest sent their sympathies. Augustina had been admired by his associates, most especially by those at the New Year's Eve party. Guillermo accepted their sympathies readily. He was grieving for her loss, grieving for what could have been...had she not met Joshua Young.

The anger clouded his vision. Rejection wasn't something he was used to. He couldn't stomach it. Had he not taken care of things when he had, everything would have been ruined. A lifetime of building, growing, and working his way up the ladder would have been washed away in a single relationship.

Now the rumors were spreading like a California wildfire. The FBI was at it again. New allegations. New charges. A warrant for his arrest. Not for killing the beautiful Augustina. No. Even the FBI believed the suicide bit. But Guillermo was wanted for another murder. The ironic thing was he hadn't even killed the not-so-Special Agent Stephen Dubois. But it didn't matter how many campaign contributions or private donations he promised, the cowards wanted out, out, out. Only he couldn't afford to lose a single contact. Not now.

"It is time to put some pressure on the FBI," he said.

Salvador looked up. "So close to the funeral? Are you certain? The *federales* are everywhere."

"Yes. I need him. I need to know what he knows. We cannot wait any longer."

"Consider it done. Anything else? Would you like me to get your lawyer on the line?"

"No." Guillermo could get that report later. He didn't want to spoil his mood.

"Perhaps some quiet time? Should I send in Catalina?"

Guillermo shot his assistant a murderous look. He didn't want a woman. Women ruined everything. He wanted revenge. Revenge on Agent Madsen. Revenge on the FBI. But more than all the money in the world, he wanted revenge on the man who started it all. The man who ever dared look at his woman twice.

"I want Señor Young," he said more calmly than intended. "I want him now. Nothing more. Nothing less. Am I understood?"

Salvador fidgeted. "They are close, sir. His flight leaves soon. They are waiting for the right moment to grab him. We shall have him by the end of the hour, I am sure of it."

Guillermo considered that a moment. He smoothed the front of his black suit in an attempt to smooth his temper as well. "You are a confident one, my friend. Let us hope you are correct. Now go. Make the call. It is time to set things in motion."

"Understood."

"Oh, and Salvador?" Guillermo finally turned away from the window. "When they find Señor Young, bring him directly to me. There are some things I wish to say to him."

Salvador smiled. "It is nice to have you back, sir."

Sadie smiled as she and Josh entered a very crowded coach section. It was hard to believe she was leaving *with* Josh.

The plane was packed. She pulled the baseball cap over her eyes and pushed down the aisle. Deputy Croff sat first, taking the window seat. Sadie went next, hobbling into the middle seat. Josh took the aisle and Harrison sat across from him. The two seats next to Harrison were empty, the only empty seats on the plane as far as Sadie could tell. One of the perks of flying on the government's dime, she guessed.

"That was a little crazy," Josh said, struggling to adjust his seat belt with his bad arm.

"Very." She grabbed the seat belt for him and latched it. They'd been whisked in and out of cars, through a special security counter, and straight to the plane with hats pulled low and heads kept down. Between her and Josh's injuries, they were quite the pair. "Though I'd rather do that than go through regular security," she added. Another perk.

"Ha. True."

She studied Josh a moment, trying to see his familiar smile through the unfamiliar blond beard. She missed Josh, the real Josh. Not that he didn't look good. He always looked great, especially in a suit. Poor guy. He hadn't been able to change since the funeral. But between his blond hair and brown contacts, it was like waking up to his unfamiliar face the first time in Sam's cabin.

Just like he did then, he asked, "Are you okay?"

She rubbed her eyes. It seemed like everyone kept asking her that. "Yeah. Sorry. I'm just tired."

"Me, too." He leaned into his blue seat and closed his eyes.

Sadie sat forward to look out the small window. The furthest she ever traveled was to San Diego to visit Damien. Her mom's dream was to take her two kids to Buenos Aires where she'd grown up, but California was the best she'd managed. That's the way it was growing up with a single mom who made ends meet with a department clerk's wage.

Sadie was a little sad she didn't have a window seat to say goodbye to her Montana mountains, but since she also insisted on sitting by Josh, and since Deputy Croff and Deputy Harrison insisted on sitting next to their assigned refugees, Sadie was stuck looking over Deputy Croff's romance novel. Technically she'd get another glimpse of the Rocky Mountains during their layover in Denver, but after that it was pure Smokies. *Tennessee here we come.*

She was proud of herself for not crying. She was even more proud she'd been tear-free for a whole hour. It's probably the longest Josh had seen her go without crying. Not really, but it felt like it lately. It was high time to convince him she really wasn't a weepy, emotional basket case. He'd become her rock amidst a shifting tide, but now that her life was on a better path—or at least a safer one—she was ready to be her own rock again. Or maybe even his. Wouldn't that be nice?

The flight attendant's voice came over the speaker starting the routine. Sadie turned to watch her through the crack between the seats. She didn't like sitting on the front row where she couldn't see the 150 passengers behind her. With the loud engines revving up, she couldn't hear them either. It was unsettling. Why couldn't Agent Madsen put them in the back of the plane instead? They'd be out of the way back there, too, only then she would be the one watching all the rows instead of being the one watched. She had more than her fair share of unseen eyes watching her the last month.

The man in the row behind her looked up from his airline magazine. He gave her a quick smile, but his bushy mustache twitched with curiosity. Sadie faced forward again and tried to relax. Josh's eyes were closed, Harrison's were halfway there, and Croff was well into her book. They weren't bothered by the 150 strangers behind them.

Deep breath.

It dawned on Sadie why she had the jitters. This was her first time in public since Guillermo kidnapped her. It didn't matter where they sat on the plane, it didn't matter what happened that morning with the redhead. Everything was being taken care of. Everything was fine. They were safe.

She took in another slow breath. Perfectly safe.

Only…

What if they weren't?

"Are you sure you're okay?" Josh raised their intertwined hands, bringing attention to the fact that she was squeezing the life out of his.

"Sorry." She eased her grip.

He eyed her, concern etched on his face. He wasn't worried about himself. He wasn't worried about his sprained arm or how close he'd come to a far worse fate. He wasn't even worried if someone on the plane knew exactly who he was like they had at the funeral. No. He was worried about *her* of all things.

"I love you," she said over the roar of the engine. His brows creased further and she quickly added, "I'm fine. Really. Go to sleep."

Deputy Croff lowered her book, exchanging a glance with Harrison on the other side of Josh. Sadie ignored both Marshals, pushed up the armrest, and wiggled under Josh's arm into the least painful position she could find. It was lucky she was on his good side. He hugged her, kissed her forehead, and lay back against the seat.

Sadie did her best to hold still so he could sleep. He'd stayed up later than her to finalize plans with Madsen—plans she just tossed out the motel window. But she didn't want to sleep. Or close her eyes. For some reason, she felt the need to get up and walk around.

Her tender ribs ached in her crooked position, yet she refused to move. Josh's arm shielded her from the cold air blowing directly above. She hoped Tennessee would be as warm as Mississippi was supposed to be, even in January.

Tennessee.

Mississippi.

Something didn't sit right. How was it possible after Josh stayed up half the night finalizing their plan—not to mention the three days before that—Madsen was able to completely shift gears in five minutes? How could Madsen have thought through every tiny detail like Josh always did? He couldn't have. Not that fast.

What if by changing plans, Sadie put them in more danger? What if Madsen hadn't researched all of Guillermo's real estate ventures that quickly? For all they knew, Guillermo owned property in Tennessee, a house in Knoxville or cabin or something, and that's where he was hiding now. Had anyone checked *that* in the motel? No. She knew they hadn't. Because ever since she and Josh agreed to Tennessee, everything had been a whirlwind. New tickets. New plans. Seventy-three minutes.

Harrison had three seats to himself even though the rest of the plane was jam-packed. The other passengers should have been complaining, and yet they weren't. An empty window seat of all things. How long would it take them to know something was different about the people in the front row? Or did they already?

Sadie carefully inched out from under Josh, tweaking her casted foot as she stole another glance around. She peeked in between the seats. Nobody looked their direction. Nobody except the man with the mustache seated directly behind Josh. He lowered his airline magazine and smiled at her again.

She turned back quickly and pulled her hat lower over her eyes. A baggy sweatshirt and a hat. How was that supposed to hide her when a blond beard and contacts hadn't hidden Josh? True, no one had seen her with her hair so short since Guillermo nearly scalped her—it barely curled out under the hat—but still...the man smiled at her too quickly. And that bushy mustache. There was something familiar about him. She'd seen him somewhere before, hadn't she? She searched her memories, coming up short.

Think!

Josh was breathing deeply, well on his way to sleep, but Harrison leaned forward and shot her a warning glance. The deputy hadn't said more than four words as they rushed through the airport. "Keep moving" and "Blend in." It wasn't hard to decipher which one he silently yelled now.

Closing her eyes, she sat back and worked to slow her breathing. How long before she quit looking over her shoulder? Too long. Yet not looking started everything the last time. She'd been too trusting, too naïve. Even when her mom told her people were spying on them, Sadie dismissed it.

She lowered the wall of memories long enough to remember the way Mr. Ugly laughed at her.

"You're so stupid, beautiful. It was a test. And guess what? You failed!"

She shivered against the plane's regurgitated air, knowing she should stop the memories while she could, but the wall was already down. Everything came faster and faster: the man watching her in the Blue Moose; the men following her on the ski slopes; Salvador reciting every move she and her mom made down to the precise movie her mom rented for their girls' night.

By the time Sadie reached that dark Mercedes, Guillermo didn't need her journal. He already knew every step she'd taken, every incriminating word of every phone call. Yet he brilliantly used her own words to convict her.

Her pulse pounded in her ears. She begged her mind to make it stop. She squeezed her eyes tight, trying to envision Whitefish Lake, her place of solace, but Guillermo's dark face was no longer in the Mercedes, it was right before her.

"I shall truly enjoy the game of hunting him down."

Her chest constricted. Killing Josh was just a game to Guillermo, a game he refused to lose. If her old locker-partner could be working for him, any of the 150 people behind her could be. Hunting Josh.

She turned, searching the passengers she could see. But what about the ones she couldn't? What if the man in leather was there? Or Luis? Or Salvador?

No. It wouldn't be them. She knew their faces too well. Of course, she was supposedly dead. But still, Guillermo would use someone new this time. It could be anyone.

The mustached man behind Josh's chair looked straight at her. There was a smile in his eyes, but there was no mistaking the malice.

Her heart pounded against her broken ribs. She felt more alive than she ever had.

His eyes flickered to the sleeping woman next to him, and then he shook his head imperceptibly. It was a message for Sadie, only she didn't know what. With a smile that sent a shiver down her spine, he raised his magazine and hid again.

Just like the skier in leather had.

Just like Guillermo had.

Suddenly she couldn't breathe. She whirled around and searched the window. *We have to get out of here.* He could be planning anything. He could have a gun, a knife.

We have to get out of here!

Part of her was telling herself she was overreacting, another was telling her to run. Fast.

The pain won out. She stifled a cry and sank lower in her seat. She checked the window again. Sealed. She searched for an exit. Too far. She checked the watch she didn't have. Why hadn't they taken off? The flight attendant finished minutes ago, yet they hadn't budged. How far was Denver?

Too far!

She peeked over her shoulder again. The mustached guy stared at her with a long, hard stare. He was no longer smiling, but his eyes hardened into a thin, cold line.

It's him! she gasped. Guillermo's man. She'd known it the second she saw him.

In the same choking breath, she tried to talk herself out of it. *It's all in your head. All in your head!*

Josh sat up. "Sadie?"

The mustached guy could have anything. A gun. Guillermo's knife. Four other men working with him. Or 150.

Her breathing turned into rhythmic stabbing against her ribs. Her vision started to go dark, and she felt herself spiraling out of control. But she couldn't stop.

She turned another time. Josh turned as well, curious. The man went back to his magazine, pretending to ignore both of them.

That's when Sadie knew. The mustached man wouldn't attack them now. He would wait like the redhead had. He would stalk them in Denver. Drag out the game until Sadie was alone. Or worse…

…Josh was.

Josh leaned close. "What's wrong?"

If it wasn't that man, it was one of the other passengers. Or were there two? Or 150?

She sank deeper in her seat.

Josh turned and took over the search. That set Harrison and Croff off. All three scanned the rows up and down looking for nobody knew what.

Sadie kept telling herself it was all in her head, but what if it wasn't? She never thought Josh would get a gun pulled on him at the funeral. She never thought her mom was being stalked. She never thought Guillermo was who the feds said he was. She never thought *anything* before it was too late.

"Who is it?" Josh whispered in her ear.

"No one," she said, begging it to be true. Her heart raced a mile a minute. Her breathing punched her lungs over and over again. The majority of the first ten rows were looking their way now. Something was wrong, and everyone knew it.

Blend in! she yelled at herself. *Blend in!*

Too late. The dominoes were set in motion. Even if she calmed down, she'd attracted attention. People didn't like other people looking at them on airplanes. Especially panicked, heart-racing people.

Harrison stood, sizing up the situation. The flight attendant walked stiffly toward him and told him to sit down.

"What did you see?" Josh asked Sadie again.

"Nothing," she answered. Her voice came out as a wheeze. Her throat swelled, cutting off her air. Each beat of the heart was a stab to her cracked ribs.

Josh spoke hurriedly to Harrison and the flight attendant while Croff grabbed a doggie bag and shoved Sadie's head between her knees.

"Breathe," Croff demanded.

Tears streamed down Sadie's cheeks and rolled onto the blue carpet.

Blend in! Blend in! Blend in!

The pain was unbearable. With her head down, the plane began to spin. Her ears rang with a high-pitched scream. Even if the 150 people hadn't noticed them before, they had now. She could hear the concerned voices.

Another flight attendant joined them. And then another.

And then it happened.

The man with the mustache rose. "May I be of assistance?"

Sadie's hands flew over her head, anticipating the blow. He wouldn't wait. He would strike now. Would it be her or Josh?

"No," Harrison replied sharply. "We have this under control. Sit down, sir."

"I'm a doctor," the man insisted. "I can help."

A doctor. A redhead. A friend.

Sadie couldn't breathe. Waiting. Tensing. Praying.

Make it stop!

"Stand back, sir. Now!" Harrison warned.

Sadie didn't know what the mustached man did, because her head was down and Josh was pleading with her to calm down—or at least explain what was wrong. But he kept stroking her hair. Over and over and over again. Like Guillermo had. Stroking. Whispering. Which meant any second he would pull a knife on her.

"Don't touch me!" she shrieked, voice far too raspy to convey her desperation.

Josh's hand flew off of her.

The plane began to dip forward. She looked around wildly. Nothing had moved. It was her.

All of it was her.

"I have to get out of here!" she cried, throat hoarse with tears. "Please. Make it stop!"

CHAPTER 7

Sadie stared at a huge, gray mop.

She sat on the cement floor of an airport janitorial closet, leaned against a wall. She wasn't crying. She wasn't even hyperventilating anymore. She was just staring. Every once in a while she blinked. That was it. Technically she was breathing, too, but it didn't feel like it.

Josh sat against the opposite wall next to the mop and yellow bucket, staring at her even though there was nothing left to see.

She felt completely empty inside. Hollow. Like she'd shoved her brain in neutral and if she put it back into gear—forward or reverse—it would shatter into a million pieces. So she stared. Neutral. At Josh's mop.

The last hour, or however long it had been, was a blur. Emptying the plane. Emptying this section of the airport. The FBI was efficient if nothing else. Or was it the U.S. Marshals? She didn't know, and she didn't care.

She barely made it off the plane before her body quit. She stopped at a door and could hobble no more. Neutral. She didn't know where the door led except away. Before she opened it, she made sure to tell Josh goodbye. Yet he followed. He always did.

He just didn't get it.

Most of the 150 people would have no problem identifying him now. Her, too. Just that fast, she made them the most popular people on the plane.

Harrison and Croff, along with half the Missoula PD, had the fun job of narrowing the list down for questioning. Last update Croff gave them, they only questioned two passengers: the mustached doctor and another guy from the back of the plane who went ballistic when he found out he would miss his connection. Neither turned up anything the tiniest bit suspicious. Not even a parking ticket. They were free to join the other 148 waiting for another flight to Denver.

Scratch that. 147. Sadie wasn't going. Neither was Josh apparently. 146. Which meant Harrison and Croff were stuck in Missoula, too. 144. All three of them were waiting for her to move. Forward or backward. Something other than neutral. But there was no way she was getting back on that plane. Which meant no Denver. Or Tennessee. She was sitting. Staring. Hollow.

Empty.

Her gaze dropped to her wrists. Though the welts were healing, the faint red lines were like a slap in the face. A slap that said no matter where she ran or where she hid, she'd never be free of Guillermo's chains. For the rest of her life, she would be his prisoner, looking over her shoulder, behind her back, through the crowds. She would never feel safe again. He made sure of it.

Her ribs weren't broken. She was.

Her ankle wasn't broken.

She was.

That's what the doctors forgot to tell Josh.

That's what the doctors forgot to tell her.

The slashes on her wrists blurred beyond recognition. "This isn't me," she whispered.

Josh said nothing, but she could feel his arms wrap around her even though he sat three long feet away and wasn't touching any part of her whatsoever—taking the "Don't touch me!" thing literally. Considering how she yelled it on the plane, she didn't blame him. But she knew he wanted to hold her right now. His face said so. Which is why she could feel his arms around her. It was nice.

Empty, but nice.

Of course, she could also tell he was terrified. His face said that, too. One of the lousy things about having a transparent face was that it never lied. If it had, maybe she would have invited his securing embrace. But he looked petrified, frozen like she was, only by a different fear.

She was the one that changed his carefully thought out plan today. *She* was the one that selfishly endangered his life by freaking out on the plane. And ultimately, no matter how much she didn't want it to be true, *she* was the one that betrayed Josh's name to Guillermo in that dark Mercedes. She should have protected Josh like he would have protected her. But no. She didn't. One little gun and she caved, forever destroying his life.

She was a coward. She was nothing.

Just like Christmas evening.

Just like now.

Acid burned her throat. "This isn't me," she lied again. Hot tears streamed down her face because no matter how many times she said it, she couldn't make it true. This *was* her. Every last bit of it. This is who she'd become. Broken. Empty. Nothing.

Someone opened the door. Deputy Croff. Sadie's eyes stayed on the gray mop, but Josh jumped to his feet. "Media?" he asked.

"No," Croff said. "Everything's under control. It was labeled a medical emergency, and everything's been dismissed. Your luggage is here, so we're ready. How are things in here?"

Josh didn't respond. At least, not verbally. Sadie didn't check to see what wondrous things his expression said now. Disappointment? Disbelief?

Disgust?

Deputy Croff scrunched down next to Sadie. "Are you ready to go?"

Sadie didn't blink. Didn't move.

"We've got a car and a wheelchair waiting as soon as you're ready."

A car? Now they were driving to Tennessee? With her luck, she'd have a nervous breakdown before Wyoming. Then what? Insane asylum? Straightjacket?

And then she caught up to the second half of what Deputy Croff said. A wheelchair.

Because she was broken.

"Airport security cleared the area," Croff went on. "There's no one around. It's just the four of us. You're safe, Sadie." She straightened and extended a hand, waiting for Sadie to put herself back together and shift back into gear. Forward. "Are you ready, Mrs. Peterson?"

Sadie's gaze dropped to her left hand having forgotten about the ring. It hung clumsily from her finger. It didn't fit which, in a way, was fitting. She didn't belong with Josh. She'd stolen him from another. Someone who would have kept his name safe. The ring felt unbearably heavy.

She looked at Josh's wedding ring wondering if he felt the same way, wondering if he was desperate for some way to hit the reverse button and back out. Probably not. He didn't know how to protect himself any more than she did. But if he was waiting for her to make the first move, he would have to wait a long time.

She liked neutral. Neutral was easier. Neutral didn't hurt. Neutral was safe. Neutral meant staying in the janitorial closet, possibly forever. That was her now. Path-of-least-resistance Girl. Janitorial-closet Girl.

Deputy Croff looked at Josh for help. He sat back on the cement floor, staining his nice church suit with who knew what.

"We're staying," he said.

"Here?" Croff glanced around the small supply closet as if she'd never considered the possibility.

"Yes."

The Marshal glanced back and forth between them, panicking now that her walking targets were no longer walking. And in such a public place? Airport security couldn't keep this part of the terminal closed forever, could they? Sadie guessed the thoughts racing through Croff's head. Including her next question. "For how long?"

Forever, Sadie thought at the same time Josh said, "As long as it takes." Which basically meant the same thing.

Croff finally took the hint. She shut the metal door. Then Sadie listened as Croff had the exact same conversation with Harrison, only with Croff playing Josh's part.

Harrison didn't take the news well that the four of them were moving into Missoula International Airport's janitorial closet. But the way Croff chewed him out right after convinced Sadie that Josh had picked the right deputy for her.

Josh picked.

Because she couldn't.

Broken.

"Sadie?" Josh said softly.

She refused to look away from the gray mop, refused to blink, knowing that if she did either it would break her. So much for being Josh's rock. The only rock she'd become was a huge boulder he was trying to hold up while treading water. He'd never be able to keep them both afloat. At this rate, he wouldn't last much longer. If only she could convince him to let her go, he could save himself.

"You know it's okay, right?" he said.

Did he mean that it was okay they were moving into a janitorial closet, or that Deputy Croff just chewed out Deputy Harrison? Did he mean it was okay she screamed at him on the airplane, or that she was losing her mind? Or how about his sprained arm? Was that okay? Or that she'd shut down a wing of the Missoula airport? Or how about the fact that she'd ruined 150 lives; strike that, 500 lives if she included those from the funeral. Add to it Sam's family who no longer had a cabin and Josh's family who no longer had a son. Her mom. Damien. How many was that? She couldn't keep up.

Or could he possibly mean that any day now—if they were lucky—the FBI would find Guillermo, convict him, imprison him, and then break the news to him that he hadn't killed her after all. She would be forced to stare into those murderous eyes as she testified against him, hoping by some miracle he would forgive her enough to let her live a normal life after she destroyed his.

Was that okay?

Could that ever be okay?

Because from where she was sitting, on a sticky cement floor, staring at a mop next to the fake husband she barely recognized, she was pretty sure nothing was okay. Nothing would ever be okay ever again.

"You know we don't have to go anywhere," Josh said. "We can stay here as long as you want."

She swallowed. He was pushing her over the edge. By saying she could stay in neutral he was actually forcing her to shift gears.

Forward.

Her breathing sped up. Her throat burned.

"This isn't me," she said so softly no one could have possibly heard.

Except he did.

His fake-brown eyes filled with tears. "I know."

That did it. That forced her over the edge. Her eyes closed and her bottom lip trembled.

Josh ignored her earlier request. He kicked some boxes out of the way, crawled over, and completely enveloped her as a flood of tears exploded hard and heavy.

CHAPTER 8

They stopped that night in Billings. Sadie slept most of the ride, or at least she pretended to. Josh wasn't sure. When she was awake, she nodded at the right times and smiled when pressed. But mostly she looked out her frosted window, which would have been fine except she kept her arms folded the whole time, keeping her hands tucked away from him. Anytime she fell asleep it was against the window, not him. The day had taken its toll on her—the week, the month—and he wanted desperately to help, only he didn't know how.

He kept his left hand on the seat between them, like a teenager in a movie theater begging the girl to notice. A few times he caught her staring at his hand. Not the one laying on the seat like a lame offering, but the other one. The bad one. Beyond that, it was like he didn't have another hand. But he kept it there, hoping if they could stay connected somehow, everything else would work out.

Yet as the night wore on, her arms folded more tightly and she leaned further and further away. Even her casted leg was tucked as far under the driver's seat as she could manage. It felt like they were back in Sam's cabin and any minute she'd bolt out the back door into the knee-deep snow.

Harrison and Croff took turns driving, hoping to make it to Wyoming the first night. Once it was dark they were forced to a crawl. It wasn't snowing, but it might as well have been. Giant snow drifts blew across the I-90 stretch. By nine o'clock it was impossible to see anything. The three of them—four if Josh counted Sadie's blinks—agreed to stop for the night. They pulled into Billings and found a small motel.

Harrison let the car idle and looked over the seat at Josh. "You have to come in with me."

"Okay." Josh waited a second for Sadie to turn. When her eyes met his, he smiled. "I'll be back in a minute."

She smiled, too, but it was empty. She was there in body only.

Hoping a good night sleep would help, Josh opened his door and ran after his bodyguard through the bitter wind.

"We need a room," Harrison said to the motel clerk. "Preferably two queens."

Josh stomped his feet on the mat and looked out the glass doors. He hoped Croff wouldn't make Sadie come inside while she set up their room. There wasn't a chair anywhere in the lobby, and he couldn't imagine Sadie wanted to hold herself up on crutches for that long. Surely Deputy Croff would let Harrison watch Sadie for a few minutes. They had to have some compassion.

"You wouldn't have three beds in a room, would you?" Harrison asked. "Or two beds and a couch? Croff's going to make me sleep on the floor. I just know it."

Josh's head jerked up. Two beds he could understand—not that he needed a whole queen to himself; a double or single would have been plenty. But three didn't make any sense. Unless Harrison thought...that... His stomach dropped. *Oh, no.* One room for the four of them?

"Wait, wait, wait. Hold on," Josh said, rushing forward. "One room won't work. We need two rooms tonight," he said to the woman behind the desk. "Two *separate* rooms."

"No," Harrison said. "Just one." He lowered his voice. "I don't care how much privacy you and Sadie want, there's no bending the rules. Croff and I aren't letting you two out of our sight, so get used to it. We're all adults here. Besides, Croff and I have seen our share. Believe me."

Josh's face went hot. "I meant two rooms as in you and I in one, Croff and Sadie in the other."

Harrison grabbed Josh's arm and pulled him aside. "You guys are married," he whispered.

"No. We aren't."

"Fine, but you're supposed to be. I thought you two are dating."

Josh gritted his teeth, wondering why Madsen hadn't filled Harrison in on this little aspect of Mormon culture. Then suddenly he wondered if *he'd* filled Agent Madsen in on this little aspect of Mormon culture.

A pit formed in his gut. *Tennessee!*

Josh was the one who set up their side-by-side apartments in Mississippi, not Madsen. Madsen might not have even noticed. Josh had no idea what was set up for them in Knoxville. For all he knew, the four of them were moving into one tiny apartment. With three beds. Or worse...two.

Josh groaned, picturing his parents' reaction to that one.

Shoving thoughts of Tennessee aside—he'd fix that later—he focused on the problem at hand. But there was one thought that overshadowed the others. If Harrison and Madsen were clueless, what was Sadie expecting for tonight? For the next month? The next year? After all, like Harrison said they were 'married.' Most married people cohabitated.

He shook his head. She knew him better than that, didn't she? They talked about his religion in the nursing home, but not that aspect of it. He hoped she knew enough about his church and the firm 'wait' clause he'd committed to. Considering her blatant distance in the car, he hoped it was a moot point. This wasn't the time or place to go into the Law of Chastity with Harrison *or* Sadie.

He stepped back up to the desk. "We'll take two rooms," he said firmly. "Two queens each please."

As Josh and Harrison left their room ten minutes later, Harrison was still smirking. Josh finally explained the reason behind the separate rooms, and the U.S. Marshal couldn't let it go. "So you're telling me you've never—"

"No," Josh snapped, temper flaring. That was the last time he was answering. Four times was bad enough. He was trying to give the deputy all the respect and appreciation his title deserved, but the guy was making it difficult. Josh had more important things to worry about than his sex life— or lack thereof.

"What about Sadie? Has she ever—"

Josh whirled around so fast Harrison fell back a step. His hands flew up. "Sorry. I'm done. That's cool. I was just curious."

As Josh knocked on Sadie's door, he struggled to rid Harrison's second question from his mind. He had no idea if Sadie had been with other men. Probably. With a boyfriend like Guillermo, most likely. His heart sunk. Definitely.

It doesn't matter, he told himself. Then he told himself again. And one last time to make it stick.

Deputy Croff opened the motel door a crack. Even though she phoned two minutes earlier saying they were ready for dinner, she wasn't wearing her thick winter coat.

"Sadie said she's too tired for dinner," Croff said. "Sorry."

Josh looked behind her. Their room was dark. Sadie had gone to bed. Though he was selfish enough to be disappointed, he told himself it was for the best. It was time to be done with the long, horrible day.

"Alright," he said. "You want us to pick up any dinner for you?"

Croff smiled. "No thanks. See you guys in the morning."

Sadie said little over breakfast. She ate little, too. Just a cup of coffee and a piece of toast. Josh watched her, unable to do anything else. After a couple bites, he pushed his waffle aside, feeling his appetite waning as well.

Time. He kept telling himself she just needed time.

They both did.

They fell into a pattern. Drive. Stop for gas. Drive. Stop for lunch. Drive. Drive. Drive.

Croff suggested they take a break and do a little sightseeing. When Josh asked Sadie if she wanted to see Mount Rushmore her mouth said, "If you want," but her eyes said, "No." That was fine with him. He wanted to get her as far away from Montana as possible. The faster the better.

Though Josh originally planned to help with driving, he didn't offer, and Croff and Harrison didn't ask. Croff read while Harrison drove, and Harrison slept while she drove. Josh lost all desire for communication with anyone but Sadie, who spoke less than the two deputies, making for a very long, very quiet day.

He couldn't bear to leave his hand on the seat anymore, knowing he'd crossed the line from wanting to help her to needing reassurance he wasn't losing her altogether, this time to some unforeseeable force in her mind. Yet with every mile, he could feel the distance growing between them. So he switched from leaving his hand on the seat to going through every possible thing to help her once they were in Tennessee: namely, therapy—and not just the physical kind. He planned on finding the most highly-qualified, highly-recommended counselor.

But even those thoughts couldn't keep him company forever. As they passed a sign for Nebraska he thought about his family. He leaned forward in his seat. "Do you have a map?"

Croff handed back an ancient GPS. Josh zoomed out of their spot on I-90. Just as he thought. They were driving in a perfect parallel line north of the Nebraska border.

Sadie looked at him for the first time in an hour. "What is it?"

Josh scanned the cities of Nebraska, trying to remember where his brother was serving his mission. He hadn't thought to ask for Jake's address from his parents. Not that it mattered a whole lot since Josh couldn't write him. Plus Jake would be off his mission in April. He'd be home soon enough. Not that Josh would see him.

Josh punched a button to take them back to their current location. "Nebraska. My little brother's on his mission there."

Sadie sat up. "I forgot. Do you want to stop and see him?"

"No. That's okay. I was just curious to see how close we are."

"Probably really close. Let's stop. Can we stop?" she asked Harrison.

Harrison gripped the steering wheel. "No."

"Yes, we can," she said. "Josh didn't get to say goodbye to his parents. He should at least say goodbye to his brother."

Josh was backpedaling. "That's okay. We can't see Jake anyway. Missionaries aren't allowed to have visitors—especially family."

"But you haven't seen him for two years!" Sadie sat on the edge of her seat. "I'd love to meet your brother, any of your siblings actually. How far away are we?" She took the GPS from Josh and flipped back to Nebraska.

Josh wanted to kick himself. It was the most emotion he'd seen in her all day. "Even if we were driving through his town—which I can't seem to remember—I wouldn't stop. They're really strict on the *no visitors* thing. Besides, Jake only has a few months left."

She continued to scan the map. "I'm sure if they knew the situation they'd let you see him. Who knows how long it will be before you see him again? We have to stop."

Josh couldn't help himself. He was suddenly considering the possibility of seeing Jake, not for his own sake, but for Sadie's. Was that so bad? Bend the rule a little? He rubbed his itchy beard. Like she said, Jake's mission president would understand the strange situation. His little brother probably didn't even know anything that happened to Josh in the last three weeks, let alone his complicated future.

If it would make Sadie happy…

The thought of introducing his crazy, fun-loving brother to Sadie, the girl who used to be that way, was enticing enough to have Josh searching the map with her. He checked all the names hoping something would ring a bell. Omaha? Grand Island? If he could just remember where his brother was serving, he was certain the mission president would make an exception. Just this once. See Jake. Make Sadie happy.

But…

No contact. None.

Harrison glared at Josh in the rearview mirror. Madsen would have Josh's head for this. Same with Josh's parents, who weren't rule breakers. And after the funeral, Josh vowed not to be either.

He looked into Sadie's large, expectant eyes. "I really don't think we can. But it's okay." He smiled, hoping she believed him. Hoping she knew he was resolved and happy with this new life he'd chosen. "I just wondered how close we were, that's all."

She studied him a long, silent moment. Then she blinked rapidly and turned back to her frosted window. "Not close enough."

Sadie was still looking out the window when the sun set, but every few minutes she shifted positions. By the tenth time, Josh couldn't stand the silence anymore. "Are you feeling okay?"

She barely looked at him. "Yeah. I'm fine. You?"

"Fine."

He continued to watch her. She leaned to the right a moment and then back against the seat. A minute of that and she leaned forward slightly as if trying to find a spot that didn't hurt.

"Are you sure you're fine?" he asked. "We've been driving a long time. Do you ribs hurt? Or your leg? Probably both, right?"

"I'm fine. Really." She gave him a tiny smile. "You?"

Small talk. He hated it. Next they'd talk about the weather. "When did you take your medication last?" he asked.

"When did *you*?" she shot back.

He jerked up. "What? I don't have any medication."

Her expression hardened. "Neither do I."

Josh stared at her. He couldn't believe it. Sadie threw out her pain medication. He could see it in her defiant eyes. Why would she do something like that? No wonder she was so uncomfortable.

"Sadie…" he started.

"I'm fine."

"At least tell me you're doing your breathing exercises."

"I'm fine," she said, turning back to the window.

Fine, fine, fine. Only she wasn't. Nine hours on the road and even *his* ribs and legs ached.

"What about dinner then? You didn't eat any lunch and you barely ate breakfast. Are you hungry?"

"No. Why? Do you want dinner?"

"Yes." He leaned forward and spoke over the seat. "In fact, I think we should stop for the night. Is there a city coming up?"

Harrison grumbled something under his breath, but Croff nodded. "We're about twenty miles from Sioux Falls. We can stop there."

"We've come 1,061 miles since leaving Missoula," Harrison said. "We still have 1,113 more to Knoxville and you want to stop? Now? At 5:18 PM?"

Josh glared at the deputy in the mirror. "Yes."

"Great. Just great."

"Look on the bright side," Croff said. "We're almost halfway."

"Halfway," Sadie whispered.

Josh glanced sideways. The relief in her voice was almost palpable. He nearly took her hand which she'd left on the seat—probably accidentally—but didn't. He wasn't sure if she still wanted space.

They bypassed several nice hotels in Sioux Falls and pulled into another small motel, more run down than the first. It had two cars in the parking lot, which made the anticipated smoky rooms and lumpy beds worth it. The VACANCY sign was missing the letters *C* and *A*. Had circumstances been different, Josh would have pointed out the irony of the title "VANCY" over the run down motel. He and Sadie would have laughed and poked fun of the place that was as far from "fancy" as any he'd seen. He didn't.

As he reached for the handle to follow Harrison to the lobby, something inside him snapped. He turned back. "What sounds good for dinner?"

Sadie shrugged. "Whatever you want."

"Italian?"

"Whatever."

"Pizza? Mexican?" He had no idea what kind of food Sadie liked. He'd only eaten a few non-hospital meals with her and the longer she shrugged it off—shrugged him off—the less it felt like he knew her at all. "Thai? Steak? Cheap Chinese takeout?"

Her eyes lit up on the last one. Perhaps a memory of being in Sam's cabin with Trevor, Sam, and Kevin, eating horribly cheap Chinese food. But just as quickly it passed. "Whatever you want. You choose."

Josh was out of ideas. Harrison crossed his arms angrily on the curb. A light snow fell and the wind blew sideways into the open car door. It was freezing, but Josh couldn't stop himself.

"Sushi? Burger and fries? Ice cream?" *Just say something!* "Or maybe fast food. Does that sound good? Or hot chocolate? Or how about Mongolian barbe—"

"Italian," she interrupted.

Josh stopped mid-barbeque. "Italian? That sounds good?"

The little sassy spark returned—small as it was—along with the tiniest sliver of a smile. "Yes. Don't hurt yourself. Italian sounds great. Thank you."

Josh smiled. Sadie wanted Italian. It was a stupid, trivial thing, but he was beaming as he strode inside the motel lobby. *Don't hurt yourself.* The strong-willed, spunky Sadie he'd fallen in love with was still in there somewhere.

By the time Josh and Harrison dropped off their stuff and made it to Sadie's room, Josh was fully grinning. His stomach growled and he was glad he insisted they stop when they had. He even stopped by the lobby to ask for the best Italian restaurant in town. The man at the front desk recommended the 'quaint' little place across the street. 'Quaint' sounded as wonderful as *Don't hurt yourself.* It sounded normal. Josh was desperate to do something normal with Sadie. If he pretended Croff and Harrison were dating—or even better, weren't there at all—it almost felt like he was picking Sadie up for a date. Their first.

He finger-combed his fake-blond hair before knocking on their door.

Like the night before, Deputy Croff was the one to crack open the door. And like the night before she wasn't wearing a coat, the lights were off, and Sadie was nowhere to be seen. The look on Croff's face broke the news before she could.

"Sorry, Josh," Croff said. "I tried."

He stared in disbelief. "But she said Italian. She told me she wanted Italian." It was the first direct answer she'd given. Their first date. It wasn't even six o'clock!

"I know. I'm sorry."

"And she hasn't eaten all day." He tried to keep his voice to a whisper, and yet failed to mask his disappointment.

"Neither have I," Harrison growled under his breath.

Josh stared at the snow beneath his shoes, trying to tell himself Sadie was just avoiding the crowds, not him. That she didn't want to be around people tonight. Not him. While his mind might believe it, his heart struggled.

"What do I do?" he whispered more to the heavens than the U.S. Marshals.

Deputy Croff studied him a long moment. She quickly checked over her shoulder and then swung the door open wide. "Try harder."

CHAPTER 9

Guillermo threw the report across the room, splaying papers everywhere. "Where is he?" he roared.

Salvador cowered. "His name is on the flight list: Joshua David Young. But he never showed, sir. He has not returned to school even though the semester already began."

"What about home?"

"We have no way of knowing. As of yet, we have been unable to determine his family's whereabouts."

"Why?"

Silence filled the apartment.

Guillermo turned slowly. "That was not a rhetorical question. I demand an answer."

"We are struggling to find his family's information, but Mr. Young is not in Spokane. I am certain of it. We watched every passenger on every flight to Spokane. He could have rented a car to return, but those reports are coming up empty as well."

"Why has he not returned to his schooling?"

"Because…" Salvador winced.

"Spit it out!"

"I think, sir…it is because the FBI is protecting him."

Guillermo breathed deeply to keep from blowing a gasket. He ran his hands through his jet-black hair. "Why? That is the question we must answer. Señor Young had no contact with Augustina after he left her on New Year's Day. He went back to his Mormon girlfriend, so why is the FBI guarding him? Why did they move him?" His blood began to boil. "He has no reason to fear me!"

"Except you want him dead," Manuel said from across the room.

Guillermo whirled around. "You think you are so clever, little brother? No one knows I want Young's blood. Unless one of you has been squealing like a newborn piglet—which if that is the case, I will find out. Better come clean now."

Manuel clamped his mouth shut. Guillermo watched him another moment to make certain, but Manuel looked innocent enough.

With a few deep breaths, he started again more calmly. "Salvador, my well-paid friend, I want the young mouse found now. Not tomorrow. Not the next day. Now. Whatever Señor Young thinks he knows must be silenced, and it must be silenced today. Do you understand?"

Salvador's head bobbed. "Yes, sir."

As Salvador left, Guillermo pointed at his brother. "You. Come with me."

Manuel groaned. "Oh man, what'd I do now?"

Sadie hadn't been asleep after all. When Josh entered the dark room she was sitting on top of the covers fully dressed staring at nothing. But as Croff flipped on the lights and she spotted Josh in the doorway, she smiled. It was the same empty, vacant smile she'd given him since the airport, but he took it as welcome enough and walked in.

With a call to the front desk, he got the number of the Italian place. Unfortunately 'quaint' little Italian places didn't deliver. He refused to leave to pick up the food and risk the chance Sadie wouldn't let him back in.

Neither could he bear to ask what she wanted to eat again. So with one more call, he found a pizza place to deliver salads, breadsticks, and some pizza. Quasi-Italian.

When the food arrived, Croff and Harrison did their best to give Josh and Sadie some privacy, which meant the deputies sat on one bed watching TV while Josh and Sadie sat on the other. Not quite a date, but not all bad either.

Sadie and Josh faced each other. Her neon green cast was stretched out across the bedspread. The rest of her was curled into a ball, arms hugging her knee. She hadn't touched her pizza or Josh's hand, but she was talking. Finally.

"Tell me about your mom," she said.

"You met her," Josh said with another bite. "She's awesome. Talkative. Sometimes a little on the crazy side. What do you want to know?"

She traced the lines on the quilted comforter. "Not that mom."

Oh.

There were only a few things Josh remembered about his real mom and those were cemented in his mind.

Suddenly he wanted to change the subject. He wanted to keep the conversation light and happy, something that could bring back Sadie's smile. Yet he was sick to death of small talk. If she wanted to know about his real mom then…

"She walked out when I was five and Jake was two," he started. "I only saw her twice after that. One of those times…was at her funeral."

"Funeral?"

He nodded.

"I'm sorry," Sadie whispered. "I didn't know."

He shrugged it off. "From what my dad tells me, she was pretty outgoing in her younger years. But the last few years she became"—he paused to find a better word; sadly, there wasn't one—"volatile. My dad thinks she had an undiagnosed mental illness she refused to get help with."

Sadie went quiet. It looked like she wanted to say something, so he waited. She tucked a short, dark curl behind her ear. "How volatile?"

"Nothing like—" He stopped himself in time, refusing to throw Guillermo's name at her now. Instead, he considered how unfair it was that the few memories he had of his mom weren't the pleasant ones. "Nothing horrible. Mostly a lot of yelling. I remember her punching my dad once, which, considering he was twice her size and a police officer, was pretty gutsy."

Sadie's fingers ran slowly over the burgundy comforter. Josh studied her, thinking that even in her subdued state she was still the most beautiful woman he'd seen. Her olive skin was lit by the two lamps, and her short, dark curls framed her face like they'd been cut for that purpose, and not because Guillermo sliced a section of her hair off to have "something to remember her by." But her lashes were what held Josh's attention. They were thick, long, and very feminine, even though she wasn't wearing any makeup.

Her dark eyes lifted. "How old were you when she died?"

"Seven."

"That's so young." Her hand brushed his knee. "I'm sorry."

He nodded, but his thoughts were more on her brief gesture than her words. He wasn't sure if it was a sign that he could hold her hand again or if she still needed space. Before he could decide, she withdrew into her ball, arms wrapped around her good leg again.

Space.

"How did she die?" she asked.

"Car crash. She was drinking pretty heavily and it was raining. When she hit the tree, my dad thinks she was doing upwards of sixty."

Sadie flinched. "Wow."

"Yeah, but it's my dad I feel sorry for. He was on duty at the time and ended up being the first on the scene. They were divorced by then, but still..." Josh set his pizza aside, no longer wanting any more. "That's when I knew that even if I wasn't a Mormon, I'd never touch a single drop of alcohol."

Sadie's gaze wandered to his arm like it had several times before. Before he left his room, he unwrapped it and left the bandage behind. It still ached and had swelled to something fierce. If he moved it the wrong way, pain shot up and down both directions, but he was sick of her staring at it. Another day or two and it would be fine. But unwrapping it hadn't done anything to keep it from her worry list. He shifted his weight to hide it behind his body. Her eyes tried to follow.

"Drinking's not all bad," she said. "Sometimes it's nice to escape and dull the pain. Like right now, I…"

Josh couldn't move as he waited for her to finish. His mind wanted to analyze her words, but he couldn't allow it.

She looked up, as if suddenly remembering that she wasn't alone. "Sorry. Never mind."

He shrugged, not sure what to say. He knew Sadie drank. At the New Year's Eve party, he had watched her sip her champagne with Guillermo. It shouldn't have surprised him that she might want to dull some of the pain—or all of it—if she could now. If they'd gone out to dinner, he might be sitting across from her now as she consumed such relief.

The thought made his head hurt.

As unfair as it was, the conversation forced his thoughts where they shouldn't have gone. He started to compare Sadie and his mom, and the comparisons were chilling. His mom joined the LDS Church for his dad so they could be united in faith as a couple—like Sadie insisted she would do for Josh. Like his mom, Sadie couldn't fully understand how much was involved in that commitment. Josh wasn't holding her to her promise—obviously the decision to switch religions was completely hers—but at the same time, if she changed her mind he was back to where he was on New Year's, questioning the reality of a long-term relationship with her. His religion meant too much to him. He couldn't spend a life divided between his beliefs and the woman he loved. While Josh knew some couples made it work, he was more like his dad than anyone, and if his benevolent dad couldn't make it work, Josh had no hope whatsoever.

"Why don't Mormons drink?" Sadie asked.

He looked up. She watched him steadily, guessing some of his thoughts.

"We have a commandment called the Word of Wisdom. It asks us to stay away from alcohol, tobacco, tea, and"—he cleared his throat—"coffee."

"Commandment? It's that serious?"

He nodded.

"Is it hard?"

"No." He smiled. "But people don't believe me when I say that. I know some Mormons struggle with the Word of Wisdom, but between growing up in the church and watching what happened to my mom, I never wanted otherwise. Even when Kevin and Trevor started drinking, it was never a temptation. Sam would tell you the same thing. Honestly, most of it grosses me out."

Harrison snorted from the other bed. "That explains some things."

Josh glanced over. It was a commercial and both deputies were listening in. Not wanting more of Harrison's digs to surface, Josh scooted Sadie's untouched plate toward her. "Are you ready for some pizza?"

"No, thanks. I'm not hungry."

"But you haven't eaten all day."

"I'm fine. Really."

"Are you cold then?" She was still wrapped tightly in her little ball.

"No."

"So we've come full circle?" He nudged her leg playfully. "You're not cold. You're not hungry. We might as well be at the cabin. Kevin would call you Ice Woman, and Trevor would force you to eat Lucky Charms."

A shadow crossed her face. "When will you see them again?"

"You mean when will *we* see them again?" he said, trying to ignore her huge slip of the tongue. "Soon. Very soon."

She traced more lines on the comforter.

Having to sit back and watch her fight her internal battles—especially the ones she lost—was killing Josh. She was shutting him out and probably didn't realize it. She was back to survival mode. Which was fine, only...

He sighed. Only there was no only. It was fine.

"Why now?" she whispered.

"What do you mean?"

"Why did I have to meet you now? Six months ago or a year ago, why couldn't we have met then when I was myself? Why now? When I'm like this?"

"You're still the same person, Sadie," Josh said gently. "That person isn't gone."

She blinked rapidly. "What if she is?"

"Then I have a feeling I'll like her better on the other side. From the first day I met you, I've been blown away by your ability to fight this—to fight him. I mean, come on. What guy could resist a girl who kicked through a wall of a burning cabin?"

"He's got a point," Harrison said from the other bed. "That was sweet." Croff elbowed him. "What?" he said. "I read the report."

Sadie refused to look at any of them. She kept tracing the lines.

Josh lowered his voice, hoping Harrison and Croff would take the hint and quit eavesdropping. "Sadie, I chose to be here. I still choose to be here. I have no regrets. I love you," he whispered. *Please don't shut me out.* He didn't know if he was saying the right or the wrong thing, but he decided to ask the question at the center of his concern. "Do you still love me?"

"Yes."

It came without any hesitation. He took a quick breath. That was something. "Then...do you believe when I say that I love you? Not the you you want to be, but you today? Right now?"

That time it took effort for her to answer. The TV droned on in the background as she drew tiny swirls. Finally, she answered. "Yes. I just don't know why."

That he could deal with. "Trust me. I do. But if you can't take my word for it, give me time to show you. Just..." He sighed. "Just don't shut me out anymore. Please."

His hand slid toward hers, crossing the invisible line that separated them. But he stopped short, determined the last few inches were hers to cross.

She stared at his hand, deliberating. And then her hand moved. The second her cold skin brushed his, he slid his fingers around hers and squeezed tightly. They could do this. They were going to make it through.

"So when you want to dull the pain," she said quietly, "what do you do?"

I don't. Sometimes it felt like there was no end to this nightmare. But then Josh remembered the agonizing hour in the janitorial closet, plus all the other dark hours from the past weeks, and he knew that wasn't entirely true. There was one place he could always turn when life became unbearable, and it wasn't at the bottom of a bottle.

"I pray," he said. "Or read my scriptures. Or both."

She weighed that a second before her large eyes lifted to his. "And does it help?"

He nodded slowly. "Every time."

CHAPTER 10

Sadie shut the door behind Josh and Deputy Harrison. She walked back to her bed, carrying the heavy bible Josh left with her, his 'quad' he called it. She still couldn't believe the change that came over him in the last ten minutes. Watching him explain his book of scriptures was as animated as she'd ever seen. But at the same time, he'd been nervous. So nervous he forgot his goodnight kiss on the way out.

She stroked the cover. The scriptures were made of soft leather, a deep blue like his eyes were supposed to be, with elegant silver-lined pages. She wondered if blue was his favorite color. Seems like she should know something like that since they were 'married.'

Then she spotted silver writing on the bottom of the blue cover. She ran her fingers over the words: *Joshua David Young*. They were beautiful.

"These are my scriptures," he had explained. His finger ran down the spine, listing off the titles. *"The Holy Bible, the Book of Mormon, Doctrine and Covenants, and the Pearl of Great Price. It's four books in one. Quad."*

Sadie recognized the first book, obviously, and remembered her aunt and uncle telling her a little about the Book of Mormon. But the third and fourth she knew nothing about.

Though Josh placed a slip of paper where she was supposed to read, she opened his quad to the very first page, curious. She skimmed the title page of the Bible and stopped on four words: Authorized King James Version.

She groaned.

Croff looked up from her novel. "Something wrong?"

Sadie thought back to her childhood when their pastor switched from the KJV to the newer, easier-to-understand NIV, a version that actually resembled English. Reading the King James Version was like reading Shakespeare. She despised Shakespeare. She should have known this wouldn't be an easy fix.

"Nothing," she said. "Sorry."

As Croff went back to her novel, Sadie was tempted to crawl under her covers and try to sleep. However, sleep wouldn't come easily. The nightmares were growing steadily worse, and her whole body—and mind for that matter—ached for relief.

She couldn't help but think a few drinks could put a haze over everything and dull the pain since she'd thrown out her medication in Billings. But that was a cop-out. She was a social drinker at best. Plus, Josh had confidence in this way. She had confidence in him.

Dull the pain.

She flipped to a third of the way back to the page he marked. For a moment, she was distracted by all the colors. It looked like Josh took a highlighter to certain verses—which he had, it just surprised her. There were green, blue, red, and bright yellow verses. Sometimes a whole paragraph was colored and other times a certain word or phrase.

Curious, she flipped through other parts of his quad. Several pages were colorful like the first, others were completely blank. Every once in a while, a verse or two would jump out at her, highlighted to do just that. There were a few pages with his writing in the margins, notes and thoughts written at random.

It was like being given a glimpse into Josh's soul. A very personal glimpse, she realized. As if reading his journal uninvited like Guillermo had.

Quickly, she flipped back to the right page and read Josh's short note.

John 14:27. One of my favorites. Hope it helps. Love you.
Love, Me

Sadie studied his sweet but simple note. Why was he sticking around? Any other guy would have skipped town by now. He was too good to her. Nothing like any other guy she'd dated. Thankfully.

She took a deep breath. John 14:27.

Maybe if she'd gone to all the Sunday school classes her mom signed her up for she might remember that verse. Still, she couldn't make herself find it on the page. She was scared to see what Josh—or God—might say to her, as if somewhere in the Bible it said, *By the way, you really are going crazy.* Or maybe, *Don't look out those curtains right now. Guillermo has two men stationed in the parking lot.* There was also the possibility it would simply say, *Give up. You can't be fixed. You chose Guillermo and now you're going to hell.* She rubbed her eyes feeling like she was already there.

Focus, she told herself. How bad could it be?

She searched for verse 27. It was easy to find since it was bright yellow and the only verse marked that way. She made a quick mental note: bright yellow = one of Josh's favorites. It was tempting to flip through his huge book and find everything yellow, but again she knew she was stalling.

Forcing her gaze downward, she put her finger on 27 and imagined Josh's calm voice reading the verse.

Even in the cumbersome King James language, she recognized the verse immediately, but this was the first time it knocked the air from her lungs.

Peace I leave with you, my peace I give unto you:
Not as the world giveth, give I unto you.
Let not your heart be troubled, neither let it be afraid.

Sadie stared at the yellow words. Josh was giving her peace, telling *her* not to be afraid.

Him.

The guy running for his life.

Something inside her shattered. The words blurred. She bit her trembling lip to keep her emotions from taking over. If she started to cry now, she'd never stop.

Reaching over, she turned off the lamp and hugged his bible as she slid under the covers.

The first time Sadie woke, she had died a quick, painless death. Just a simple bullet to the heart. Better than other dreams. Still cradling Josh's bible, she convinced herself that sleep was better than reality and fought her way back into it.

The second time she woke gasping for air. Pain shot through her ribs. She held her sides, rocking back and forth to ease the pain, but the dream had been too real.

"What's wrong?" Deputy Croff asked groggily.

Another bullet. Another blizzard. Another Guillermo. There were more people in this dream, which was asking for trouble. Sadie had dragged her mom into the blizzard with her, too scared to go alone. Together they ran through the woods. Together they'd been found.

She shuddered, remembering the moment she realized Guillermo wasn't shooting her this time. Thankfully she woke up before the bullet hit her mom, but the look of terror on her mom's face left Sadie's heart and head pounding.

"Nothing," Sadie said. "Sorry. Go back to sleep."

She curled herself around the quad scriptures again. If it hadn't been pitch black she would have opened it to that page, but she let Josh's voice read the words to her again.

My peace. Don't be scared, Sadie. My peace. My peace.

The third time her eyes flew open after the gun fired but before the bullet reached her. At least she'd been alone. That was good. Still, she searched the black room until she found a blue screen in the corner. The movie was done, but the TV was still on. The clock next to her read 12:28.

She stretched a little and looked down the empty couch. Guillermo was working late again. She shook her head. *Workaholic.* Not that she complained. He devoted all his daytime hours to her. When else was he supposed to get work done?

Suddenly the contents of the dream clarified in her mind. The bullet hadn't been aimed at her at all. It had been aimed down at the snow, at someone in the snow.

She leaped from Guillermo's couch and ran to the curtains, peering into the dark. Guillermo, Mr. Ugly, and a smaller man stepped back from view. A body lay in plain sight, perfectly illuminated in the moonlight.

She stared into the eyes of Agent Madsen's young partner, Stephen Dubois. She knew it would be him down there. The young FBI agent wasn't dead yet, but it wouldn't be long. Blood flowed from his stomach, staining the snow a deep scarlet.

He spotted her in the upstairs window. "Help!" he groaned.

She didn't move. She couldn't. She was locked in place, watching in terror as the color slipped from his face. Pale to gray to pure white.

"Please!" he begged.

Tears streamed down her face, already knowing she wouldn't. She couldn't risk Guillermo finding her. Her life mattered more than the young agent's. As punishment, she was forced to watch the life slip from his eyes, turning them to glass.

"What have you done?" someone said behind her.

She whirled around expecting Guillermo, but it was Josh. The hatred in his deep eyes was like a dagger to the heart.

"You just let Agent Dubois die," he said. "You could have saved him, but you did nothing. How could you be that cruel, that horrible?"

She started to cry. "You don't understand. I couldn't. I had to save myself. But it was too late anyway. He would have died even if I—"

"How do you know?" Josh shouted. "You didn't even try!"

He stepped away from her, disgust darkening his countenance until he vanished from the room.

Her whole body shook. Josh was right. She hadn't tried.

She spun around and searched for her phone. Maybe it wasn't too late. Maybe Agent Dubois was still alive. She wouldn't be a coward this time. She would save Madsen's partner.

She dialed the police and without waiting yelled, "A man has been shot! You have to come fast! Please—"

Someone yanked the phone from her hands.

Her arms flew over her head, shielding herself from the blow. But it wasn't Guillermo. It was Mr. Ugly. "You're so stupid, beautiful," he said, hurling her phone out the window. "We didn't kill anyone. It was a test. Only a test. And guess what. You failed!"

As he threw his head back with a laugh, she ran to the window. A test? No. She'd seen the blood. She'd seen the—

A scream pierced the night air.

Hers.

It wasn't Dubois laying on the snow, but another man. One she cared infinitely more about. His bleached-blond beard hung open in a silent scream. But it was too late. She could never change—or forget—the way Josh stared up at her with the glass eyes of a dead man.

"Sadie!" Someone grabbed her shoulders and shook her. "Sadie! Wake up!"

Her eyes flew open. Deputy Croff stood over her in the soft lamplight.

Sobs erupted hard and heavy, exploding against each and every rib. Sadie buried her face in the pillow and cried the adrenaline away.

CHAPTER 11

"You'd be surprised how common this is."

Croff gave Sadie a glass of water and sat next to her on the bed. Even though it was four in the morning, the deputy offered to call Josh. Sadie knew he would come because he always came, but she didn't want him to. She was a big girl. Maybe not, but she desperately wanted to pretend like she was.

"I've seen this kind of thing a lot actually," Croff said. "If you think about it, my job is to protect witnesses waiting for trials of highly-powerful people, people who pay others to hunt witnesses down. Most of these witnesses have already been threatened or severely injured. Some have been nearly killed like you. So let's just say you're not the first person to wake me up in the middle of the night screaming." Croff yawned on cue. "I'm used to it."

Sadie wiped the last of the moisture from her cheeks, finding comfort in that knowledge. It's not that she wanted other people to be living in constant fear like she was, but it was nice to know she wasn't the first person to go crazy.

"So what did they do to…you know…get through it?" Sadie asked.

"First, they learned to trust me." Croff went to her bed and pulled something out from under her pillow. A gun.

Sadie jerked back. That was the last thing she expected. But even more surprising was when Croff held it out to her.

"Touch it," Croff said.

Sadie's eyes popped open. "No! I can't just—"

"Touch it." Croff pushed the gun closer to her. "I want you to feel its power. So far you've only witnessed its power to impose fear, but I want you to feel its power to protect."

Sadie reached up. Her fingers grazed the cold, notched metal. The power to protect.

"I won't bore you with the details of my training," Croff said, "but let me say, they spend an incredible amount of time training us to fine-tune our senses. We're trained to detect danger from a mile away. I'm the best deputy in my zone," Croff added, sliding the gun back under the pillow. "Even better than Harrison. I've never had a single person under my care harmed in any way, shape, or form. Neither has Harrison. We're the best of the best."

Sadie felt like she was five years old and her mom was giving her the don't-be-afraid-of-the-boogie-man talk. Only this wasn't her mom. It was a six-foot-tall woman with the training and confidence of the United States Marshals. And Madsen.

"I'm not telling you this to brag," Croff said. "I don't need help with my self-esteem. I'm telling you so you'll believe me when I say you and Josh are perfectly safe. I don't know if it will help with the nightmares, but at least when you're awake you should know nothing will happen to you. We'll get you to that trial. I promise."

Trial.

Sadie's stomach twisted. She hugged Josh's scriptures, dreading what waited in her future, not in her dreams, but in reality. Murderous eyes across the courtroom. Murderous intentions across the country. She was terrified of the retaliation once Guillermo found out she was alive.

Sensing she'd struck a nerve, Croff laid a hand on her arm. "It'll be okay. You're stronger than you think."

"No, I—"

"You are," Croff insisted. "But in the meantime, you're completely safe."

Sadie took a deep breath that both hurt and gave her strength. "Thanks. I know it sounds empty, but I mean it. Sorry I woke you up."

"Anytime."

Croff smiled and slipped back into bed, but before rolling over, she went up on an elbow. "You might not want to hear this, but I'll say it anyway. I think you need counseling. It's part of our job to get you set up, and not just with housing, but with the proper counselors."

Sadie fidgeted with the corner of Josh's bible. Talking about counseling was as bad as talking about the trial. Yet the worse she got, the more people kept dropping the word, waiting for her to pick it up.

"We won't be in Tennessee for another day," Croff continued, "so you don't have to decide now. But in my experience, counseling helps a lot of people through the bad times. It even prepares them for the hard times to come."

"I don't know. It's not that I have anything against counseling, it's just that I'm not...I'm not really..."

"One of *those* women?" Croff finished. "Look, I read your file. I read the things that jerk did to you. But I'm guessing none of us know the half of it. All these nightmares are a sign that he left some huge scars on the inside. Going to counseling doesn't make you weak. In fact, I've been to a few sessions myself."

Sadie's eyes widened. "Really?"

"Yeah. Childhood stuff I won't bore you with," Croff said. "But counseling doesn't take away your strength and independence. Just the opposite. It makes you stronger because you refuse to let that jerk spend any more time in your head. It means you recognize that something is broken inside you, and you need some help putting it back together."

Broken. The word she couldn't escape.

"The doctors fixed your ankle and ribs, right?" Croff asked. "You still have to heal, but they found the problem and adjusted things so your body could do the rest, right?"

"Yeah."

"This is the same. Vasquez and his goons fractured something deep inside of you that can't be seen on any x-ray or MRI. So...let's find someone who's trained to look past those tests, figure out where it hurts, and set it properly so you can heal."

A doctor. For some reason, that sounded a hundred times better than a shrink. And Croff went to one. If it meant going a whole night without dying or getting someone killed, maybe it was worth it.

"Okay," Sadie said. "I'll think about it."

"Good." Croff smiled. "Don't misunderstand me, though. Josh is right about the Bible. I don't know where you are on your journey with God, but wherever it is, God can find every last broken shard that no doctor or counselor can. God can heal you, body *and* soul. Not only that, but He'll make you stronger for it."

Sadie's head snapped up. The words sounded familiar. And then she remembered where she'd heard them. It was almost exactly the words Josh spoke in a prayer when she was unconscious in the snow, some special blessing he'd given her. In it, he promised she would heal, body and soul, through God's love.

Croff's smile grew. "Get some counseling and don't quit reading. That's my advice. Both will help you beat Vasquez. Oh, and one last thing before I get off my soapbox..." She yawned again. "Don't tell my boss I told you to read the Bible. I'd like to keep my job." Then she pulled the covers over her shoulder and went to sleep.

Sadie sat another moment, taking it all in. Doctors. Healing. God.

Slowly, she cracked open Josh's book and found John 14 again.

As she reread the bright yellow verse, the words began to change. Suddenly it wasn't Josh's voice saying them to her, but a deeper, more commanding voice.

Peace I leave with you,
My peace I give unto you.

Her gaze stopped on the word *my*. She put Josh there before, knowing how desperate he was to share his peace with her. But that's not how it was written or intended. Backing up further, she found a verse colored in red.

I will not leave you comfortless: I will come to you.

And another.

If ye shall ask any thing in my name, I will do it.

That wasn't Josh speaking. It was Jesus.

Have I been so long time with you, and hast thou not known me?

Her heart started beating strong and steady. Starting at the beginning of John 14, she read each and every verse, each and every word, stopping, thinking, weighing. By the time she reached 27, the full power of the message swelled inside her.

Peace I leave with you, my *peace I give unto you:*
Not as the world giveth, give I unto you.
Let not your heart be troubled,
Neither let it be afraid.

She closed her eyes, letting the words resonate in her mind. Peace. *His* peace. Even more powerful than Josh's. She could feel it wrapping around her. Warm. Quiet. Enduring.

With a sigh that reached down to her soul, she set Josh's bible on the nightstand and drifted to sleep.

In the morning, Sadie meant to thank Josh for his verse, but the second she saw him, all thoughts of last night vanished. "It's you!" she blurted.

He laughed and rubbed a clean-shaven cheek. "Yeah. It's me."

"And you thought she wouldn't notice." Harrison dropped their bags in the lobby. "Alright. If we push hard we can make it to Knoxville tonight."

Sadie ignored Harrison as she studied Josh's waves of now-dark hair, restored to its original color—or at least close to the original. It was a couple shades darker now, matching hers. She couldn't figure out how he ever found the time or open place to dye it after he left her last night. But he had. And his eyes. That was the best part. They matched the sky again. No more dull-brown contacts. No more lies. He looked like he had when she first met him. Handsome. Confident. Josh.

"I was going to wait until Tennessee," Josh said with a shrug, "but I got sick of the whole mountain-man look. Do you mind?"

She hobbled to him, pulled his face to hers, and kissed him soundly.

Josh froze. He didn't wrap his arms around her like he normally did. He didn't even kiss her back. He just stood there, frozen.

She quickly backed down, realizing how silly it was. She shouldn't get excited about something so small. It was a beard and contacts. Very silly.

As she glanced around, her cheeks warmed. She'd not only thrown herself at Josh in front of their escorts, but the other motel patrons eating their continental breakfasts. It just felt so nice to have Josh back to himself, almost like part of her was back, too. Almost like the blond man in her nightmare hadn't been Josh at all. Very, very silly.

"Sorry," she said.

Josh shook his head. "Don't apologize. You just caught me off guard. After the last few days, I thought…" A slow grin spread on his clean-shaven face. "Don't apologize. In fact"—he pulled her back to him—"feel free to start every day like that."

CHAPTER 12

Even as they got back on the road, Sadie couldn't quit staring at Josh. It was pathetic that something so seemingly small bothered her so much. So she felt bad it took her that long to remember his bible. She pulled the heavy book from her purse. "Thank you for the verse last night. It was perfect. I finally got a few hours of sleep."

"A few?" Josh turned. "Croff said it was a rough night, but only a few?"

"Maybe the worst is behind me."

He smiled. "I figured as much after breakfast. How many pancakes did you eat?"

"Two. Or maybe three."

His blue eyes lit up. "It was four. What are you, part camel?"

"Four?" she choked. "Are you sure I ate four?"

"Yeah."

"Well, at least they were small."

Harrison eyed her in the rearview mirror, letting her know they weren't all that small. Was the entire world watching her eat? Had she been that bad?

"Fine. I'm part camel," she relented. "Although I'd rather you called me Kermit."

Josh laughed. "You mean Gumby?"

"No. *Anything* but Gumby."

She leaned into the seats and took Josh's hand, pleased to see him back to his teasing ways. Maybe the worst was behind him, too.

"So what do you have for me to read tonight?" she asked.

He turned. "Huh?"

She picked up his scriptures and stroked the beautiful blue cover. "I think I bent a few pages last night—sorry—but I'd like to borrow it again if you don't mind. I think it helps."

"It does? Okay. That's great. Really great." He squinted and scratched his cheek. "What exactly did you have in mind?"

It was the most talkative she'd seen Josh. They spent all of Wisconsin talking about his scriptures and beliefs. His favorite book was the Book of Mormon with the New Testament a "close second." When she asked what the different highlighted colors meant, he flipped through the pages and showed her. Reds were for everyday reading, yellows were his favorite—like she guessed—greens were people and places, and orange verses were the ones he memorized in a youth seminary class that, for some reason, required him to wake up at 4:45 AM every day. Lastly, the blue ones were from his mission to Scotland, another topic that got him talking a mile a minute.

He kept apologizing for talking so much, but she wouldn't let him stop. Not only did it pass the time and keep her mind off things, she loved watching the way his left brow pulled down as he considered something, or how his eyes danced when he talked about a favorite belief. Kevin once told her how much Josh's religion meant to him, but it wasn't until they crossed that long, snow-covered stretch of I-90 that she realized just how much.

Mostly, though, it reaffirmed how totally and madly in love she was with him. From that first day in the cabin, she knew Josh was different from any other guy she'd met. His depth amazed her. Enough that by Illinois, she was looking forward to following through on her promise. She would be a Mormon someday. Hopefully someday soon.

"There's Chicago," Josh said in a break in conversation. "Have you ever been?"

Her stomach dropped. "No."

"I went when I was ten. It's awesome. We went up the Sears Tower—or Willis Tower or whatever it's called—and out on Navy Pier." He strained his neck to see out the window, trying to catch a glimpse of the skyscrapers. The buildings were growing by the minute. Looming. Daunting. And traffic was slowing to a crawl.

Her pulse picked up. Her lungs started to constrict. She could feel herself plummeting. *Not again,* she begged. *Please no.*

"I've always wanted to see Chicago," Croff said from the driver's seat. Harrison was sound asleep against his window, snoring softly. "I hear it's a beautiful city."

"It is," Josh said. "I loved it."

Sadie stared down at her scarred wrists.

Josh leaned forward between the seats to point. "Look. There's the Willis Tower. What if we stop in Chicago? We could even stay the night here, explore, and walk around." He glanced down at Sadie's casted foot. "Or maybe just hang out at the Cheesecake Factory. You'll love Chicago, Sadie. Navy Pier is"—he scrunched down to see past the mass of buildings—"on the other side of all that. I know it's cold out, probably really cold out, but it would give us time out of the car. What do you think? Are you ready for a break?"

Only then did he turn to look at her. As soon as he did, his face fell. "You don't want to stop," he said.

She closed her eyes briefly. *Stop. Go away. Get out of my head!* she screamed at the memories.

"It's fine if you don't," Josh said. "I just thought your ribs could use some time off."

She wanted to say yes. Heaven knew she'd said no enough for one trip. She hated taking this away from him, but...she just barely got her feet under her again. She didn't want Guillermo memories pushing her over the edge, which meant Josh would plunge in right after her.

If she wasn't so weak, maybe they could stop, but...

"It's really cold," she said, deflecting. "Plus Harrison wouldn't want to. He thinks we can make it to Tennessee tonight."

Excuses. Even she wasn't buying it. But her breaths were coming faster, her palms cold and sweaty, as the buildings loomed above them. Would the memories always control her like this?

"Hey, whoa." Josh leaned forward to peer at her. "What just happened?"

She was a horribly selfish person. Why couldn't she be strong for him?

"Sadie? Don't shut me out."

"Spring." She glanced out the window, watching the snow flurries whiz past. "We were going to come here this spring once the weather turned warm. He wanted..." She closed her eyes. "He wanted to show me Chicago."

"He," Josh said, "as in...*him*?"

The memories slammed into her. She and Guillermo stood by the floor-to-ceiling windows in his massive ski lodge, watching the snow blanket everything in sight. *"Come spring, hermosa,"* he had said, *"we shall walk every step of the Magnificent Mile. You must see the tulips in bloom. Es cielo en la tierra, heaven on earth. Just like you."* He had pulled her close and kissed her to take away the chill of the storm. The memory sent a shiver down her spine.

"Wait," Josh said. "Why would Guiller—he bring you here?"

"He comes every spring to follow a hedge fund. He meets with some group for a week in April. He has a place here." She looked at the mass of buildings, wondering which one it was.

"Are you sure? I don't remember you mentioning Chicago to Madsen."

Horrified, she twisted back to Josh. "Because I didn't. I forgot. Technically, it's not Guillermo's place. It's his uncle's. But he comes every spring." Her heart pounded. "And he said only a few people know about it, so he's not bothered with distractions and calls and..."

Adrenaline shot through her veins. She peered out the window as her mind raced. She struggled to remember how Guillermo described the place, the street, the overbearing doorman, and the upper corner suite with the white marble, praying she had enough details.

Ignoring every pain and doubt, she leaned forward and shook Harrison. "Wake up. I need your phone."

"You shall see, Manuel. I will come back stronger than ever. Who knows, maybe I shall run for office someday. Governor Vasquez. How does that sound?" Guillermo straightened his tie and studied himself in the mirror like he always did. He was the vainest man on the earth. "Or maybe *Presidente?*"

Manuel snorted. *President? Of the United States?* His older brother was not only vain but delusional.

"I just need time," Guillermo went on. "And a little positive publicity to come out of all this. In a way, I need this investigation. Time in the papers. Vindication. Proof that the FBI's allegations against me are false. You just wait, *hermanito.* I shall come out of this stronger and better."

"You need a reality check," Manuel muttered.

Guillermo whirled around. "Do not forget that if I go down, we all do."

"Down? What's more down than this?" Manuel motioned to the over-stuffed uptown apartment so "spacious" he'd spent the last five nights sleeping on the white marble floors. "We might as well be under house arrest. We can't go anywhere, see anything, call anyone, or even scratch our heads. The only time I left was to go to the lobby to get the mail. That's. It."

Guillermo smiled. "You are lonely, little brother? Salvador, Manuel is lonely."

Salvador, Guillermo's little puppet, laughed a fake laugh. Typical. "Poor *hermanito.*"

Manuel gritted his teeth. *I hate you. Both of you.* One of these days, the words would escape his lips regardless of the consequences. The longer all of them were holed up in that tiny suite, the faster that day was coming.

Guillermo picked up his wine and swirled it a moment. "What do you think, Uncle? Shall I run for president?"

"*Bien, bien,*" their uncle said without glancing up from the *Chicago Times.*

"And you, *hermanito?*" Guillermo turned his sights on Manuel. "Will you vote for me if I run for office?"

Manuel slid down in his leather chair. He wasn't answering that question. Not if he wanted to live another day.

Guillermo slammed his goblet down. He crossed the room and put both hands on the arms of Manuel's chair, bringing his face—and nasty breath— inches away. "You did not answer, *hermanito?* Will you vote for me when I run for president?"

Maybe it was the cramped quarters. Maybe it was the late hour. Maybe it was sleeping on hard tile for a week. Whatever the reason, Manuel did the last thing he should have. He answered truthfully.

"I think if *you* think you can run for president, you know less about America than I do. You were born in Venezuela. Your entire family is Venezuelan, not Americano. You have as much chance of being president as Mickey Mouse."

"And in case *you've* forgotten, little tiny brother of mine," Guillermo hissed in his face, "I played their game. I am a full-fledged American citizen now." He stood back and brushed down his black suit. "You are nothing."

"And you have a warrant for your arrest!"

Guillermo's eyes turned coal black in the lamplight. "They cannot arrest me for a murder I did not commit. I will be freed of Dubois' murder within the week, and they are not intelligent enough to know about *mi amor's* untimely death. Within a week, I shall be whomever I choose to be. So perhaps you should stop this treasonous talk and admit where your anger truly stems from. You are jealous of me."

Manuel jumped to his feet. "Only people born in America can be elected president. And who do you even think you are to—"

He never had a chance. Guillermo's fist swung too fast, too expertly. It exploded against Manuel's cheek.

Manuel flew back. His shoulder hit the chair first. Then the rest of him hit the hard tile.

Once the initial shock wore off and the lights cleared from his vision, he felt a warm trickle of blood ooze down his nose to his upper lip. He didn't bother wiping it away.

Sneering, Guillermo crouched next to him. "I may become president of anything I choose. I may have been born in Venezuela, but you are forgetting something." His smile twisted into something evil. "Laws can be changed. Or bought."

The blood from Manuel's nose dripped freely onto the perfectly-polished marble. With luck, he'd bleed to death in this new prison. Not that a soul in the world would care. His uncle hadn't even looked up from the paper, and Salvador sat across the room, grinning at him from afar.

It was karma.

Manuel deserved this. He didn't save Sadie when he could have. Even when her dark eyes begged for mercy in that cabin, even when he knew she was innocent and didn't deserve to burn alive, even when he knew he could have saved her without Guillermo knowing, he locked her in the bathroom and walked away. Just because Luis threw the match didn't mean Manuel wasn't responsible for her death. Sadie was the only person in the world who thought he was better than his older brother, and he killed her for it.

He deserved this.

"Salvador," Guillermo said, "send in Luis. I think Manuel needs a reminder of which side he belongs to."

"Oh, please no." Manuel would rather another punch to the face. He'd already seen Luis' hand—or stump since it was fingerless now. Regardless of the fact that Guillermo was killing Sadie, she was still *his* girlfriend and *his* property. When Manuel reported finding big, fat Luis in the cabin, dragging Sadie up the stairs to claim her before her death, Guillermo hadn't taken the news well. Manuel was glad to have saved Sadie from that much at least. But once Luis recovered from the finger thing, he was sure to take revenge on Manuel for ratting him out.

Maybe Manuel should have been the one to burn in the cabin.

"Don't be what he is," Sadie whispered from his memories. *"You're better than this."*

Those dark eyes would haunt him until the day he died.

Luis got what he deserved. Now it was Manuel's turn. Guillermo would probably force Luis to unwrap the whole gory mess for dramatic effect. Guillermo loved dramatic effect. Manuel spit blood onto the tile. If it was blood Guillermo wanted to see, let it flow.

Salvador was only gone a few seconds when he walked back in, hands in the air.

"What is going on?" Guillermo asked. "Where is Luis? Why is—"

Guillermo stopped. A man followed Salvador into the suite. He was older with a gray goatee, and he wore a dark business suit.

The man in the dark suit flashed a gold badge as two dozen men in black swarmed in behind him, guns sweeping the room.

Manuel finally wiped his nose with his sleeve. Then he stood. He wasn't scared by the sight of a full SWAT team. In fact, there wasn't an ounce of fear in him at all. Just joy. Inexplicable joy.

The FBI had found Guillermo.

Suddenly Manuel was the one with the smug smile. Even if his brother took him down with him, it was worth it to be here for this moment. Guillermo was going down.

Agent Madsen walked right up to Guillermo. "Look who's back in the country."

There was the slightest trace of fear in Guillermo's black eyes, but it only lasted a second before he warmed up.

"Señor Madsen," Guillermo said with a smile. "How wonderful to see you again, my friend. It is a little late in the evening for a social visit, but not for good friends, no? Tell me. How may I assist you today?"

Madsen shook his head with a smile of his own. "I've waited a long time for this. You're under arrest."

They were ten minutes outside of Knoxville when the call came. It was one in the morning, Croff was driving, and Sadie was half-asleep. But as soon as Harrison's phone went off, Sadie sat up quickly—too quickly.

Biting back the pain, she watched the deputy's reaction to the only call any of them had received since the funeral. Harrison nodded, grunted a few times, and then turned.

The second Harrison looked at Sadie, she knew.

Guillermo had been arrested at last.

CHAPTER 13

Croff pulled into the driveway, and Sadie still couldn't move. Her thoughts were too muddled to care about their new house. The house was small, but Guillermo was arrested. It was nearly pitch black, making the color hard to see, but Guillermo was arrested. Harrison and Croff started unloading their stuff, but Guillermo…was…arrested.

Because of her.

Josh squeezed her hand in the dark car. He hadn't said anything since the call but watched her steadily.

"This is good," she said, breaking the dark silence. "Right?"

"Very good. Are you okay?" Josh asked.

She wanted to nod, but her thoughts were racing, trying to imagine Guillermo's reaction to the FBI storming his place in Chicago. She couldn't wrap her mind around it. She, Josh, and their bodyguards could have been staying down the street from where he was right now. *No*, she corrected. *Where he used to be*. Now he was in jail. Locked up. Arrested.

Because of her.

Would he piece things together? Would he figure out who told the feds about his uncle's place? Did anyone besides her know about it? At the very least, the FBI hadn't or they would have searched it already. It was impressive Madsen figured it out with her sketchy memories. Very impressive. But still… How long would it take Guillermo to figure out it was her? That she was alive?

Did it even matter if he was locked up?

And what charges had Madsen drawn up? Last she heard, the FBI lacked sufficient evidence for anything but her own attempted murder. If she was 'dead', they couldn't arrest him for 'attempted' murder, which wiped out that charge as well.

Unless…

Madsen told Guillermo she was alive.

Her breath caught. *No!* Madsen wouldn't. He promised. It had to be charges for Agent Dubois' murder. Somehow Madsen found enough evidence to pin it on Guillermo.

She closed her eyes. She knew this day was coming—or at least she hoped it would. She just never dreamed it would be so soon. Only a month ago, Guillermo was the man of her dreams: perfect, charming, doting. Now he was behind bars—which he deserved, it was just surreal how quickly life shifted from white to black, from light to dark. It's like she was in another nightmare, only one that never ended. The only thing anchoring her to reality was Josh.

Worry lines creased his dark brows.

"This is good," she whispered again. "Right?"

"Very good," Josh said. "For you especially. And your mom."

"And you," she added, realizing Josh had the most to gain in Guillermo's arrest. The hunting would stop. Guillermo was locked up, caged, restrained.

She hoped.

Josh smiled, though it was tight. "This is the beginning of the end. Maybe you'll sleep a little better tonight."

Or worse. Guillermo would be raging mad, and then what? How would he retaliate? She wanted to believe he couldn't, but she doubted little iron bars could stop his wrath. Yet… She took another painful breath. There was a reason she and Josh were on the other side of the country. If only everyone was.

Josh turned her chin toward him and looked deeply into her eyes. "It's going to be okay." His face, lit by the surrounding house and street lights, looked as calm and confident as his words. "We should be celebrating. You did it. You made this happen."

I did.

Why did the words cause her stomach to knot?

"Come on." He unhitched his seat belt. "It's late and it's getting cold. We'll know more in the morning. Try not to think about it right now. Let's get you inside your new house."

He got out and walked around to open her door. Taking her crutches, he helped her stand. It took more effort than it should, but her bones, joints, and muscles protested the unbelievably-long day. She was one big ball of pain, and she cursed herself for throwing out her meds.

She blinked hard to focus through the darkness. This was their new home, after all, keeping them hidden—hopefully—until the trial, which was coming all too soon.

The air in Knoxville wasn't warm by any means, maybe upper thirties, but it felt warm in comparison to the Montana wind that blew so cold it burned the skin. Their new house was small and square, almost squat. A single, dim porch light hung over a small, paint-chipped porch. The house looked pre-Civil War. There were two huge, leafless trees in the yard, one in front, one behind the house, hovering over the roof like a black umbrella. There wasn't a single flake of snow in sight, which was the best thing Sadie had seen all day.

Deputy Croff walked past them with another load of bags. "The house is rigged with a top-notch security system," she said. "A great setup."

Sadie nodded. Maybe that would help her sleep. Maybe.

She started to walk, and then noticed Josh. He was looking down the dark road where there were more squat houses under more leafless trees. There was something off in his eyes, though she couldn't quite place it.

"Are *you* okay?" she asked.

He snapped back around. "Yeah. Sorry. Let's get you inside."

Croff and Harrison continued shuttling bags back and forth. Josh quietly led Sadie up the sidewalk. With a grunt, she hopped up the two wooden stairs and crossed the threshold of their new home.

One step in and she stopped. In spite of the musty smell, the interior was surprisingly cute in a farm-house kind of way. It was furnished with a blue-checkered couch and welcoming oak furniture, making it easier to ignore the not-so-cute shag carpet. Off to the left was a blue and white kitchen, and to the right, a hallway leading to the bedrooms. The inside was definitely better than the outside.

She pushed herself into the kitchen and slumped onto one of the oak chairs, feeling every minute of the sixteen-hour day. Unfortunately slumping jarred her ribs and she was forced to lean sideways to find a bearable spot. That kinked her leg which she quickly tucked under her chair. She was a twisted mess, probably looking as awkward as she felt. Had she planned ahead, she would have landed on the couch instead of the hard oak chair, but it was ten feet away, much too far. She wondered if Madsen had the foresight to stock the house with Motrin. A lot of Motrin.

Josh didn't sit, though. He walked through the house checking every inch of the hallway.

Sadie couldn't help but wonder what kind of place Guillermo was in. She really needed to quit thinking about him, but she had no idea where he was or what came next. Trials were supposedly long, drawn out performances with several court dates spaced over months and years. Madsen was never more specific than that, including how soon she would be flown back to Montana to start testifying.

Her head throbbed. She rubbed her eyes thinking she could sleep right there. But just as she was about to rest her head on the table, Josh came into the kitchen.

"Two bedrooms," he said, shaking his head. "Only two. And there's just one bathroom, one tiny bathroom. I can't believe this."

Sadie finally placed his expression. He was disappointed. He expected something nicer and newer, bigger even. She didn't know, and with

Guillermo's arrest, she didn't care. Maybe that's what Josh was thinking, too. This checkered, squat house was another reminder how Guillermo ruined their lives. For all she knew, Josh lived in a mansion in Spokane. This house was barely bigger than her apartment.

As Harrison came in with another load, Josh strode over to him. "Did Madsen say where you and I are supposed to stay?"

Sadie's head snapped up. "Stay?"

Harrison dropped the last of the bags inside the door. "Right here. This was the only address listed, so deal with it. Which bedroom do you want your stuff in?"

"There are only two," Josh said.

Harrison's jaw clenched. "Which one?"

Josh no longer looked disappointed. His whole body was rigid as he stared his bodyguard down. He was mad. Fuming. "Madsen," he muttered. "I knew it. The only thing he got right was the piano."

Piano? Sadie turned as much as her body allowed. Sure enough, in a dark corner of the living room was an upright piano. That was a pleasant surprise, but not enough to distract her from Josh.

"What's wrong?" she asked.

He barely looked at her before turning to Harrison. "If there were two floors and two bathrooms, maybe. But this?"

Harrison folded his arms. "I'm not going anywhere."

"What's wrong?" Sadie asked again.

Josh opened his mouth to respond but clamped it shut. He grabbed the deputy by the arm and pulled him down the hallway. They spoke in fierce whispers which looked like it could erupt into a full-blown fistfight any second.

Croff leaned against the blue couch. "There are plenty of pillows and blankets," she called. "One of you can take the couch."

Sadie took in the size of the blue, checkered couch. It wasn't even a full-sized couch, which meant it couldn't fit either of the six-foot-tall men. Or Croff, who was just as tall.

Suddenly, she understood. The small house. Two rooms. One couch. Four adults. The math didn't add up.

Mustering up the last of her energy, she stood and hobbled down the hallway. "I'll take the couch since I'm half the size of all of you. I don't mind, though. I'm so tired I could sleep on cement."

Josh shook his head. "No. We'll find somewhere else for tonight."

"Wait? You're leaving? Now?"

"Yes. I'm sorry." His blue eyes searched hers. "Will you be okay?"

"Yeah, but…why?"

Harrison swore under his breath. "No way! I'm not finding some lousy motel at two in the morning!"

"You're right." Josh gave Sadie a quick peck on the cheek. "Try to sleep. See you in the morning." Then he walked past Harrison, past Croff and their bags, and out the front door.

Sadie followed him with her eyes. Through the window, she watched Josh open the passenger door of the car and get in. He inclined the seat all the way back, as if he intended to sleep right there in the car. It stopped at a sixty-degree angle, not nearly flat or large enough for him to get comfortable. Yet he tried anyway.

"What is he doing?" she asked. When no one answered, she looked at Harrison. "Why is he sleeping in the car? What did I do?"

Harrison growled softly. "Sleeping in a car was *not* part of the job description. Does he really expect us to live out of a car for the next who knows how long? Just for some…some…moral code? She won't even sign the papers!" He swore again. "I'm not doing this!"

"What moral code?" Sadie asked. "What's going on? Why is Josh sleeping outside? I said I'd take the couch."

Harrison turned his glare on her. "Why don't you ask *him*? He's *your* husband. Do you even know that guy at all?"

His words were like a stab to the heart. She stared out the dark window.

Croff picked up a blanket and threw it at Harrison. "Get out there. Now!"

"There's no alarm on the car," Harrison said.

Croff grabbed his arm and marched him forward. "We've had three long days, deputy. Let it go. We'll sort it out tomorrow."

Harrison broke free of her grip. "I don't get paid enough," he muttered as he stormed outside.

His last question lingered on Sadie's mind long after the door slammed shut.

Do you even know that guy at all?

CHAPTER 14

Josh should have asked for a key or the code for the alarm. Once the sun hit the leafless trees of Tennessee, he was ready to get out of that cramped, freezing car. A thin layer of frost blanketed the windshield and front lawn. He blew on his hands. But it wasn't until he was on the porch that he remembered he was locked out. Or at least, he better be. A locked door and impenetrable security system was the least the U.S. Marshals could do to keep Sadie safe on the night of Guillermo's arrest. But he was cold enough to try the handle anyway.

Locked.

He pressed his face to the cold window, wondering how long before Sadie or Croff woke up. Then he spotted a small, gorgeous Hispanic sitting on the piano bench. Sadie was awake already. Sort of. She stared out a far window with a faraway gaze.

He knocked softly. She looked around, smiled, and grabbed her crutches. It was amazing what that woman could make look good. She wore an oversized sweatshirt and leggings. Her short, dark curls were a little on the wild side this morning, which he loved. Watching her push across the room, he decided she could be a crutches model.

She punched in the alarm code and opened the door. "Good morning," she said with her large smile.

Having Guillermo behind bars was working its magic already. Her eyes were bright and alive.

"Morning. How did you sleep?" he asked.

"You're asking *me* how I slept? How did you sleep?"

He fought the urge to stretch the kink in his neck. It had been a long night. Lots of shifting to find a comfortable, warm position. It didn't help that every hour Harrison cursed him under his frozen breath.

"I slept fine. Have you looked outside this morning?"

Her eyes widened in panic. "No. Why?"

"Oh, nothing bad. I just wanted you to see something." He grabbed her hand and led her to the window. The sky was deep blue and cloudless. Sadie's house was situated on the upper part of a hill, giving them the faintest glimpse of gray mountains beyond the tall line of trees. "I didn't know if you'd seen the Smokies yet."

"Oh…" she breathed. "They're beautiful."

"You better like hiking better than skiing, Miss Dawson, because I seriously need to conquer a mountain—I mean, when you feel better," he added, remembering her green cast.

"You'll be happy to hear that I love to hike. My brother and I hiked in Glacier National Park all the time. Maybe we can hike in the afternoons, *after* your classes."

"When you feel better," he amended. "So how's the piano?"

Sadie headed back to the piano bench, and he followed. The upright piano was blonde in color and looked as old as the house. She sat on the bench and plunked out a simple C chord. He winced. It was horribly out of tune yet, for some reason, she smiled. "It's awesome. How did you get something like this in the deal?"

He slid next to her on the bench and tried a few notes of his own. It was awful. The octaves didn't match within a half-step. Once they got it tuned, hopefully it would hold a pitch. That would be job number one tomorrow. Or number two. He still had to find a place to stay.

"Madsen was feeling generous," he said. "Or desperate. I'm not sure which."

He slid an arm around her tiny waist, glad she was on his good side. "I wasn't expecting you to be up yet. What time is it?"

"Just after seven."

"And you're awake? Wow. Kevin would be proud."

She elbowed him softly.

Sitting that close to her, he noticed the dark circles under her eyes, which sobered him quickly. "More nightmares?"

Her fingers grazed the white keys. "Not many."

He hoped last night's news would help. Maybe tomorrow he could convince her to find a counselor. Add it to the list. He swept a dark curl off her soft cheek. "What were the dreams this time?"

"The usual."

Which he didn't know because she wouldn't tell him. "Sorry," he said anyway. It was weak and useless, but he had nothing else to offer. Except… "Did the new verses help?"

She brightened. "Yeah. Thanks. I fell asleep holding your book again, though. It's getting beat up. I'll probably have to buy you a new quad at the end of all this. I'll try to be more careful next time—assuming you're okay with me keeping it awhile longer."

He pictured her sleeping with his scriptures clutched in her arms and smiled. "Absolutely."

"Oh, and…um…" She twisted her loose wedding ring. "Is there anything in your scriptures I can't see? I mean, anything private you don't want me to read?"

He panicked for a moment, wondering if there was a note from his old girlfriend, Megan. Even if there was, he had nothing to hide. Megan was in the past. "No. Read whatever you want."

"Okay. You wrote some notes on some of the pages, but I didn't want to read them without your permission."

"Oh, yeah. Sure. Be my guest."

She tried a few last painful notes before giving up on the piano. Scooting closer, she snuggled into his side and laid her head on his shoulder. He caught the faint scent of roses, the scent of her hair. The house was silent and peaceful, and so was he.

"Do you plan on sleeping every night in the car?" she asked.

"No. I'll work on finding a place to stay tomorrow."

"Tomorrow?"

"Yeah, it's Sunday, so it'll have to wait. And we should get your ring sized," he added, as she twisted it again to make the diamond face front—job number four. It was going to be a busy day. "How do you keep that thing on?"

She closed her hand in a fist. "See. It works wonders. Wait a second." She straightened and looked up at him. "Shouldn't you be in class tomorrow?"

"No."

She shot him a dark look. "Josh…"

He stifled a sigh. It's not that he didn't like school, he did. It was just the last thing on his mind. But Sadie was determined to see him graduate. He had no idea how many strings Madsen pulled to get him into senior level classes at UT-Knoxville—or if Madsen lined up a senior project similar to the solar-powered microcar Josh nearly finished at Washington State—but his grades were sure to plummet in his distracted state.

"Come on," she said. "You already missed a week. They're expecting you tomorrow. 8 AM sharp."

"If I can miss a week, I can miss another day." *Or a month. Or a semester.*

"I guess," she sighed. "What about tonight? Can I take a turn sleeping in the car?"

"Ha. With a broken leg and ribs? I don't think so. No. Harrison and I will find a motel tonight."

She played with her dangling ring another moment. "So, you really aren't staying here with me?"

He shook his head. "I don't think I should. It's just that...I don't think it's..." His knee started to bounce. Why hadn't he explained this earlier? "I mean, I don't think you and I should be...here...together. For so long."

"Why?"

"It's so small, and in Mississippi we were supposed to have adjoining apartments, but Madsen didn't know. And I know technically we're not here alone, and we're supposedly married, but..." He stopped, hoping she would jump in and rescue his ramblings. Instead, her large, dark eyes studied him without blinking. She was going to make him spit out each and every word. "I don't think we should live together, Sadie."

There. He said it.

"O-kay...?"

"It's just not..." He struggled to find a good word. "...appropriate."

"Appropriate?" she repeated, reminding him how awkward that word could be. "I guess I figured since we're married we would at least live in the same house."

"I know. Maybe we shouldn't be married."

She backed away from him, looking hurt as well as confused.

"Wait. That didn't sound right," he said. "I want to be married to you. It just makes not living together complicated. We don't need any nosy neighbors wondering why Harrison and I sneak out of here at night."

She was silent long enough for the room to grow unbearably warm.

"I didn't realize how strict you were with all that," she said at last. "I figured since I stayed at the cabin—"

"—where there were stairs," he pointed out.

"Stairs? There's a rule that if there are stairs separating you and your girlfriend it's okay?" There wasn't a hint of teasing in her tone. She was completely serious. She didn't know what to expect from him. Neither did Harrison. Or Croff.

Suddenly Josh saw himself and his rules from their point of view. Maybe he was as ridiculous as they thought he was. Too strict. Too careful. After all, Sadie stayed three days at the cabin with him and his buddies. What would Kevin or Trevor say to him right now? They'd say he was blowing things out of proportion—like always. *It's harmless,* they'd say. *Just stay in the other room if you're worried about it.* Sadie needed him close by. And maybe it was harmless. Especially with Croff and Harrison staying with them around the clock.

But then again…

His parents would freak if they found out Josh and Sadie were living together. They would never approve. Neither would Sam, which told Josh he'd chosen well enough.

"I don't think there's anything specific enough for our situation," he said. "But the Jacksons have a 'No Girls' rule at the cabin."

"Really? Why did you guys let me stay then?"

Josh almost hadn't, but then he remembered. "Because we weren't dating then. That changes things."

"Oh."

What he would have given to read her thoughts. The realities of dating a Mormon. Then again, maybe he didn't want to know.

Without warning, she leaned in close, closed her eyes, and pressed her warm lips to his. Like the other morning, her kiss caught him completely off guard. At least this time he recovered quickly. His fingers were torn between wanting to cradle her soft face and wind through those short, wild curls. He chose the curls. Her soft lips were moist and incredibly inviting. Her hands wrapped around his waist and pulled him closer on the bench.

Just as his head started to spin, she broke off the kiss. It was another second before he found the strength to open his eyes.

"So," she whispered, "you don't trust me to stay away from you?" An ironic question considering her nose touched his, and the rest of her wasn't much further.

"After a kiss like that?" he choked. "More myself than anything."

"Really?" One of her brows rose. "I better be on my guard then."

Though his neck grew warm, he laughed. She was teasing him. It was nice to see this side of her again. He kissed her nose and sat back before his thoughts ran away from him. "You're something else, you know that?"

"So are you." She reached up as if to run her fingers through the back of his hair, but she stopped short and dropped her hand in her lap. "Exactly what is allowed?"

"This." Josh squeezed her hand. "And this…" He tilted her chin up and gave her a firm but brief kiss. "And that's probably it for couples who aren't married—really married."

She tried to smile. "Okay."

They lapsed into another silence, more awkward than before. It was eating him alive. He finally had to ask.

"Do you hate me or think I'm crazy? Weird, eccentric, overzealous? Harrison thinks I'm the strangest man on the planet."

"I think you're different," she offered. "A little old-fashioned maybe, but I like it." She leaned against him. "I love it, actually."

"You do?"

She flashed another radiant smile. "Yeah. It's cute."

He stared at her, amazed at her adaptability. Dating. Marriage. Cohabitating. Not cohabitating. Mississippi. Tennessee. Not to mention she just saved his pride. "Hmm. I can live with cute. Manly is more preferable, but at this point I won't push my luck."

She laughed. "How about gentlemanly? Is that better?"

He rubbed the back of her hand. "Much better."

Josh heard Croff stirring in the back room. She emerged with her hair wrapped in a towel. "Morning," she said, heading into the kitchen. "How did everyone sleep?"

"Fine," Josh and Sadie said together. Then they looked at each other and smiled at their ridiculous answer.

Croff rummaged through a few cupboards and found the coffee. She pulled out the pot and asked, "You guys want any?"

"None for me," Josh said.

"Me neither," Sadie said.

Josh glanced sideways but said nothing. Sadie loved her morning coffee. Which reminded him of something else. He checked his watch and thought about the other awkward conversation they needed to have.

"Hey," he said, "since today is Sunday, I thought I'd find a church service to attend somewhere."

Her eyes widened. "Oh?"

"I'll just go for a little bit. I'm pretty sure Harrison will kill me when I tell him—and frankly, if I thought he'd stay behind, I'd tell him not to come—but I think I need to regroup, re-center, or I don't know. I just need to go. Are you okay if I leave for a bit?"

Sadie paled. "What?"

"I won't stay long," he said quickly. Maybe long enough to meet the bishop and warn him of their unique situation.

"Okay…" Her pained expression reminded him of everything she'd been through in the last three days. A funeral—hers. Hospital. Ribs. Leg. The redhead. The plane. The long drive and a new house. Saying goodbye to her mom. Her ex-boyfriend arrested. Her new boyfriend abandoning her at night. She was living on no sleep and the fear of being killed, and Josh was leaving her. For church. Maybe he was as clueless as Harrison thought.

"If you don't want me to go, I won't," he said, and then wondered if that would be the case next Sunday or every Sunday. How soon before he stopped going altogether?

"No. You can go. Just…don't you want me to go with you?"

He finally understood. The promise she was determined to keep. "No. You stay here and sleep. You've had a long week—not to mention a bad night."

"And you haven't?" she shot back.

Yes, but it's my church.

And then he realized why she was doing it. Guilt. Ever since she decided she was ruining his life, she overcompensated by trying to give him every last thing he wanted—school, his brother, Jake, his church, no coffee—

without any regard for herself. Maybe on another day, he would have jumped at the possibility of taking her to a Mormon service, but he was too tired to deal with the fact she was going for the wrong reasons.

"You don't have to do this, Sadie."

"Yes, I do."

"No. You don't."

Her dark eyes narrowed. "Yes. I do."

"Look, I know what you're trying to do, but I don't want you to—"

"What?" Her chin jutted out. "You don't want me to what?"

The sting in her voice cut off his words.

"Look, I'm trying hard not to be insulted, Josh, but why don't you want me to go to church with you when I told you I would? Do you think I'm too weak to do anything, or too horrible of a person to want religion? Which is it? Because either way, it's a slam. And don't forget…" The look in her eyes caused the hairs on his neck to stand on end. "You're a horrible liar."

That wasn't much of a choice: too weak or too evil? He couldn't back-pedal fast enough. "I'm sorry. I didn't mean to suggest you *couldn't* go. I just figured with the long car ride and everything else, you'd want a day without people and crowds and—"

She nodded. "Too weak. I'm so broken you have to run around and protect me from everything. Is that it? Because I thought that was Croff's job."

Deputy Croff froze. Her eyes went to Josh, looking as shocked by the sudden attack as he was.

"It's Croff's job," Josh said penitently. "I'm sorry. I didn't mean anything."

Sadie glanced over her shoulder and remembered Croff in the kitchen. Her shoulders dropped. "No. I'm the one who's sorry. I'm just being difficult. Forget it. Go to your stupid church. I'll be waiting here for your grand return."

The word *stupid* sounded in his ears long after it should. She was just upset. She was exhausted, in pain, and everything else. Frankly, so was he.

But…her words were nearly verbatim what his mom yelled before storming out of their life forever.

He stared straight ahead at the old piano.

She slipped her hand into his. "I'm sorry, Josh. I'm just tired. Please don't…" She blew out her breath. "I'm really sorry. I didn't mean it."

Only she had. It was the most honest thing she said in three days.

She bent down into his line of vision. Once she caught his gaze, she straightened, taking his eyes with her. "You know I'm not a morning person, especially without my coffee. If you don't want me to go with you today, it's fine. If you don't want me to live with you, it's fine. It's all fine. Just ignore me, okay?"

"Sadie," he said, stroking her soft cheek, "I want to be with you all the time. Today. Tonight. Forever. It's just…" Just what? How could he explain something to her when he didn't fully understand it himself?

"I'm not the only one shutting people out," she whispered.

He stared at her. She was right.

With a quick breath, he took both her hands in his. "I want you to go with me today. In fact, I want it more than anything. I want you to read my scriptures—to love my scriptures—and quit drinking coffee, and everything else, but I'm scared you're doing it just to make me happy, which if that's the case, it won't."

"It won't?"

"No!"

"Good. How soon do we leave?"

"Sadie…"

She cocked her head to one side. "Would you stop being so difficult? I want to be with you, too. I want to have a day without funerals, running, hurting, or thinking about men behind bars plotting revenge on everyone I love. But more than that, I want to know who you are and what makes you happy, what makes you you. " Her shoulders lifted a little. "I'm jealous you can sleep without nightmares. I'm jealous you aren't constantly looking over your shoulder even though you were the one attacked at the funeral. I want your peace. If your religion is where you get it, then is it so wrong to see if it gives me any?"

Things shifted for Josh. Sadie wanted to go to his church, was fighting to go, and he was pushing her away. He had a few choice words to describe himself, but before his hopes soared, he had to double check.

"You're sure you want to go with me right now? To church? Today?"

She rolled her eyes. "You have issues."

Placing both hands on his cheeks, she said in a slow, clear voice, "I. Want. To. Go. With. You. Today. As in now. Is that clear enough?"

He smiled between her hands. "I think so."

Special Agent Stephen Dubois stared at the cement walls. Still blurry.

Not good.

It had been six days now, or was it seven? And those were only his conscious days. Who knew how long he'd been sitting in that smelly, rotten prison cell.

The cut above his eye pulsed. Though he couldn't see it, he could feel how swollen it was. The surrounding skin throbbed with pain. Knowing his luck, what started out as a minor injury would end up being the thing that killed him. After what he'd been through, that would be his luck. He could see his death certificate now:

Cause of Death: Minor laceration above the eye (Very minor)

But between the fevers, the shakes, and the cold sweats, he was sure it was turning into something far worse. Staph? Blood poisoning? And just three measly blocks from the U.S. Consulate in Casablanca, Morocco. He could crawl there if someone would give him a chance to explain.

"I'm a United States Federal Agent!" he yelled through the rough bars. "Just give me one call! Just one! Can anyone hear me? *¡Tengo dinero! J'ai* *de l'argent!* Or…" With temples pounding, he struggled to remember the Arabic equivalent—probably why he hadn't received help yet. "I have money! A lot of money! Call the consulate if you won't let me call the States. They'll tell you who I am!" He waited for a response. "Does anyone speak English?"

Swearing loudly, he sat on the cot that smelled worse than the urinal. He'd failed the FBI, failed Madsen, and he'd failed with Guillermo. His wife would never know what happened to him. Who cared that he'd made her rich? Who cared that his two girls would never have to think twice about paying for college or anything else for that matter? He would slip quietly into the next life in some small cell in Morocco, and only Guillermo and his henchmen would know the truth.

He balled his hands into fists. He would get revenge somehow. Revenge was undefeatable which meant, until he found it, so was he. Guillermo turned his carefully planned scheme upside-down, but Dubois could do the same. He'd come so close before. The power he longed for when Madsen botched Miss Dawson's Christmas interrogation, Dubois had found a week later. He couldn't quit now. He would become the agent Madsen never dreamed he could.

"I have money!" he shouted again.

Dubois had one last thought before the fever consumed him. If he ever got out of that rancid, smelly cell, if he ever found a way back to Montana and into the FBI, he was going to kill Guillermo Vasquez.

One way or another, Guillermo Vasquez was going to die a thousand deaths for this.

CHAPTER 15

An hour later, Josh surveyed the four of them. He wore wrinkled slacks and a tie. Sadie was in a black sweater and pants—pants hiked above her neon green cast. She had heavy crutches under her arms and heavier circles under her eyes. Croff was sipping her second cup of coffee, and Harrison, wearing a business suit, looked the most prepared for church as long as Josh ignored the murderous scowl on his face or the way he kept fingering the gun inside his suit coat.

Josh wasn't exactly getting a "blend in" vibe from them. Maybe when their stuff arrived from Washington and Montana they would look more church ready.

Maybe.

Josh walked toward Croff. "Are you sure you don't need help?"

"No!" She waved him away. "Stay back. I've almost got it."

He grunted. When Madsen said no computers or phones, Josh hadn't realized their bodyguards would be the ones to enforce it. Josh was left talking Croff through Mormon.org to find the nearest congregation.

"Okay," Croff said. "I think I found it again. It says 'Wards and Branches.' There's only one listed at that location."

"Right. And you're sure it's 9:00 AM for the start time?"

"Nine," Harrison muttered. "On a Sunday. After the night I had."

"Yes. 9:00 AM," Croff said.

Josh nodded. "Alright. Then we should go."

Croff shut her laptop. "Okay. Let's go over this one last time. Who are you?" she asked, pointing to Sadie.

Sadie straightened. "I'm Sadie Peterson. My husband and I were just married and moved here from…" Sadie squinted. "Provo?"

"Yeah," Josh said. Provo was the most populated Mormon area he was familiar with. That would hopefully help them avoid the name game of, *"Hey, do you know…?"* Mormons loved the name game. If anyone asked specifics about where in Provo they lived, he was dead in the water. They all were. Of course, that was pretty much true with any questions they could be asked in the next hour. He brushed the wrinkles from his pants. Maybe the whole church thing was a really bad idea.

"My husband is attending the University of Tennessee," Sadie went on. "He's finishing an Engineering degree before he gets his MBA." She shot Josh a look, daring him to disagree. "We're happy to be here."

She sounded convincing enough. Josh almost believed her.

"Are you sure I should go by Sadie?" she asked. "Maybe I should switch to my real name, Sarah, since it's so common."

"No," Croff said. "Last names are hard enough to remember. Witnesses do better keeping their original first names. I promise it will draw less attention than if Josh called you by the wrong name in public. So…" Croff pointed at her neon cast, "what happened to your foot?"

"Skiing accident."

Josh turned with a smile. "Really?" They hadn't discussed that one yet. "But you hate to ski."

"Which makes it all the more believable," Sadie said with a smirk.

Josh laughed. "Good point."

"And what about your arm?" Croff asked Josh.

His smile faded. "My arm's fine."

"Then stop cradling it."

He dropped it, unaware he had been. It just felt better in the horizontal position.

"What did you guys decide?" Josh asked the two deputies in return.

Harrison grunted. "You're sure they'll even notice four new people at this church? How do you know how many people attend that congregation? You've never been."

"They'll notice," Josh said. "Most congregations are around 250 people and usually close-knit. Everyone knows everyone."

"That's it." Harrison crossed his arms. "The deal's off. We're not going."

"It's fine," Croff said. "We're going late for a reason. Besides, Josh and Sadie need to get settled into their community. This church is Josh's community. They need to work on blending in. It'll be fine. So, what do you think? Sadie and I as relatives?"

Hispanic Sadie had to stretch to reach 5'0 and African American Croff had to slouch to get to get to 5'11. Josh shook his head. Though it pained him, he looked at Harrison. "No. I think it has to be us."

He stepped close to his bodyguard, standing shoulder to shoulder with Harrison. "What do you think? Can we pass as brothers?"

Sadie grimaced. "I don't think so. Deputy Harrison's hair is lighter and his build is different. Plus there's the age difference. Josh is twenty-four and Harrison is…"

"Forty-one," Harrison said.

"Seventeen years," Sadie said. "It's too much. What about cousins?"

Josh nodded. "Cousins it is."

"Cousins who are best of friends in spite of their age difference," Sadie added with a knowing smile.

Harrison choked on his toast.

"If that's the case," Josh said, "I should probably know your first name."

"Frank," Harrison said.

"Frank? No way," Josh said. "It sounds fake. Can't you come up with something more modern?"

Harrison glared at him. "That's my real name."

Sadie laughed. Josh would have, too, if he wasn't pinned by Harrison's glare. "Oh. Sorry. Frank."

"You can call me Deondra," Deputy Croff said, "which is my real name, so don't slam it. So, we have Josh and Sadie Petersen who were recently married and moved to the area to attend UT-Knoxville. They live next to Josh's cousin, Frank, and his gorgeous, adoring, fabulous girlfriend, Deondra."

As ridiculous as it sounded, it had to be good enough.

Sadie took Josh's hand. "Are you sure we shouldn't pretend to be Mormon like you?"

"Yes," he said. "We have enough lies to keep track of." Plus, with the way they were dressed, and the way they were sure to answer questions, it was the safest option.

Hopefully, all this wouldn't matter anyway. Josh's plan was to sneak them in and out of the church before any good-intentioned Tennessee Mormons decided to befriend—or convert—any of them.

He checked his watch again. If they showed up exactly eight minutes late, they should miss all chances of interaction. That way if the local ward ran on Mormon Standard Time, the service still would have started. Or if by some chance they ran on time, eight minutes was early enough they wouldn't be caught in the foyer for the sacrament, giving chance to any conversations out there. Today was all about avoiding people. He owed Sadie that much.

"We should go," he said.

"Isn't it a little early?" Croff asked.

Josh checked the time again. "There could be traffic, or we could get lost. No. I'd rather go now and wait in the car."

"Or circle the block a few times if needed," Harrison added.

"Yeah. Good idea." Josh took a deep breath. "Good idea."

Sadie squeezed his hand. "You're nervous. But it's okay. We'll behave."

They didn't get lost. There wasn't any traffic. And they had to drive in a circle for five minutes to kill time. Yet as they pulled in exactly eight minutes late, Josh wondered if Croff got the time wrong after all. It was a full-sized church, but there were barely a dozen cars in the parking lot. No one was going in or out of the church either.

They parked along the side of the church, just in case, and Josh hurried around to open Sadie's door. In spite of the fact that her left pant leg was hiked up over her neon cast, she looked beautiful. Her black, hand-knit sweater brought out her dark eyes, and her curly hair was tamed into a feminine wave.

She stopped, went up on tiptoes, and whispered, "It'll be fine. Relax."

He breathed deeply. *Relax. What's the worst that can happen?* Unfortunately, Sadie was a walking testament to that question.

Croff and Harrison's gazes swept the surrounding trees and bushes as they headed for the back door. So did Josh, though for different reasons. It was too quiet. Too empty.

Stake Conference maybe?

The four of them entered an empty hallway. Josh heard faint voices singing ahead of them—an opening hymn. There was a service after all. He led them toward the music, and they entered a large foyer with three possible doors leading to the chapel. The last thing he wanted to do was choose a door right up by the pulpit. He needed to find one near the—

Sadie grabbed his arm, fingernails digging into his wrinkled shirt. He looked down into her wide eyes. "What is it?" he whispered.

"Listen," she said.

Then he heard it. The singing voices were piped into an overhead speaker, coming into the foyer loud and clear.

In Spanish.

Josh listened another moment. They were singing "Redeemer of Israel," but it definitely wasn't the English lyrics he knew.

The others looked at him for an explanation. Maybe it was a special musical number. But as soon as the song ended, a man's voice came over the speaker, talking in the fastest Spanish Josh ever heard.

He finally realized what happened. "When you looked at the times," he whispered to Croff, "did it have the word 'Spanish' next to it?"

Croff paled. "I thought that meant I could read the start times in Spanish. I'm so sorry. I didn't realize it meant…this."

Josh sighed. That's what he got for not doing it himself.

"I think they're praying," Sadie whispered.

Josh bowed his head, mind racing too quickly for more reverence than that. This was hardly the ideal situation to introduce Sadie to the gospel. How could he explain doctrine when he didn't understand what was being said? But by the time they made it back to the house, searched for another congregation—through Croff—and drove around to find it, they'd probably miss any other start times.

It had been too good to be true. Sadie in church. He should have known.

"Maybe we should go," he said softly.

"No. Let's stay." Sadie winked up at him. "Maybe you'll learn a thing or two."

He couldn't believe it. His stomach was tying its millionth knot, yet she was suddenly all smiles. He straightened. "Alright. We'll sneak in after the prayer."

Once he heard the round of "Amens," he cracked open the nearest door. He'd chosen well. The door was in the far corner of the chapel. He pulled it open and grabbed Sadie's hand, forgetting she needed it to work the crutches. She gave it a little squeeze, and then let him walk in on his own.

They might as well have dropped an atomic bomb for the attention they drew. There were thirty or so people in this Spanish-speaking congregation, with a fourth of that being children under the age of twelve. Which meant the four of them substantially added to the size of the group. The Branch President—or at least that's who Josh guessed stood at the podium—stopped to smile in their direction.

"*Bienvenido,*" he said into the microphone, bringing the last of the eyes around.

So much for blending in.

Harrison glared at Josh, yet without missing a beat, Sadie waved. *"Gracias,"* she said.

"Bienvenido," others in the congregation muttered with smiles. "Welcome."

Josh managed a small wave and moved to the closest bench. He entered first and took Sadie's crutches so she could hop in after him. Croff and Harrison followed, holding hands as if it was the most natural thing in the world.

As the Branch President got back to his announcements, Josh looked around. A few people continued watching them. He could almost hear their silent questions. *Are they new? Just visiting? What callings can we give them?*

A woman in the row in front of them turned and said…something. Josh didn't catch a single word. Two years of high school Spanish. A lot of good it did him. But she spoke so fast. So did Sadie who gave a quick—and hopefully rehearsed—answer.

As Sadie sat back, Josh looked at her expectantly. She repressed another smile. She was loving this. She was in *his* turf, but she was the only one who understood a single word. The Branch President could have been solving the world's deepest mysteries, or worse, spreading all sorts of false doctrine up there, but Josh would never know because Sadie went mute and he was too frazzled to ask.

Right then and there, he decided to add a Spanish class to his schedule. Immediately. Then he focused on getting himself and his 'friends' through the next hour.

The Branch President sat down, and people around the room picked up their hymnbooks. The sacrament song. The four of them followed suit. Josh nearly shouted hosanna when he saw Spanish lyrics inside the hymnbook. At least he could pretend he spoke the language.

As he flipped to page 118, he read the title: "Asombro me da."

He scanned the notes, trying to discern which hymn it was. Music, at least, was one language he understood. Noticing the chords, he figured out the sacrament song was "I Stand All Amazed," one of his favorites.

There was no organist or pianist up front, which meant that when a woman stood up and hummed a note, it was their cue to start singing. Under normal circumstances, Josh would have jumped up and offered to play the piano for the small congregation. Back in his student ward, he was not only Elder's Quorum Counselor, but official Sacrament Meeting pianist as well. However with his bad arm, Sadie, Spanish, and his irritable bodyguard, he stayed put and started singing a cappella with everyone else. It was a little rough at first as people struggled to match pitches, but then the voices started to come together.

He didn't sing loud, not because he was butchering all the words, but because he wanted to hear Sadie's voice. She had a beautiful voice, and hearing her sing one of his favorite hymns brought warmth to his soul.

This hymn was new to her, the words were new to him, and singing without accompaniment was new to the rest of them. Yet by the time they reached the chorus, their small congregation of thirty sounded pretty good. Even Croff and Harrison joined in as best they could, a true sign they were trying to blend in.

As the second verse started, however, Sadie's voice dropped off. Josh glanced sideways and was startled to see her eyes glistening. She stared blankly down at the hymnbook. "You okay?" he whispered.

"Do you know what this says?"

He tried to remember the words to the second verse. He didn't know if the translation was an exact one, but obviously the powerful message translated well enough.

> *I marvel that He would descend from His throne divine*
> *To rescue a soul so rebellious and proud as mine.*
> *That He should extend His great love unto such as I,*
> *Sufficient to own, to redeem, and to justify.*

Oh, it is wonderful that He should care for me
Enough to die for me!
Oh, it is wonderful,
Wonderful to me!

Josh thought about Sadie's situation, her state of mind, the little he knew of her quest to find God, and her recent lack of self-confidence. A lump formed in his throat. He squeezed her close and said the only thing that sounded sufficient.

"Yes."

CHAPTER 16

The forty minutes passed in a haze.

Josh's attention span was short, and his mind wandered often. He only understood one word in a hundred, which didn't help. Sadie seemed transfixed by everything, making his mind wander even more. He had no clue if she liked what she was hearing. She could walk out of that church and vow to never return. But her face…her expression… She was enthralled, and his mind kept jumping a year ahead, and then ten. And then fifty.

To contrast, Croff and Harrison looked bored beyond tears. Josh couldn't imagine what it was like to not only have the language barrier, but the religion as well. What an intro to Mormonism.

Though it went against every instinct, as the closing hymn started, he nudged Sadie. She blinked, breaking her long trance.

"We should go," he whispered.

Her eyes widened slightly, but she nodded. She passed along the message. Harrison breathed an audible sigh of relief. Croff picked up Sadie's crutches.

With a final glance around, Josh Petersen, his wife, his cousin, and his cousin's girlfriend made their quiet escape.

That didn't stop every person from watching them leave.

"What happened to your hand?" Agent Madsen asked.

Luis, a huge man both vertically and horizontally, sat back on his all-too-small chair. Madsen was surprised the chair didn't collapse under his massive weight. Two scars ran diagonally across Luis' left cheek, but he dropped his wrapped-up hand below the table, hiding it from Madsen.

"What does my hand have anything to do with anything?" Luis said.

"It might have a lot to do with your questioning. How did you lose your fingers?"

"In a game of poker."

Madsen laughed dryly. "Very funny. You're very funny"—he almost said Mr. Ugly, borrowing Sadie's description—"Mr. Ortiz. I'm hoping you'll be more cooperative, though. Unless you want to spend the rest of your life in prison."

Luis chewed on a red coffee straw. He didn't look to be in any hurry.

"Fine." Madsen leaned forward. "We'll talk about your hand later. How about we talk about what happened the night of January 5th, at Guillermo Vasquez's cabin."

Luis picked something in his teeth. "Nothing happened. Nothing at all."

"I have a witness who says otherwise. She identified you at the scene, standing outside in the snow just after midnight. She heard four shots, and my partner has been missing ever since, so would you like to try again?"

"Augustina is dead. Good luck using her testimony in court."

"I have her testimony recorded," Madsen said. "She told me everything that happened. But come to think of it, since she's dead, I bet the jury will give her testimony extra credibility. Perhaps they'll stick around for another trial, one that involves *her* murder. I'm sure they'd love to see you for that one, too."

Luis straightened. "Look, we didn't kill that FBI agent or anyone that night, okay? It was all a setup to test Augustina's loyalty to G."

"What do you mean, you didn't kill Agent Dubois *that* night? Does that mean you killed him another time?"

A sly smile spread across his scarred, round face. "You're good. Very good. But I'm not talking."

Madsen stood and gathered his papers. "Well, I tried," he said to the other agents. "Good luck in court, Mr. Ortiz."

"Wait!"

Madsen turned slowly. It was moments like this that made him love his job. People were so predictable. Especially when it came to a possible life sentence.

"Okay, so we might have roughed up your little agent," Luis said. "But he was alive and kicking last I saw him. G had some deal going on, but I don't know what. The only thing I know is that night was also a trap for his *chica*, Augustina. He didn't trust her. He wanted to see what she'd do if things turned ugly. So we shot a couple blanks into the snow to see if she'd rat him out. I guess his instincts were right. Tell me, how soon did she come squealing to you? Days? Hours?"

"Days?" Madsen shot back. "Miss Dawson was dead in days, remember?"

"Oh, that's right. I heard about that. She killed herself, right? Burned herself alive in some cabin?"

Madsen had the overwhelming urge to reach across the table and punch the guy. While Guillermo made his quick escape, he left the dirty work of killing Sadie to this over-confident henchman. As beautiful as Sadie was, she was lucky to have avoided Luis' lust-filled, greedy hands. If not for Manuel, she might have suffered a worse fate than she already had, but for the sake of questioning, Madsen decided to play along.

"Tell me, Mr. Ortiz," he said, sitting again. "Why would Miss Dawson want to kill herself two tiny days after the incident with the shots?"

"I guess she couldn't live without G, huh? He broke up with her. It musta broke her heart." His mouth twitched with his lies.

"You don't often win in poker, do you," Agent Madsen said, "because I'm thinking it was the other way around. I think Guillermo found out that Miss Dawson came to me about the murder of Agent Dubois, and Guillermo decided to get rid of her—to 'dispose' of her." Madsen purposely used the word the informer gave him.

It worked.

Luis flinched.

Knowing he'd baited him, Madsen decided to reel him in. "I'm starting to think her suicide wasn't a suicide at all. I think Guillermo had her killed to cover his tracks on the 5th. Maybe Guillermo is behind the fire at the Jackson cabin. Maybe he put her there." Madsen stared Mr. Ugly down. "What do you think?"

Luis' tan face no longer looked so tan. "G was out of the country when she died."

Madsen smiled. This was easier than he thought. "That's right. He was. He left a day or two before the fire. Thank you for reminding me. He must have hired it out. Paid someone good money to finish the job. Now…who do you suppose he hired to pull off a thing like that? Killing his beautiful girlfriend? Destroying two different million-dollar cabins? Someone with a history of arson maybe?"

Luis wiped the sweat from his forehead. Guillermo didn't have a criminal record, but Luis did, and arson was only one of the many things on his list.

"You're crazy," Luis said. "There's no way G wanted her dead. She broke up with him."

"I thought you said he broke up with her."

"Whatever. If G wanted that Augustina chick dead, I would have been the first to know. He didn't. He didn't. He…" Luis swallowed and glanced around the small room. "Okay, fine. He might have. But I haven't heard a word about it. Not a thing. I'm clean on this one."

Madsen shook his head. Guillermo certainly hadn't hired Mr. Ugly for his brains. But until Sadie was back from the dead, her attempted murder charge would have to wait.

"Perhaps your memory will improve with time," he said. "Or perhaps your desire to protect your boss will lessen with time. But for now, let's return to the night of the 5th. What happened to Agent Dubois?"

"There's nothing more to say. Your guy was alive and healthy last I saw him. Whether G did something after, I don't know."

Luis' color was back, his confidence returned. He believed what he was saying, which didn't make sense.

Madsen's pulse pounded with rage as he thought about Dubois' widowed wife, Katrina, and their two girls. Guillermo would not win this one!

His voice rose. "How long are you going to cover for Vasquez? Didn't he lose that privilege when he took your fingers? Aren't you ready to see him pay? I know he was behind Dubois' murder. I know he was behind Miss Dawson's murder, but I need someone to help me prove it. That someone can be you."

Luis' jaw clenched, though his eyes darted back and forth, deliberating.

"Did you deserve to lose your fingers?" Madsen pressed. "What did you do that was so bad Guillermo took such drastic measures?"

"I tried to take something that wasn't mine," Luis said softly. "Something of Guillermo's. Only nobody takes his stuff without paying. Especially not something like *that*."

Madsen thought about Sadie's testimony, and the revulsion swelled inside him. Still, he pressed. "What?"

Again, Luis clamped his mouth shut. With time, Madsen hoped the bitterness would win out, the fear would win out. Something. Interrogation was an art, knowing when to push and when to pull back. For now, Madsen pulled back.

"Sorry to pry again. Right now, I have the murder of my partner to deal with, and an eyewitness identifying you at the scene."

"A dead witness," Luis said.

Madsen leaped to his feet. "Will you take your chances with that in court? Knowing that, in the meantime, I'm still investigating Miss Dawson's death? Knowing I'll find out everything you've ever done for Guillermo

Vasquez, every last little thing he's hired you to do? Are you ready for that? Or…" His finger jabbed the table, "are you ready to help me bring G down once and for all? Are you ready to see him pay for what he did to you?"

Luis sat back, fat hanging over the chair. His black eyes never left Madsen, though Madsen could tell he was working through his options. There weren't many.

"I can protect you," Madsen said. "You could live a peaceful, comfortable life, Mr. Ortiz. But you and I have to become good friends first. We have to learn to trust each other."

Luis' black eyes finally met his. "Alright. I'll do it."

Half an hour later, the paperwork was done.

"You won't regret this, Mr. Ortiz," Madsen said. "You'll be well protected."

"I hear I get a paycheck for doing this. How good is it, 'cause G was paying me pretty good?"

It was always the first question these guys asked. "You get some, but not enough. Get a job."

"I have a job. My job is to rat out G. Seems like you should pay me a pretty penny for that."

"Considering your alternative is prison," Madsen said, straightening his papers, "you don't get a say. You might be entering WITSEC, but you'll be watched closely. The Marshals are not only protecting you, but they're about to become your new parole officers."

"Parole officers?" Luis' eyes narrowed to a menacing glare. "I'm not sure it's worth it if I have you watching my every move. I might as well be in prison."

He was bluffing. Not that it mattered. He already signed over his life.

Madsen stood. "I'm warning you, Mr. Ortiz. If you so much as sneeze the wrong way, I'll slam you behind bars so fast you won't know what hit you. Your underhanded days are over. No more drug deals. No illegal anything. You're on a very short leash. You have a job to do, and I expect you to do it without issue. But if you betray my confidence, if you try to go back to your old scheming ways, I might do something worse than throwing you in prison. I'll turn you loose in Vasquez's organization and make sure he knows you ratted him out. He burned the love of his life when she came to me. Imagine what he'll do to you."

Luis reached out his good hand. "Sounds like we have a deal."

CHAPTER 17

Josh loosened his tie. "What did you think of church?"

Sadie bit her cheeks to keep from smiling. His curiosity finally won out. She hadn't said a word about the service on the drive home, and neither had he. But she knew he was anxious to find out what he missed.

She hopped over to a kitchen chair and sat at the small table. Her ankle was killing her, her ribs as well, making the oak chair feel harder than it was. Harrison was already conked out on the couch, and Croff was engrossed by something on her laptop, giving Josh and Sadie some privacy.

Postponing his question, she studied him from a distance: his dark wavy hair, broad shoulders, and deep blue eyes. Josh always looked good, but she especially loved him in a suit and tie. Of course, she figured that much out at the New Year's Eve party. She smiled in sudden memory. Speaking of which, he still owed her some Rachmaninoff. Once the piano was tuned…

He leaned against the wall, arms folded as if trying to look casual and full of patience, but his face belied him. His brows were pinched, his neck muscles tight. She was reading open, almost pained curiosity.

What did she think of church?

Sadly for him, she was in a teasing mood. It was wonderful to feel so light after such a heavy week. She couldn't just give in now. Not yet.

She rubbed a spot on the oak table. "It was nice."

"Nice?" The rest of his question hung between them. *That's it?*

"Yes. It was nice."

Though she was giving him a hard time, church really had been nice. She wasn't sure what she expected. The Mormon service was more relaxed and yet more formal at the same time. The words hit home more than she ever dreamed they could, as if they were directed to her. Like the verses from John.

And that hymn…

Asombro me da. I Stand All Amazed.

The words still encircled her. *Tan indigno. Cuán asombroso. Rescate.* If any soul needed rescuing, it was hers. And the melody. So lyrical, so moving. She just didn't know how to explain any of that to Josh. But if the last few days were any indication, she was going to love his religion.

He shook his head. "You know you're killing me, right?"

She laughed. "Yes. Sorry. Those three people spoke about families. One of them talked about families lasting forever, but only if they were…" She squinted, not sure how to translate the word.

"Sealed? In the temple?"

"Yeah. I think that was it."

He perked up. "That's one of the doctrines I love most. Families are central to everything we do, but it's not just in this life. We can live together as families after death, husbands and wives, children and their parents. It doesn't have to end at death."

That's what she thought she'd heard. She half-remembered her aunt and uncle mentioning something like that once. Sadie had spent an unusual amount of time pondering death lately. One of her biggest fears was losing those closest to her. She loved the idea that, no matter what Guillermo did to her or her loved ones, they could all live together beyond this life, hanging out every day in the clouds or wherever.

"The last guy talked about how to be a good husband. It's too bad you couldn't understand," she added playfully. "You could have gotten a few pointers."

"Really?" Josh smiled. "And what exactly can I improve on, Mrs. Peterson?"

Her gaze dropped to his bent, cradled arm, to his hair not quite the right shade, to his wrinkled clothes and tired eyes, and suddenly she couldn't find her voice. The man talked about husbands taking care of their wives the same way Jesus took care of His people. A tall order, yet Josh was already there. He'd put his life on the line for Sadie more than once, and even beyond, he treated her more selflessly than anyone she ever met. And what had she done for him in return?

"Nothing," she answered.

Apparently he had less confidence in his husbanding abilities than she did. His dark brows shot up in surprise.

Her throat started to burn, but she forced a smile. "It's true. You're already perfect."

The house grew silent. Josh looked at her without blinking. She stared back, hoping he would join her at the table. Her small house was drafty and cold, even with her black sweater, and she could have snuggled into him. A little nap on his shoulder sounded heavenly. But for whatever reason, he stayed leaned against the wall, staring. Not in a bad way. Not at all. Just intense, focused. He was thinking about something, and from his intense gaze, she guessed it was her.

That's when she realized that even more than liking the way Josh looked, she loved the way he looked at her, like there was no one else in the room, in the world. In fact, she liked it enough she gave the answer he was waiting for.

"I really liked church today. I'd like to go with you again if that's okay."

"Yeah?" He shoved his hands into his pockets and pulled them out again, only to turn around and shove them back in. "That's great. Sure. I'm glad you liked it. I'm very, very..." He blew out his breath. "You really liked it?"

It was cute when he tried to contain his emotions, especially his thrilled ones. He was an open book, which was vastly liberating after dating Guillermo.

"Yes," she said. "But for your sake, maybe next time we should try an English service."

"Next time?" Harrison jerked up from the couch, heavy lines etched on the side of his face. "There's not going to be a next time. We're not going anywhere. Today proved it's too dangerous to go anywhere with you two."

"How?" Sadie asked.

"Too many people. Too many questions."

"There were only thirty people," Josh said, "and nobody asked any questions."

Harrison glared at Sadie. "You didn't tell him about the woman?"

Josh whirled. "What woman?"

Sadie finally understood the evil look Harrison shot her during church. "How much Spanish do you understand, Deputy Harrison?"

"Enough to know she asked point blank where we lived," Harrison said, "and you told her!"

"She did?" Josh asked. "You did?"

"It's fine," Sadie said. "People will eventually find out where we live, and it would have only piqued her curiosity if I'd said, 'Sorry. I can't tell you. That's classified information.'"

Harrison's fist slammed on the coffee table, making her jump. "You said too much. She asked too much. If it wouldn't have attracted more attention, I would have hauled you two out right then. But I'm putting my foot down now. You two aren't going anywhere, not even to get the mail."

Sadie felt her blood pressure rising. She probably should have shut up, but she was fed up with Deputy Harrison's attitude. "It was *one* lady, and all I said was that we lived on the south side of town."

"On a hill. In a small house."

She winced. She'd forgotten that. Still…how many small houses were on hills in the south part of Knoxville? Thousands. At the same time, she was bugged Harrison never mentioned his Spanish fluency before.

The deputy folded his arms. "If we hadn't left when we had, we would have been swarmed by other people anyway. Eager boy there said as much this morning. It's too dangerous."

"I meant swarmed in a good way," Josh said. "Mormons are overly-friendly."

"Exactly. Which is why we're not going anywhere. I forbid it," Harrison added with less strength than his words implied.

Sadie's temper flared. Maybe Josh should have spent more time picking his own bodyguard instead of worrying about hers. Sadie's temper flared.

"Until I sign those WITSEC papers," Sadie said, "I'm under the jurisdiction of the FBI. Agent Madsen told us to move in and move on. We have no idea how long we'll be here. It could be weeks or years. Madsen told us to find jobs, go to school, work, shop, and blend in. So that's what we're going to do. Blend in."

"And as *I* remember," Harrison said, rising to his feet, "Madsen said your ex knows half the Hispanic population. What makes you think he doesn't know the people in that church?"

The possibility sucked the air from her lungs. How did she know? She didn't. No one did.

"Madsen was talking about Montana," Josh said more to Sadie than Harrison. "Guillermo doesn't have any business dealings in the South. There's a reason we drove 2,200 miles."

"Really?" Harrison snapped. "I thought we drove 2,200 miles because—" He bit off the last of his sentence, but the message was still delivered.

Because Sadie had a breakdown. That's why.

Josh straightened. "We were coming to Tennessee regardless of whether we flew or drove. This is where we belong."

"Not Mississippi?" Harrison challenged. "Not well-researched Mississippi?"

Josh took a step forward. "Do you have a problem with the situation, Deputy?"

"Yeah, I got a big problem. In the four days since I met you, you've proven how reckless you both are. You at the funeral. Her on the plane. In church. You're both walking red flags, which is why the FBI brought us in. We're responsible to keep you alive. We're here because we're the best. But we need full jurisdiction to give you full protection, and yet she won't sign the papers, proving her complete and utter disregard for the seriousness of this situation. I don't see you begging her to either. So yes, I have a huge problem with the situation. I'm in charge, but I'm not officially in charge."

"That's right," Josh said. "You're not. Can you blame her for not signing yet? The second she does, Guillermo will know she's alive, and if he can't find her, he'll go after her mom and brother. While Sadie is flown back and forth, jerked back and forth for the trial, she'll have a madman after everyone she loves."

"Which is why Croff and I are here!"

Sadie hugged her tender ribs. She didn't jump into the conversation because, in their own way, both men were right.

"Temporary or not," Harrison said, "I'm being paid to babysit the two of you, and if I say you're not going—"

"Hey!" Croff shouted, cutting him off.

All three turned. Sadie had forgotten Croff was in the corner of the room with her laptop. Sadie waited for Croff to reprimand Harrison for his sudden dictator-like lecture, at the same time she braced herself for Croff to echo Harrison's words. But Croff was too engrossed by something on the screen.

"You guys might want to see this," Croff said, waving them over.

Josh and Harrison joined her by the computer, but Sadie didn't move. She didn't like the look on Croff's face. Something was wrong.

As Josh read the screen, lines creased his forehead. After another minute, his eyes lifted to Sadie's, heavy with worry. There was something on that screen he didn't want her to see, but something she probably needed to know. It was bad news—definitely bad news—which meant it was about Guillermo.

Her ex-boyfriend had been arrested less than 24 hours and already there was bad news? Her chest tightened. Had he escaped? Gone ballistic? Figured out who ratted him out?

Who did he hurt this time?

She closed her eyes and took in three slow, painful breaths. With effort, she pushed herself off the oak chair and hobbled over to the laptop.

Croff turned the screen.

Guillermo's black eyes smiled up at Sadie.

Sadie fell back instinctively. *It's just a picture. Just a picture.* She summoned the courage to look at the computer screen again.

The photo of Guillermo was a regular, smiling photo, as if it was snapped during his latest business venture. Below was the newspaper article that held everyone's attention.

January 18.

KALISPELL, Mont. — Real estate mogul Guillermo Vasquez was arrested Saturday in Chicago, Illinois, to face a murder charge in a deadly Kalispell shooting.

Vasquez was taken into custody just before midnight in an upper Chicago high-rise, an FBI spokeswoman said. "Vasquez was arrested without incident by FBI agents with assistance from the Chicago PD."

Vasquez will be taken directly to Montana to face charges in federal court.

"He's not guilty," Lawyer Keith Brandy told reporters earlier. "We look forward to getting his name cleared."

The FBI previously obtained a murder warrant for Vasquez in the Jan. 5 shooting of one of their own, 39-year-old Stephen Dubois, FBI Special Agent and father of two young children. Police say Dubois was working near the scene of Vasquez's cabin when he went missing.

The FBI spokeswoman said the motive appears to be retaliation for an FBI investigation into Vasquez's real estate dealings.

"Mr. Vasquez is wanted for murder," Special Agent Bruce Madsen said early Sunday. "We are pleased he was taken into our custody in a peaceful manner."

Vasquez has no previous criminal record. According to his lawyer, "He never will." Brandy was retained by Vasquez's family on Sunday morning and was in contact with Flathead County District Attorney and the FBI Fugitive Task Force.

Initial court proceedings are set to begin Wednesday.

Sadie's ribs ached, reminding her to breathe. She kept telling herself this was good. This is what they wanted all along. Guillermo was arrested peacefully. No one was hurt. She should have jumped for joy.

She didn't. And neither did Josh.

Because the clock was ticking. Things were happening fast. If initial court proceedings started Wednesday, her time to decide was running out. Madsen would force her hand any day. Sooner or later, she'd have to choose justice or safety, whether to share what little she knew of Dubois' murder or not, and she had the feeling it would be sooner.

"I never thought of him as the type to go peacefully," Josh said, studying the screen.

That's because Josh only knew one side of Guillermo, the private side, the violent side. The public side was like his picture: a smiling, benevolent diplomat. She could picture Guillermo schmoozing the reporters even now: *This is just a big misunderstanding, friends. Do not worry yourselves. It will all clear up with time. I am innocent, my friends. Completely innocent. By the way, that is a fabulous tie, sir. Where did you purchase it?* That was the Guillermo she'd fallen in love with, the only side of him she'd seen.

Before he tried to kill her.

As if pulled by a magnet, her gaze lifted to his picture again. Even though he smiled, she could feel his black eyes boring into her, like he was inside the computer looking directly at her and her treachery.

You turned me in, he seemed to say. *You ratted me out. You and you alone, so I will make you and everyone you love pay.*

She faced the window. The sun shone brightly, reminding her she wasn't in Montana or Chicago or anywhere near Guillermo. He was locked up, hopefully for life. And she was in Tennessee, possibly for life. So was Josh. Goosebumps still ran down her arms. She tried to rub them away.

"I don't suppose this means we can go home?" she asked. It was wishful thinking more than anything, but Harrison whirled on her.

"You just don't get it," Harrison said. "Vasquez will be more dangerous than ever. He'll be looking for retaliation, payment for what's been done to him. He'll be searching for any last person who had the tiniest part in putting him behind bars. This is his most dangerous time."

"Most dangerous?" she squeaked.

"Yes! You'd be shocked what these crime bosses can accomplish behind bars. Usually very little changes in their organization. He'll still be running things, calling the shots. Hunting."

Mamá! Damien. Kathy. Peter!

Every possible face of every possible victim flashed before her eyes, ending with the mind-numbing image from her dream of Josh's glass eyes staring up at her.

Tears clogged her throat. "When will any of us feel safe again?"

"When he's dead," Josh muttered.

Sadie's eyes widened. Josh's face matched his dark words. Yet it was true. If Guillermo was just as powerful in prison, what was the point of locking him up? Why should she sign papers and return from the dead if his wrath wasn't tempered by iron bars? But above everything else, why in a million years would she ever let Josh go home? The answer was, she wouldn't.

They were stuck in Tennessee forever.

Josh put an arm around her and pulled her tight. Her forehead fell against his chest, and she focused on the steady rise and fall of his breathing.

144

"Sorry," he whispered. "It's not true. There will come a day when you'll feel safe. For now this is good news—great news. The beginning of the end."

In her mind, *the beginning* loomed larger than *the end.* Neither did she miss the way he didn't include himself in his optimism.

"It'll be okay," he breathed.

His words didn't comfort her. Instead, they made her mad. Why was he always the one comforting her? He was the one who wasn't safe, and she was sick of her own weakness.

She straightened. "Sorry. I have to quit letting this get to me. This is good news—for both of us. We should be happy." She forced herself to smile. It hurt her cheeks, but it worked. He returned her smile.

"The beginning of the end," he said.

There it was again. She was starting to loathe that phrase.

Needing something other than Guillermo to think about, she asked, "Are you hungry?" Food sounded horrible, but distraction sounded divine.

"Uh...sure."

Leaving her crutches behind, she used the wall and couch to limp her way into the kitchen. Josh followed.

"Madsen said the house was fully stocked with food," she said. "But I don't think there's much. Maybe stuff for sandwiches, like PB&J and cold cuts. What sounds good?"

Josh was giving her a strange look. "I don't know. What sounds good to you?"

An end to her nightmare. She stole a glance over her shoulder. Croff and Harrison were still huddled around the computer, faces taut.

"PB&J," she said.

Josh opened a drawer and rummaged through the cupboards. Sadie grabbed out the peanut butter and found the jam in the fridge. Croff whispered something to Harrison. Something that made Harrison shake his head. The guy looked stiff as a board. Why were they still reading the article?

Josh opened every drawer. "I can't find a knife."

"I think I saw one in there. Can you hand me one?"

She grabbed the loaf of bread at the same time Josh reached for it. "I'll make the sandwiches," he said. "You go sit down."

Holding up her heavy cast made her leg ache, but sitting meant waiting. Waiting meant thinking. Thinking meant Guillermo.

"No, I got it," she said.

"Are you sure?" The corners of his mouth turned up. "I might roast marshmallows to perfection, but I make a killer PB&J."

Sadie thought about Josh sitting next to her on the hearth of Sam's cabin, about Trevor making grilled cheese, and Josh teasing her endlessly. She almost lost herself in the memory, almost forgot Croff and Harrison were huddled around the article. Almost.

She took the knife from him. "Tempting, but I'll take my chances. Do you guys want a sandwich?" she asked over her shoulder.

Neither deputy heard.

"What choice do we have?" Croff was saying.

Harrison folded his arms. "Not many if we can't fly. Which means we'd have to leave now and drive through the night."

Sadie's ears perked up. "Leave? You guys are leaving already? The temporary permit doesn't expire for a few days."

"We're all leaving," Harrison said. "Hopefully."

"What? Where?" she said. "We just got here!"

Croff left her chair and approached the kitchen slowly, as if to keep from spooking Sadie. "Guillermo's being flown to Montana for trial, Sadie. Madsen hasn't said yet, but I'm sure he'll need you. I don't think he can wait any longer. The end of his email said he'd be calling soon."

"We're just trying to figure out how to travel this time," Harrison added dryly.

"What?" Sadie said, pulse thickening.

"The newspaper said initial court proceedings begin Wednesday," Croff said. "That's you, Sadie. Both of you, actually, since the FBI is using Josh.

146

The first briefing with the prosecutor should be Tuesday." Croff gave Sadie a sad smile. "It's time."

The air rushed out of Sadie's lungs. Three days. In three days, she would be alive again.

In three days, she would see Guillermo again.

The knife dropped, splattering peanut butter on the checkered floor.

CHAPTER 18

Madsen didn't call for two more hours. Josh watched Sadie chew her fingernails down to the skin, deciding whether to sign the WITSEC documents or not, whether to be alive or not.

It was devastating to think they went through the whole funeral charade to buy Sadie and her mom one lousy week of peace. If they'd known it was going to be that short, they never would have agreed.

The phone rang, and Croff jumped up. She spoke to Agent Madsen first. Then she handed the phone to Sadie. Sadie's face went white. She held it for several seconds before shaking her head. "I can't." She shoved the phone at Josh.

Josh took it reluctantly. "Hello?"

Madsen sighed. "I need to speak with Miss Dawson."

Sadie curled up in a ball on the couch, staring at nothing as she retreated to that dark place in her mind where she ventured alone.

"Not right now," Josh said.

"I suppose you'll do. How are things in Tennessee?" Madsen asked.

"Short. Very short. Is it true?" Josh asked. "Are you asking us to leave already?"

There was another deep sigh. "I need Miss Dawson in Kalispell Tuesday afternoon at the very latest."

Josh pinched the rim of his nose to keep cool. "You realize we'd barely make it if we left now, pushed hard, and drove through the night. It takes thirty-six hours to drive, that's without stops. You can't expect us to—"

"Then fly."

Sadie's head lifted slowly, blankly, having heard Madsen perfectly. The pained look on her face tore Josh to pieces.

A burst of anger shot through him. He moved into the kitchen. Madsen was fully aware what happened on the plane—no doubt he'd dealt with the fallout—yet he had the gall to ask Sadie to fly?

"Not in a million years," Josh whispered. "You'll be lucky to get her back in a car. Do you realize how much pain she's in when she travels? We've barely been here twelve hours, and you honestly expect us to turn around and drive across the country again?"

"You'll be back in Tennessee by the end of the week—or later, I suppose, if you insist on driving. Technically, Mr. Young, you don't need to come with her. We won't use your testimony until later, which means you could stay in—"

"Over my dead body!" Josh yelled.

"Which is what I assumed." Another sigh. "I know you may not believe me, but I'm sorry you've had little time to get settled. And yet I've been more than patient with Miss Dawson on my end. I can't wait any longer. I didn't expect to find Vasquez this quickly, but this is good news, don't you agree? Don't you want him locked away forever?"

"Obviously. But..." Josh lowered his voice, "do you realize what happens when he finds out she's alive?"

"We plan to move her mother and brother the second she signs the paperwork."

That was something at least. But even that wouldn't stop Guillermo from hiring hit men to track them down—all of them. Already Sadie couldn't sleep at night.

Josh glanced back at her. She still stared straight ahead.

"I just don't understand why she needs to be there Tuesday," he said. "Can't you start the proceedings without her testimony? I thought the initial trial was a formality anyway, to make sure Guillermo knows the charges against him. We thought it would be months before she was needed. Not days."

"May I be frank with you, Mr. Young?" Madsen said.

As if he hadn't already? "Yes."

"I don't have time for this. I have a killer and crime lord in my custody that I've been trying to nail for two years. I have him. He killed my partner. I will *not* let him slip away again because my witness is too scared to see him. I can't coddle Miss Dawson anymore, and quite frankly, neither can you. I need her now!"

Sadie blinked hard. Josh backed up realizing Madsen's voice was still carrying perfectly across the room. He couldn't back into the hallway fast enough.

"So it's your job to get her on board," Madsen ranted. "You have exactly one hour to do it. I'm going to have a hard enough time pushing the paperwork through the Attorney General's office to get her in Marshal's full-time protection by Tuesday. There's a lot of red tape getting someone into the WITSEC."

"But why Tuesday?" Josh asked again. "Why so soon?"

"Because! The judge wants to know the witness is truly going to testify and not back out. Her time is up!"

Josh was all the way to the bedrooms when he stopped. He was too steamed to lower his voice, but he tried anyway. "May I be frank with you, sir? We just had her funeral on Thursday. Thursday! Her mother just got settled, and we're not even settled. And Sadie's not..." He almost said stable, but prudently redirected. "...herself. If you put her in front of Guillermo when the scars from last time haven't even healed—"

"What better time to put her in front of a judge? No one can deny her injuries when they see her."

"Sir!" Josh shouted. "She's a person, not a pawn. If you play this too hard, you could lose her for good." His jaw clenched. "And me, too."

Madsen went silent a moment. "What do you mean?"

"Sadie and I are a package deal."

"But I thought you said—"

"I changed my mind. I'm not testifying without her. I'm not bringing her back alive without her consent. I'm sorry, but she comes first."

Josh could hear Madsen breathing heavily. Josh, too. While he had him listening, he decided to press. "Can't you have your prosecutor explain the situation to the judge? Somewhere private where Guillermo's lawyers won't overhear and won't know she's alive? I'm sure the judge will understand. She just needs a little more time." His voice dropped to a whisper. "Have some compassion here."

"Has she remembered anything else?" Madsen asked.

That caused Josh to pause. "You mean from the 5th?"

"Yes."

The four shots. The three men in the snow on the night of Dubois' murder. "I don't think so. Not that she's told me."

Madsen swore under his breath. Josh shook his head. This wasn't a good sign. If Madsen didn't have more evidence, if he was relying strictly on Sadie hearing those shots and seeing those three men, he wouldn't convict Guillermo of anything. Josh knew enough about law enforcement to know that.

"Tell me you have more evidence than just Sadie," Josh said. "She didn't see anything that night. She heard the shots, but that's it."

"I have more."

"Like?"

"It's classified."

Josh bristled. The agent wasn't making things easier by any stretch of the imagination. "Will you at least say if it's some-*thing* or some-*one*?"

"Someone. But," Madsen said quickly, "even with this person on board, it would be a huge risk to have the initial court appearance without Miss

Dawson fully signed on. She's my best chance for getting a murder conviction. She's my credible witness. The other witness is…"

"Shady?"

Madsen didn't answer, which Josh took as confirmation.

So Madsen got one of Guillermo's guys to turn against him. That was good. That was great! Any trial of this magnitude needed an insider. Sadie's fear from the beginning was that she didn't know enough—and she didn't. Guillermo shielded her from his business dealings, which meant she was risking her life and others to offer very little to the trial. But if Madsen found an insider…

Josh was dying to know who. He knew less of Guillermo's contacts than Sadie did, especially who'd be willing to rat him out. The only one he could think of was Guillermo's little brother who, Sadie was convinced, made the anonymous tips to the FBI that saved her life. Even in the cabin, Manuel tied her up in a way that allowed her to eventually escape. They still weren't sure if that was intentional or not—a last way to defy Guillermo—but without Manuel, Sadie would be dead.

Whoever Agent Madsen found, Josh suddenly understood his urgency. If the prosecution got details from an insider about the murder of Dubois and Guillermo's other illegal behavior, they could use Sadie as their credible witness to back it up. Combined with her testimony of Guillermo's violence toward her, it could be enough to get a lasting conviction.

Madsen's plan had potential. And promise.

"What if she sends a written testimony?" Josh whispered.

"No!" Sadie shouted.

Startled, Josh turned. She stood behind him in the hall, holding out her hand for the phone. A little flustered, Josh handed it over.

"Two weeks," she said without preamble. "I'll sign the papers in two weeks. I'll work on my statement and do whatever you need, but I want two weeks. Deputy Croff said that's when the real trial stuff begins anyway, so you can have me in two weeks. Not a day sooner."

Croff nodded emphatically behind her.

Josh wanted to ask if Sadie was sure. Two weeks was still a short time to get her back on her feet—literally. Her cast wouldn't even be off yet. But there was a determination in her eyes, so he bit his tongue.

Madsen said something. Sadie nodded and said, "Fine. If they can't stay, we'll manage without them. We'll be fine."

Josh followed her gaze and froze. Sadie was looking at the two deputies. His stomach dropped. *If they can't stay...* Their temporary papers expired Thursday. That meant Josh and Sadie would be without bodyguards for ten days.

"Sadie, wait!"

She held up a finger, cutting him off. "Just so we're clear," she said into the phone, "the second I sign those papers, my mom and brother are on a plane headed here." A few more words were exchanged. "Understood. See you in two weeks."

Once she ended the call, she looked at Josh for a long moment. "I had to," she said.

Josh's thoughts raced. Ten days without Croff and Harrison sounded like an eternity, but as long as Guillermo didn't know she was alive, they should be fine. He hoped. And really, even with signed papers, Croff and Harrison weren't a 24/7 thing forever. They were just there to see them through the worst of the trial stuff.

Though it took a second, he nodded. "I trust you."

Her dark eyes hardened. "No, you don't. Nobody trusts me—which they shouldn't. Even I don't trust me." Sadie huffed tiredly. "But I had to do it."

"I trust you, Sadie," Josh offered softly.

"No. You don't." And before he could argue, she grabbed her crutches and said, "I need a nap." Then she pushed herself into her room and shut the door.

Josh stared at the closed door. *No, you don't?* What did that mean? He trusted her. It's Guillermo he didn't trust.

Croff and Harrison watched him, waiting for him to break the tense silence.

"Does this really mean we're without protection in the interim?" he asked.

Croff looked at her partner before answering. "I'll check with our boss, but…it sounds like it."

"You know this means she'll be alone at night," Josh said. "Plus any times I'm gone during the day. What am I supposed to do? I can't stay here. I can't." Had Sadie thought through that? He hadn't until just now.

No, you don't.

Did he trust her? The guilt started to eat at him. Did he trust her to make the right decisions in her state of mind? If so, why hadn't he pushed the phone back at her and let her deal with Madsen? She had no problem sticking up for herself with Harrison earlier. And why hadn't Josh thought she'd be up for church that morning? She survived and escaped Guillermo plenty of times on her own. If that wasn't reason enough to trust her…

He shook his head. He was doing it again. Overprotective, over-reactive, overbearing.

"Let me do some asking around," Croff said. "I'll see if we can apply for an extension without her signature. At the very least, we're here until Thursday. It will be okay."

Then why didn't Croff look okay? Why did Josh feel sick?

He studied Sadie's closed door. A nap sounded heavenly to him, too. Actually, hibernation sounded heavenly. The last four days were wearing on him, plus the month before that. But if they had two weeks before the hard stuff started, they should probably get settled.

Josh turned to Harrison. "Now might be a good time to find a place to stay tonight."

"Didn't Madsen tell you?" Harrison said.

"Tell me what?" Josh asked. He couldn't handle any more bad news.

"That even Mormon boys catch a break."

Josh's brain was too fried to compute.

Harrison nearly smiled. "Madsen didn't forget your little moral code. Your place is across the street, two houses down. I'll get the bags."

"The mayor guy called."

Guillermo picked at a piece of dirt on his orange suit before looking up. "Which one?"

"The one I hate," Manuel said.

"Which one?"

"The bald one."

"Ah, yes." Guillermo smiled. "And how is my old friend?"

"He wanted to let you know that things are turning in his favor. He doesn't need your support in the campaign this fall."

Guillermo's smile faded. That was five now. His contacts in Montana were backing out like mad, skittish cowards afraid of being linked to him and his supposedly-sullied reputation. He still couldn't believe he was sitting where he was, behind a glass partition. It never should have happened. But there was a snag getting Agent Dubois out of that Moroccan prison, which, ironies of irony, meant Guillermo was stuck in his. And his business associates wouldn't wait. They wanted out, out, out. The election was ten months away!

Something had to happen. Something fast. It was time the FBI cleared his record once and for all. It was time they quit wasting their time protecting useless engineering students and started protecting their own.

"Is that so?" Guillermo finally answered. "Well…we shall see. Anything else?"

"That's five now," Manuel said.

Guillermo stiffened. "You are keeping track, little brother? Perhaps you wish to take over my job. Perhaps you think I will not be returning. Is that it, *hermanito*?"

Manuel glared at him. He hated the diminutive title. That's why Guillermo kept using it. Guillermo tapped the glass. "I am still trying to decipher how I am on this side while you are not."

"I didn't kill anyone. That helps."

"My, my," Guillermo said. "Such venom. It does not suit you, *hermanito*. What happened to *innocent until proven guilty*? I have been convicted of nothing. I *will* be convicted of nothing. This is merely an…inconvenience."

Manuel rolled his eyes. "You drive me nuts."

Guillermo glanced at the beefy security officer behind his brother and decided to risk it. By law, the officer couldn't record or use anything against him. But still. He was careful not to use names. "How is our friend with the finger ailment?"

Manuel flinched. He had no stomach at all. "I don't know where they put him. Maybe he's in the cell next to yours."

"Not that I have heard. They cannot hold him long. They have no evidence. When he is released, tell him to see me here. Pronto. Make sure he knows."

"Why should I?"

Guillermo's eyes narrowed. Just enough to deliver the message.

Manuel fidgeted behind the glass. "Fine."

Guillermo ran through his mental list and nodded. He saved the most disconcerting question for last. "Any news on our young mouse?"

Manuel stole a glance over his shoulder. The security officer didn't blink. Still, Manuel looked uncomfortable. Speaking of Luis was one thing. Speaking of Joshua Young was another entirely. Yet Guillermo had a business to run regardless of where he slept at night. And really, Señor Young's nickname suited him well. He fled the funeral like a mouse flees at the first sign of danger.

The disturbing part was how closely the FBI was protecting the little mouse. What exactly did Joshua Young think he knew about Guillermo? Was it possible Augustina called him before her death from a remote phone Guillermo hadn't been tracking? Possible, but not likely. Was the FBI trying to pin her 'suicide' on Guillermo? If so, how? If Joshua Mousy Young was their best hope, it was a thin prosecution at best. Nothing Guillermo's defense lawyer couldn't break through.

Although Joshua took Augustina in after the Christmas Day incident…

A ball of anger formed in his stomach. "The mouse must be trapped and squashed. Immediately."

Manuel glanced at the security guard again.

"They do not care what you say!" Guillermo snapped. "Out with it!"

Even then, Manuel leaned close to the mic and lowered his voice. "He's not at BYU. His roommate at Washington State said a couple guys came and got his stuff, but he's not there either."

"And his friends from the cabin?"

"We're working on it."

"Work faster. What of his family?" Guillermo asked.

Manuel shrugged.

Guillermo cursed under his breath. Of all the luck, the guy's father was a cop, and his family had one of the top thirty most common names in the U.S. But still…how hard could it be to find them?

"Remind my employees that mice are not allowed in my house. Ever. They are not allowed anywhere near my house. Think harder and work faster. When mice get scared, they flee home to the nest. Start with the home nest and work out from there. You find the nest, you will find the mouse."

"And if he's in WITSEC?" Manuel asked.

"Why would he be?"

Manuel rolled his eyes. "Oh, I don't know. Maybe because you threatened to kill him at the funeral. Why didn't you take him out then if you wanted him dead?"

Because he needed to know if the FBI was protecting him, and they were. "Tell the men to fix my rodent problem immediately. It is top priority." Guillermo sat back. "That is all. You may go now."

"Oh, *I* may go? Unbelievable." Manuel glared at him. "Maybe I wasn't finished."

"Is that so? What have you more to say, *hermanito?*"

Manuel leaped forward and pressed his nose to the glass. "Why am I being followed?"

"Why not?"

For a long minute, Manuel glared at him. Then he turned to the officer. "I'm done."

Guillermo grabbed the microphone, laughing. "Oh, come now, brother. You know why. I must make sure you do not forget who you are."

"Oh, yeah? And who am I?" Manuel said.

"A man fortunate to be born into the same family as I."

Manuel never appreciated Guillermo's humor. His eyes grew cold. "Don't forget which side of the glass you sit on, *hermano*." He spat the word.

Guillermo tapped on the thin barrier. "This is only temporary. You watch and see. All of this will work to my advantage. The press is covering it well. My supporters are protesting. Once the FBI clears my record, my friends will realize what a joke this whole investigation is, no? They will never believe another FBI accusation again. And then they will come crawling back to me. Every last one of them."

Manuel snorted in derision. "Good luck with that. I'm leaving."

"Just a moment. There is one more thing."

"What?" Manuel asked without turning.

"I need you to make a call for me."

"No, thanks."

"Manuel!"

Guillermo didn't use his brother's name often, but when he did, Manuel knew enough to respond. He turned slowly. Guillermo's smile grew.

"I think you shall want to make this one."

CHAPTER 19

"How's your house?" Sadie asked. "I don't even know which one it is."

Josh gave Sadie a quick peck on the cheek before sitting across from her at the kitchen table. He grabbed a warm waffle and plopped it on his plate. He was starving. "Pretty much the same as this one only maybe a smidge smaller."

She gave him a strange look. "A smidge?"

"Yeah. Is there something wrong with 'smidge?'"

"I've just never heard a grown man use it since Jimmy Stewart."

"Great." Josh poured syrup over his waffle. "How long have I been saying smidge and nobody told me?"

She laughed. "You never said it in front of the guys. I can guarantee it. Kevin and Trevor would have never let you live it down."

Josh waited a second for her expression to fall at their mention. When her large smile remained he went on, pleased. "True. So, are you up for some errands today? There's a bunch of stuff we need to get done, like finding a bank, getting your ring sized, finding you a doctor—"

"—and a counselor," Croff added. "I found one who's highly recommended."

Sadie scowled at both of them. Then her dark eyes widened. "Wait. What about your classes?" She twisted around to look at the clock on the oven. "No! It's after ten! Josh!"

He took a few bites. "Oops."

Her hands went on her hips.

He avoided her heavy glare. "I already missed the first two. The last one starts in twenty minutes. Bummer. I'll never make it."

"Josh! You slept in on purpose."

He winked at her. "I don't sleep in, remember. That's your thing." Or it used to be. "Don't worry. I'll go eventually. Just not today. There's too much to do. So...are you up for some errands, or do you want to hang out here with Deputy Croff?"

"No errands," Harrison said. "No way. We're all staying put."

Josh ignored him. He wasn't fighting about this again. They already hashed it out this morning.

Sadie looked out the window with a faraway gaze. The sun was shining and the sky was a crisp blue. The few clouds would be gone in another hour. There was talk it might hit sixty degrees today. Sixty! In January. Josh already loved Tennessee. He couldn't bear to spend an entire day inside like Harrison insisted. He was itching to get out.

"Do you think she's okay?" Sadie asked softly.

"Who?"

"My mom."

Josh nodded. "Yeah. I'm sure she's fine." They would have heard if she wasn't. Hopefully.

Sadie continued to gaze out the window. "What if we just go?" The way she said it made it sound like she wasn't talking about errands. It made it sound much farther.

"Go where?" Josh asked.

"I don't know. Anywhere. Exploring, maybe."

"Yeah?"

She turned back. "Yeah. I don't know Tennessee and neither do you. Let's find out what makes it tick."

He started to smile. "Sounds good. We can explore after we run some errands."

She pulled a face. "Errands? That's no fun. Unless…we explore campus while we're out. I bet the campus is lovely." Josh fought the urge to roll his eyes, but she grabbed his hand. "Come on. If we're running errands, we should figure out where your classes are for tomorrow."

"I guess that's fine," he relented. "Your doctor's office is right around the corner from the stadium."

It was her turn to scowl, which made him laugh. It was a war of wills. But before she could back out, he turned to Deputy Croff. "Don't suppose you'd let us explore in peace today?"

"Neither of you are going anywhere," Harrison said. "Neither are we. Everything on that list of yours can be done from right here, so drop it."

Croff jumped in. "Now wait a second. Technically, they're settled, Deputy Harrison. They need to get used to these new identities, and we have a pile of paperwork to extend our jurisdiction two weeks. Even when they sign the papers, we won't be here 24/7. They need to adjust to being on their own. Today seems as good a day as any." She looked at Josh. "Assuming you guys stay in the area and keep a low profile…"

"We will," he said. "I promise."

"Then I don't see a problem," Croff said.

Harrison slammed his coffee down. "It's *not* fine."

"What about the Attorney General's office?" Croff said. "It's going to take us all day. Come on. Give them some space. It's not like they'll wave any red flags."

Sadie crossed her heart exaggeratedly. "We'll be good."

"No," Harrison said. "End of story."

Croff straightened to her full height, making her look more commanding than her already commanding height. "They're going, and we're staying. That's an order, deputy."

Harrison's eyes turned to tiny slits. "An order?"

"Yes."

So Croff outranked him. The room dropped a few degrees. Harrison glared at Josh and Sadie from across the room. Josh was in too good a mood to let that bother him. A smile threatened to escape. He and Sadie could explore on their own. He felt like a little kid whose mom extended his curfew an hour.

Croff started for the hallway. "I'll grab the keys and the GPS."

"We don't need the GPS," Sadie called. "We'll find our way."

Josh turned in surprise. "Do you have some super-human navigating powers I don't know about, Ice Woman?"

"Maybe." Something in her dark eyes spoke mischief, or maybe just spontaneity. Whichever it was, Josh was more than willing to go along.

Harrison sat up. "It's bad enough you're going without us. I demand you take the GPS. You can't risk getting lost at a time like this. That's not too much to ask."

"He has a point," Croff said. "I'll grab it."

With GPS in hand, Josh and Sadie stepped onto the small and peeling porch. Sadie tipped her head back and let the sunshine light her olive skin. She was glowing.

"Why do I suddenly feel like swimming?" she asked.

"Because to someone from Montana, sixty degrees is swimming weather." He took her hand. "Come on, Mrs. Peterson. We have some exploring to do."

As soon as they got in the car, Sadie tossed the GPS in the backseat. "Just because we have it, doesn't mean we have to use it," she explained. "Damien and I drove up in the mountains all the time growing up, never knowing where we were headed. It's the only way to truly explore."

Josh smiled, loving her more by the second. He put the car in reverse and pulled out onto their quiet street. He avoided a few neighbors earlier that morning leaving for work, but right now the street looked dead.

As they pulled up to the first four-way stop, he looked right and left. There were too many trees and hills to see more than a few hundred yards. He wasn't sure which way led to town.

"I...uh...should let you in on a little secret," he said. "I'm not much of an explorer. I'm a planner. What do you suggest?"

Her eyes lit up. "A game. At each intersection, we'll take turns choosing which way to go."

"A game?"

"Yes." She was nearly bouncing in her seat, making him worry about her sanity. They could end up in Georgia today, and he had the feeling she wouldn't care. He glanced in the rearview mirror to make sure the GPS was still there. And then he wondered if Sadie's new house was programmed into it since he didn't know—

Her hand shot up and covered the mirror. Then she turned those large eyes on him. "Come on. You need to learn to trust me."

She probably didn't realize what she'd said. She was in too good of a mood to remember her rebuke from yesterday, but he remembered. "You're right. Which way?"

Without looking either direction, she said, "Go right."

They wound through old neighborhoods and past well-groomed parks. At each intersection they took turns deciding where to go next: right, left, or straight. Without trying, they ended up driving along the beautiful Tennessee River which ran along the east part of Knoxville.

Sadie flipped on the radio and settled on a station that made Josh cringe. Country. She swayed and sang to the beat, which was cute and all, but still. Country? In the time it took for a single light to turn green, someone died and their girlfriend left them high and dry. Josh hated country music. No, he loathed it.

He wasn't exactly sure how to broach the subject, so he decided to hit it head on. "You're not a country music fan, are you?" *Please say no. Please say no.*

"Yeah. Why? Aren't you?"

A guitar twanged in the background, cementing his revulsion. "But you're a musician. How can you stand it?"

She chuckled. "Wow. That's harsh. There are plenty of awesome musical country songs out there. Here. Let me find another one."

She reached for the radio, but he grabbed her hand. "No. This is"—he was about to say fine, but something about a guy's old pickup truck surfaced— "painful! I can't take anymore."

He punched a button and got another country station. He punched again. More country. He flipped through station after station. Country, country, and more country. "What is going on?"

She laughed. "You're in Tennessee. What did you expect?"

"I should have known this state was too good to be true." He flipped the dial again and found a classical station. "Ah, sweet bliss."

Her laughter turned to giggles. "I had no idea how strongly you felt about country music. This might be an issue between us. Wait!" she cried. "There's a sign for UT. Campus is that way. Go left. Left!"

Josh drove straight through the light.

"Josh! You were supposed to turn."

He pulled off on the side of the road and gripped the steering wheel. After a moment, he faced her. "Why are you so dead set on me going to school?"

"Why are you so dead set against it?" she said. "I thought you liked school."

"I do, but it seems like the last thing I should be worrying about right now with you, the trial, and…everything."

She shrugged. "So?"

"I'm jumping in at the last semester of the engineering program. It would be like a runner coming into a marathon at mile 24. What are the professors going to think? What kinds of strings did Madsen have to pull to make my credits transfer? What about the other students in the program and my senior project? What are they going to do now, throw me into a group so I can graduate? From UT-Knoxville?"

Whatever joy was in her eyes before dissipated. She stared down at her hands. "I'm sorry."

"No. Stop. That's not it. I *want* to be here. I chose to be here. I want to be with you listening to music all the time—minus the country music. That's what I'm trying to say. I don't want to be taken away from you with school. When I'm in school, I get intense and focused. A little OCD even. It can drive people crazy."

"I like intense," she offered softly.

She was trying to lighten the mood again, and he wanted to go back to their game of teasing and forgetting real life. But he couldn't.

He stroked her soft cheek. "Sadie, shouldn't we be focused on you?"

"No! I'm sick of everything revolving around me. It's your turn. You just feel guilty. Come on. I'll help you study and everything. I graduated from college with high honors. I'm smart. I'll help you through it."

"High honors?" He studied her with new-found respect. "Wow. I'm impressed."

"High-ish," she admitted sheepishly.

He laughed but then sobered again. She wasn't going to back down, but neither had she addressed his concerns. "In theory," he said, "finishing my bachelor's sounds like a great idea. In practice, it's awkward. Mile 24."

"But it could be awesome. You'll never know until you try. Besides, it's my turn in the game. You have to go where I say, and I say we go that way." She pointed toward campus.

"You realize my turn is next. What if I turn us back around?"

"Then I'll turn us around after that."

"So we're at an impasse?" he asked.

She leaned across the seat and kissed him. Not a quick kiss either. At first it was slow and gentle, giving him a chance to appreciate the softness of her glossed lips. But then her fingers wound their way to the back of his hair.

Just when his head started to buzz, she pulled back and looked up at him through her dark lashes.

"Are you sure we're at an impasse?" she whispered.

Those darn eyes of hers. They were messing with his head. He was putty in her hands, and she knew it.

"You know," he said, "I was thinking we should check out campus."

She smiled and sat back. "I thought so."

He shook his head. Waiting for the next car, he flipped them around and drove toward campus. "You're shameless. You shouldn't have that much power over me. You don't play fair."

"It's not my fault you're so easily persuaded. I could never change Guiller…"

She caught herself a second too late. Josh watched her face darken with something that churned his stomach with rage. She could have never changed Guillermo's mind. That's what she was going to say. How long before his power over her faded? Or would it?

He squeezed her hand. "Hey. You okay?"

She blinked, coming back to the present. She took a deep breath and forced a smile. "Tell me about your senior project back home."

Amy Hancock wiped her hands on the towel before grabbing the phone. She hit the answer button and checked the caller ID. Had she only done the two things in reverse, she might have been saved. Unknown number. She didn't have time for solicitors. She readied her speech as the person on the other line greeted her.

"Good evening. May I speak with Mrs. Hancock, please?"

"This is her." Amy tried frantically to remember how Kevin got rid of solicitors, something from an old *Seinfeld* episode. She wasn't fast enough.

"Hello, Mrs. Hancock. This is Ivan Mansino, from the *National Geographic Magazine*. Have you ever heard of us?"

Amy picked up her keys and wallet. "I'm really not interested. Thanks."

She started to hang up but heard him shout, "Wait! I'm not selling anything. I have good news for you—for your husband actually."

She held the phone to her ear. This guy had literally ten seconds before she hung up.

"A photo of your husband's has been selected as a finalist in this year's contest. His name is Kevin, right?"

"Yes," she said, sufficiently distracted. "Where did you say you worked?"

"The *National Geographic.*"

"A picture of Kevin's? Really? Which one?"

"It's a phenomenal shot of a snowboarder silhouetted by the last rays of day."

"Really? Kevin didn't tell me he entered any photo contests." Of course, knowing Kevin he'd just come home one day and plop the *National Geographic* in her lap, turned to the right page. Her mind swung wildly from excitement at Kevin having won *anything* to guilt for razzing her husband about spending so much time—and money—on that hobby of his.

"And you said he's a finalist?" she said, setting her keys down. "How many entries are there? What does he get if he wins?"

"There are seven finalists. It's a monetary prize of five thousand dollars, plus a full page spread in our November issue."

"What? That's great! I can't believe Kevin didn't tell me!"

"He probably doesn't know. It says in the notes that his friends entered him in this contest. Sam Jackson and Joshua Young."

Sounded like something Sam and Josh would do, the ultimate friends surprising Kevin. Kevin was going to flip out when he found out. And *National Geographic* of all things. Amy was fully grinning.

"Sam and Josh are Kevin's friends," she said. "Does it mention Trevor?" Although if it didn't, she wouldn't have been surprised.

"Oh, yeah. Trevor's name is by the others. Trevor...uh...sorry. I'm struggling to read my own handwriting."

"Fillion. Trevor Fillion. This is so great!"

"Yes. It really is." She could hear a smile in his voice. "The winners will be announced at an awards banquet in Washington DC this July. If your husband's photo is selected, we'll fly both of you out for the weekend. I'll send you a packet with more information in the mail. Perhaps you should wait until then to tell your husband about the contest. It seems his friends want it to be a surprise."

"I won't say a word. Don't worry." Kevin was always surprising her with things. It was nice to turn the tables on him for once. She was practically jumping up and down.

"Good, good. There is one last thing I need from you," the man said. "Before I can process this, I need permission from the subject of the photo so I can officially send it to the next stage. The caption says it's a photo of Joshua Young. You mentioned Josh was Kevin's friend, but do you happen to know Josh yourself?"

"Yeah. I know him really well."

"Perfect. His face is showing, which means I need his permission to use the photo. Actually, he and I have been corresponding by email since he's the one who submitted the photo. He sent me all the paperwork just a week ago. However, when I emailed him yesterday about the permission, it kicked the email back to me and said his account was deactivated. I can't process this until I get his signature. Do you happen to know another way I can contact him?"

Amy felt sick. Josh was gone—long gone—with no plan of return. "Can one of the other friends sign for him? Josh is…uh…kind of unavailable right now."

"I wish they could, but since it's his face, I need his specific permission. You know how it goes. Legal garbage. It'll be my hide if he shows up on the cover without proper paperwork."

On the cover? she rejoiced silently. Kevin's picture could be on the cover. *I knew it!*

Amy bit her lower lip, thinking. Phone calls to Josh were out. Apparently so were emails. Why did it have to be him in the picture? Why not Trevor who was ten times better at snowboarding? This always happened. Kevin needed this. He needed a breakthrough. They desperately needed the extra money since her car was going to die any day.

"Actually," she said, "I'm not sure how to contact Josh right now. It's...complicated. I'm sorry. I..." She squinted, trying to think of something else. She had no idea how long Josh would be gone with that girl. Longer than a month, at least. Possibly a year. Nobody knew. Except... "What if you asked his family?" she offered. "They'll know how to contact him."

"Oh. I suppose that would work. Do you happen to have their number?"

"I think so. Hold on." If she remembered right, Josh's parents were in her contact list. She quickly scrolled down the massive list and found them: Peter and Kathy Young. She breathed a sigh of relief. Surely they could get Josh the email, and he could sign over the release.

She read off their phone number slowly. "I'm sure they can help."

"Great. Thank you very much, Mrs. Hancock. I hope to see you in DC. In the meantime, if I need something else, I'll make a note to only contact you, so your husband won't know. We want to keep this a surprise. I always love a good secret."

Amy grinned. "So do I. No worries on my end. My lips are sealed."

CHAPTER 20

Knoxville was a giant maze of hills, trees, and rivers. Campus was no different. Old, red buildings lined the skinny streets and huge leafless trees hung over the student-filled sidewalks. The campus looked older than most of Spokane in a way that made Josh feel like he'd stepped back in time.

Students crossed the street in front of the car with heavy coats and scarves. Yet Sadie's window was down and her face tipped back to enjoy the winter sun. *Perspective.* Tennesseans didn't know what cold was.

Josh's stomach growled. "Are you hungry?"

Sadie kept her eyes closed. "Yeah."

"Good." He leaned over and called out her window. "Excuse me. Where's the best burger place around here?"

"Josh!" Sadie laughed. "What are you doing?"

The light was still red. A mass of students was crossing in front of them. They had time. "College students always know where the best burgers are, trust me. Besides, Mrs. Peterson, I think it's time you and I had our first date. What do you think? Can I buy you lunch?"

Her smile grew. "Okay. But only if it's the best burger around."

A few students bent down to see in their car. "Fat Harry's," one said. "Definitely Fat Harry's." Then the guy stopped and looked at Sadie. His eyes took in her stunning beauty a moment and he melted into a smile. "Oh. Hey. Hi."

"You like Fat Harry's?" Sadie asked.

His smile grew. "I love it, and I think you will, too." Then he had the audacity to wink at her.

Josh glared at the guy. Really? Was he really going to hit on 'married' Sadie with Josh sitting right there? She was gorgeous, but still.

Punk.

The girl next to the punk student disagreed and named an organic turkey burger place. That erupted into a full-blown discussion on the corner of campus. But by the time the light turned green again, the overall consensus was still Fat Harry's down on Main Street.

"Thanks," Sadie said. "Can you tell us where the engineering complex is?"

The flirty guy pointed them in the right direction, and Josh was only too happy to head that direction. Even then, it took four more stop lights of Sadie poking her head out to ask for clarification before they found the engineering section on the northeast section of campus. Josh wasn't thrilled to be committing himself to this school thing, but he had to admit Sadie's way of finding things beat using a GPS, hands down.

He slowed to a stop, taking in the group of engineering buildings. They looked welcoming in an odd sort of way.

"Want to walk around?" Sadie asked. "We could meet a few of your professors."

"I didn't bring my schedule. I wouldn't even know where to start. No. This is great. I'll come early tomorrow to figure the rest out."

"Really?" she said. "You'll go to class? You'll try to graduate?"

"If you make me."

She gave him a quick peck on the cheek. "I am, but if you want, I'll come with you. I'll even hold your hand."

"Careful what you offer. I might take you up on it, and we'll see how much you like Algorithm Analysis and Automata."

She grimaced. "That's a real class?"

"10 AM tomorrow."

She patted his hand. "Good luck with that."

He laughed. "You'll be happy to hear I signed up for a Spanish class, though."

She turned. "You did?"

"Yeah. I changed my schedule this morning. I figure it's time I try to keep up with you—or at least die trying."

"Wow. Eres muy considerado."

"Uh…what?"

She leaned over and kissed him softly. *"Te amo."*

"I understood that one." He stroked her soft, olive skin. "I love you, too. Alright, Mrs. Peterson. Are you ready to have the world's best burger?"

"Yeah. Are you still okay without GPS?" she asked.

"Are you?"

"We're about to find out. Go right."

When they passed the same cute Main Street for the third time, Sadie got desperate. Reluctantly she pulled the GPS from the backseat. Sadly, not even Mr. GPS knew where Fat Harry's was.

"Let's find somewhere else," she suggested. "We can't be too much longer or Harrison will call Knoxville's PD to find us."

Josh drove slowly along the old downtown, and Sadie soaked it all in. Shops were stacked one next to the other: specialty shoe stores, small coffee shops, and bakeries. Between brick pavers and small verandas overlooking the street, the city had timeless southern charm. She loved it.

She scanned every restaurant looking for a place worthy of their first official date. She was giddy Josh even cared to ask her out. He wasn't taking her for granted.

Without warning, he stopped in the middle of the road. No stop sign. No jaywalkers. He just stopped.

"What did you find?" she asked.

He put the car in reverse and backed into a parallel parking spot. Sadie looked around. She liked spontaneous—she loved spontaneous—but it didn't seem like Josh. The only food-ish thing she could see was the bakery.

He pointed to a purple sign behind them. "There's a jewelry shop."

As he jumped out and jogged around to get her door, Sadie took in the jewelry window display. Bright, glimmering signs hung from the rafters with large, block letters: ENGAGEMENT RINGS.

Her heart stopped.

Josh opened her door. "Um…" She swallowed. "Why are we going to a jewelry store?"

"To get your ring sized."

The ring. The *old* ring. Her heart started again. "Are you sure we should? I feel bad. What will your mom do when I give it back?"

"Size it again. I don't think it's too complex of a design."

Even though she'd memorized Kathy's ring, she twisted it around to face front. It had two simple gold bands, the wider of the two with a marquise-shaped diamond. It didn't look too complex. But if it was, she could live with the bigger size. She was getting used to keeping her hand in a fist.

Josh put a few coins in the meter and helped her hop down the sidewalk toward the store.

"Something smells good," she said. Looking around, she spotted a Mexican café tucked in between the bakery and the jewelry shop. "Oooh. Do you like Mexican?"

"I love Mexican," he said. "You?"

"Yes. Let's go there after."

Josh didn't even get the jewelry store door all the way open before a salesman jumped up and approached them. He was a middle-aged, eager-looking man, wearing a navy vest and bow tie.

"Welcome to Lewis Jewelers," he said. "How may I help you?"

"We need to get her ring sized," Josh said.

There was a flash of disappointment as the salesman realized the young couple was already 'ringed,' but he recovered quickly. "I'd be happy to help you. My name is Gregory, Master Jeweler."

Master Jeweler? That was a fancy title for the short, balding man.

Gregory led them over to a counter where row after row of diamond rings sparkled beneath the glass-top display. Sadie's stomach tightened. It was awfully shiny in there. She blinked a few times to clear her vision. Josh took her crutches and offered her a stool by the counter.

"Alright," Gregory said. "Let's see what we have here."

Sadie held out her hand and tilted it slightly. Kathy's ring slid right off.

"Wow. That is a problem." Gregory picked up the ring and held it close to his face. His eyes narrowed, and he looked up suddenly. "This isn't stolen, is it?"

"Stolen?" Sadie choked. "No. Not at all."

Gregory admired it from every possible angle. "This ring is from the mid-nineties, either '95 or '96. So is yours, sir." Again, he eyed them suspiciously. "I doubt you two were married in 1995. You were probably barely born then. Are you sure they weren't stolen?"

Sadie couldn't believe it. They'd been in the store less than a minute, and he'd pegged both of their rings. He really was a Master Jeweler. But unfortunately, she was fresh out of lies. Two stolen rings wasn't a great way to start their stay in Tennessee. He could easily call the cops.

She was still stressing over an answer when Josh said, "My parents were married in late '95. That one there is my mother's ring. I'm wearing my father's. They gave them to us as gifts. Wow. How did you guess the year that easily?"

Sadie's shoulders relaxed. The truth. She forgot how much she loved the truth. Gregory relaxed, too.

"Ring styles change," he explained. "I can usually guess within a year or two. But we can't have your mother-in-law's diamond slipping off your finger now, can we?"

Sadie shuddered. "No."

Gregory made small talk while sizing her finger, asking the typical small talk questions. Where are you from? Are you in school? Sadie and Josh sounded more and more confident in their answers. Even when he asked a new one, "How long have you two been married?" Sadie quickly replied, "A month."

Josh glanced at her in surprise. They hadn't discussed that one yet, but it seemed right. They met after Christmas.

"I thought so," Gregory said. "I can always spot the newlyweds. You smile at each other when you think no one is looking."

As if planned, Josh and Sadie smiled at each other. Gregory rolled his eyes.

Once Gregory got the right size, he sent Sadie's ring to the back room.

"About how long will it take?" Josh asked.

"Depending on what work Brandon has," Gregory said, "probably less than a half hour. You're"—he paused to smile at Sadie—"more than welcome to browse the store while you wait."

"No. That's okay." She grabbed Josh's hand. It felt strange to hold his hand without the ring on her finger. It was strange how quickly she'd become acclimated to marriage. "We're going to try that Mexican place next door."

"Hey, have you heard of Fat Harry's?" Josh asked.

"The burger joint? Sure. It's around the block in the basement of the bookstore."

"Yes! That explains why we couldn't find it." Josh grinned at Sadie with boyish enthusiasm. He really wanted that burger. "We'll be back after lunch to pick up the ring."

As they started to leave, Gregory jumped up. "Wait. If I might make an observation, Josh, I don't think your beautiful wife wants to get that ring sized. I think she wants a new ring."

Josh turned slowly and looked at Sadie. His blue eyes widened to the size of baseballs. "You do?"

Her face went red hot. "No. No!" Why would the stupid salesman say something like that? "I love your mom's ring."

Gregory smiled a knowing smile. "If I may be so bold, I noticed you eyeing the rings in this particular case. Specifically"—he leaned sideways, opened the glass case, and pulled out the top display—"this one."

Horrified, she looked at the display box that held six diamond rings. She wanted to crawl under a hole. Until that moment, she hadn't even realized she'd been looking at them. But she had. Specifically the ring he picked from the box and held out toward her.

The ring was white gold, with a wide, square-shaped diamond. What she loved was how deeply set the diamond was within the gold, making it subtle and unique. She'd never seen anything like it.

How had Gregory known?

Stupid salesman.

He held it closer, tempting her to slip it on her now-bare finger. Josh continued to study Sadie with a deep, penetrating question. Heat rose in her cheeks.

When she found the courage to look at him, she realized his unasked question wasn't for her at all. He was asking it of himself.

Does Sadie want to marry me?

For real?

Her pulse hammered in her chest. He wasn't thinking, *Do I want to marry Sadie?* which was scary enough on its own. But it's almost like he was trying to gauge how badly she wanted to slip that diamond on her finger, as if he'd already answered the second question in the positive.

Nerves tingled all over her skin. One month. She'd known Josh one month, and he wanted to marry her?

What was he thinking? What was *she* thinking, glancing at wedding rings?

Gregory waited patiently, almost smugly, having nailed another observation on the head. He probably went to school for reading expressions, spending months in training on how to follow a woman's line of vision. Not only the general direction Sadie was glancing, but the exact ring she admired unconsciously. The ring that sat suspended a foot away, begging to be worn.

Stupid, stupid salesman.

"No," Sadie said, regaining the use of her voice. "I don't want another ring. I-I love the one I have. I don't need another. Really. Thank you."

She couldn't help it. Her eyes flickered to Josh.

His expression fell. He was disappointed. There was no other way to explain it.

Her heart pounded in her ears. Josh wanted to marry her. Her. While she tried to find the ground beneath her feet, stupid Gregory, against her wishes, took her hand and slid the ring on her finger.

"What do you think?" he said with the gentleness of a zoo trainer trying to keep from spooking a new animal.

Sadie held her breath and summoned the courage to look. She turned her hand slightly to let the light reflect off the perfectly square diamond.

Her breath unhitched.

She didn't like it. The ring. She didn't like it! She smiled in utter relief. While she loved the concept of the inset diamond, once on her finger, it overpowered the setting. And really, the diamond was too large anyway. Too showy. She wanted something more subtle. More classy.

Actually, she wanted to get out of there.

Fast.

She slid the ring off her finger. "No. I don't like it. It's too—"

"Showy. I agree," Gregory cut in, already scanning his glass cabinets for another. "Hmmm. I know just the one."

Sadie should have stood up. She should have moved as fast as her broken body could carry her. She was headed down the path of no return. Yet, she didn't. And as Gregory searched for another ring, neither did Josh.

"Ah, yes. Here it is," Gregory said. "I think you'll like this one."

"Wait," she said. Before Gregory slipped the next ring on her finger, she had to know.

She looked up into Josh's deep, blue eyes, trying to ask him if this was okay. If he seriously wanted to head down this path. He smiled briefly, trying to pretend indifference, trying to look unaffected, but in that moment, he confirmed it. He wanted her to try on that ring.

He wants to marry me.

The room spun. She kept her gaze locked on his, needing something to anchor herself. Half of her craved a moment of privacy to have the conversation they'd never had. Marriage. A real marriage. The other half was grateful Gregory was there to prevent it. Her thoughts tripped over themselves, vying for her attention, jumping further and further into the future. A future with Josh. Was that what she wanted?

Yes.

The answer came so quick and untethered, it caught her off guard. She couldn't imagine the future without him. Already he was part of her past, present, and immediate future. He acted like he was in this for the long haul. And she wanted him there for the long haul. One month and she knew enough of him to know he was a better man than she'd ever dated, ever met, ever deserved.

Why wouldn't I want to marry him?

The question made her stomach drop because she couldn't find an answer.

Josh.

Forever.

"May I?" Gregory asked softly.

Before Sadie could prevent it, she was grinning. Broadly. Josh seemed to register the change in her and a slow smile spread across his features. She turned back to the counter and held out her left hand.

Twenty minutes later, she'd tried on a dozen rings. She and Josh were acting more 'newlywed' than ever, stealing quiet smiles when Gregory wasn't looking. Josh looked thrilled by this new course of action, which made her inexplicably happy.

"Hypothetically speaking," Josh said leaning against the counter, "which one do you like best?"

Sadie had no idea. Guillermo always picked out her jewelry. Diamond necklaces. Earrings. Her style was to grab what was on the clearance rack. But hypothetically...

She glanced over the five rings she'd narrowed it down to. Each had a similar theme. Square diamond. White gold. Subtle elegance. Each had something she liked, but none were quite right. "Hypothetically..." she started again, "I like the diamond on that one and the band on this one."

Gregory nodded as if he was thinking the same thing. "That one is too gaudy, too Elizabeth Taylor. And this one's not Elizabeth enough."

Whoever trained him in the art of jewelry needed a raise.

Gregory looked at Josh. "You know, we do custom rings."

Custom.

For some reason, the word snapped Sadie back to reality. Custom meant expensive. Expensive meant money. Money they didn't have—Josh didn't have. Even if they got a living stipend from WITSEC, it surely didn't cover wedding rings. Wedding rings after a month!

Sadie picked up the nearest ring box and saw the price tag. She gagged. She could buy a small car with that. What were they thinking?

She pushed away from the counter. "No. Sorry, Gregory. I was just looking. It's fun to look, you know? But I already have a ring, and it's a great ring. A beautiful ring, and I really, really love it. So I don't think I should be looking at any others. I love the one I have. I...um..." She tucked a dark curl behind her ear. "Is it sized yet?"

Though frustrated by this sudden turn of events, Gregory went to the back room. Thankfully, Brandon was finished. Kathy's ring fit perfectly. The sizing hadn't changed the look of it either, and Sadie felt like she could breathe again. Mrs. Josh Peterson was hard enough to get used to. If there ever came a day when she was asked to be Mrs. Josh Young, she'd deal with it then. For now, she slipped her hand into Josh's again and relished that everything felt back to normal—or at least as normal as it would get.

"Thanks for your help, Gregory," Sadie said.

"Anytime. Before you leave, how is your ring, Josh?" Gregory asked. "I didn't ask if you wanted to try on any."

"Me? Try some on?" Josh glanced around the store, eyes wide in panic. "No. Um…no. This is great. We're all set. Aren't we set?" he asked, gripping Sadie's hand. "Yeah. I think we are. Don't you?"

Sadie smiled. So maybe Josh wasn't ready to think about marriage either. Maybe she jumped the gun thinking he wanted more. They were just playing around.

She smiled at Gregory, feeling a little victorious. The master salesman hadn't completely sweet-talked them after all.

"Yes," she said. "Thanks for your help, Gregory."

He eyed them a moment before pulling a business card from the counter. He gave it to Josh. "Here's my information. When you two get engaged, come back and see me."

Sadie's jaw went slack. In contrast, Josh stiffened next to her.

Gregory went on, unaffected. "I'm not sure what kind of game you're playing, but before you pop the question to this lovely young lady, come back and I'll have the perfect ring ready—the one she really wants. And I'll make sure to have one for you as well."

Sadie studied the pink carpet. Gregory knew they weren't married. How long did it take him to figure it out? And how?

Josh mumbled something like, "Sure. Yeah. No problem. Um…we gotta go. Now."

He grabbed Sadie's hand and they fled the jewelry store. They passed the Mexican café and went straight to the car. No lunch. No words.

Josh put the key in the ignition, but he didn't turn it. The two of them stared straight ahead.

"Harrison would kill us right now," Sadie finally said.

"Yeah. I think our acting needs some help," Josh said. "How long do you think it took him to figure us out?"

"Not very long. It's scary."

"Very scary. And yet…" Josh said, slowly. "Not all of it was bad."

Sadie's eyes flickered sideways. Josh continued to stare straight ahead, but the tiniest smile lit his features. She faced front again, pulse picking up, as they lapsed into a silence that was more uncomfortable than it should have been. She didn't dare scratch her face for fear if she moved it would launch them into *the* talk. They were perched on the pinnacle of a cliff, and there was no going back once they jumped.

Josh jumped first.

"So?" he said, facing her.

"So…that was fun," she offered. Because in truth, trying on rings had been fun. A lot of fun. Too much fun.

"Yeah."

Carefully, he reached up and cradled her cheek, eyes intent on hers. "You know, we really haven't talked about…us."

"I know."

"You know that I love you, right?" he said. "That I'm seriously in love with you? And the longer it goes, the easier it is to think…to think…" He didn't blink. "That maybe…"

"We could do it?" she whispered. "Us? Forever?"

He smiled. "Yeah."

His thumb stroked her cheek, bringing warmth to her soul. She should have known Josh wouldn't push her into this. His whole persona was gentleness. He wanted to talk about marriage, not force the idea on her. It helped her breathe a little easier.

"So, what do you think?" he said. "About us, forever?"

"I think…" She closed her eyes briefly, needing time to think clearly without getting lost in his deep eyes. "I think it's too soon to know what I think."

"Yeah." He said the word, yet she didn't miss the disappointment in his voice. It tugged at her heartstrings. Josh wanted to marry her.

Why?

She reached up and took his hand. "I'm sorry, Josh. You're everything I want and more in a"—she cleared her throat—"in a husband. And you're so amazingly good to me and wonderful and everything. But…"

"It's too soon. I know." He smiled sadly. "In spite of what you might think—and what my brain tells me when I'm with you—I agree."

"You do?"

"Definitely. We haven't even been on a first date."

She laughed as some of the tension released in the air. "Seems like we should at least have a date first, right?"

"Should we pinky swear on it? No marriage talks until at least…" He pursed his lips. "One date. Maybe two."

She wanted to laugh again, but part of her didn't know how serious he was. He was the type of guy that, once he knew what he wanted, went for it full force. And if he wanted to marry her…

"We should probably make it three," she said. "Just to be safe."

He held out his pinky. "Three dates."

"Four," she said, desperate. No couple should talk about marriage after three dates. "Definitely four to be really, really safe."

"Four. You got it."

She still wasn't sure how much was just him teasing her, but they interlocked pinkies, sealing the deal. Then Josh completely surprised her by leaning over and kissing the tip of her nose.

"You are *so* beautiful," he whispered. "Do you know that?"

The compliment came out of nowhere. Not that she minded. She tucked a dark curl behind her ear. "Thanks."

His finger traced the skin of her lips a moment. Then he pulled her toward him and pressed his lips to hers. As the heat of his kiss soothed her soul, the possibilities swirled in her mind, making her heart flutter. They could do it. Them. Forever. But before she could change her resolve—or he could forget his—she broke away.

"Let me ask you," he said. "Is there any situation in which a drive around town is considered a date?"

Her eyes narrowed. "No."

"Now wait, I think it could. For example," he said with a quirky smile, "if the couple listened to some horrible music, played a game or two, and conducted a cutting-edge survey of the local population? Sounds like a date to me."

He was creative. She had to give him that much. "I guess under the right circumstances it could be considered a date—*if* it was with the right guy." Besides, that left her three more. She could handle that.

"I thought so. And are you still hungry?"

"No…" she lied, sensing where he was headed.

He grinned and snatched the keys from the ignition. "Yes, you are. Prepare yourself to be wowed, Mrs. Peterson, because you're about to have the best burger of your life." His smile grew. "Date number two."

CHAPTER 21

Wednesday came whether Sadie wanted it to or not.

She played a different chord on the piano, going minor instead of major. She always gravitated toward the minor, probably a sign of something dark inside her. Oh, well. The song sounded better that way.

She plunked around the black notes another minute. The piano tuner did a great job of whipping the old beast into shape. It felt wonderful to have music to occupy her thoughts now that Josh was in school full time. Yesterday, she'd set about organizing her house and kitchen. That helped pass the long hours. But even with the joy of music back in her life, her thoughts still strayed where she didn't want.

Guillermo.

She plunked harder. Louder. Another minor chord. She even threw in a few ugly diminished ones. Yet one name screamed in the back of her mind.

Guillermo.

He was in the courtroom right now, being read the formal charges. She needed more than notes to push him from her mind. Maybe lyrics.

Purposely leaving her crutches behind, she hobbled into her bedroom. She was getting better without crutches. Hopefully, the doctor would agree at her appointment today and let her graduate to a walking boot. She planned to do everything in her power to convince him she didn't need the bright green cast anymore either. It was getting old and gross, and she was sick of the attention it drew.

Using the furniture and walls for support, she practiced putting some weight on her ankle. It hurt less than she thought it would. Her ribs only hurt now when she laughed or coughed too hard. She was definitely on the mend.

Grabbing her notebook from her nightstand, she made her way back to the piano bench. Croff watched but said nothing. The longer Sadie spent with Croff, the more she liked her. Deputy Croff knew when to talk and when Sadie needed space. Today, she definitely needed space.

The song she was writing was a new one—a depressing one if truth be told. All she needed was depressing lyrics to match the dark tone. She tapped her pencil, thinking. Guillermo's dark eyes crept up on her, as if she was in the courtroom, too. She'd seen enough crime dramas to have the whole thing visualized: him sitting properly, staring right at her.

She started scribbling.

When will you leave my mind?
When will you stop haunting my dreams?
I hate you!
I hate you!
I hate—

She stopped, took a deep breath, and scratched it all out. Croff looked up, curious but still silent. Sadie stared at her messy page. She didn't need lyrics. She needed her journal back. She craved her old paper friend, the one she used to tell everything to, but her journal caused too many issues. No. Lyrics would have to do. She clutched her pencil and started again.

Will you ever leave me alone?
Will I ever find peace?
Why can't you just plead guilty today and save me from testifying
against you?

She stared at the last line. Way too many syllables, but it was her favorite line by far. Surely there were other people out there in her same predicament. Maybe she'd write the WITSEC theme song.

Sighing, she set her paper aside. With her neon green cast stretched out on the piano bench, she reread the messages everyone wrote to her. Kevin and Trevor's made her smile, like always, but her eyes stayed on Kathy's.

Don't think you're not worth all this because you are—Kathy

Sadie traced the bumpy words. "I need a job."

"Two days of Josh in school, and you're bored? Maybe you need a better hobby." Croff held up her half-crocheted blanket. "Want to give it a try? Or we could watch a movie?"

"No. If music can't help me escape, nothing can." It was going to be a long day. Month. Year.

"A trial can do that to you."

Sadie looked up. So Croff was thinking about it, too? Nobody said a word about Guillermo's trial over breakfast that morning or any time since. Sadie wondered if Josh was thinking about it, too. Hopefully it wasn't distracting him from his classes. He was already behind enough.

"You could take a nap," Croff said. "I think I heard you up a couple times last night. I'm sure you're tired."

"No." Sleep was the absolute last thing she wanted. As scary as reality was, it was better than her morbid imagination. She'd forgotten what it was like to sleep through the night.

"Your appointment with Dr. Greenwood is in an hour," Croff offered. "That will keep you busy."

Sadie looked at her neon cast. "Maybe."

She stood and started another trip, this time around the living room in a large circle. It was a Jane Austen thing to do, taking a turn about the room, but she needed the exercise, the hope of distraction.

"What can you tell me about the trial today?" she finally asked.

Croff set her crochet aside. "It's more a formality than anything. The judge wants to make sure Guillermo is informed of all the charges, and that he knows his rights. If Guillermo wants to end things quickly, he can enter a guilty plea today, which I don't picture him doing."

Sadie thought about the apology Guillermo left on Kevin's phone after hitting her on Christmas. Though he feigned true remorse, in reality, he blamed his explosive behavior on the FBI.

"No," Sadie agreed. "He'll never plead guilty. Whatever happened that night with Agent Dubois, in Guillermo's mind, it's someone else's fault. He's never been guilty of anything. He'll probably blame it on Mr. Ugly."

"Who?"

"Luis. The guy Guillermo sent to watch me in the cabin. He's the one who threw me over his shoulder...to..." Sadie shuddered.

"I remember," Croff said softly. "The guy is a pig."

Sadie felt nauseous like she always did when she thought about Mr. Ugly. She'd been tied up, helpless, and Luis loved it. Guillermo would definitely throw Luis under the bus today if it would save his own hide. Luis probably already had a criminal record.

"There's another part of today..." Croff said. She played with a stray yarn a moment as if hesitant to say. "The judge will decide if Guillermo will be allowed to post bail."

"Bail?" Sadie cried. "They can do that?"

"Yes. The judge decides if he's released or if they keep him in custody while he awaits trial."

"So, he could get out?" The room swayed. "Today?"

"Yes, but I don't think that will happen," Croff said quickly. "This is a serious case, and the prosecutor should be able to convince the judge that Guillermo's a high flight risk. They struggled to find him once. The judge won't want to have to find him again, hopefully."

Guillermo could be on the streets in an hour. All that work finding him, and he could just disappear again. Her lungs started to constrict.

"That's about it for the trial today," Croff went on. "The real stuff happens during the preliminary trial. That's where the judge will want to see you and get your testimony. Have you given more thought to finishing those papers? I know you have eleven days, but that doesn't mean you can't sign them early."

Sadie shrugged. "What happens if I haven't decided before the preliminary trial? Technically the trial could happen before my two weeks are up."

"The prosecution will have a hard time convincing the judge they have enough evidence for a full conviction without you. Depending on the judge, he might dismiss the case."

"Why did Madsen give me two weeks then?"

Croff shot her a withering look. "Did you give him a choice?"

"No. I guess not." Sadie hugged herself.

"The more likely thing," Croff said, "is whoever Madsen found to testify knows enough about that night that Madsen is feeling confident to get through all the preliminary stuff. Hopefully it's a good sign he's not bothering you."

Sadie hadn't even thought of that. Hope soared inside her. "Whoever it is, they must know a lot. Maybe Madsen won't need me at all."

"Don't get too excited," Croff said. "Madsen needs you. He just might not need you for eleven days. That doesn't mean you can't sign the papers early. It takes time for them to clear the Attorney General's office."

Sadie took another step. A little less pain. Another step. Less pain than the time before. Step. Step. Step.

Croff stood and joined her on her small walk around the room. "Look, I know WITSEC sounds daunting and permanent. And while it's sometimes long-term, other times it ends up being a temporary thing. In my experience, it's always the best means to an end."

"Which end?" Sadie leaned against the checkered couch. "You must think I'm horrible and such a coward for not wanting to testify against him."

"Not at all. I'm not sure what I would do in your shoes. Stay under the radar, out of sight, dead, and keep yourself, your mom, and brother safe—

possibly. Or…risk all of your lives to bring Guillermo to justice for a crime you heard but didn't see."

Sadie was surprised by how well Croff articulated it. "Yes, but it's not just that. I really don't know very much. He kept me sheltered from everything. I met a few people and heard a few shots. How does that make me the star witness? His lawyers are never going to let it stand."

Croff cocked her head to the side. "Give Madsen some credit. Give the judge and the jury some credit, too. If they've spent any time on organized crime, they understand these crime bosses. It's very typical for the men to choose women who are naive to their underhanded business dealings. In fact, many times they choose women who will turn a blind eye so if they're ever pulled in for questioning, they can legitimately say they know nothing. Guillermo was testing you, testing to see if you'd turn that blind eye the night of Dubois' murder, and you didn't."

She almost had. Going to Madsen was one of the hardest things she'd done.

"I think the judge will understand why you don't know more than you do," Croff went on. "With luck, Madsen has found more evidence. You'll just be backing up Guillermo's character. Your testimony is stronger than you think." Croff smiled. "So are you."

Sadie studied her hands. "I should just sign now. Josh wants me to—at least, I think he does. He won't say."

"Don't be so certain," Croff said. "It's always a risk sending a witness into a trial like this, and if Josh's dad is a cop, Josh has seen the reality of the criminal justice system. It's less than perfect. WITSEC is set up with several fail-safes, but it still has its loopholes. Josh can't guarantee your safety. He knows the second Guillermo finds out you're alive and testifying against him, he'll go ballistic. I'm not so sure Josh is ready to risk you for justice. I'm guessing he doesn't want *you* to go through the pain of sitting across from Guillermo in a courtroom, let alone testifying against him. I'm guessing Josh would love to keep 2,200 miles between you and Guillermo for the rest of your life, and…I can agree with that."

"But…"

Croff folded her arms. "But I'm in law enforcement. What do you want me to say? My temporary permit expires in two days, and my boss refuses to renew it. I can't keep you safe unless you sign. What if Guillermo finds you guys? Even if he doesn't, what if he gets off scot-free and turns his vengeance on the next person? How will you feel when you could have stopped another attack? Another heartbreak? Another murder?"

Sadie winced. The weight of Dubois' murder already rested heavily on her shoulders. How could she live with herself if Guillermo went free and killed more people?

"I'm sorry to be so blunt, Sadie, but that's the reality you have to face. In a way, you're in a lose-lose situation. Risk yourself, your family, and Josh, or stay low profile, but possibly risk others later. You have to decide which option you can live with. And nobody will judge what you choose."

"Madsen will. So will Harrison," Sadie said.

Croff smiled. "Okay. Nobody *else* will."

As she left Sadie by the couch and went back to her crochet, Sadie pictured Guillermo in his Armani suit in that courtroom, schmoozing everyone, including the judge. For all they knew, that judge was already on his payroll. Wasn't that partly what Madsen was trying to nail him for? Bribing government officials? How would he ever be convicted? He could be on the streets in an hour, and Croff and Harrison could be gone in two days.

She clasped her hands together and stared up at the ceiling. *Please let him plead guilty today. Please. Please. Please!* Even as she prayed, she knew it wouldn't work. Not even a direct command from God would sway Guillermo if it meant negative publicity.

Besides, who was she to ask God anyway?

She heard keys in the lock, and the front door opened. Josh and Harrison came in.

"Hey," she said brightening. "How was scho…?"

One look at Josh and her voice dropped off. His face was grim, almost pale. Something was wrong. Then she noticed Harrison on the phone. There was only one person she'd seen Harrison talk to on the phone. He was talking to Madsen. The initial trial was over.

Harrison nodded a few times but didn't respond. Sadie closed her eyes again and prayed harder. *Please, please, please,* she begged without a single ounce of hope. *At the very least, don't let him get out on bail. Please!*

"Okay. I'll let them know." Harrison ended the call and looked up. "Guillermo pled not guilty today. The preliminary trial is scheduled for next Thursday."

"Bail?" Sadie whispered.

"No bail. Thankfully," Harrison said.

Her breath unhitched. It wasn't perfect, but it was something. The trial was eight days away. Guillermo would be retained until then. So why did Josh look so disturbed? He was staring at the shag carpet.

She sidled up next to him. "What's wrong?"

He pulled her in for a long hard hug that pinched her ribs.

"Josh?" she said, more worried.

"We found out who Madsen got to testify against Guillermo," Harrison said for him.

"Who?"

Josh's arms tightened around her. His chest heaved. She looked up into his face, now flushed in anger. It took him a moment to answer.

"Luis Ortiz," Josh said.

Sadie stopped breathing. Then she shook her head. "Wait. You don't mean Mr. Ugly. He can't...No. He won't testify against Guillermo."

Harrison nodded.

Her mind raced, trying to fit the pieces together. It was odd and made her ill, but she still didn't understand why Josh was so infuriated. Until it hit her.

"What did they offer him for testimony?" Sadie asked.

Josh's jaw clenched. "His freedom."

CHAPTER 22

Sadie felt like she'd been kicked in the ribs, like when Luis had. No air. No explanation. Just pain. Blinding, dizzying pain.

Luis went free.

"No," she breathed. "No."

Josh nodded, looking sick. "Madsen offered Luis Ortiz amnesty in exchange for his testimony. He already entered WITSEC."

Sadie felt herself go on overload. "He walks? He's being protected? He has a bodyguard and, and…" She waved her arm. "All this?"

None of them answered. They didn't have to.

"But everything he did to me…" Her ribs. Her wrists. Her life!

"Plus everything he almost did," Josh added, teeth clenched. "It's all forgotten. Erased. Forgiven."

"Not erased," Harrison said. "Just set aside to take down Vasquez. It's choosing the lesser evil. This is common. Many witnesses in WITSEC are criminals themselves, just lesser criminals."

"Lesser?" Sadie breathed. She leaned on the couch for support. Mr. Ugly walks. He was free.

Harrison put a hand on her shoulder. "It's just how this goes. That guy knows enough to bring Guillermo down. But I also know what he did to you. I'm sorry, Sadie."

She looked up. It almost sounded like compassion, almost like Harrison cared that the man who attacked her in Sam's cabin, who tied her up, kicked her down the stairs, and nearly took advantage of her was going free.

Josh shook his head, muscles tight with fury. "I don't get how that's the best option, or why that guy deserves a bodyguard. Can't he testify from prison?"

"In theory, yes," Harrison said. "In reality, he has no reason to."

"But he tried to kill her!" Josh cried. "And worse! Doesn't anyone care?"

Croff joined them by the window. "It's not that they don't care, Josh. But who ordered Luis to kill Sadic? Luis was simply acting on Guillermo's order. It's choosing the lesser evil."

"Evil is evil!" Josh spat.

Though Sadie hated the situation as much as Josh did, she could see the value of it. "They're right, Josh. Luis is the follower, not the leader. He knows a hundred times more about Guillermo's organization than I do. Luis is on the inside. He can do what I can't."

"But at what cost, Sadie?" Josh's face twisted in pain. "Even *you* don't know what you looked like when I found you."

Her eyes widened.

His jaw clenched and unclenched as if working to keep his emotions in check. He lifted her hand and traced the red scars on her wrists. "Or what you looked like the day after that." He paused. "Or the day after that. That guy deserves to hang for what he did to you. They all do."

Josh hadn't talked much about the day he found her. After dropping from the upper window of the cabin, Sadie collapsed under a pine tree and let the cold and pain push her into a deep hypothermic coma. Josh searched the woods for twelve hours without success. It wasn't until he grabbed Sam's dog, Rocky, that they found her. But she was unconscious and, for a full day after that, completely unaware. The word everyone used to describe her was gray. Josh and her mom stayed by her side, unsure if she'd survive the night. For over a day, they fretted about the cause of her widespread injuries, imagining the worst. And then Josh found out it was worse than he'd imagined when she gave the full report to Madsen: Guillermo *and* Luis. She didn't even let her mom stay for that part.

Sadie felt the pain of every injury, but Josh had *watched* it. Who was she to say which was worse? So she put herself in Josh's shoes. What if he had been the one in the hospital bed, beaten and bruised, and she had been stuck in the chair? What if things with the redhead had gone worse and that gun went off? Already she was haunted by Josh's minor injury. What if he'd been nearly killed like she had?

It was one thing to be the victim. It was another to watch helplessly from the sidelines.

She wasn't the only one with scars.

He continued to trace the lines on her wrists. She pulled free and slid her arms around his waist. His chin rested on her head, and his arms enveloped her like a cocoon. He held her for a long time, squeezing the life out of her—or into her.

"It's okay," she whispered. "We're going to beat him. One way or another," she promised with every ounce of her soul, "we're going to beat Guillermo."

Josh and Harrison crossed the grounds, heading to Josh's second class.

"Are you sure?" Josh asked. "I mean, it makes sense. I'm dying that she's going to be alone all the time now."

Harrison pulled him to a stop. "If it was my girlfriend, I'd do it. Actually, I'd park myself on her couch with a .22 Magnum. But if you're not willing to do that, this is the next best thing. It will give her—and you—a little peace of mind."

"She'll kill me," Josh said. "You don't know how strongly she feels about this. It might be more work than it's worth. By the time we get it settled and trained, you guys will be back."

"Maybe. But you have no guarantee she'll ever sign those papers."

"She will."

Harrison shot him a look, and Josh sighed. Sadie already backed out once. Who was to say she wouldn't back out again? And then what?

"What can she do?" Harrison said. "Once it's done, it's done."

"Never speak to me again. I'm telling you. She'll freak. Unless..." Josh jerked up with a sudden thought. "There might be a better option. Can I borrow your phone?"

"No."

Josh quickly told him his plan. By the end of it, Harrison handed over his cell. "I could lose my badge for this."

"What can they do?" Josh asked. "You have an untraceable number."

"Fire me."

"Good point. I'll be fast."

Josh dialed the number from memory and held the phone to his ear. "Hey, buddy," he said with a smile.

"Josh?" Sam said. "Is that you? What's up? Is something wrong?"

"No, no. Everything's great. I just have a small favor to ask. Actually, it's kind of a big favor. A big, smelly, hairy favor."

Sadie stood in the doorway, deliberating. Deputy Croff was at the kitchen table with a cup of coffee, and Josh was at school with Harrison. If she didn't do it now, she never would.

She limped into the kitchen. "Can I borrow your phone?"

Croff looked up, instantly suspicious. "Why?"

In the week Croff had been Sadie's protector, Sadie had grown to love her. She was compassionate and a friend. She'd been furious when her boss denied them an extension. Starting tomorrow, Sadie and Josh were on their own. While Sadie dreaded sleeping alone in that old house—really dreaded it—she was determined to have another week of peace before Guillermo went after everyone.

But that's not why Sadie needed the phone.

A chill ran down her spine as she thought of her most recent dream. It was by far the worst nightmare of all. Guillermo hadn't been the shooter. Josh had. She would never forget the moment he turned the gun on her.

"I think I'm ready," she said. With a quick breath, she said what she couldn't believe. "I want to make an appointment with that counselor."

Deputy Croff said little about Sadie's change of heart. Not at the house. Not as they drove. The only thing she'd done was grab the phone from Sadie and demand the receptionist fit Sadie into the counselor's schedule today. Croff could be pushy when she wanted, but she explained that since she was leaving tomorrow, and since the doctor refused to remove Sadie's cast yesterday, Sadie couldn't drive. Once Croff mentioned the U.S. Marshals, the receptionist had little choice but to pencil them in.

As they drove, Sadie wondered what she could discuss that wouldn't bring the past back with a vengeance. Seeing a counselor seemed like it would make the nightmares worse, not better. But she was desperate enough to try.

Her counselor was a small man with an olive green suit and glasses. He welcomed her into his office with a wave of his hand. "Sit wherever you want, Mrs. Peterson."

Straight out of the movies, his room had a long, flat couch with a square pillow. On the walls hung every tranquil picture imaginable: waterfalls, rain forests, and butterflies. But the one that caught her eye had a deep blue sky hovering over gorgeous white, snow-capped mountains. It looked like home.

Sadie chose the chair next to his desk, a simple, upright chair. He sat across from her.

"I have a confession to make, Mrs. Peterson," he said. "I'm not much of a talker. I'm hoping you'll do most of the talking today."

"Like what?" she stalled. It was lame to stall, but so was seeing a counselor.

"Tell me about yourself, why you're here, what's your story. I see you're married. Do you have children? Tell me a little about your family."

She looked at him. She had a mom and a brother she couldn't mention, plus a fake husband. What was she supposed to say?

Her gaze went to the door. Maybe it wasn't too late to back out. Even if she wanted to talk—which she didn't—she wasn't allowed to say anything anyway.

"Or how about your foot?" he said, sensing her hesitation. "How did you hurt it? Or do you have any hobbies? Favorite color? Really, anything. You start and I'll stop." He smiled, probably trying to make her feel more comfortable.

It didn't work.

She looked up at the rocky mountain landscape on the wall. A huge wave of homesickness overwhelmed her. Her mom. Damien.

"How does the whole confidential thing work?" she asked.

"Anything we discuss here won't be discussed with anyone, anywhere, ever."

"Ever?"

He nodded.

"Then I have a confession for you." Keeping her gaze on that snow-capped mountain, she finished softly. "I'm not Mrs. Peterson."

"Please don't tell Josh I went today," Sadie said as she and Croff drove home.

Deputy Croff glanced sideways. "Okay."

Sadie played with the strap on her purse. "I'll tell him sometime. I just...I want it to come from me."

"Understandable. And how was it?"

Sadie smiled. "He wasn't kidding when he said he wasn't a talker. You should have seen his face when I told him everything."

Croff laughed softly. "And were you a talker?"

Sadie nodded, surprised with herself. "Most of it blurted out of me in completely random order. I kept remembering more pieces of the story. I tried to go back and fill in the blanks. It probably didn't make any sense. He only said a few things, and mostly it was to say, 'Wow.'"

"Wow?"

Sadie thought about the stunned look on his skinny, little face and laughed. "Yeah. Wow. Hopefully next time he'll have more to say."

"Yeah. About that..." Croff glanced sideways. "I kinda made you another appointment for tomorrow morning."

"What?"

"Harrison and I don't have to report to the local office until noon. With a little arm-twisting, I got you an appointment for first thing tomorrow so I can drive you."

"Really?"

Croff shrugged. "I feel awful leaving you. I'm glad they're letting us work in the local office, but...well...if you see a dark Ford Focus circling the block, don't freak out. It's just me checking in on you."

Sadie didn't know what to say. Her eyes started to burn, and she blinked rapidly. "Thank you. And I don't just mean for tomorrow. Thank you for everything. I'm going to miss having you around. Will you two definitely be the ones who come back?"

"Are you kidding? Do you think I'd let anyone else take over?" Croff said.

If they weren't driving, Sadie would have given her a hug. As it was, her heart swelled. "Thank you, Deondra. For everything."

They lapsed into silence as they drove home. When Sadie looked over again, the deputy was grinning.

"What?" Sadie asked.

"No advice. No comment. No professional help whatsoever," Croff said. "Just...wow? How much does that guy make an hour?"

Sadie laughed. "Too much. I might have to drag my amazing U.S. Marshal bodyguard with me tomorrow. Maybe you can show him your gun. See if that gets more of a response out of him."

Much to Sadie's dismay, her counselor came prepared the next day. She hadn't taken Deputy Croff into the room with her—a huge mistake—which meant for an hour, he made Sadie answer questions, the hard ones that hurt. At the heart of it, he wanted to know what she was most afraid of, and he wouldn't take "death" for an answer.

But even worse, he gave her homework. She had to write down the entire Guillermo story, start to finish, in a brand new journal he bought just for her.

Stupid counselor.

CHAPTER 23

Katie Young picked up her sled and headed home. It wasn't fair it got dark so early in Spokane. She and Olivia only had one hour after school before it was too dark to sled. The first decent snow in two weeks, and all her parents gave her was one measly hour. She kicked a clump of snow as she headed home.

Katie wiped her runny nose with her glove forgetting she'd taken a dive in the snow on the last run. She smeared freezing snow all over her face.

She glanced over her shoulder to see if Olivia was laughing. She wasn't. Katie and Olivia always walked each other halfway home. They stopped at the exact middle sidewalk square before they parted ways. They counted it out one day to make sure it was fair. 139 sidewalk squares to Katie's house. 139 to Olivia's. It was their tradition. But tonight was especially cold. And dark. Olivia was long gone. She must have taken off the second Katie left. Snow on the face wasn't half as funny without a best friend. It was just freezing.

The street lamp above her was burned out, making the street even freakier now that Olivia was out of sight. Katie picked up her speed. Her purple sled was awkward enough she couldn't quite jog, but she tried.

She cleared the bend and spotted a man walking toward her. His chin was tucked in his coat, so he hadn't noticed her. She jumped sideways into the deep snow to clear a path for him and nearly face-planted. People in her neighborhood always stopped to chat with each other, regardless of the weather. Especially adults. They were the worst.

How's your mom? How's fifth grade? My, how you've grown!

Katie was way too cold to be polite. Holding her purple sled up to hide herself, she crept quietly through the deep snow in Maxfield's yard, hoping to avoid chit-chat.

The man looked up as he passed. He smiled briefly but kept walking.

Whew!

She jumped back on the sidewalk and started for home. Another minute and she'd be inside with a mug of hot chocolate—assuming Drew didn't drink the last of it.

"Hey," the man suddenly called. "Aren't you Josh's little sister?"

She skidded to a stop. No such luck.

"Yeah," she said over her shoulder. Even though she knew it was rude, she started for home again. Her toes burned, which didn't make sense because they were freezing. They were going to fall off any second.

The man ran to catch up. She kept walking, hoping he'd take the hint. He just fell in line next to her, keeping up with her brisk pace.

"I thought I recognized you," he said. "You've grown up since I saw you last, but you still have your pretty blonde hair."

Katie's gaze flickered sideways. She didn't remember him at all. The guy wasn't old, but neither was he young.

Creepy.

As if reading her thoughts, he said, "I'm Josh's old buddy from high school. Gavin. Gavin Jenks. Don't you remember me?"

She tucked her chin in her coat and picked up her pace, half-tempted to drop the sled and run the rest of the way home. Josh had too many friends.

"Nope," she said. "Sorry. Bye."

He jogged to keep up with her. "You know, I haven't seen Josh in a while. It'd be fun to catch up with him. Do you know his number?"

"No." *Go away.*

"Bummer. Where is he these days? Is he still at Washington State?"

A sudden thought twisted her stomach. Since the day she was born, her cop dad gave her the same lecture over and over: *"Don't talk to strangers. Don't talk to strangers. Ever. Do you understand? Don't give them information. Don't give them numbers, addresses, nothing! Even if they say they know you, trust your gut."*

The lecture was fresh in her head since he had repeated it the night before, only that time he added another ten minutes onto it. *"If anything ever feels wrong, you run fast and come tell me and Mom, okay? Trust your gut, Katie."*

It wasn't exactly wrong for Gavin to ask about her brother. It was just weird that, of all her brothers to ask about, he wanted to know about the one who broke up with Megan, quit school, and took off to somewhere no one would tell Katie. The only thing she knew was there was some big secret that meant she might not see Josh for a long time. She hated being the youngest. Nobody ever told her anything. Gavin was asking the wrong person.

But...her stomach.

Her gut.

It felt like it weighed thirty pounds.

Without meaning to, she slowed to a stop. Gavin smiled. If she listened to her gut, she was in serious trouble. Of course, her dad was a paranoid freak. One too many cop moments.

She hugged the sled and calculated. She was only four houses from home. If needed, she could scream. She had an amazingly loud scream, ask anyone. Her family or some neighbor would hear. Wouldn't they?

"Oh, wait," Gavin said. "That's right. Sam told me Josh left Washington State. Where'd he end up?"

Gavin knew Sam. The knot in her stomach unhitched a little. Katie liked Sam. He was her favorite of Josh's friends. "Josh is at BYU, I think." She thought she heard her mom say that to someone.

"BYU?"

"Yep. Good old BYU." She started backing up. "See ya."

Gavin grabbed her arm, pulling her to a stop. His fingers dug into her thick coat, his expression turning dark. "You wouldn't lie to me, would you, Katie?"

Run! her gut screamed.

"Let go!" she said, trying to push him away. "Let go of me!"

His grip tightened. "Look, I'm done playing games. Josh isn't at BYU, and I think you know where he is. I need an answer, and I need it now. So give it to me, and I'll let you go. Where is Josh?"

Her heart pounded in her chest. "I don't know, I promise." Terror rushed out of her and sped up her words. "I'm really, really late, and my mom is waiting for me. So are my big brothers and my dad who's a cop with a gun—a huge, ginormous gun he likes to shoot at people. He's probably getting his gun out now because he's really mean and likes to—Let go of me!" she cried, as his fingers dug deeper.

"Not until you tell me where—"

It happened. Katie let one rip. She screamed at the top of her lungs without planning to. Her body just took over. The scream was so loud it hurt her own ears. The cold constricted her throat, making it a high-pitched siren in the silent, snowy night.

Gavin's mouth dropped. His grip loosened, but for only a second. Then his huge hand clamped over her mouth.

"What do you think you're doing?" he hissed in her ear.

She screamed again. No sound came out.

He glanced over his shoulder at a dark car parked a few houses down. The car lights flipped on and started rolling toward them.

Katie tried to back up. His grip tightened. She thrashed around, but her boots slid on the ice without making progress. In terror, she looked from the approaching dark car, to Gavin, and back again. One word blared over and over in her mind:

Kidnap.

"I'll ask one more time," he whispered. "Where is Josh? And I swear if you scream again, I'll kill you."

His hand moved off her mouth one inch so she could speak.

She couldn't feel her arm anymore because he held her so tight. She was going to die. She was only ten years old, and she was going to die. Katie heard of kids being kidnapped, but she would never last that long.

Tears leaked from her eyes. "I told you, I don't know. No one will tell me. Please don't hurt me," she begged, even though he already was. His fingers dug into her coat. "Please. No one will tell me where Josh is."

She took one last chance.

"Help!" she screamed. "Help me!"

His hand clamped over her mouth so fast she fell back. But not far. His other hand snatched her to him, squeezing the air from her lungs.

"You have a death wish, kid?" he hissed. His hand no longer covered just her mouth but her nose as well. She couldn't breathe. Couldn't. And he was dragging her backward, away from her house, away from her family, toward that dark car. "So be it," he said. "You and I are quietly getting in that car, and you're going to—" "

"Katie?" A loud shout shattered the neighborhood. It was her mom. "Katie?!"

Katie didn't think. She just moved.

She bit down on Gavin's hand and rammed her heavy snow boot into his shin. He cried out, grip loosening.

It was enough.

She dropped like a rock and scrambled along the sidewalk. Gloves, knees clawed the snow. When she was clear, she jumped up and took off, booking it for home. She flew over the snowy sidewalk in spite of her heavy boots.

"Get back here!" Gavin yelled.

She sped up, passing Maxfield's hedge.

Headlights lit the path in front of her. Tires peeled out on the icy road. The car was coming. Chasing her. So was Gavin. She could hear his footsteps.

Oh, please, oh please, oh please!

Her boots hit a patch of ice, and she slipped. Not far, but she screamed again. Louder.

"What do I do?" Gavin yelled at someone. The driver in the car.

Katie struggled to stay upright. The forward momentum kept her moving.

Three houses.

Two houses.

"Katie?" Her dad's voice yelled that time. "Katie, where are you? Katie!"

"Dad!" she screamed.

"Get in!" someone new shouted, this time behind her. "Let her go, Brett. Just get in! Let's go, let's go!"

The car screeched to a stop, and a car door slammed shut. More slush splashed under car tires.

Katie risked a glance over her shoulder. The car was headed for her. She was on the sidewalk, but the car was going to run her over.

Suddenly she was flying. The car was ten feet away, but someone picked her up.

Her dad.

He threw her over his shoulder and ran. Her head and body bounced as he sprinted the length of their driveway in one breath. He took the cement stairs to their house two at time and, before she could blink, she was thrown on the hardwood floor of her entryway. The front door slammed behind them.

Her mom dropped to her knees in front of her, hands fluttering around her face. "Are you okay? What happened? Katie?"

Katie's mind was mush, trying to keep up.

Her siblings rushed into the living room, panic written on their faces. Their mom waved them back.

Katie watched her dad. He crouched down next to the front window, gun held high. He whipped out his phone and dialed. "Curt, Curt," he huffed. "I need help. Fast! They found us, Curt! Please! Fast!"

The lack of breathing caught up to Katie. She gulped for air, trying to figure out what just happened. What was still happening. Gavin, or Brett, or whoever he was, where was he now? Where was the car? Would they start shooting? Would her dad?

Why did they want Josh?

She couldn't pull her eyes away from her dad. He was in socks—drenched socks—peering out the front window, finger on the trigger. He was shouting at Curt through the phone. Curt was his boss. Curt ran the whole precinct. And her dad was yelling at him.

"They found us Curt! They found us, and they're here!" He nodded frantically. "Yes. At the house! Please, go fast. I don't know how much time we have. They tried to take Katie. The man almost got her in the car. They tried to take Katie!"

They tried to take Katie.

The words unlocked something deep inside her. She started shaking. Her stomach. Her legs. Her shoulders. Everything turned into an earthquake determined to detach her limbs from her body.

They tried to take me.

She wanted to rush to the window. She needed to see where the car was, where Gavin was. Her spasmodic body wouldn't release her.

"Katie," her mom said, holding her face. "Katie, look at me. Are you okay? Katie?"

"He tried to take me," Katie whispered.

"Oh, baby." Her mom grabbed her into a tight embrace that smothered her. Katie didn't fight her.

"They're heading down the far side of the street," her dad said. "I don't know. I can't make out the plates." He perched on the balls of his feet. "Send Tony down Madison to head them off. Go fast! They have to be pushing sixty."

Katie couldn't bear any more. She covered her ears and buried her face in her mother's arms.

They tried to take me.

CHAPTER 24

The second Sadie heard the front door open, she shoved her new journal under her bed. She was barely through Christmas Day and already exhausted, but she met Josh in the living room with a smile. She still hadn't told him about seeing the counselor.

"How was class?" she asked.

"Fine, but I'm glad it's the weekend." He shrugged out of his jacket and looked around. "How are you doing without Deputy Croff?"

Sadie hugged herself, feeling the loss of another person in her life. Thankfully, this was just temporary. "Fine."

Josh's blue eyes clouded with concern. "And how do you feel about being alone?"

"Alright." At least right now. Nighttime was another story, but she wasn't about to tell him that. The only thing keeping her from going insane was knowing both of their houses were equipped with the world's best security systems. It would have to be good enough.

She hobbled over to him and wiggled into his arms, laying her head against his broad, warm chest.

"Because if you need me," he said, stroking her hair. "I mean, if you're not comfortable or worried at all, I could maybe—"

She put a finger to his lips. Though she'd briefly considered it, and as comforting as it would be to have Josh sleeping on her couch at night, she wouldn't allow him to compromise. "You can't stay here. I'm fine, but what about you? Maybe you're the one I should be worried about?"

"No worries. I sleep like a log. Just ask my old roommate." He kissed her fingers and pulled her against him again. "But if it's too much for you, let me know. I'm not far away, and I can…I'll come if you need."

She smiled. His sense of duty and sense of propriety warred inside him. "Thank you, but I'm a big girl. I'll be fine."

"I know you will. I know. But, uh…" He paused long enough she looked up into his face. "I kind of did something without asking you first."

"What do you mean?" she asked.

The doorbell rang, and Josh winced. "Don't hate me, okay?"

Sadie looked at the door in shock. Not only was someone there— someone Josh seemed to be expecting—but she was pretty sure she could hear barking. Loud barking.

He left her and went to the front door. The second he opened it, the barking doubled. Sadie flew to the door and saw Josh scrunching down on the porch in front of a large box. No. Not a box. A kennel. A dog kennel. Sadie looked up as a man walked down her driveway toward a large delivery van with every type of dog painted on the side.

The barking picked up volume.

"What did you do?" she asked again. There was a dog in that kennel. A dog! She didn't even like dogs. "You bought me a dog?"

Josh jiggled the handle on the kennel, trying to open it. "Just remember that I love you, and you love me, and I only did this so you'd feel more comfortable at home alone all the time."

"You bought me a dog," she said again, not sure if she should laugh or cry. The front of the kennel was turned away from her, so she couldn't see much, but it was huge, at least two feet tall. And barking like a maniac.

"Not just any dog."

Josh finally got the wire door open, and a huge, black lab sprung onto the porch.

Sadie's hands flew to her mouth. "Rocky?"

"Hold on, boy," Josh said, struggling to get hold of Rocky's collar before he took off. "Let's get you inside."

Sadie followed them in. Once the door was shut, Josh let go. Sam's dog jumped up on Josh first before running over to Sadie, nearly knocking her over in her stunned state. Then he was back to Josh again. He jumped and pranced around both of them. Josh tried to pat his back, but the big black beast wouldn't hold still.

Sadie couldn't believe it. At Sam's cabin, she'd been less than enthusiastic about Sam's black lab. She'd never been a dog lover, but for some reason, Rocky adored her right from the start. He'd been instrumental in saving her life at least three separate times. And he was here. In Tennessee.

Rocky finally stopped at her feet, panting heavily with excitement. Sadie crouched down and patted his back.

"You're coming to my rescue again, boy?" she whispered.

His tail wagged a million miles a minute. With a bark, he took off to explore her house. Sadie watched in amazement.

"How did you get him here?" she asked.

"Believe it or not," Josh said, "it was Harrison's idea. When he found out we would be without bodyguards for a week, he suggested we get a dog. But I knew it couldn't just be any dog. After everything Rocky did for you—for us—I convinced Harrison to let me make a phone call. By the way, Sam says hi."

Sadie whirled around. "You got to talk to Sam? No fair!"

Josh smiled. "Only for a second. Don't tell Madsen. We just talked long enough to ask about borrowing Rocky. Long enough to find out he asked that Elizabeth girl out."

"He did?" Sadie clapped her hands. "Yes!"

Rocky couldn't decide where to go or who to get attention from first. He zigzagged in and around everything. Barking filled her small house.

After a moment, Josh slipped his hand around Sadie's waist. "You don't hate me?"

"Are you kidding?" She threw her arms around his neck. "This is perfect. Thank you."

Rocky pranced around their feet a full hour before he calmed down enough to sit for more than half a second. Even then, the slightest sound or movement made him hyper again.

After dinner and homework were done, Sadie and Josh cuddled on the couch for some Star Trek. Josh was determined to convert her into a Trekkie. Rocky finally wore himself out and snuggled in next to her. The original episodes were the cheesiest shows Sadie had ever seen, but she loved the opportunity to tease Josh about his nerdy obsession.

Rocky slept that night at the foot of Sadie's bed. Having him brought back the memories of being at the cabin—the good memories.

But in the morning, when Rocky still was going wild, Josh and Sadie decided to get out and do more exploring. It wasn't the perfect sunny day they had earlier in the week, but it was in the low fifties, so they grabbed their coats and headed straight to the heart of the mountains, the Great Smoky Mountains.

Rocky sat in the back seat, head and tongue hanging out the window. By the time they reached the national park, Sadie also had her window down and head partway out like Rocky, minus the wagging tongue. She stretched to see the tops of the mountains. Josh, however, was more interested in her, short curls blowing in the wind, olive face lit with joy.

She turned and caught him staring. Blushing, she sat back. "It's different," she said. "I mean, I know it's different, but it feels like we're driving into Glacier Park right now. Maybe God really does love me."

Josh's brows rose. "What do you mean?"

"Putting me so close to the mountains. We could be in Mississippi right now, but somehow we ended up outside the largest mountains in the East. It can't just be a coincidence."

He broke into a smile. "You're not going to turn Julie Andrews on me and start singing about hills coming alive, are you?"

She closed her eyes to the sun. "I might."

He laughed. "As long as it's not country music, sing to your heart's content."

"I'm going to convert you one of these days. Mark my words, Mr. Peterson, but you're going to love country music before I'm done with you."

Once inside the national park, Josh stopped at the first intersection, waiting for instructions. Sadie had already tossed the park map in the back seat, a map he would have memorized by now. "Which way?" he asked.

"How do I even choose?" she said, eyes taking in every ounce of the scenery. "I bet there are hundreds of trails in here. I'd give anything to go hiking today, but this stupid foot says otherwise. Oh man, look at that bridge there," she said pointing. "That is gorgeous!"

"I think I better park before you and Rocky climb out the windows."

She tried to swat Josh, making him laugh again.

They found the bridge off a side road to the north. It was nothing special as far as Josh could tell, just a simple wood bridge spanning the roaring mountain river, but Sadie's eyes were bright and alive. Josh wasn't sure how her doctor ever told her no on Wednesday, but apparently her foot needed a few more weeks to heal. At least he gave her a better walking boot because she was already halfway to the bridge by the time Josh got Rocky's leash on.

The air was crisp and fresh with pines. And cold, much colder than the lower elevations in Knoxville. Snow patches dotted the surrounding rocks and mountainside. The higher up the mountain, the heavier the snow. Josh zipped up his coat, glad he'd brought it.

The bridge led to a trail that wound through trees and climbed up the mountainside. Rocky was headed for that trail, but Josh yanked him to a stop at the center of the bridge.

The river roared below them. Sadie leaned against the wood railing, watching the river tumble over the huge gray boulders. Her eyes darted around, trying to take it all in.

Again, Josh studied her over the scenery. He'd always loved the outdoors. He and his buddies grew up playing football on front lawns and skiing all winter to stay outside. But in Montana, all he'd seen of Sadie was the girl who hated—loathed—skiing. Her aversion to skiing was vastly misleading because right now, she looked like a total outdoors girl. He loved it.

She breathed in the fresh mountain air. "This is home."

"I can tell," he said fondly.

The sun caught her dark hair, bringing out her beautiful auburn highlights. Her cheeks were rosy from the cold. He was tempted to grab her hand to warm his up, but hers were tucked deep in her pockets. Plus, he didn't want to disturb her reverie.

She glanced sideways, realizing he was watching her again. "What?"

"You're happy," he said, unsure how else to explain it.

"Is that so shocking?"

"No. I just haven't seen this side of you before. You're as hyper as Rocky."

She smiled. "Sorry. It's just that some of my best childhood memories are exploring the Danny On Trail above Whitefish with Damien. We'd find rivers like this and climb for miles trying to find the beginning. By the time we made it home, we'd be soaking wet and filthy, so we'd shower super fast before my mom got home from work. It was the best."

Like Sadie, Josh's gaze followed the river as far up the mountain as he could before it curved out of sight. He pictured Sadie climbing those huge gray boulders with Damien—with himself—and determined that come spring, when she was healed and the temperature was right, they'd find the top of that river.

She slipped her cold hand into his and snuggled into him. "You don't know how bad I wish we could hike today. As soon as this cast is off, you better watch out."

"Is that so?"

She grinned up at him. "Yep."

Rocky tugged on his leash, trying to head up the trail that was tempting all of them, giving Josh a sudden idea.

"Why wait?" he said. "Let's go."

"I can walk a little," she said, "but I was thinking a real hike where we start early in the morning and pack a lunch." She scowled down at her walking boot. "I don't think I'd make it very far today. But I guess we could go a little ways if you don't mind going slow."

"Or…we could try something a little unconventional. Do you trust me?"

Her brows lowered, letting him know that she didn't trust him at all. "Why?"

He faced away from her and scrunched down. "Climb on."

"What?"

"On my back. Climb on. We're going for a hike."

"What? No. No, we can't." Her eyes betrayed her and gazed longingly at that trail. "Where would we go?"

He laughed. She was as transparent as the sunlight. "We're finding the beginning of this river."

"You're crazy. You're insane!"

"As if you didn't already know that." Still crouched, he pointed to his back. "Come on. The day is young. Rocky's ready. I'm ready. So let's go."

"I'm too heavy. You'll get tired."

Josh rolled his eyes. She was less than 5'0 and weighed nothing. "You're insulting my manhood here. Hold Rocky's leash and climb on."

She took an apprehensive step forward. Grabbing her hands, he made the decision for her. He pulled her arms over his shoulders and stood.

With her arms and legs clutched around him, her cheek was right next to his. He turned and smiled at her, just inches away. "Hmmm. This is better than I thought." He gave her an awkward sideways peck on the cheek. "Much better."

She laughed. "You're crazy."

"Which is why you love me. You ready?" he asked.

"As I'll ever be."

CHAPTER 25

The trail didn't follow the river long before it veered to the right. The woods next to the river were damp and snowy, so Josh and Sadie postponed their quest to find the top of the river and stuck to the basic trail.

Sadie clung to Josh's shoulders and Rocky's leash as Josh carried them higher and higher up the mountain.

Considering it was technically still winter, Josh was surprised by all the hikers they passed. Most of them wore heavy backpacks and the men wore huge, scruffy beards, as if they were in the mountains for the long haul. But if anyone got weird looks, it was Josh with Sadie on his back. That didn't stop them.

Unfortunately, the higher they climbed, the more Josh huffed. He couldn't help it. His breaths came out in white puffs of smoke that he tried to swallow to keep her from noticing. It didn't work.

"Put me down," Sadie said. "You're going to give yourself a heart attack."

He worked to breathe through his nose, but he wasn't getting enough oxygen. *Come on body. Don't fail me now.*

"Josh. We have to stop. Look, there's a bench up there. Let's stop for a minute."

"No, I'm fine. It's just the altitude." Even though his lungs were burning and his bad arm killed from holding her up, he couldn't stop. She was so close to him, so warm against his back, and so dang cute. He remembered back when he'd carried her at the bottom of the ski lift after she'd slipped on the slushy snow. And he thought that had been fun. Now that her cold cheek was pressed to his and her arms were wrapped around him like a spider monkey, he could hike all day.

Sort of.

Sadie started squirming and twisting her legs. "Put me down. I'm serious. We've gone far enough."

"No. We have to keep…" Another breath. "…going."

"This is great right here. Please," she begged.

He shook his head with another huff.

Suddenly her fingers raked through the hair at the back of his neck, sending chills down his spine. "Pretty please," she breathed in his ear.

Josh flinched as her hot breath snaked in his ear. What the heck was that? Maybe carrying her for so long wasn't such a good idea. Not with her that close, tempting him with that—

Something pinched his shoulder. Hard.

Instinct took over. He jerked back, arms flailing, and suddenly her weight was gone. He had dropped her.

"Sadie, no!" Josh cried, whirling around.

She wasn't flat on the ground like he expected her to be. She was standing next to him, laughing her head off as Rocky pranced around her.

"You're so gullible," she said. "I love it!"

"Sadie!" He rubbed his ear. She had purposely distracted him with that hot, breathy voice. "You could have been hurt!"

"I knew what I was doing," she said, slipping an arm around his waist.

He didn't doubt she knew *exactly* what she was doing. He kept rubbing his ear. "Don't do that to me."

"Are you sure?" She winked up at him. "I think you kind of liked it."

He shook a finger at her, trying to fight off a smile. "You have way too much power over me. You better be careful. I'm not sure I can handle this mountain girl side of you."

"Oh, you can't. Trust me."

He chuckled. She was something else. "You do realize this is a date. Date number three to be precise."

That stopped her cold. She looked up at him, wide-eyed, with the same horrified expression she wore after trying on rings.

"Keep this up," he continued, "and I'll count that Star Trek episode as a date and end up dropping to a knee right here, right now."

"You wouldn't."

"I might."

"You're crazy," she said even as she backed up.

"We've already established that. You were warned."

Josh started to bend one knee, lowering himself inch by inch to the frozen ground. Though he wasn't planning to pop the question, part of him was tempted. The longer he spent with Sadie, the easier it was to envision the two of them as a permanent thing.

"Stop!" She grabbed his hand and yanked him up. "Quit teasing me."

"Then don't breathe in my ear."

"Deal. Now come on. I think I can make it to that bench all by myself."

Rocky tugged them up the trail. Sadie made surprisingly good time with that new boot of hers. And that's when Josh decided that instead of Kermit, Gumby, or even Kevin's nickname of Ice Woman, there was a better nickname for Sadie: Mountain Girl.

As they sat, he slipped an arm around her shoulders. "Why didn't I see this side of you when we were skiing?" he asked.

She rolled her eyes. "Because I hate skiing. Obviously."

"But skiing and hiking are basically the same thing. Mountains. Trees. Fresh air. Even snow," he said, pointing to a huge patch near their bench.

"Except with skiing you slide uncontrollably down the mountain instead of putting one solid foot in front of the other. I've never face-planted in the snow when I was hiking."

"Are you saying you've face-planted otherwise?"

She elbowed him. "Skiing and hiking are two totally different things." Her eyes suddenly widened. "Oh, no. Don't tell me Megan liked to ski."

"Megan?" Josh wasn't sure how his old girlfriend entered the conversation. "I don't know. Maybe. But I think she only skied because I did. That kind of sums up our relationship actually. She did a lot of things because she thought I wanted her to."

Sadie pulled Rocky close and rubbed his black fur. "I should be that way more often."

"No," Josh said firmly. "You shouldn't." He thought about her over-exuberance to join his religion. If she wasn't doing that for herself, it wouldn't last. "I didn't like that about Megan. I wanted her to be her own person with her own thoughts. I dated her for a long time, and in the end, I felt like I really didn't know her."

The light faded from Sadie's eyes. "You, too?"

Josh squeezed her cold hand, refusing to let Guillermo ruin this moment. "Good thing we're not like that, right? I know you hate to ski, and you know I hate…"

"Country music," she finished with a smile. "Whew! I think we're safe."

The wood bench was cold, and Josh scooted closer to Sadie to warm up. A few more hikers passed them, but now that Sadie wasn't his little spider monkey, they received waves instead of strange looks.

Sadie leaned into Josh and looked out over the view. A moist fog clung to the mountainside, making it hard to see beyond their little corner of the Smokies. "Up here it's easy to believe in God," she said after a minute.

"Yeah." Josh thought about how many prophets went to the mountains to pray. God was definitely in the mountains.

"How can people say all this happened by chance? It's too beautiful, too perfect." She fidgeted with the zipper on her black coat. "But…"

He looked at her. "But?"

"But…" She bit her lower lip. "I'm not sure how to say it."

Josh felt himself tense up. "Just say it."

"If God exists, if He can make something this beautiful and peaceful, how can He let people like Guillermo run loose? Why doesn't He kill them off? And what about the people who hurt little kids, all the abusers in the world? How can God let them live?"

It didn't escape Josh's notice that she said Guillermo's name. Though it was a small thing, it was progress. But her question was a hard one—hard, but perfectly valid. Rocky barked at a few passing hikers while Josh figured out how to respond.

"Seems like God should do something," he said. "But the thing is, people have their agency, the ability to choose right or wrong. God can't—or at least, He won't—take that away from them."

Her dark brows furrowed. "Meaning?"

"If He came down here and started zapping people it would create utter chaos."

"As if there's not chaos already."

"True," he said, "but it would be different. Heavenly Father respects our right to make choices. He won't force us to do anything, even if it's the right thing."

"Because…?"

"If He immediately punished us when we did something wrong, we'd get conditioned to do the right thing simply to avoid punishment. Like Pavlov's theory with the dogs," he said, rubbing Rocky's back. "We'd be doing the right things for the wrong reasons, and then it wouldn't be right anymore. So I guess He lets us make our own choices, even if sometimes those choices hurt other people."

"Really hurts them," Sadie whispered. "Maybe He could just wipe out the bad ones."

"Yeah, but where does He draw the line? I know you're going to do something bad so I'll take you out? He doesn't work that way."

"I guess it makes sense," she said, even as her shoulders slumped.

Josh lifted her chin. "Don't forget, He's still a god of justice. Evils will be punished, if not now, sometime in the eternities. Justice will be served. It just doesn't always happen in this life."

"But the next life seems so far away," she said.

Some days, maybe. Others, not so much. They'd come too close, too many times with Sadie, but Josh kept that to himself.

"So you're saying that, regardless of what happens in the trial," Sadie said, "Guillermo will pay for what he's done to everyone? Eventually?"

"Yeah."

"I guess that's something." She rubbed behind Rocky's ears. "If only justice could happen now."

"It might."

She shot him a dark look.

"Or it might not," he conceded, thinking about Mr. Ugly getting off scot-free. "I guess that's why we have the Savior. He can take away the pain of what happened now while we wait for justice and mercy to kick in. Though it seems impossible to believe, when you put your problems in the Savior's hands, everything is easier. The problems might not go away"—it felt like Guillermo would never go away—"but the Savior can make it bearable."

Her eyes lifted to his. "Is that what you're doing? Putting our problems in the Savior's hands?"

He flushed, suddenly hating himself. "Not as much as I should be. I…" He sighed. "I have some anger issues when it comes to your ex."

She smiled sadly. "I noticed."

The guilt ate at him and he couldn't hold her steady gaze. Instead, he looked out over the vast mountainside. "You asked me once at the bonfire about Christian forgiveness. Honestly, I don't think I've ever struggled with forgiveness before I met Guillermo." He turned back and studied Sadie's perfect face, the curve of her soft cheeks, and her dark eyes that lit up when she smiled. How was he supposed to forget the bruise that encompassed her left eye, a larger one on her shoulder delivered after she'd passed out, her broken ribs and ankle, or the way she'd looked when Josh found her nearly dead—first in Sam's truck and then two weeks later under a pine tree?

He reached up and stroked her cold skin that had healed perfectly. If only hearts healed so easily.

A scripture filled his mind, haunting him further. *"Love your enemies. Bless them that curse you...for he maketh the sun to rise on the evil and on the good."* If anyone had reason to hate others it was the Savior. He had endured the ultimate betrayals and yet, He was the one who gave the command, *"Love your enemies."*

"Sometimes," Josh whispered, "I wonder if I'll ever be able to give this over to the Savior. I know I'm supposed to." He paused, feeling vulnerably honest. "I just don't know how."

She leaned into his hand, smiling through shining eyes. "Me neither. Maybe we could work on it together. We could say a prayer or something right now."

"Yeah?" They had started praying over meals, and he loved Sadie's ability to talk to God as if He was in the room with them. But they hadn't prayed yet in non-food times. "That would be great."

He straightened and glanced up and down the trail. No one else was coming, so he took her hand and bowed his head. "Do you want me to say it or you?" he asked.

"You. But don't forget to pray for our families. They need it as much as we do."

Josh was on a high as they drove home. Between the mountain, the piggy-back ride, and that amazing moment with Sadie, he was on cloud nine. Things were finally falling into place.

As they pulled onto their street, he noticed a strange car in their driveway. It wasn't Deputy Croff's, but it looked an awful lot like...

He slammed on the brakes. "No, no, no."

"What is it?" Sadie asked. Then she saw what he did. "Is that...your mom?"

Josh lifted his foot off the brake and let the car coast into Sadie's driveway. He pulled up next to his family's minivan.

Seven Young family members piled out.

CHAPTER 26

Sadie opened the car door. Her mind couldn't compute what her eyes told her. Josh's family was in Tennessee. And then she didn't have time. She jumped out of the way as a blonde girl rushed past her.

"Josh! Josh!"

"Katie?" Josh picked up his sister and swung her around. "What are you doing here?"

Josh's mom came up behind them. "We thought we'd check how things were going out east." Kathy gave Sadie a hug. "How are you, sweetie?"

"I'm stunned," Sadie said. "What are you doing here?"

"It's a long story. Let's wait until we're inside." Though she was smiling, the way Kathy said it made Sadie's stomach drop. They would only be here if something happened.

Something bad.

Two more siblings plowed over Josh, two teen boys. Peter was right behind them with the last of Josh's siblings, Lauren, who looked seventeen or eighteen. Lauren gave Josh a fierce hug, only unlike like the others, she wasn't smiling. Her face was tight, her lips were trembling as if she was on the verge of tears. Josh missed it.

Laughing, he tried to grab all his siblings for a massive hug. "Sadie, I'd like to introduce you to my crazy family. That tall obnoxious one here is my brother, Drew. This one here is Mike," he said, ruffling his dirty blond hair. "And there's Lauren, and"—he shook his head—"Man, I can't believe you guys are here."

His siblings laughed nervously. All except Lauren who hadn't let go of Josh's torso. Sadie wanted to smile at them, but she couldn't break away from Lauren's desperate embrace. Sadie knew that embrace only too well. Fear. Misery. A desire to escape the world.

Guillermo did this.

Sadie didn't know how, why, or when, but her worst nightmare had come true. Guillermo found Josh's family.

She quickly searched each face and limb for injury as Josh continued.

"Lauren's a senior in high school," he said. "And my youngest sister there is Katie, the blonde I told you about."

Finally Sadie managed a smile. Katie looked like an older version of little Sophia, the small girl who flirted with Josh in that monstrous ski lift line.

Sadie looked from sibling to sibling. Who were in Tennessee. She couldn't see any injuries. Maybe Guillermo hadn't found them after all. Other than Lauren's expression, there was little else to tell Sadie this was a bad thing. Maybe Madsen sent them to Tennessee as a precaution. If that was the case, why weren't her mom and Damien there, too?

"It's so nice to meet you," she said, suddenly remembering her manners. "Josh has told me so much about you guys."

"Well, he hasn't said anything about you," Mike said.

Josh tried to smack him, but Mike jumped out of the way.

"Except when he cried himself to sleep every night after he left Montana," Drew added with a grin.

Josh took another swipe. Both brothers ducked out of the way. Katie bounced around all of them with a huge smile.

"We have one more brother, Jake," Katie explained to Sadie. "But he's on a mission in Nebraska, so he's not here right now. But he's coming home early!"

"You mean, coming *here* early," Lauren corrected softly. "Jake can't go home anymore."

Josh whirled around to his parents. "Jake's coming off his mission? Now?"

Kathy scowled at her kids. "Girls, I told you not to…" She sighed and looked at Josh. Her eyes started to water.

"Mom?" Josh said, fear lacing his voice.

"Jake is…" Kathy started. A knot formed in Sadie's stomach when Kathy couldn't finish.

"Jake's flying into Knoxville tomorrow," Peter said gravely.

Josh's face went white. "But he has four months left."

Another look passed between Josh's parents. The longer it went, the harder it was for Sadie to breathe. Guillermo. She leaned against the car for support. Guillermo did this.

Kathy waved her hands at her youngest two kids. "You guys help Dad get the bags. Let's get inside so we can talk."

Katie and Mike took off and explored Sadie's small house, ducking in and out of the few rooms in a matter of seconds. Rocky followed them, thrilled to have more people to dote over him. Drew and Lauren, however, squeezed onto the checkered couch next to their mom. Kathy put an arm around Lauren, who quickly buried her head into her side like she was three-years-old and not eighteen. Peter and Josh grabbed oak chairs from the kitchen.

Guillermo, Guillermo, Guillermo.

Sadie couldn't rid the chant from her mind. Her stomach churned with something vile. She took a chair and sat directly opposite the couch, bracing herself for the news. Josh sat next to her, grabbing her hand in a tight embrace. His hands were cold and rigid.

"Alright. What happened?" Josh asked.

Kathy looked at Peter before she started. "There was an incident at the house. With a man. And Katie." Josh nearly jumped out of his seat, but her hands flew up. "We're all fine. Katie's fine, but…"

"But?" Sadie breathed.

Kathy's lips twitched, betraying her carefully controlled front. She swallowed once and looked up at Peter, eyes suddenly swimming with tears. "I can't," she whispered.

Peter took over, rehearsing the brief encounter with Katie and the man on the sidewalk. Josh confirmed that he didn't know anyone from school named Gavin, and Sadie felt more and more ill.

"When I heard Katie scream," Peter said, "I ran up the stairs. I can't believe her scream carried all the way inside, but I heard it clear as a bell from our basement three houses away."

"That's because Katie has the loudest scream in the world," Drew said. "The kind that makes you go deaf."

"Drew," Josh's mom said in quiet warning. She glanced over to where Katie and Mike continued to explore Sadie's house with Rocky. It was a small, echoing house. It would take very little for Katie to overhear.

As Peter continued, explaining about bursting outside and seeing a man holding Katie, Sadie's chin dropped to her chest. Guillermo found Josh's family. Who next?

"I threw Katie over my shoulder and ran," Peter went on, "fully expecting them to start shooting. I could hear the men in the car yelling at each other, but the car peeled out and they left. I called Curt, but—"

"It's no big deal," a little voice squeaked.

Sadie turned. Little Katie stood in the far corner, looking much younger than ten. She'd slipped back into the room without anyone noticing.

Josh's face darkened. "No big deal? Katie!"

Katie's shoulders lifted. "It wasn't. I'm fine."

Josh opened his mouth to argue, but Sadie kicked his leg. No need to frighten Katie more than she already was. She was trying to act brave, keeping her chin up and strong, but her hands were clasped tightly, and her shoulders were too high. The episode shook her up, but she couldn't admit that to a room full of older siblings.

Josh's dad sighed. "Curt sent men right over, but they didn't find the car, and the FBI doesn't have any record of a Gavin or a Brett working for Guillermo. Do you know anyone by those names, Sadie?"

She had identified twenty-two of Guillermo's contacts, but none by those names. She managed to shake her head.

"I'm not surprised," Peter said. "The FBI questioned a few neighbors. The Maxfields said they'd seen a car like that driving slowly around our street the day before. They thought it was suspicious because it was parked outside after the snowstorm, which they aren't supposed to do with the snowplows."

"So why didn't they call it in?" Josh cried.

"Because no one wants to think the worst, Josh," Kathy said gently. "People want to think the best of their world. They want to feel safe. Most things slip past people without notice. It would have slipped past the Maxfields, too, if they hadn't heard what happened to Katie."

Without warning, Katie ran across the room and buried her face in her father's stomach.

"Katie was very brave," Peter said, stroking her blonde curls. "Very brave."

The house grew painfully silent as Josh and Sadie tried to process.

"So they were watching your house," Sadie said. "Guillermo sent men to Spokane. To find Josh. Only when they couldn't find him, they found..." As she looked at Katie, tears welled up inside her, hot and bulging. Guillermo was kidnapping children now? Would he stop at nothing?

"But how did Guillermo find you—me—us?" Josh asked. "Your number is unlisted. You double-checked all that before I left!"

"Obviously we missed something," Peter said.

Sadie started trembling. Her insides, her hands, everything started to shake as if someone dumped a bucket of ice over her head. What else were they missing? With them? With her mom? With everyone? Her stomach churned with possibilities.

"When Dad finished talking to his boss," Josh's mom said, "he told us to pack. We were terrified because Lauren wasn't home. She was at a friend's house studying."

"Christopher's," Drew said under his breath.

Lauren still didn't look up from the brown, shaggy carpet.

"We weren't sure if the men knew where Lauren was," Kathy went on. "Thank goodness they didn't. We picked her up and didn't stop driving. We drove all night and through the day and…" She shrugged. "We're here."

Just like that. Josh's entire family walked away from their lives.

"Katie did the perfect thing," Peter said, still clutching her tightly. "If she hadn't screamed or fought back…" His voice broke, and he couldn't continue.

Sadie felt like throwing up.

Little Katie looked up at her father. "Can we stop talking about it now? I don't want to hear anymore."

Sadie wanted to reach out and hold her tight. She understood Katie's need to quit talking about it. The urge to run from the memories was overpowering to the point of insanity. But the memories followed you no matter where you ran. She wondered how long before Katie realized that.

Josh's tone softened. "I'm sorry, KitKat. Maybe you should go in the other room and play with Rocky. I still have some questions for Mom and Dad."

"You can go in my room if you want," Sadie offered softly. "Josh bought me a picture book of Tennessee with lots of pretty mountains."

Katie shook her head against Peter's side. Her bottom lip started to quiver, and she covered her face. Within seconds, her tiny body heaved great sobs that echoed through the house.

Peter rocked her back and forth. "It's okay, sweetie. Everything's okay now."

Sadie swallowed to keep her own emotions from erupting. It wasn't okay. It would never be okay. Not with Guillermo.

"Katie gave the description of the man to Agent Madsen," Kathy said softly. "He's working on it, but…"

"It never goes anywhere," Josh finished angrily. "Guillermo covers his tracks well." He turned to Sadie with a look she easily read. *I could kill him.*

Katie's shoulders continued to convulse.

"Agent Madsen told you where to find us?" Josh asked.

Peter blew out his breath. "Not exactly. Madsen wanted us to stay put. He offered to have men patrol the house and keep a watch out. He was worried that if we took off, we'd arouse more suspicion. I told him—well, I won't say what I told him, but the gist was that we were leaving. He tried to talk us into Arizona or somewhere far from here, but—"

"It's my fault," Kathy cut in. "I'm sorry but I begged to come here. Agent Madsen didn't want us to because of the chance of us leading Guillermo here, but we took all the kids' devices away. They have no electronics and won't until this is settled. We promised Madsen we were cutting all ties. I just…" Josh's mom blinked rapidly. "I had to know you two were safe. I had to see you with my own eyes."

"Even then," Peter said, "it took the Chief of Police and several security clearances to convince Madsen. Technically, since neither of you have signed papers, you're not under WITSEC control yet. There was little he could do to keep us away. But we promise to be careful," he added to Sadie more than anyone. "If you're concerned at all, we'll find somewhere else. Kathy's always wanted to see Maine anyway."

"Or Italy," she said, looking at Katie. "Or Siberia."

"No," Sadie said. "Please stay. We want you here. Right, Josh?"

When Josh didn't answer, she glanced sideways. He was staring down at the carpet like Lauren was, like he hadn't heard Sadie. With a shake of his head, he jumped up and started pacing. Back and forth he went across the small room, raging.

"What kind of psychopath goes after little girls?" he asked. "What would he have done with her? She doesn't know anything!"

Sadie couldn't bear to watch Josh have a breakdown. Not him. She twisted the yarn on her sweater while a boulder lodged itself in her throat. She needed to apologize to Katie who had no reason to be hunted by an evil, violent man like Guillermo. She needed to but couldn't.

"How come everyone still thinks it's that Guillermo guy?" Drew asked. "I thought he's in prison."

Josh whirled around. "Because he's still calling the shots! He has men who carry out his orders. He tells them what to do, who to find! She's only ten!"

"It's okay, Josh," his mom said, only she wasn't looking at him. She wasn't even looking at Katie. She was looking directly at Sadie. "It's okay. It's over now."

Sadie shook her head angrily. "No, it's not." The first of the hot tears escaped, streaking down her cheeks. "I can't believe he…" The words stopped again. She covered her lips to keep them from trembling. "I'm so…so sorry, Katie. I'm so sorry everyone. Peter. Kathy." A hiccup exploded against her tender ribs, and she winced. When she found the courage to look up, she said the words that hurt the worst. "I'm sorry, Josh."

Without hearing, he continued to pace, hands running through his hair over and over again.

Josh's mom reached across and grabbed Sadie's hand. "We don't blame you. None of this is your fault. You have to believe that."

People kept saying that, and yet it wasn't true. This was completely her fault! Sadie chose Josh over Guillermo, and Guillermo would forever make him pay. Make his family pay.

Make everyone pay!

Suddenly Katie pushed away from her dad and ran across the room. She flung herself at Sadie. Sadie barely got her arms open in time to catch her. Then little Katie hugged Sadie tightly as her body shook with giant sobs.

Sadie was too stunned to do anything. Josh's family looked shocked, too, as Katie's tears soaked Sadie's sweater. Sadie had only met Katie a few minutes ago, yet Sadie's arms reacted before the rest of her. They closed around Katie's small body and squeezed with all the fierceness she dared. Her chin rested on Katie's head, wetting Katie's blonde curls with her own tears.

"It's going to be alright," Sadie whispered. "We're going to beat him. We're not going to let him win anymore."

Katie looked up with red, swollen eyes. "How?"

The impulse came so fast and strong, Sadie couldn't fight it. "Excuse me," she said.

She pushed Katie up and hobbled as fast as she could toward her room. She didn't make it. Privacy or not, she couldn't wait another second. In the hallway, she pulled out the phone she always carried but had yet to use and dialed the only number she was allowed to dial.

"Hello, Miss Dawson," Agent Madsen said. "What can I help you with?"

"I wanted to let you know that I'm ready now." She took a quick breath. "I don't need to wait. I'm signing the papers right now."

CHAPTER 27

"Wait!"

Sadie heard Josh run after her, but she waved him back to finish her call with Agent Madsen. She couldn't let Josh change her mind. Not now.

"Yes," she said, heart beating out of control. "I'll send the papers when they're done."

Josh grabbed her hand. "Guillermo will know you're alive. Just wait a second. Let's talk first. Please, Sadie."

His face was one of sheer torture. She had to turn away. He let go of her, allowing her to clutch the phone two-handed.

"Miss Dawson," Madsen said on the other line, "I'll do everything in my power to keep your name out of the records going to Vasquez's lawyers. I can't prevent it forever, but you should have some time before Guillermo knows you're alive. I'll give you a warning before the documents go out."

She nodded. "Whatever it takes. I'm ready."

Josh was still watching her when she hung up. So was his whole family. Before she could change her mind, she went to her room and grabbed the papers from her dresser. A pen was already waiting. With a quick prayer, she added her initials to each page and her signature to the bottom of the last one.

It was official. She was testifying against Guillermo Vasquez.

With another signature, she entered WITSEC. Her life was no longer her own.

She stared at her two signatures. There was no going back.

Josh stood in her doorway looking like he'd been sucker-punched. "Do you even want to talk about this?" he asked, pained. "Do I even get a say?"

She walked the papers over to him. "Guillermo has to be stopped. He can't go on like this anymore, and I can't stand by and do nothing anymore."

"He's going to go ballistic, Sadie," he whispered. "When he finds out, he's going to—"

"Which is why I'm here with you." She couldn't bear to think about flying back for trial days, or how Croff and Harrison would ever sneak her in and out without her getting killed. She'd worry about all that later.

Josh pinched his eyes. "What about your mom?"

"Tomorrow is Sunday. Madsen said it will take at least four days for the paperwork to clear the Attorney General's office. He'll tell my mom the situation and ask if she wants to be relocated immediately or wait until Guillermo's lawyers see the proposed witness list." Her breath hitched. "With my name on it."

"No," Josh said firmly. "Your mom needs to come here now. So does Damien."

"I know. That's what I told Madsen," Sadie said. "As soon as my paperwork clears, which should probably be Thursday, they're on the next flight. My mom is coming Thursday. I can't believe it."

"And you're okay with this? With Guillermo knowing?" Josh didn't look okay by any stretch of the imagination, but adrenaline still coursed through her veins.

"Yes. Everyone will be here. Everyone will be safe. It feels right for the first time. I can finally tell the world who Guillermo is." She squeezed his hands. "I'm sorry I didn't talk to you first, but I knew if I didn't sign it right away, I'd lose my resolve."

He brushed a stray curl from her forehead. There was so much agony in his expression.

"Please trust me," she whispered.

He took a deep, slow breath. "I do. If you're at peace with this, then…so am I. Where do I sign?"

"Are you sure you want to do this?"

His blue eyes narrowed, although he also smiled. "You're asking me now?"

After adding his signature below hers, he pulled her to his chest. She concentrated on the steady drumming of his heart. It was going to be okay. They could do this. She could do this.

Peter cleared his throat in the hallway. Josh quickly backed away from Sadie. "That was very brave of you, Sadie," Peter said.

For all his law enforcement years, she guessed Peter understood what she'd done better than anyone. She shrugged. "I had to do something." And right now, it felt like she'd just given up her life to protect others. At best, the next several years would revolve around this trial. At worst, she wouldn't live that long.

"I'm still proud of you," Peter said. "We all are. Well…" He looked around her small house. "I hate to ask this of you two with everything else going on, but is there a place for all of us to sleep tonight? We've had a long two days, and I think a good night's sleep will work wonders. We'll work on finding a place to stay tomorrow."

"You guys can stay at my house," Josh said. "It's not far from here."

Peter's brows rose. "You have your own place?" He might as well have heaved a massive sigh of relief, making Sadie grateful she turned down Josh's offer to sleep on her couch.

"Yeah," Josh said. "Two houses down."

"But you won't all fit there," Sadie said. "His house is like this one. Why don't some of you stay here with me and Rocky?"

"Can we?" Katie said, sneaking in behind her dad. Her eyes were still red, but she'd stopped crying. "Can I stay here with Sadie, Dad? Please?"

Josh shot Sadie a strange look, probably thinking what she was. Why had Katie latched onto her so fast?

The rest of Josh's family crowded into the small hallway behind them. The old hallway wasn't built for eight people, yet no one seemed to mind. Maybe with six kids, they were used to small spaces. They waited for their dad's verdict.

"No," Peter said. "We don't want to be in your way."

"Oh, you won't be," Sadie said. "I promise. Josh's place is smaller than this. You'll never fit, even sleeping people on the floors. Honestly." She smiled down at Katie. "I'd love the company."

"What if the boys come with me," Josh said, "and the girls stay here?"

Peter nodded. "Sounds good. Thank you, Sadie." Turning, he said, "Alright, boys. Bring in the girls' stuff, and then Mom and I better head to the grocery store. We're about to eat Josh and Sadie out of house and home."

Adjusting his suit and tie, Josh slipped out of his house before the boys were dressed or done with breakfast. He showered extra early, hoping there would be enough hot water to go around. Mike was notorious for his long showers.

While Josh was happy to have his family safe and sound in Tennessee, it was a logistical nightmare. Even if they combined tables and chairs between the two houses, that gave them four chairs for eight people to eat every meal. And Jake was flying in later that day. Nine people. Yet it would be a day or two before his parents could find a place big enough for them to stay. It was going to be chaos. Josh looked forward to some quiet time with Sadie at church today.

He crossed the street. It was probably a good thing they hadn't met any of their neighbors yet. Most looked like single people with busy lives. Madsen was right. Married people attracted less attention. People at school assumed Josh didn't want to socialize since he was married. They were nice, but most the guys in his program were single, and the girls didn't give Josh a second glance, which was perfect. Still, he was careful leaving his house, going out a back door and slipping through the woods to emerge further down the street, as if he'd just gone on a morning walk. He wasn't sure how he'd ever explain the strange living situation that suddenly got a lot stranger. When Marcela and Damien showed up Thursday, they would have to rent the whole block to keep neighbors from talking.

As he headed for Sadie's, he thought about last night when Sadie had knelt with his family for night prayers. There was something inexplicable about that image, and he was smiling well before he reached her driveway. His smile grew when he spotted her on the front porch, waiting for him.

She wore a blue skirt and feminine pink sweater that accentuated her curves. She was going to church with him again. Not only was she going, but she was excited. Her short, dark, curly hair was pulled back with a single pin, which left her flawless face exposed to the world.

Holding her hands out to the side, she said, "Is the cast too obnoxious? If so, I can wear pants."

"Your neon cast will be the last thing people notice." He skipped up the stairs and kissed her softly. "You look stunning today, Mrs. Peterson. How did you sleep? Or did you with everyone crowding in? I heard Katie ended up sharing a room with you. Tell me that's not true."

Sadie smiled. "Yes. She is so sweet."

"Oh, man. I'm sorry."

"No, seriously. I love her already. She told me all about her friends at school. Did you know there are eighteen boys in her class, but only ten girls, which is entirely unfair because everyone knows boys are more obnoxious than girls, and if anything, they should have more girls than boys so Mrs. Padrosky won't have to scream at them every day?"

Sadie said the whole thing in one hurried breath like Katie always did.

Josh cringed. "I'm really sorry. Katie's a little on the talkative side."

She laughed. "She's wonderful. But the best part was when she stopped to take a breath—or at least, I thought she stopped to take a breath. The next thing I knew, she was snoring softly. She'd fallen asleep mid-sentence."

Josh shook his head with a laugh. "Oh, KitKat. Luckily she sleeps like a rock."

Sadie squeezed his hand. "So did I."

"Really?"

She nodded, practically glowing. "First time in a while actually. It was nice. Very nice."

Josh couldn't believe it. If anything Sadie's nightmares should have been worse after signing the papers, not better. She really was at peace with her decision. On the hike, she finally confessed that she'd started seeing a counselor. Maybe that was helping, too, although that was just as hard to believe considering the only thing the counselor did so far was ask her to write her story down in a new journal. Or maybe having Katie in her room or Rocky or—

"I think my prayers are working," Sadie said.

Josh flushed. Or that. "Your prayers and mine, and probably others, too. Speaking of which, we should go if we're going to make it to church on time."

"Now? Don't you want to wait for your family? The girls are inside getting all prettied up, although Lauren's convinced her hair will never straighten in Tennessee."

"No. My family's going to the English-speaking ward. They'll stick out less there, plus it starts in an hour. They need the extra time. Mike was still in the shower when I left."

"So..." she said slowly, "aren't we going with them?"

Josh leaned against the railing. "I thought you wanted to go back to the Spanish branch."

"Why would I? You didn't understand a word."

"Yeah, but I'm taking Spanish now."

Her dark brow cocked. "You think you've learned enough this week to understand a full service?"

"Maybe not everything," he admitted, "but if I listen closely I bet I can pick up quite a bit. I'll have you know I took two years in high school. It's all coming back to me."

"Really? *De cierto quieres ir a la iglesia española o estás listo para inglés?*" She rattled the whole thing off in one second flat. It flew past him in a blur.

"Uh…what?"

She smiled. "I didn't think so. English it is."

"Wait. You did that on purpose. You talked faster than you normally do."

She laughed. "No, I didn't. Let's wait inside. "

Josh followed her in. He could hear his sisters and mom working out Lauren's hair drama in the bathroom. He sat at the kitchen table as Sadie grabbed a glass of water.

"Are you sure?" he said. "You seemed to like the Spanish Branch. Plus we need to be careful about the two of us in public. If we walk into a new ward with six other people, we won't exactly blend in."

"Like we did last week?"

"Okay, but we already made our grand entrance there. People will be bored of us now."

Sadie held her glass of water, regarding him. Then she did it again. She fired off another rapid sentence in Spanish that flew by so fast he barely translated the first word by the time she was done.

"Um…" Josh cleared his throat. "Could you slow down a smidge?"

Her smile grew. "No. But I'll write it down for you. It will be your homework."

Lauren came in the kitchen, hair in a towel even though she was dressed for church. "She said she thinks it's nice that you're trying, and you're really cute. But honestly, she doesn't deserve you. When are you going to wake up and realize it?"

Josh's mouth dropped. "Lauren!"

Sadie's gaze dropped to the floor. Lauren didn't bother to look at either of them as she pulled cereal from the counter.

"Lauren," Josh said. "That was rude. Apologize right now."

Josh's sister shot him a dark look. "Why should I?"

"Actually," Sadie said softly, "she just translated what I said. It was a perfect translation, too."

"Sadie!" Josh said in exasperation. What was she thinking saying that? That he'd wake up and realize she didn't deserve him? What was all that about?

She ignored him and spoke to his rude sister. "I'm impressed, Lauren. You must have taken a lot of Spanish."

Lauren grabbed the milk. "I'm in AP Spanish right now. Or I should say, I *was* in AP Spanish. Now I'm in nothing."

With the bowl of cereal in hand, she went back to the bathroom.

"Lauren!" Josh called.

She shut the bathroom door.

His mouth worked for a moment before he found words. "I'm sorry, Sadie. She's not usually like that. I don't know what's gotten into her."

"You don't?" Sadie sat next to him. "How about the last three days?"

"That's no excuse."

"Actually, it is. You walked away from your senior year of college for me. Lauren was yanked from her senior year of high school—plus her boyfriend—for all this." She looked around her small, drafty house. "She just slept on a cold floor, and her little sister was nearly kidnapped by a lunatic. Right now, she has no idea if or when she'll ever go home. She didn't even get to say goodbye to her friends," Sadie added pointedly, "so be a good brother and cut her some slack."

Though Josh softened, he was still ticked. "That's still no excuse."

"What's no excuse?" his mom asked, coming out of the bathroom.

"Nothing," Sadie said, shooting Josh a warning glance. "We're ready whenever you are."

"With a miracle, we should be ready soon. Thankfully, Lauren decided on a ponytail. Thank goodness we're only going to an hour of church," she added loud enough to carry down the hallway. "Can you imagine if she had to go to Sunday School and Young Women's looking like that? What an outrage?" She rolled her eyes with a sigh. "I don't know what's gotten into her today."

Josh started to open his mouth, but Sadie kicked him under the table. He bit his tongue even though he didn't want to.

His mom looked out the window with a faraway gaze. "I hope church goes fast today. I can't believe I get to see Jake in just four hours."

Josh's mood darkened to match Lauren's. "Me neither."

"This is the best you can do!" Guillermo shouted.

His lawyer cowered. "I'm working on it, sir, but the trial starts next week, and frankly, the list of charges are coming in steep."

"From some measly engineering student?" Guillermo cried. "He knows nothing!"

"I told you, Mr. Young isn't listed here—at least not yet. But they're gathering evidence, and"—his lawyer winced—"I think they might have you this time."

"You think so?" Guillermo's eyes narrowed. "I will not spend another night in this hell hole. I will be released today. Do you understand?"

"Yes. But you've been saying that for four days."

Guillermo's fist slammed on the table, making his lawyer jump. "Because it is true!"

His lawyer glanced over his shoulder before leaning forward. "May I be frank, sir?"

Depends on how long you want to live. Guillermo kept the thought to himself, knowing it wouldn't bode well considering where he was and who might be listening in. But his whiny little lawyer was grating on his nerves.

If he didn't pull together something fast, everything Guillermo had built in the last fifteen years would be destroyed, dropped charges or not. He smoothed down his orange suit. "Go ahead. Be frank, my friend. Surprise me."

"How do you know this Dubois guy isn't dead?" his lawyer whispered.

"Because I know."

"Are you certain? Your brother made it sound like—"

"My brother is the most incompetent being in all mankind!" Guillermo snapped. First Young slipped through his fingers and now Dubois. If Salvador hadn't been locked away like Guillermo was, awaiting charges on Dubois' murder like Guillermo, this whole mess would have been cleared a week ago, Joshua Young would have been dead a week ago, and that whole debauched mess with Young's family never would have happened. But with Salvador *and* Luis held on murder charges, Guillermo was running out of men able to carry out a simple order. He needed Dubois returned immediately.

"Dubois is alive," Guillermo said as calmly as he could. "He must be. My brother must check again."

"Your brother was not hopeful," his lawyer said.

Guillermo gritted his teeth so hard they nearly cracked, trying to keep from spewing a mile-long list of obscenities. Dubois couldn't be dead. He couldn't be. Because if he was…Guillermo was dead.

"There is one more thing," his lawyer said. "I think…"

Guillermo looked up. "Yes?"

"I think…um…"

"Spit it out!"

His lawyer leaned over the table. "They have a new witness. Someone that I think…might be…"

"What?"

"One of your men," the lawyer said with a wince.

"It cannot be. My men would not dare!" Guillermo snatched the papers from him. The metal cuffs dug into his wrists, but he didn't care. He glanced

241

through the list of charges quickly. Most of it was concerning Dubois' disappearance and 'murder.' There were some conspiracy charges, drug dealing nonsense, and money laundering fluff, but even those were flimsy. Then he stopped. A sentence sounded so close to the truth, it made his blood boil.

"After a severe blow to the head, the victim was stripped down to his under garments and thrown in a wooden box."

Only three people knew about that moment with Dubois: Guillermo, Salvador, and Luis.

"I know who it is." Guillermo's fist formed around the charges, crumpling the papers. "The squealer. I know who it is!"

"Wait! I need those." His lawyer grabbed the papers and smoothed them out.

Guillermo's mind raced faster than he could keep up. He glanced at the clock. Time was running out.

"You listen to me," he hissed, "and you listen close. You need to be ready to pounce on the FBI. I want them taken down for this frivolous murder charge. I want Señor Madsen's head on a chopping block. No, I want his whole department shut down! There will no longer be an FBI office in Kalispell. Do you understand? And I want to see my brother immediately."

"You can't. They've restricted your—"

Guillermo rose to his feet, coming inches from his lawyer's nose. "You tell my brother his time is up!"

His lawyer gulped. "And this new witness?"

Guillermo's eyes narrowed to small slits. "I shall deal with the new witness."

CHAPTER 28

The Knoxville airport couldn't contain the Young family's enthusiasm, which put Deputy Croff and Harrison on edge.

"Can you tone it down a bit?" Harrison snapped outside the security gate.

It was a hard request of Josh's siblings and mom considering they hadn't seen Jake in nearly two years. But they tried. Technically, the two deputies weren't supposed to be there. The paperwork hadn't cleared the Attorney General's office yet, but Deputy Croff called after church to check in. When she heard Josh and Sadie's plan to go to such a public place, she flew through the roof. Josh was fully prepared to stay home with Sadie and let his family pick up Jake alone, but Sadie dug in her heels. She wasn't letting Josh miss out on any possible family event. Not if she could help it.

The guilt thing really had to stop.

Then Deputy Croff and Harrison showed up on their doorstep, insisting they escort them. They didn't have clearance to do so. They were coming as "friends." Armed friends.

Airport security refused to let their entire family go to the gate. Not surprising. But they were allowed two people. Josh was stunned when his parents suggested he be the one to meet Jake. Seemed like he should be the last one to go considering he forced his brother to cut his mission short. But Harrison flashed a badge, and the two of them headed past security. The rest of his family, including Sadie and Deputy Croff, stayed behind in an out-of-the-way spot.

Josh walked through the maze of people with Harrison on his heels.

"He's tall," Josh said. "Probably taller than me now. He has dark hair, but not as dark as mine. And he'll be wearing a suit and tie. Probably the only guy wearing a suit on the plane. Just look for a twenty-year-old who's dressed as a business man. You won't miss him."

By the time they made it to the gate, people were already unloading. Josh checked every face, waiting. Then he spotted him, the guy with the super short hair talking animatedly to the passenger next to him. Jake didn't look upset or angry his mission was cut short. He looked like a missionary. Grinning. Exuberant. Full of life.

Josh shook his head with a smile as he watched his brother try to convert the passenger deplaning next to him. Jake had probably talked the guy's ear off the whole time, going through the Joseph Smith story and committing him to baptism before they ever took off.

Jake looked up and spotted him. "Josh, hey!"

Hefting his heavy bag on his shoulder, Jake ran over to Josh and Harrison. Josh gave him a huge hug, pounding him on the back. Like he'd guessed, his brother was taller than him now but skinny as a reed.

"I can't believe you're here," Josh said.

Jake laughed. "Tell me about it. I couldn't have predicted this to save my life, bro. Tennessee? What the heck?"

Josh sobered quickly. "I know. I'm sorry. About cutting your mission short, and bringing you here, and…" He sighed. "It's such a mess."

All smiles, Jake pounded him on the back again. "No worries. I only lost a few months, and Tennessee is pretty cool from what I've heard. But you better believe I'm expecting the story of a lifetime."

Josh's muscles relaxed. Leave it to crazy Jake to laugh it off. "That I can do. Come on, let's find the family. They're dying to see you."

Josh took his brother's bag and started through the masses. Glancing over his shoulder, he noticed the passenger still following Jake. If that wasn't strange enough, Deputy Harrison and the man were talking like they knew each other. Then it dawned on Josh why.

"They sent you a bodyguard?" Josh asked.

"Sweet, right? Dad's request. Hey, Cliff," Jake said to the older passenger. "This is my big brother, Josh. The guy who started it all."

Josh stopped to shake Cliff's hand. "Thanks for getting my little brother here safely."

"No problem," Deputy Cliff—or whatever he was called—said. Then he went back to talking with Harrison, something about a winter in Colorado.

Josh's brother watched them a moment before elbowing Josh. "I'm telling you," he whispered, "the story of a lifetime, bro."

"How much do you know already?" Josh asked.

"Not much. Mom and Dad called yesterday morning and told me some of what's going on. But they were a little...um..."

"Freaked?" Josh offered.

"Yep. About all I got was, 'Josh met this girl who's great but is in a ton of trouble, and now her ex wants to kill Josh—literally—and he just found our house. Oh, and you have to come home now only you can't go home. What do you think of Tennessee?'"

Josh winced. "Man, I'm really sorry. I had no idea it would ever get this bad. It's just that Sadie's ex is..."

"No worries. Seriously," Jake said. "The Lord works in mysterious ways. Maybe there's someone who needs me in Tennessee. But man, you should have seen President Cassidy's face when he talked to that FBI dude. And I thought my mission president was intimidating. It was sweet. So..." Jake looked around the airport, "where's this girl who stole my brother's heart?"

Josh led him through the crowds until he spotted their family down a level below the elevators. Sadie was talking to Katie. Deputy Croff stood close by scanning the heavy airport traffic for potential threats. Sadie's hair was down again and curled in waves around her face. It was starting to grow out and just reached her shoulders. She wore a dark sweater and slimming jeans.

"Which one is she?" Jake asked.

Josh pointed. "The short one."

Katie looked up and waved frantically. "Jake! Jake!" she shouted.

Deputy Croff shushed her, but the message was delivered. The entire Young family spun around and started waving like mad. Sadie looked up as well and smiled her large, dazzling smile.

Jake whistled softly. "Nice."

"Back off," Josh said, elbowing him. "The rest of the family's bad enough." Josh stepped onto the escalator, but turned to still talk to his brother. "Oh, and you should probably know something. Sadie's not a Mormon."

Jake's smile faded. "Huh?"

"Oh, and..." Josh held up his left hand, flashing his dad's wedding ring.

Jake's eyes popped open. "What?"

Harrison nudged him. "Keep moving. Don't stop. Keep moving."

Jake stepped on the escalator behind Josh. "What the heck is that?" he whispered. "You're married to a non-Mormon?"

"No—and yes, but mostly no. It's a long story. We're not really married, but Sadie's interested in the church. In fact, she's been with me twice and says she wants to join."

Jake smacked his arm. "Dude, I about had a heart attack. Don't do that to me!"

Both of them watched Sadie as they descended the escalator. Sensing she was the subject of conversation, she tucked a curl behind her ear and spoke to Deputy Croff.

"So this is good, right?" Jake said. "The two of you can live happily ever after and all that."

Josh didn't answer immediately. Church had gone well again today—really well. Like the week before, they came late and left early. But there was an unexpected bonus of having his family in Tennessee. Josh and Sadie were no longer the focus. They were just part of the gang, the huge

"Peterson" family who moved in. The English congregation was large enough that few people noticed them anyway.

Sadie had listened quietly through the service while Katie held her hand. Then halfway through the first speaker, Sadie leaned over and whispered, *"I've heard of him."*

"Who?" Josh had asked, embarrassed he hadn't been listening as closely as he should. It was just so strange to be in a church across the country with his family and Sadie. It made it hard to focus—especially with the local missionaries sitting two rows in front of them.

"Alma," Sadie whispered, only she said Ahl-ma, instead of the more popular nasal pronunciation. *"I read about him last night. His name means 'spirit' in Spanish."*

Stunned, Josh whispered back, *"You're in the book of Alma? Did you skip ahead?"*

"No. I'm in the Mosiah part, but it talked about Alma listening to Abinadi, the one who was burned." Again, her pronunciation was A-bi-nah-dee instead of A-bin-a-di, but that's not why Josh stared at her. She only had his difficult-to-read Book of Mormon for ten days and already she was a third of the way through? Most people took years to read it the first time.

When he asked how she was that far, she explained that she read it when she couldn't sleep. *"It's interesting,"* she said with her eyes on the speaker. *"I've never heard any of the stories before, so I'm not sure I understand it, but I like it. It's fascinating."*

She was fascinating. Her face was radiant, and she seemed at peace in a sea of Mormons. Yet through the whole service and ever since, a pit sat in Josh's gut. It was the opposite reaction of what it should be. But it wasn't until she remarked how much she loved the closing hymn that he realized why.

It was too easy.

Church. Scriptures. The whole thing. Josh went on a mission. He'd been a life-long member. He knew conversion was never that easy. There was always a glitch, often big ones. Yet Sadie was Miss Eager Beaver, Miss I-love-it-all!

His brother still watched him.

"Let's hope," Josh said. That she was doing it for herself and not him. That she wanted it for herself, and not because guilt was driving her to it. Josh left her on New Year's because of their religious incompatibility. What if Sadie was trying to prevent him from leaving again? And could he leave her again if things went sour spiritually? He played with the ring on his finger, hating both answers.

The whole airport echoed with cheers of, "Jake! Jake's home!"

Josh's mom ran up the escalator to get to them. She bypassed Josh and threw her arms around Jake. Within seconds, it was a mob of hugs, kisses, and tears.

Harrison and his new buddy, Cliff, tried to get them to tone it down. It was like stopping a buffalo stampede. The only thing they succeeded in doing was herding the family to a far corner of the airport where there was less traffic.

Sadie and Croff stood outside the group, smiling and enjoying the celebration. Josh wandered over and slid his hand in Sadie's.

"Wow," she said. "You and Jake could be twins. It's crazy."

"Yeah. We get that sometimes." Josh listened to his brother comment on how much his younger siblings had grown. Mike insisted on comparing heights, even though he was nowhere near Jake's height.

"It's so crazy to have him home—I mean here," Josh said.

"I'm sure. How mad is he?" Sadie asked.

"He's not. Not at all."

She twisted the strap on her purse. "But you two looked at me, and then Jake yelled something."

"Oh, that?" Josh said. "He's not mad. Trust me. Well, at least not in the way you mean. Just to warn you, Sadie, returned missionaries are an interesting breed. They're dangerous for the first few months. You should probably keep your guard up."

The color drained from her face. "What?"

Josh laughed. "Don't worry. He's the happiest of my family to be in Tennessee. Come on. He's anxious to meet you."

Josh tugged her through the mass of arms and tears. Jake noticed them and broke free.

"So this is Sadie?" Jake said, reaching his hand out with the kind of sly smile that reminded Josh how strikingly beautiful Sadie was. She attracted male attention everywhere she went. He still couldn't figure out how he caught hers.

She smiled warmly. "Hi, Jake. It's so nice to meet you. We almost stopped by and saw you on our drive across the country."

"Really?" Jake said. "Why didn't you?"

Sadie turned and gave Josh a dark glare.

Josh threw his hands up. "Come on, bro. Don't throw me under the bus."

Jake laughed. "I was just teasing, Sadie. Visitors are frowned upon in my mission. But hey, it looks like we got to meet after all. From the little I've heard, it sounds like you and my brother have had an interesting month."

She gave a tired smile. "You have no idea."

CHAPTER 29

Getting dinner on the table was an orchestrated event that involved all eight members of the Young family. Sadie was in awe. They worked in sync as if they had formal training. Josh and Jake were on mashed potato duty. Kathy took the gravy. Peter carved the roast while Lauren whipped up a salad. The three youngest set the table with everything from napkins to ketchup for the roast—an interesting tradition. All with little prodding from the parents.

Sadie did her best to help where she could, grabbing utensils and salt and pepper while secretly falling in love with Josh's family. There was little room for all of them in her tiny kitchen, yet none of the kids tried to shirk their responsibilities.

Katie tripped Drew on his way to the table, Jake and Lauren got in a lettuce fight, and Sadie loved every second. The only thing not in sync was Rocky who kept getting in the way. He loved the crowded family scene as much as she did—maybe more.

The second Katie finished setting the table, she ran over to the piano. Though she'd already played several songs for Sadie earlier in the morning, she started a new one, Bach's "Prelude in G."

"Wow," Sadie said, adding ice to the glasses. "She's good."

Josh winked at her. "You would know. Hey, KitKat," he called, "tone it down so we can hear ourselves think."

"No," Sadie said. "I don't mind. She plays beautifully."

Katie stuck her tongue out at Josh. He shook his head. "You're creating a monster. You know that right? Now KitKat will never leave you alone."

"I don't mind." Sadie always wanted a little sister—any sister. "How did she get that nickname anyway?"

Katie jumped off the piano bench and ran back. "When I was born, Drew couldn't say my name, so he called me KitKat."

Josh's teen brother turned several shades of red. "It wasn't me. If I was going to call you anything, it would have been—"

"Hey!" Peter called. "Don't start. Get drinks for everyone."

"You know, KitKat," Josh said, "*Sadie* is just a nickname, too."

Katie grabbed Sadie's hand, forcing Sadie to set down the ice. "Really? What's your real name?"

"Sarah. Actually, my full name is Sarah Augustina Dawson, which makes my initials…"

"S. A. D." Katie said. "Oh. I get it. Sort of."

Sadie smiled. Katie had Josh's ability to twist her face in confusion. "When I was in first grade," she explained, "some obnoxious boys figured out my initials spelled SAD, so they started calling me Saddy. But my girlfriends came up with Sadie since it's way cuter. Now everyone calls me Sadie, except my mom who calls me Augustina. She's always called me my Spanish name, though." So had Guillermo.

Josh set the mashed potatoes on the table. "Sadie's mom is coming in three days, KitKat, so you'll get to meet her."

"And my brother, Damien, too." Sadie leaned against the counter, heart swelling to overflowing. Soon they would have everyone safe with them.

Katie looked around the small house. "Where will we fit everyone?"

"We'll be living somewhere else by then," Peter said.

Katie's eyes widened, and her mouth formed a huge circle. "Oh! Oh my gosh! Sadie, Sadie!" She tugged on Sadie's shirt. "When you marry Josh, your initials will be S. A. D. Y. That sounds just like Sadie!"

Sadie's face flamed hot.

Not *if* you marry Josh. *When.*

Josh's brows shot up. He locked gazes with Sadie before a grin lit his entire face. The house fell silent as the rest of his family looked back and forth between them. Sadie waited for Josh to say something. His family must think they were crazy for not correcting Katie. *If.* Not *when.* But Josh didn't. His face spoke for him, and he was thrilled by the unexpected coincidence.

Did he even think they were an *if* anymore?

Thankfully, his mom broke the silence. "Come on, kids. Time to eat."

The younger kids headed for the couch and floor, while the rest of them scrunched around Sadie's small table.

Lauren stood behind her mom a moment, as if calculating if she was considered a kid or an adult.

Sadie scooted closer to Josh. "There's room by me, Lauren."

"No, thanks." Lauren grabbed a plate and joined the younger siblings on the floor. It wasn't a complete cold shoulder, but it still stung. At church it had been the same. Lauren didn't like Sadie much—not that Sadie blamed her.

Josh glared at Lauren. Sadie nudged him under the table. It was fine.

As Drew walked past, Jake grabbed him and wrestled him into a head-lock. "Who said you could grow up while I was gone, huh?"

Drew squirmed free. "Dude, don't mess with the hair! The hair!"

Sadie laughed. Drew's hair was buzzed short and incapable of a messy do. She still couldn't believe Jake hadn't seen his family for almost two years. He fit right back into the rhythm of things. And Josh served a mission, too.

After the prayer and in between the chaos of serving everyone, Sadie asked, "What kinds of things did you do on your mission, Jake?"

Jake grabbed the carrots. "Preaching. Teaching. Loving. Learning."

"Oooh," Drew taunted, "Jake turned into a poet."

"Watch it, tall boy," Jake called. "I can still take you down."

"You wish," Drew muttered. He made the mistake of reaching for a roll. Jake grabbed a towel, twisted it up, and snapped it on his thigh. The towel cracked, and Drew jumped back with a yelp.

"Boys!" Kathy cried. "That's enough."

Josh leaned close to Sadie. "Have I apologized yet for my family?"

She laughed. "No. And don't. I love it."

When their mom wasn't looking, Jake tossed the wet towel on Drew's back. Drew jumped around with a glare. "Oh, you're so goin' down."

"You wish."

Jake turned back and adjusted his tie. "Sorry about that, Sadie. What I was going to say was that I spent most of my mission teaching people about Jesus Christ and His restored church on earth."

"Oh." That was the most straight-forward explanation she'd received. "Will you go on a mission, Drew?"

Josh's sixteen-year-old brother froze. His Adam's apple bobbed up and down. "Yeah."

"Me, too," Mike added from the floor.

All four boys. Sadie couldn't believe it. Josh went to Scotland and loved it. His best friend, Sam Jackson, went to Peru and loved it. Jake went to Nebraska and loved it, even though Sadie couldn't think of much lovable about Nebraska, especially for a twenty-year-old guy.

"Where did you go on your mission, Peter?" she asked.

A quick flash of pain crossed his wrinkled face. "Sadly, I didn't make it on a mission. I've regretted it for...well...a very long time."

Kathy rubbed his arm, eyes going soft. "That's why he's determined to see his boys serve."

"I'm sure it's a hard decision," Sadie said. "Some of my friends in high school went on mission trips with their churches. They'd go for a week or two, sometimes a whole summer, but two full years away from"—she wanted to say *this*, but instead said—"your family. Is it worth it?"

"Yes," Josh, Jake, *and* their mom answered at the same time.

Sadie's eyes widened. "You Kathy? You did a mission?"

Kathy smiled. "Girls can be missionaries, too. I served in the Philippines. It's an honor to teach people about Christ. It's humbling to see people who already have so little give up everything for Him."

Sadie ate for a few minutes, taking it all in. Josh. His family. A religion that demanded so much of them and yet made them so happy. Her thoughts strayed to the family portrait that hung on the stone fireplace of Sam's cabin. Though she only knew Sam, his family and their glowing smiles had held her attention for hours. She'd never put a finger on why. Yet Josh's family had the same cohesiveness and... Again, she couldn't put a finger on it. Joy? Light? Nothing sounded right.

She picked up her water and realized Josh was watching her. He wore the same expression he'd worn after church last week. She blushed under his admiring gaze.

Jake elbowed him. "Stop drooling, Joshy boy, and pass the roast."

Sadie's blush deepened as his family laughed.

"Careful what you say there," Josh quipped. "It'll be you soon."

"No way!" Drew called. "That requires Jake finding a girl who can stand to look at his ugly face for more than a second."

Jake whirled around and chucked his roll across the room, smacking Drew on the chest. Kathy cried out in dismay. But as Sadie laughed again, she found the word she'd been looking for:

Peace.

Like her, every person in that room had their entire life thrown into upheaval. Yet they joked and teased each other as if the whole world were at peace. As if they were okay with the horribly inconvenient curve ball life had thrown at them.

The longer Sadie was around Josh and his family, the more she craved their peace.

Josh squeezed her hand. "You're in your own little world again. What are you thinking about?"

She shrugged, not knowing how to explain it.

As they ate, Jake shared stories from his mission. Now that Sadie knew him better, she saw less resemblance between him and Josh. He had the same square jaw, dark hair, and piercing, blue eyes, but his brows were wider, his face thinner, and his build more Kevin-ish. Jake was faster to laugh than Josh and, like Kevin, he rarely didn't have a huge smile on his face. About the only time was when Sadie explained her story. Even then, Jake was quick to tell her it was going to work out and that the Lord would turn it to good somehow if she only put her trust in Him.

Peace again.

When Josh didn't think Sadie was listening, he told Jake to cool it.

Jake sat back and rubbed his stomach. "Good food. Man, I've missed this." Then he looked Sadie directly in the eye. "So, Sadie, when are you getting baptized?"

The room skidded to a halt. Everything froze except the kitchen table, which suddenly jumped, jostling the dishes. Sadie looked at Josh, pretty sure he just kicked his brother under the table.

Jake turned in surprise. "What? I was just asking."

"Don't," Josh said.

Sadie thought about Jake's question. Baptism. Something she hadn't considered before, but it only made sense that she would need to be baptized if she was going to take Josh's religion seriously.

"I don't know," she said. "When can I?"

Josh dropped his fork.

"Well," Jake said, "how many lessons have you had with the missionaries?"

"What?" she asked.

"None," Josh said. For some reason, the muscles in his neck were tensed. "Don't, Jake."

Jake didn't take his eyes off Sadie. "What are you feelings about the Church by now? You've been twice, and it sounds like you're reading the Book of Mormon. What do you think?"

"Jake," Josh growled again.

Sadie wasn't sure why Josh was suddenly upset, but she still answered. "I've liked everything I've heard so far. I still feel like I don't know very much, but the messages have been amazing, and the feeling there is...I don't know. Peaceful. Everything I've learned has been interesting, especially the Book of Mormon. I really like it."

"Enough to take the next step?"

"Jake," Josh said, jumping up. "Can I talk to you for a sec?"

Josh pulled his over-eager, fresh-off-a-mission brother into the hallway. Even then, it wasn't far enough. Feeling Sadie's eyes on their backs, they moved onto the front porch. Then Josh pulled the front door shut.

"What are you doing?" Josh whispered.

Jake had the audacity to look surprised. "What? I was just asking."

"Look, you're not a missionary anymore. Give Sadie some space, alright? She has a lot going on right now. This isn't the time."

"Why? She seems genuinely interested. I was just trying to—"

"I know what you were trying to do." Josh fought to control his temper. His brother meant well. Sort of.

"Okay, fine. I'm sorry. But..." Jake leaned against the railing. "Can I ask you something? You were the only one in there who wasn't okay with the conversation. Sadie was fine. What are you so afraid of?"

"Nothing."

"I'm not buying it. Mom said something earlier, and I think I just caught a glimpse of it. It's like you..." Jake shook his head. "Never mind."

Josh folded his arms. "Like I what?"

"If Sadie's so interested in the Church, why haven't you invited the missionaries over to teach her about it?"

Josh gritted his teeth. His stepmom had cornered him after church. She'd seen Sadie's obvious interest in sacrament meeting, and she—along with everyone else—was anxious to know why Josh wasn't throwing her into the waters of baptism. "You're seriously asking me why I haven't had the missionaries over here?" Josh said.

Jake rolled his eyes. "Come on. You could meet with the missionaries at the church or somewhere else public if you don't want them coming here. So what's the real reason you haven't asked Sadie to take the lessons?"

Josh closed his eyes to consider Jake's question honestly. "Alright. You want to know why? Because right now everything's going great. She's reading the scriptures, going to church, and loving everything. But one wrong step, one wrong push, and she'll get offended. And then what?" Josh held up his left hand. "I'm a little committed here. What happens if she gets scared off? Where does that leave me? I love her, Jake. Deep down love her more than I've loved anyone. What am I supposed to do if she decides the Church isn't for her? Where does that leave us? I just walked away from my whole life for a relationship that still might not work."

Jake's hands flew up. "Hey, I'm sorry. I didn't mean to butt in."

"You didn't, Elder Young?"

"Okay," Jake said with a laugh, "maybe a little, but I've talked to enough investigators to know when they're into it or not. Sadie seems genuinely interested. Besides, you told me she wants to join the Church. I figured that meant she'd already had a few lessons. They're kinda required, you know."

Josh rubbed his temples, fighting off a sudden headache. "I know. She's told me several times she wants to join."

"So…?"

Josh leaned against the railing, taking in their limited view of Knoxville. The night was coming quickly and a cold chill with it. He twisted his wedding ring around and around.

Jake bent down to look at him. "Dude, what are you so scared of?"

"I left her on New Year's because of the difference of religion. What if she's doing all this so I don't leave her again? What if there's no real motivation? What if it doesn't last? What if she hates me later because of it, resents me later, hates herself because of it? What if—"

"She's mom?" Jake cut in. "Seriously? From the little I've seen, Sadie's nothing like Mom. She's never going to do what Mom did. Come on."

Josh looked up at the heavens. Had it really come back to that? Their real mom walked out on their dad because of religion—or at least, that was the reason she screamed—but Josh had already dealt with all that garbage. After New Year's, he talked through everything with his stepmom. Sadie wasn't like his real mom. Not even a little bit. She wasn't.

And yet...what if she was?

The front door opened slowly. Josh turned as Sadie walked out on the porch. He straightened, realizing he'd stormed out of dinner and left her alone with his crazy family.

"Hey, sorry," he said. "I just..."

He stopped. Her cheeks were wet. She was crying.

Panicked, his gaze dropped to the old rickety windows that let in every draft of air. Josh stared at the window panes which were thinner than ice, feeling sick. Sadie had heard every word he'd said.

Jake must have realized the same thing because he started backing up. "I'm sorry, Sadie. I didn't mean to make you uncomfortable."

"*You* didn't," she said calmly, watery gaze pinned on Josh.

Josh felt lower than dust. Everything she heard, his family had heard, too. He wanted to kick himself for the embarrassment he caused her. It looked like she wanted to kick him, too.

"Uh..." Jake said, "I'll leave you two alone."

Sadie grabbed his arm. "Stay, Jake. If you don't mind."

From his expression, he looked like he minded very much. He knew Josh was in trouble and didn't particularly want to stick around for the verbal lashing he was about to get.

Sadie stared Josh down a long moment before turning to his brother. "Jake, would you mind telling me what your real mom did since Josh won't?"

Jake's expression begged Josh for a rescue.

"No," Josh said. "I'll tell you."

He reached for her hand. She folded her arms. A cold breeze blew onto the porch, made all the colder by her glare. He didn't know how to begin, but he tried.

"I told you my mom left because she had issues. Some of the issues were hers...but one of them was with my dad's—our—religion. She joined our church when they were dating because she thought it would make him happy. But a year or so later, she stopped going to church and living all the rules. She started drinking heavily and doing a lot of things he didn't."

Sadie blinked more tears down her olive cheeks. Her only response.

"She resented the rules that separated them," Josh plowed on, "plus the time he spent serving in the Church. She thought it was tearing their marriage apart and..." Josh looked at Jake who looked incredibly sorry for bringing it up. Jake had been too young to remember much about the day she had left, but Josh remembered. He remembered more than he wanted to. "When she walked out, she blamed the Church."

Josh figured his dad was inside listening to every word. His dad could explain the situation much better than Josh, but it was time it came from Josh. Sadie deserved that much.

She gave the tiniest nod. "And you didn't tell me because...?"

"I'm an idiot," he said truthfully.

"Yes. You are."

"Uh..." Jake said, "I think I'll go inside now."

"No, Jake." Sadie wiped her cheeks. "You stay. I'm going for a walk."

Then Josh watched her turn and hobble down the porch steps away from him, her house, and his entire family.

CHAPTER 30

"Sadie!" Josh called. "Wait. Don't go alone. Please! You don't even have a coat."

She waved him back without looking at him. She wanted to say that she just needed some air, but the tears were coming too hard now. The sidewalk blurred in front of her. How many times had she and Josh talked about religion and his mom, and he'd never mentioned why she left? The betrayal cut deeper than the evening chill, especially with everything Sadie was trying to do for him…

She headed for the street, hobbling in her booted foot, reliving those words. *"I just walked away from my whole life for a relationship that might not work."*

"Please!" Josh called. "Take Rocky at least. You shouldn't be alone out there with your leg and Guillermo and…please!"

Guillermo was the last thing on her mind. Or her stupid leg.

It was bad enough to hear all of it as an unwanted eavesdropper, but Josh's entire family was there as she got lambasted by her 'husband.' She was a fool. Josh thought she was such a fool. And the way he talked about what to do if she didn't like his religion, as if he'd leave her. Again! What was that about? She thought they were past that. They'd looked at rings for crying out loud! He pretended to drop to a knee!

She was a complete idiot.

"Jake," she heard Josh beg, "please go with her. I don't think she should be alone."

"No. I'll go," someone else said. Lauren burst out of the front door, pulling on her coat. She ran down the sidewalk and across the street to catch up to Sadie. If it was anyone else, Sadie would have kindly asked them to give her some space, but she was too stunned Lauren wanted to go anywhere with her. Maybe Lauren wanted to make sure Sadie never came back.

Sadie kept hobbling up the street, heading the opposite direction of Josh's house. The sun was setting, and it would be dark soon. Truth be told, she was freezing. The night air bit through her thin sweater.

She folded her arms as she walked, unwilling to speak. Apparently Lauren felt the same way. They went four houses in silence. And then five.

"Josh loves you," Lauren finally said.

Sadie nodded.

"No." Lauren pulled her to a stop. "I mean he totally loves you. I never saw him this happy with Megan. They dated a long time, and he never looked at her like he looks at you. He really, really loves you."

"And?" Sadie said bitterly.

"And I don't know!"

Sadie started walking again, putting her new walking boot to the test. Her ankle was starting to ache, yet she didn't slow down. In another street or two, she'd be lost, yet she couldn't stop. Her thoughts replayed Josh's words over and over again. The anger swirled inside her.

Lauren was huffing to keep up with her. "Sadie, please stop."

Sadie slowed and finally faced Josh's sister.

"I've never heard Josh talk about his mom," Lauren said.

Sadie's brows lowered. "What do you mean?"

"I mean I'm eighteen, and I've never heard Josh talk about his real mom. Jake talks about her, but Jake doesn't remember her. But Josh was there when she walked out. He heard every bit of their final argument, and he's never talked about it with me. I don't think he talks about it with anyone."

"Really?"

Lauren nodded.

If Josh hadn't talked about it with his siblings, why should Sadie expect him to talk about it with her?

"He's just scared," Lauren went on. "You know that, right? He doesn't want to lose you, but he doesn't want to hurt you either. My dad always felt guilty about how unhappy his first wife was in their marriage. He blames himself for her death. He still feels like there was something more he could have done. Josh doesn't want that for you. He wants *you* to be happy."

She contemplated that for a while. He'd never given her reason to think he was acting selfishly, but...

"I just wish..." Sadie stopped, trying to figure out exactly what she wished. "I wish he just trusted me. Why doesn't he? I'm ready to have religion back in my life. I feel like I have this dark hole inside me, and I'm hoping this will fill it. I told him I would be a Mormon with him from the beginning."

Lauren looked at her closely. "Are you sure that's what you want?"

"Yes!"

"So if the two of you broke up and all of us left, you'd go to church next week by yourself?"

That took Sadie back. "I don't know."

"Would you still read the Book of Mormon if you hated Josh?"

"I think so. Maybe." Sadie's shoulders fell. "Maybe not."

"Then Josh is kinda right. It sounds like you're doing it for him—at least partially."

Was she? Sadie loved the peace she felt when she read from his scriptures. She loved the feelings she had in church. But did she love it enough to keep doing it on her own? Would she have done it if Josh didn't love it first?

She wanted to say yes but couldn't. "What's so wrong with me doing it for him? He loves it and I love him. I want him to be happy."

"But that's the problem!" Lauren said. "That's what his mom did, and it didn't last. He wants you to do it for you and no one else. Otherwise, he won't trust it. He can't trust you. Does that make sense?"

Sadie looked at Josh's little sister—his half-sister—finding her logic incredibly mature. "Yes. So what do I do?"

"Find out if this is what *you* want. Jake mentioned the missionary lessons. Missionaries' jobs are to teach people about our church. They'll teach you everything you need to know, and then you can choose if it's something you want for the rest of...well...forever."

Seemed simple enough. "Okay. I'll do it."

She wanted to give Lauren a hug but didn't know if that crossed the line of their newfound truce. She decided to take the chance. She gave her a brief hug. "Thank you, Lauren."

Lauren didn't fight her and actually hugged her back. Another chunk of the hurt broke off.

"And thanks for keeping me company," Sadie said. "I know you don't want to be here—and I don't mean on this street. I mean in Tennessee."

Lauren looked down the windy road with a look of longing. "It's not that I don't want to be here. Okay, it's kinda that. But I didn't even get to say goodbye to anyone. No texts to my friends explaining what happened. No messages. Nothing. I just up and disappeared. Who does that? What will they say?" She frowned heavily. "And now Mom's talking about homeschooling all of us. Homeschool! It's killing me."

Sadie brushed her arm. "I'm so, so sorry, Lauren. I didn't mean to ruin your life."

"You didn't."

"Yes, I did. I ruined your senior year."

"Eh..." Lauren flashed a crooked, adorable smile. "It wasn't all that hot anyway."

Sadie smiled. "Senioritis already? It's barely February."

"I've had Senioritis for a year. I couldn't wait to get out of that place. I guess I should be thanking you."

"Oh, please no!" Sadie cried. "Don't do that."

"Okay." Lauren grinned. "I won't."

Without discussion, they turned around and started back. As they passed the first square house, there was no longer the heavy awkwardness between them.

"You know I don't blame you, right?" Lauren said. "No one in my family does. You need to stop blaming yourself. You didn't know what a creep your boyfriend was until it was too late."

For a second time, Sadie was blown away by Lauren's sweet but simple words. She'd been blunt enough before that Sadie trusted she spoke from the heart now.

"No," Sadie said. "I really didn't."

"And you know Josh seriously loves you, right?"

"Yes. Amazingly." Sadie faced Lauren again. "Do you know that I love him? That I'd never do anything to hurt him?"

"Yeah, but you might want to tell him that."

There it was again. A simple, but obvious truth. Josh was terrified she would hurt him, to walk out like his mom had. She knew she never would—never could—but maybe it was time to let him in on that little secret.

"You're right." Sadie linked arms with her. "So...tell me about this Christopher guy."

Amy turned down the volume on the TV. Just as she thought, someone was knocking on the door. Probably Kevin who never seemed to remember his wallet until he was at the store.

As she opened the door, she was surprised to find two men, both middle-aged, standing there. The taller of the two held a video camera over his shoulder.

"Can I help you?" she asked.

"Are you Mrs. Hancock?" the one without the camera said.

"Yeah."

He extended a hand. "You and I spoke on the phone recently. My name is Ivan Mansino, from the *National Geographic*."

Her eyes zeroed in on the prominent badge he wore around his neck. In plain-as-day letters it said, *National Geographic*. "Oh, yes. I remember you, Ivan. What are you doing in Spokane?" Although she had a pretty good hunch. She bit back a smile. *Be demure, Amy. You don't know Kevin won yet.* Except people with cameras didn't come to doors to tell someone they lost.

"Well," Ivan said, "we have some great news, actually, and we wanted to present it to you and your husband in person. Is Kevin home?"

"No. He left a few minutes ago to grab something from the store."

Ivan turned to the man with a camera. "He's not home. What do you want to do?"

The cameraman shrugged.

"I apologize we didn't call first, Mrs. Hancock," Ivan said. "But the best part is seeing people's reactions. Do you think he'll be along soon?"

Cover photo. Amy could envision the whole thing. Some amazing night shot of Josh snowboarding with Kevin's name sprawled across the cover. "He should only be a few minutes. He just ran to grab a couple of tomatoes." Then again, knowing Kevin, he'd take a half an hour and come back with an armload of junk food. "I'll call him if you'd like."

"No. That's alright. We can wait. Do you mind if we wait for him inside? It's rather cold and, unfortunately," Ivan shot his cameraman a dark look, "Tony broke the heater in our truck."

"Ummm…" Amy wasn't too keen on having two men wait inside with her. Yet the door had only been open a minute and already her arms were frozen. "Sure. Come on in."

She swung the door open wide and walked over to shut off the TV.

Tony dropped the camera from his shoulder while taking in her small apartment. "Nice place," he said.

He was older than her—both of them were. Mid-forties at least. Most forty-year-olds didn't live in a tiny, newlywed-sized apartment. Once she and Kevin paid off some loans, they were going to buy a house. For now, the rental was a place to eat and sleep. Then she realized if the contest prize was decent enough, they might buy a house sooner than she thought.

"Thanks," she said, smiling again. "Can I get you guys something to drink?"

"Nothing for me," Ivan said.

Tony waved his hand, still taking in her home.

She stayed next to the counter, expectantly. She nearly grabbed the phone and called Kevin anyway. He was the slowest shopper ever.

When she couldn't stand it, she said, "So Kevin won the photo contest, didn't he? Or can you guys even tell me?"

Tony stayed by the front door. "Yep. He won alright. He hit the jackpot."

"I knew it!"

"But you know," Ivan said, "we're having a hard time tracking down that Josh guy to finish up the paperwork. A really hard time. And I'm thinking you know where he is, don't you Amy?"

A small shiver ran down her spine, though she wasn't sure why. "Oh. I thought that got cleared up. Didn't you talk to Josh's family?"

Ivan took another step toward her. "I spoke with his little sister, Katie. She's a cute one with all that blonde hair. But she couldn't seem to remember where Josh was either. Isn't that interesting?" His countenance darkened to a sneer. "Nobody knows where Josh disappeared to? Not his little sister. Not his best friend's wife. And now his whole family had disappeared. Not a soul knows where he is. Don't you find that interesting, Amy?"

Her throat clogged. All niceties had vanished. Ivan was way too interested in Josh. In Josh's family. She didn't even know the Youngs had disappeared. Why would they?

Unless…

Answers whirled in her mind, each worse than before. Her stomach dropped.

Oh, no!

Amy's heart pounded in her chest.

Another step and Ivan was within arm's reach. Her mind screamed at her to run, but the only door to the outside was blocked by Tony, a tall, muscular man built like a football player. She backed up and ran into the counter, and then she couldn't back up farther.

Call the FBI. Call the FBI.

She didn't know their number, but she knew 911.

"You know," she squeaked, reaching in her pocket for her phone, "I think I'll call Kevin. See what's taking him so—"

Ivan snatched her phone and hurled it across the room. It smashed against the wall, breaking into several pieces. "I don't think that's necessary," he said. "Kevin's having a grand old time at the store. Isn't he, Tony?"

Tony held up his own phone. On the small screen, Amy saw Kevin standing in an aisle of Safeway, holding a bag of Doritos under his arm while he browsed the liquor aisle.

"He's busy deciding which bottle of wine he should buy for an evening with his beautiful wife."

Amy stared at the small screen. *Kevin!* Her breaths came in short bursts.

Ivan leaned close enough Amy could smell his sour breath. "I think you know where Kevin's buddy, Josh, is," he whispered. "In fact, I think you want to tell me. So I'll make this easy on you." He pulled out a long, shiny knife. Amy felt her knees give. Had she not been pressed up against the counter, she would have fallen. He ran his finger along the blade as if to test its sharpness. "I'm going to ask you a question, and you're going to answer. The truth this time. Are you ready?"

She couldn't nod. She was paralyzed.

When he spoke, each word came out like a sentence, slow and unmistakable. "Where. Is. Josh?"

"BYU," she choked. "He's at BYU!"

Ivan shook his head. "And I thought you were going to make this easy." His knife rose.

"Wait!" she screamed. "Don't hurt me. I don't know where Josh is. I promise. He met this girl who was in some trouble. He took off, but nobody knows where. I don't think his family knows—or maybe they do now. I didn't even know his family was gone. I promise."

Ivan's eyes narrowed. "Why do I feel like you're still lying?"

A sob bubbled in her throat. Her limbs were giving out. "I'm not. I don't know anything. Please don't hurt me. I don't know anything!"

"Funny. That's what Josh's little sister said, too, but I don't believe any of you. I think you all know where he is, but you're still protecting him." Amy watched the knife rise again, coming closer than before. It rose to her neck. She didn't dare swallow for fear she'd meet the blade. "Tell me," he whispered, "why would you protect Josh more than yourself?"

The crying took over. Sobs erupted from deep inside her. Knife or not, she couldn't hold off the tears. "I don't know. I don't know! Please stop!"

"Then maybe his best buddy, Kevin, knows. What do you think, Tony?" Ivan asked over his shoulder. "Should we ask Kevin instead?"

Tony held up the screen again. Kevin was walking toward his car, completely unaware someone was following him with a camera. "Don't get your hopes up, Mrs. Hancock," Tony said. "His car isn't going to start. His battery is dead. He'll need to jump start it. That is…if he lives that long."

"Mississippi!" Amy yelled, pulling the state from out of nowhere. "I think they're in Mississippi. But that's all I know, I swear. That's all I know. Please don't hurt Kevin!"

Ivan smiled a bone-chilling smile. "There now. That wasn't so hard, was it?"

He moved fast. The knife slashed, and pain sliced across her cheek. Then he came nose to nose with her. "Next time I ask you a question, I expect your best answer the first time, Mrs. Hancock. Understand?"

Amy held her cheek, feeling warm blood mix with her unstoppable tears. She tried to nod.

"Good." Ivan stood back. "We'll check out this Mississippi thing, and then we'll be back. But here's your warning. Actually, I'll give you three. First, don't tell anyone we were here, not even your adoring husband. Second, don't tell anyone we're coming back. Tony is staying behind to keep an eye on things here, so resist the urge to break those two warnings, because we have eyes and ears everywhere. We'll know if you betray us." He pointed to the screen with Kevin to reiterate his message. "And thirdly, if Tony sees you ignore the first two warnings, we'll slice more than just your cheek. We'll take out your husband, your widowed mother, and your two little brothers. Do you understand, precious Amy?"

Her legs couldn't hold her up anymore. She sank to the floor.

Ivan crouched next to her with a dark smile. "I thought so. In case your husband asks, you fell and cut your cheek. He'll be home in twenty minutes."

Ivan and Tony headed for the door, but before they left, Ivan had one last thing to say. "For your sake and your family's, I hope Josh is in Mississippi. If not, well, you can guess. See you soon, Mrs. Hancock."

CHAPTER 31

Josh sat by the window.

It was dark out and his blood pressure was through the roof. Sadie and Lauren hadn't returned. Anything could have happened out there. It took every ounce of willpower to give Sadie the space she wanted. For all he knew, she wasn't coming back.

Then he spotted them walking up the street.

He was tempted to meet them halfway, but his stepmom gave him a warning look. She'd lectured him for ten minutes, making him feel worse than he already did. She reminded him of his answered prayer before, the one that made him go back to Sadie after New Year's.

"You were at peace that day," she had said. *"You were certain that you and Sadie would be united in faith someday. Why did you forget that answer? Where is your faith, Josh?"*

He went from two inches tall to one.

Then she chewed him out for not being upfront with Sadie about his real mom and his concerns about Sadie's spiritual motivations. Easy for her to say. Her eternal bliss wasn't at stake.

As soon as Lauren and Sadie walked up the sidewalk, his parents and Jake pretended to scan through Jake's mission pictures on his camera. The other kids were in the bedroom playing cards, trying to give Josh and Sadie some space. Some, but not all. Josh didn't know what to expect from Sadie. He especially didn't want an audience for it. They had enough audiences for one night—for a lifetime.

Then he noticed something odd. Lauren and Sadie were laughing. And for some reason, they were linked at the elbows. Considering Lauren hated Sadie before they left, Josh was even more concerned.

When the door opened, the house went quiet. Lauren and Sadie's laughter died down to nothing.

Josh crossed the room to Sadie, but he stopped just short. "Sadie. I'm sorry. I'm an idiot. I was rude and inconsiderate and—"

She hobbled the last few feet, limping more than usual from her long walk. Her arms wound around his waist, and she buried her head in his chest. "I am, too."

Josh breathed in her rose-scented hair. He was lucky she was a forgiving woman.

"Hold it right there," Lauren said. "Before you two get all comfy, there's a stipulation."

"Lauren," Kathy said. "Stay out of it. This is none of your—"

Lauren held up a hand. "Here's the deal, Josh. Sadie would like to take the missionary lessons. I explained to her what they are, and she's interested. But you're out."

"Excuse me?" Josh said.

"You're not invited. You can't go to the lessons," Lauren said. "You can't ask Sadie about the lessons. You can't even think about the lessons. If she has any questions, she'll ask one of us. You're out."

Sadie's face stayed buried in his chest, refusing to look up at him. She wanted to take the missionary lessons? Without him? Josh looked from person to person. His parents looked as stunned as he did, but Jake nodded.

"It's probably for the best," Jake said. "It's the only way you two won't drive each other crazy while Sadie figures things out."

Josh didn't like it. Not one bit. But Sadie lifted her head and looked up at him with those large, dark eyes.

271

"Is that okay?" she asked.

He stroked her soft cheek. "Are you sure this isn't just one of Lauren's crazy ideas?"

"No. I think it's the only way I can find out if this is what I want."

"You think?" Lauren said. "It *is* the only way. Got it, Josh?"

Josh ignored his gutsy little sister. He continued to look into Sadie's eyes. She wanted him to have some faith in her. Faith. The thing he lacked.

If she could take a leap of faith, then so could he.

He forced himself to smile. "Got it."

The missionaries came every day for the next few days. They came while Josh was at school so he didn't completely obsess about it. Lauren kept reminding him that he couldn't think about it. Honestly, he couldn't stop thinking about it. But he prayed for faith and patience. By the third appointment, he was finally at peace with the whole thing and able to focus on school again.

Sort of.

His parents found a furnished house to rent a few streets over, which meant the missionaries could meet with Sadie at their place instead of hers. Really, it was as if God orchestrated everything for such a need. And maybe He had.

Josh probably would have abandoned his house and moved into his parents' place, except he wasn't sure how long his family was staying in Tennessee. Josh wasn't even sure how long he was staying in Tennessee. But his and Sadie's houses were paid for on the government's dime. His parents were on their own. However, Jake decided to stay with Josh, becoming his new roommate. Josh loved the company. After his and Jake's missions—not to mention moving away for college—it felt like they hadn't seen each other much in the past six years.

Lauren begged to move in with Sadie. Wisely his parents said, "Not a chance in the world."

Besides the fact that Lauren was too young, obnoxious, and not Sadie's relative, Marcela and Damien were flying to Knoxville tomorrow. Sadie would have roommates of her own within a day.

Actually, Josh wasn't completely sure on Marcela and Damien. Agent Madsen hadn't called to confirm the flight plans. He hadn't called them about anything since Sadie signed the papers. Those papers were supposed to have cleared the Attorney General's office already, and yet Madsen had been quiet.

Sadie called him earlier that day. If they were picking up Marcela from the airport tomorrow, they needed to know when. Madsen hadn't answered. But hopefully he called while Josh was at school.

Josh slung his backpack over his shoulder and punched the code for Sadie's alarm. Rocky barked on the other side of the door, eagerly awaiting him.

It still felt strange to walk into Sadie's house unannounced. He always knocked before opening the door—discreetly in case the neighbors were watching.

Josh spotted her in the corner at the piano. She was hunched over some papers, manuscript paper from the looks of it. He smiled. He loved it when she got in composing moods. Not only that, but she sat crossed-legged now that her cast was gone. She must have charmed that doctor something fierce to get it off a week early. She wore a brace on her ankle, but that was it. Smile growing, he scratched Rocky behind the ears and joined her.

She finally looked up. "Hey," she said. "I didn't hear you come in. How was your day?"

"Fine. Any word from Madsen?"

She frowned. "No. I don't know why he hasn't called me back. I'll call again in a little bit."

Josh sat next to her on the piano bench and picked up the papers. "What are you working on?"

"Oh, I don't know. Nothing great. Just passing the time. How was your test?"

He squinted to make out her scribbled notes. Reaching up, he tried a few on the piano. It sounded awful. Then he realized her song wasn't in the simple key of C. A bunch of flats were penciled in on the left. He tried a few more notes—the right ones that time—and it sounded much better.

"I think I bombed the test," he said.

"What? But we studied for three hours! You should have aced it."

"Maybe you shouldn't have dozed off there at the end." Not that he minded. Watching Sadie sleep brought back fond memories. *La Bella Durmiente.* "I only got a 96%."

She elbowed him. "That's bombing it for you?"

He smiled. "Thanks for helping me study, babe."

She jerked back and looked at him with wide eyes.

"What?"

"Babe?" she questioned.

His neck grew warm. He hadn't realized he'd called her that. Kevin called Amy that all the time. "Sorry. Should I not call you that?"

"Depends. Did you call Megan that?"

"No."

"Have you called any girl that before?"

"No. Why? Did Guillermo call you that?"

He didn't realize his mistake until the words were out of his mouth. But the pained, blank stare didn't surface. In fact, her dark eyes lit up with a smile. "Nope. That's a first for me. I think that's why it caught me off guard." She laid her head on his shoulder. "Babe it is."

He tried a little bit more of her song before he realized what it was. "Is this an arrangement of 'I Stand All Amazed'?"

She tried to grab the papers from him. He held tight. There were a lot of extra notes, a counter melody, plus a flowing accompaniment filled with triplets, if he was reading the scribbles correctly.

She finally snatched the papers from him and cradled them close to her body. "Yes. I couldn't get that song out of my head this morning."

"Don't be sorry. It's one of my favorite hymns. Will you play it for me?"

"No! It's nothing right now. Seriously. I'm just goofing around."

"Well, when you finish your arrangement, you have to play it for me."

She glared at him. "As I recall, you still owe me a song first."

"Oh. Yeah."

She slid off the bench and stood next to him.

"Now?"

She rolled her eyes. "Don't even think about getting out of it again. You've owed me this for a *long* time."

He thought about the New Year's Eve party when Sadie sneaked in to eavesdrop on a very private jam session. She'd been stunning back then in her pulled-up hair and black evening gown. She was stunning now in jeans and a baggy sweatshirt. He'd broken his promise to her that day. He really did owe her this.

His hands hovered over the notes a moment before he had one last thought. "I'll play on one condition." He patted the bench. "You have to sit by me."

"Why?"

He didn't answer but motioned for her to sit on the right side where she wouldn't get hurt. She slid onto the bench and gave him plenty of room as he started "Prelude in C-sharp minor" by his all-time favorite composer, Sergei Rachmaninoff.

He started off well enough. He only botched a few of the monstrous chords. But having Sadie next to him was too big of a distraction. And really, Rachmaninoff was for times when he was mad or frustrated. It was hard to take the sullen song seriously when he was in a good mood. He skipped the middle section completely.

When he got to the huge chords at the end, rather than knocking Sadie off the bench, he put his arm around her tiny waist and tried to reach the upper chords from the other side. That got both of them laughing hard enough he couldn't finish. Nor did he try.

He had an unrealized desire over a month old. Hands leaving the keys, he reached up to cradle her soft face.

"What are you doing?" she said, eyes wide. "Your song isn't done."

That song was long forgotten. In its place was New Year's Eve, a dark dining hall, a black gown, and the softest lips known to man. Josh leaned close and kissed those irresistible lips, losing himself in the reality that she'd chosen him. That she was still choosing him. When he broke off the kiss, his forehead fell against hers, but his eyes remained closed. He continued to stroke her cheeks, savoring the moment.

"Do you know how long I've wanted to do that?" he whispered.

"You kiss me all the time," she whispered back.

He laughed. "You know what I mean. Since that first time I sat next to you on the piano bench, I knew…" He breathed in the scent of her. "I mean, that's when I first knew that…"

"Yeah," she said with a smile. "Me, too."

His finger trailed down to her chin, and he pulled her in for a longer, softer kiss.

For the second time, the piano bench tempted him to say things that would move the relationship forward faster than allowed. But he found a little self-restraint and sat back.

"I almost forgot," he said. "You remember the guy I was telling you about in my Spanish class? He had four extra tickets to tonight's basketball game." He pulled the tickets from his back pocket. "It's against Memphis, so it's sure to be a good one. Want to go?"

She took the tickets. "Definitely. Who are the other two for? Croff and Harrison?"

"No." Deputy Croff stopped by yesterday to check on things. She was as antsy as them for the paperwork to clear but it probably wouldn't by tomorrow. At least Croff was checking in. Josh was still bugged Madsen hadn't called back. What if there had been a real emergency? He shook it off.

"I'm not sure," he said. "It'll be a bloodbath if we tell my siblings we only have two extra tickets to a college basketball game—or any basketball game. We can either get more tickets for the rest of them, or we could just take my parents and make it a double date. What do you think?"

"Double date?" She paled slightly. "As in…a date?"

So she figured it out on her own. Grinning, he said, "Why, yes. That would be considered a date. Number four if I've counted right. That makes it an easy decision for me. Double date it is."

"But your brothers will kill you if we go without them—Drew and Jake especially."

"They'll survive."

"Josh…"

His grin widened.

"What if…" She twisted a corner of her sweatshirt. "What if I count it as a double-date, but we take your whole family?"

"Really? Date number four?"

She lowered her lashes. "Yes."

He stared at her. She didn't change the subject. She didn't run away. In fact, she looked up and locked eyes with him, practically inviting him to have *the* talk. Date number four.

He jumped off the bench. "If that's the case, I better go home and change. I have a hot date tonight."

Rocky jumped up, too, but Sadie grabbed Josh's hand. "Wait. There's one more thing."

"Yeah?"

"I know I'm not supposed to talk about the missionary lessons with you, but I have a question I hope you can answer."

"Yeah?"

Her smile faded, and he sensed it was something serious. Not necessarily good, from the looks of things. He sat next to her again slowly. The look on her face made his muscles tense. This wouldn't be an easy question.

"Tell me what you think about Joseph Smith," she said.

"Okay." He did his best to say it straight without editing or glossing over anything. Joseph Smith's story was an incredible one, filled with heavenly visits from the Savior, God the Father, and many ancient prophets. All was required to restore Christ's church in its entirety back to the earth, and Josh believed every bit of it. He loved and revered the prophet Joseph Smith. But Sadie stared at her hands as he spoke, making him horribly frightened that she didn't. Joseph Smith concerns were common. Joseph Smith concerns were detrimental.

When he finished and she still said nothing, he took her hand. "What do *you* think of Joseph Smith?"

"The missionaries told me his story again yesterday, and something struck me."

Josh suddenly understood Jake's veiled comment before bed last night. Jake said something about an awkward moment between Sadie and one of the elders. When Josh questioned him about it, Jake clamped his mouth shut. Lauren's orders.

"Yeah?" Josh asked, feeling himself break out in a sweat.

When Sadie looked up, her eyes were shining. "Have you ever had something hit close to home?"

"Yeah."

"Well, when they told me Joseph's story, it hit me. If God and Jesus cared about a simple farm kid like him, if they loved him and knew his name and came all the way to earth just to answer his little prayer, maybe they love me, too." Her shoulders lifted. "I'm not sure how to explain it. The missionaries have been teaching me to pray, and they asked me to pray about something specific. And I did. And it hit me. I think...I think that maybe God loves me." She shook her head. "Not just loves me, because He has to love me since He's God and all. But I think He knows me, too, and maybe even likes me. I swear I'll be thinking something, or I'll be worried about something, and the next minute I'll hear something or read something, and it's like He's talking directly to me."

"Yeah?" Josh had to remind himself to breathe.

"Like when I heard this song," she said, picking up her arrangement again. "I don't know how to describe it, and I don't know what I'm trying to say here. I don't even know if I'm making sense."

She was. She completely was. He wanted to jump ahead of her words but didn't, scared that if he guessed wrong, it would break him. Lauren was right to keep him away. He was a mess. So he stared straight ahead at the piano, waiting, and praying a silent, desperate prayer of his own.

She sighed and finally nudged him. "As I understand it, you're still an elder, right?"

"Yeah."

"Which means you have the priesthood?"

"Yeah."

She smacked his leg. "Would you stop saying that? You're making me nervous."

"Well, maybe there's a reason we aren't supposed to talk about this." He wiped his sweaty hands on his jeans.

For some reason, that only made her laugh. Not a very nice thing to do when he was stressed beyond all reason. But she sobered quickly and took his hands in hers—his sweaty hands. She traced the lines in his skin and said the words he never thought he'd hear.

"If we don't talk about it, how can I ask you to baptize me?"

Josh stared at her, pretty sure he stopped breathing. "You're sure?" he whispered. "I mean, you're absolutely 100% sure this is what you want?"

Her eyes shone. "Yeah."

CHAPTER 32

"Can I break the news to Elder Farron tomorrow?" Lauren asked as they walked into the basketball game.

"You just want an excuse to talk to Elder Farron," Sadie teased. "I know you think he's cute."

Lauren didn't even bother denying it. It hadn't taken Sadie long to realize Lauren had an ulterior motive for sitting in on Sadie's lessons. Poor Christopher.

"How soon will you get baptized?" Lauren asked.

"Soon, I hope. We'll ask Elder Farron tomorrow."

Lauren grinned again, and Sadie shook her head.

Josh wasn't able to get more seats by the original four, so they gave up their good seats to sit with his family in the nosebleeds.

Sadie knew Josh was a sports nut and figured with the way the Young boys were built—tall and lean—they might all be into basketball. She just never guessed how much. They were obsessed. Nuts. Out of control. All of them. Even Josh's normally-quiet dad got into the game. Every play was analyzed to the hilt. The decent shots had all five boys—plus Lauren who was just as crazy—on their feet, high-fiving, fist pumping, and roaring their approval. They weren't even UT fans—or more accurately, they weren't UT fans until four hours ago. Mike and Lauren scrounged up enough orange clothing to blend right in with the crowd.

After nearly getting trampled when a UT player was fouled, Sadie decided it was safer to sit somewhere else. She switched seats with Lauren and sat next to Katie and Josh's mom. The three of them somewhat followed the game after that, but mostly they laughed at the others, stuffed themselves with nachos, and chatted about everything non-basketball.

With a minute to go in the first half, Katie nudged Sadie. "Is that your phone?"

"No. I don't have a phone. Oh, wait. Yes, I do. I've just never heard it ring before." Sadie reached into her purse, realizing Madsen was calling her back. Finally.

"Hi, Agent Madsen," she said.

One of the UT players made a three-point shot, tying the game. The crowd went wild, and Sadie missed his reply. She plugged an ear. "Sorry. What was that?"

"Where are you?" Madsen shouted.

"I'm at a basketball game. Sorry. It's a little loud."

"Why aren't you home?"

"I will be in a little while. I just called you earlier to ask what the plan is with my mom."

"The plan is that you need to get home," he yelled. "Now! I'll speak to you then."

"No, wait," she said. "I'll go somewhere quiet so I can hear."

Josh leaned forward to look at her from down the row. She rolled her eyes to let him know it was typical Madsen drama. The guy never did things the easy way.

She started for the aisle, stepping over Katie to head for the cement stairs. That close to the half and people were crowding the stairs to head for the concession stands. She made little progress. Balancing on her good foot, she waited for a group of students to pass.

"When are my mom and Damien coming tomorrow?" she asked.

"They aren't," Madsen said.

"What?" she cried. "You promised. That was the deal."

"Things have changed, Miss Dawson. We have a problem. A big problem."

Her stomach clenched. She knew it. When she hadn't heard from Madsen, deep down she knew something was wrong. She turned and caught Josh's eye. He started climbing over his brothers to get to her.

"What happened?" she asked Madsen.

Josh caught up to her. "What's going on?" he whispered.

She covered the phone, feeling the heat build behind her eyelids. She signed those papers with an understanding that her mom and Damien would come to Tennessee. She'd been counting the days, and now Madsen was backing out. "They're not coming."

The look on Josh's face said what she felt. "Tell him no way," Josh said. "He promised you—"

"Miss Dawson!" Madsen shouted, trying to get her attention again. "Tell Mr. Young that both of you need to get home immediately. As in right now! I will talk to you then. I'll be waiting in your driveway."

Sadie felt every muscle in her body freeze. "You're at my house? In Tennessee?"

"Yes. You have ten minutes. Drive fast."

There were three cars parked in front of Sadie's house when Sadie and Josh drove up. Josh's parents stayed behind with the kids, not because they didn't want to come, but because they didn't want the entourage to follow.

Sadie couldn't think of a single good reason Madsen would come to Tennessee. Her stomach couldn't either and was tied in knots the whole drive home. Josh said little, and so did she. There was no point speculating what devastating thing had happened next.

As they pulled up, one of the car doors opened, and Agent Madsen stepped out. The glare he gave them caused a chill down Sadie's spine, even from twenty feet away. She held onto her anger and let it carry her right up to him.

"Why are you here?" she asked. "Where is my mom?"

Madsen looked around. "Why aren't deputies Croff and Harrison with you?"

"Their temporary permits expired," Sadie said. "They haven't been here since—"

"You signed the papers!" Madsen shouted.

"Yeah, but—"

"Never mind," he said, cutting her off again. "Get inside. Now!"

Three other agents followed them in. Josh flipped on the lights and grabbed Rocky who was going nuts with all the new people. Josh shut the dog in the back bedroom and then sat by Sadie on the checkered couch.

Madsen didn't sit, though. He pulled out his phone and started yelling into it. "Who gave the orders to release the deputies from 24/7 duty? I want that person fired. For now, your two deputies better be in this house in five minutes, do you understand?" He listened a moment, fuming. "I don't care about formalities! The situation has changed. Get them here now!"

Sadie's ribs started to constrict. Changing situations was always a bad thing. She tried to guess what it could be until she came to the most devastating possibility. What if Guillermo's men went after her mom like they'd gone after Katie? A wave of nausea hit her strong and hard. She pinched her eyes shut, waiting for it to pass. It didn't.

Mamá!

Madsen shoved his phone in the holster and sat across from them. The last two agents stayed by the door, guarding it. The air in the room was heavy with tension.

"You look well, Miss Dawson," Madsen started. "I see you got your cast off."

"Spare the small talk," she snapped. "Why are you here? Where is my mom?"

"Your mom is fine."

"Then why are you here?" Josh asked.

"I have some good news and some bad news."

"Bad news first," Sadie said, wondering why he always made things difficult.

Madsen raised an eyebrow. He didn't like to be ordered around. He never did. "The *good* news is…my partner, Special Agent Stephen Dubois, is alive."

Sadie blinked slowly. "What?" That was the last thing she expected.

Madsen nodded. "We found him two days ago."

"How? Why?" Josh asked. "Where did you find him?"

"We're not exactly sure how it happened. He has no recollection beyond patrolling Vasquez's cabin the night you heard those shots, Miss Dawson. The next thing he remembers is waking up in a prison in Morocco. He's been there ever since, trying to convince the warden to release him. He arrived in the States yesterday."

Sadie's throat burned. "He's alive?"

"Yes."

"Injured?" Her voice was losing power, but she had to know.

"A little worse for the wear," Madsen said, "but nothing that can't be fixed."

She breathed slowly, in and out, trying to keep the flood of tears from erupting. Dubois was alive. "Can I see him?" she whispered.

Madsen's prematurely graying eyebrows furrowed. "Why? I thought you hated him."

She had. Back on Christmas, Madsen and Dubois barged into her room at the ski lodge demanding she spy on Guillermo. When she refused, Dubois slipped a listening device in her purse that Guillermo later found and used as a reason to attack her. After the cabin, Dubois spent the next week following her and leaving messages on her phone every day. He was a pushy, arrogant, overbearing agent—even worse than Madsen—and she couldn't stand him. But…that was before she thought Guillermo had killed him. That was before he had surfaced in her nightmares over and over again, begging to be saved.

"We didn't kill anyone," Luis whispered from her memories. *"It was just a test. And guess what? You failed!"*

She had never been so thrilled to be wrong.

"I just need to see him," she said. "To make sure he's okay."

"Perhaps in time," Madsen said. "But right now he's supposed to take time off to be with his family—although he's still insisting on working. He's hell-bent on nailing Guillermo Vasquez. He can't remember how, but he's sure Vasquez is behind his kidnapping. I finally had to order him to go home last night, but he was in the office first thing, ready to work. He's furious."

"Understandably," Sadie said. "I can't imagine what his wife and kids have been through, or what he's been through." Nor could she imagine why Guillermo shipped the agent to Africa instead of killing him, but none of that mattered. "You must be so happy. Your partner is back. Isn't this wonderful?"

She turned to Josh. Josh's face was white, his entire body rigid next to her. "What's the bad news?" Josh asked.

Madsen's mouth opened and then clamped shut. He looked around her small house. "Why aren't your deputies here yet? The second you signed the papers, they were supposed to be brought back in."

"They were waiting for them to clear the Attorney General's office," Sadie said.

He swore loudly. "I don't care! Where are they?"

"Agent!" Josh shouted. "What is the bad news?"

Madsen's gaze locked on Sadie.

Josh shot to his feet and started pacing. "This can't be happening. Not again. I can't believe this is happening again! Will it never end?"

What? Sadie wanted to ask. The word didn't pass her lips because her lungs no longer had air. The obvious answer shouted in her mind, but it couldn't be true. Madsen wouldn't let it be true.

She watched Josh pace, feeling her world grow smaller and smaller. The distance between Tennessee and Montana suddenly shrank by 2,200 miles. Madsen was here. It couldn't be true. It couldn't.

"Madsen?" she whispered.

The agent's hands came together in a tight, white-knuckled grasp. "Guillermo Vasquez was just released from prison."

CHAPTER 33

Josh folded his arms tightly to keep from punching something. Guillermo was free.

"Why?" Josh said. "Why!"

"My partner is alive," Madsen said, "which means Vasquez couldn't have killed him. His lawyers pounced as if they were expecting Dubois to show up exactly when he did. The charges were dropped and Vasquez was freed before I knew what happened. I'm not happy about it either."

"Not happy?" Josh repeated. "Not happy! Does he know she's alive?"

Sadie stared down at the brown shag carpet, face devoid of all emotion. She didn't blink. She didn't move.

"I…don't think so." Madsen might have said the words, but he hesitated long enough, Josh felt sick.

Guillermo was free. Free and possibly knew Sadie was alive.

"That's why I'm here, Miss Dawson," Madsen said. "We have to strike now before Vasquez disappears or comes looking for you. Or both. It's time for you to press charges for everything he did to you. Christmas Day. Assaulting you in the car. Burning down the cabin. I have to get him on your attempted murder charges, and it has to be right now. It's the only way."

Josh whirled around. "The only way? What about everything else? Drug trafficking, conspiracy, bribing government officials?"

"It's…complicated."

Sadie still hadn't looked up. She still hadn't blinked. She stared beyond the shag carpet, retreating to the dark place in her mind. Not only did Madsen want her to testify against her ex, but now she was supposed to be the one to press charges?

Josh's mouth moved long before he could find the words. "Are you crazy? The guy is a drug lord, a crime boss with a list a mile long of prosecutable things, and the only way you can get him is with *her*?"

Madsen stood, coming nose to nose with Josh. "It's the only way I can get him because anytime I have evidence," Madsen seethed, "it's wiped out. He destroys any leads I get. I've lost all credibility, Mr. Young. My job is in jeopardy."

That took Josh back. "Your job? Why?"

Madsen looked sick himself. "I received a call from FBI headquarters this afternoon. Guillermo is suing the FBI for malicious prosecution and slander. He's been out of prison for a day—less than a day!—and already he's swarming like a vulture. If I don't get this sorted out immediately, I won't be around to finish the job. Guillermo will never be charged for anything."

"He's suing the FBI?" Josh asked. He didn't even know that was possible.

Madsen's lips tightened in a thin line.

"What about Luis?" Sadie said softly.

Josh nodded vigorously. "That's right. You have Luis Ortiz on board. Why can't you get him to rat out Guillermo? He knows more than Sadie."

Madsen's eyes twitched with something. Pain. Frustration. Josh couldn't tell. Madsen motioned to the couch. "You might want to sit again, Mr. Young."

Josh's stomach dropped. "Why?"

"There's one more piece of bad news."

What was worse than Sadie's psychotic murdering ex walking free? Already she was shutting down. So was Josh. He dropped on the couch next to her. He grabbed her hand with both of his and waited for the next hit.

"I'm going to be completely upfront and honest with you," Madsen said. He blew out his breath before continuing. "Luis Ortiz—or Mr. Ugly as you call him…"

"Yes?" Josh said, nerves strung tight.

Madsen's jaw clenched. "Mr. Ortiz was shot and killed this morning."

Josh couldn't move. For a full minute, there was no sound was in the house.

"A car pulled up next to him at a stoplight," Madsen went on. "He was shot through the head. His deputy was wounded, but not killed. Thankfully."

Josh closed his eyes to block it out, but a much-worse image waited behind his eyelids. Sadie. She was next. And her mom and…everyone. His heart pounded. He didn't want to ask, but he had to. "And Luis was in the Witness Security Program, right?"

"Yes."

Luis was in the program, and Guillermo found him. Silenced him forever. Josh whirled to the window, mind racing. Guillermo was free, Luis was dead, and Sadie was sitting on a couch in front of an open window.

"We have to get out of here," Josh said. Three measly squad cars wouldn't stop Guillermo. Not if he knew she was alive. He turned to Sadie. "We have to go before he finds you."

She didn't look at him. She was staring at Madsen, face far too calm to have processed anything. "Where was Luis living?" she asked.

"That's classified," Madsen said.

"Where?" she shouted, startling the room full of agents. Even Madsen flinched at her outburst.

"Missouri."

Sadie stood and pulled Josh up. "We're leaving."

"Hold on," Madsen said, jumping in front of them. "You're not going anywhere."

"Your program failed," Sadie said. "Your witness is dead, and we're leaving. Get out of our way!"

Madsen side-stepped, staying between them and the door. "Listen to me. We haven't been able to fully investigate, but we think Mr. Ortiz broke protocol and contacted someone from his past."

"You think?" Josh challenged, chest heaving in anger. Already he was trying to figure out which way to drive. North, south, or east. All the way to Argentina if needed.

"I have a plan," Madsen said.

Josh shook his head. "First Katie. Now Luis. Your plans have failed, and we're not waiting. So move."

"No." Madsen planted his feet. Two agents moved, blocking the only door to the outside.

"What if you have another leak in your organization?" Sadie asked.

Madsen's expression darkened. "We don't."

"Why not?" she said. "Guillermo got someone in the FBI before. He can get someone again. Maybe one of your own guys leaked Luis' whereabouts or told them where Josh's family lived."

"I told you," Madsen said stiffly, "we're investigating that."

Her chin came up. "And we told you, we're not waiting. Now move!"

Josh heard some voices outside. The front door flew open, nearly knocking over one of the agents. Deputy Harrison and Croff barged in.

"What is going on?" Harrison said.

With Madsen distracted, Josh backed himself and Sadie up, going around the far side of the couch. They were getting out of there one way or another.

Deputy Croff moved in front of them to intercept. "Where are you going, Sadie?" Croff asked.

"Move," Sadie said. Croff reached for her arm, but Sadie jerked free. "Don't touch me!"

Croff looked hurt. "Don't do this, Sadie. I know you're scared, but don't do this. Don't go off the radar. It will only make things worse. You'll be running for the rest of your lives—however long that is. And what about your families? You'll never be able to keep everyone safe."

"Neither have any of you," she shot back. "So move. Please."

Croff did, and Josh pulled Sadie close. "Get some things together," he whispered in her ear. "I'll run home and leave a note for my parents. I'll be back in a few minutes."

"Your parents?" Her eyes widened. "What will they do?"

"We'll find a place to meet them later. Let's go."

Madsen cut in front of them, puffing out his chest. "I don't think you understand what I mean when I say you're not leaving." He motioned to the extra agents, who pulled out their guns and planted themselves in front of the door. "I don't mean that I prefer you don't leave. I mean that you're not allowed to leave. We'll use force if we have to."

Josh stopped short. "What? You'll arrest us for...for trying to stay alive?"

"Just listen to Agent Madsen," Croff said. "He has a plan."

"His plan got Luis killed!" Sadie snapped.

"Miss Dawson," Madsen said, "you walked out on me twice before and what happened? On Christmas? On the day Guillermo found you? Both times you walked out, you almost died. Just listen. You have to trust me. There's another way."

"What?" Josh challenged.

Madsen's eyes darted back and forth between them before he spoke. "You need to leave, Mr. Young."

Josh dug in his heels. "Over my dead body."

Madsen's head inclined slightly. Two agents pounced. They jumped forward, grabbed Josh's arms, and threw him against the wall so hard, his head exploded with pain. But they weren't done. They flipped him around and, before he knew what hit him, pinned him with his hands behind his back, cheek to the wall, and someone's elbow in his back.

"Where do you want him, sir?" one of the agents said.

Josh squirmed with all his might. He didn't budge.

"In the squad car," Madsen said. "I'll be there in a minute."

"No!" Sadie yelled. She ran over to Madsen. "I'm listening to your plan. Please let Josh stay. We're in this together. Please. We're a team. Let him stay!"

Madsen looked at Josh, but Josh could only see half of Madsen since his face was squished to the wall. The guy's elbow dug into his back, shooting pain down Josh's legs.

"Fine." Madsen glared at Josh. "Stay, but not another word from you, Mr. Young, or you'll spend tonight on the floor of a jail cell. I can detain you for a full day for no other reason than you sneezed. Do you understand?"

Josh nodded against the wall.

The two agents released him. Josh slumped forward, drawing in gulps of air. When he straightened, the agents stayed in front of him, blocking the path to Sadie. Sadie stood by Madsen, ten very long feet away.

"I want you to come with me, Miss Dawson," Madsen said. "To Montana."

Are you crazy? Josh nearly shouted. He bit his tongue and took several more breaths. Harrison watched him from across the room as if giving the warning. *It's not worth it. Just listen.*

"Why?" Sadie asked.

"If I can get you in front of a prosecuting attorney," Madsen said, "we can get a firm set of charges drawn up. I can arrest Guillermo Vasquez on aggravated assault and attempted murder, and it will be enough to detain him until I can find someone else to take the stand against him, until I can pin Luis' murder on him, and Dubois' kidnapping, and who knows what else. But I have to have all my ducks in a row this time. I can't make any mistakes again. I was not exaggerating when I said my job is on the line, Miss Dawson. My boss doesn't even know I'm here right now. Guillermo won't stop until I lose my badge."

"I'm sorry," Sadie said calmly.

Josh's brows rose. Even Madsen looked confused by her comment.

"I am," she said. "I should have listened to you on Christmas, and I'm sorry I didn't. I should have listened to you in your car, and I didn't. I've not helped your credibility."

Madsen eye's flickered to Josh. Sadie had never felt bad before. From the beginning, she hated the FBI and their investigations. Josh didn't know what to say. He wasn't allowed to say it anyway.

"So will you come with me to Montana?" Madsen asked.

She blinked rapidly, her eyes filling with tears. "Is that really the only way to get him?"

"No," Madsen said truthfully. "We can wait until I find something else, but how long will I have to wait? That's only that much longer he's free to wreak havoc on the world—on your life and everyone else's. Even mine."

"He was doing a pretty good job of that behind bars," she pointed out.

"It will get worse. Much, much worse. He's furious now."

"And he wasn't before?"

Madsen's eyes narrowed. "Truthfully?"

She winced. She looked from agent to agent, looking very small and very frightened. Yet her shoulders stayed up as she spoke. "Do you know where Guillermo is right now?"

Josh's pulse sped up, realizing she was considering Madsen's offer. She was thinking about going back to Montana. Why? If he didn't think it would get him a night in jail, he would have asked.

"Not precisely," Madsen said. "With this new lawsuit, I have to be careful. We can't be snooping around his property or offices without a warrant. But I'm hoping he hasn't left Montana. I'm hoping he's feeling overconfident that he's gotten away with murder."

"He has," she whispered, voice cracking. She hugged herself and stared down at the floor.

"I can't let him slip through my fingers again," Madsen said. "I won't! Once you press charges, we'll check every rat hole he's ever owned."

Don't do it, Sadie! Josh begged. There had to be another way to get Guillermo without sending her to Montana, without making her take the lead against him.

"He won't know you're alive until he's arrested," Madsen said.

Josh couldn't take another second. "What if he already does?" he yelled.

As if choreographed, the two agents whirled around and grabbed his arms. They yanked hard, lifting him to his toes. "You want him gone, sir?" the one agent asked.

Madsen waved a tired hand. "No. Leave him."

They released Josh, but the heavier one shoved a finger in Josh's face. "Don't. Speak. Again. Do you understand?"

Josh's jaw clamped down, seething.

Madsen folded his arms. "I said I don't *think* Mr. Vasquez knows you're alive, Miss Dawson. There's always the chance, but by the time he knows for sure, he'll hopefully be behind bars again. I'll ship you back here or somewhere new if you prefer. But I need you to come with me now. You're my best chance. We'll fly you in tonight and take you directly to our offices in Flathead. Deputy Croff will escort you—Harrison, too, if you prefer. And if that's not enough, we'll double that number."

"Or triple," Croff said. "He won't touch you, Sadie. I promise."

Josh felt sick as he realized something horribly devastating. Everyone was speaking in the singular. *You.* Josh hadn't been mentioned once. He wasn't part of the plan. Madsen was leaving him behind.

Did Sadie know that?

She barely glanced at Croff. "What about my mom and brother?"

"My men are at their place now," Madsen said. "They're waiting for my order to move them out."

"And they'll be sent here?"

"Not after what happened in Missouri," Madsen said. "I can't risk them leading Guillermo to you. It's already bad enough Mr. Young's family is here. Keeping that many people quiet in one place is a logistical nightmare. No. They'll be sent to another secure location, and Mr. Young's family will be moved as well. Either that or you and Mr. Young need to find a new place."

Sadie's face betrayed her emotions. Her eyes started to water. "When will we see our families again?"

"When it's safe."

She swallowed. "How soon do I have to decide?"

"Now. A private jet is waiting for us. We'll be the only passengers."

No! Josh cried silently. *Don't do it, Sadie!*

She looked at Josh as if hearing his thoughts. Her expression was one of immense pain. "And you'll keep Josh safe? Here?"

"Yes. We'll keep his house heavily guarded at all times."

"No!" Josh shouted, not caring what happened to him in the next few minutes. He could barely see Sadie past the agents' shoulders, but he didn't care. He couldn't let her walk away. "Don't, Sadie. Don't go alone. Don't go at all! There has to be another way."

She smiled sadly, and a few quiet tears fell down her cheeks. "I have to. But it's going to be okay. I can do this."

Sniffing back her tears, she turned to Madsen. "I'm ready."

"Good. Go pack." Madsen looked pleased with Sadie's rash decision. Why wouldn't he be pleased? He bullied her into it. "Pack enough for four days. Maybe longer."

She started for her room.

"Sadie, wait!" Josh called, desperate. If it wasn't for the two agents, he would have run across the room and shaken some sense into her.

She stopped but didn't turn to look at him. Madsen had backed her into a corner. Already he had his phone out finalizing the plans.

"Don't do this," Josh begged. "I know why you're leaving me behind. You're trying to keep me from getting killed, but that's not a good enough reason. Not even close! There has to be another way. You keep making decisions without me. Are we a team or not?"

"I have to go," she whispered.

"Then let me come. We're a team. Don't go alone. Please!"

She kept her face hidden from him, but he could tell her breathing was short and labored. After a moment of deliberation, she shook her head.

"I'm sorry," she said. Then she walked into her bedroom. Alone.

Josh leaped forward. Just as fast, the two agents grabbed his arms and threw him against the wall, slamming into it again. Pain exploded everywhere. The room spun, and though he blinked several times, he saw nothing but swirling lights.

"What is going on?" a man shouted. "What are you doing to my son?"

Josh shook his head to clear it. A blurry figure stood in the front door, trying to get past Deputy Harrison.

The agent holding Josh called over his shoulder. "Stay back, sir."

Josh's dad held his badge high. "I'm his father, and I work for the Spokane PD. I demand to know what is going on!"

Madsen was still on the phone but pointed to the door.

"Talk to your son outside," the agent said.

He yanked Josh away from the wall and dragged him across the room. Josh rubbed his head, trying to clear the spots from his vision. His head pricked with pain.

As he was pushed outside, he saw Croff and Harrison by the window.

"Do something," he begged. "Please."

Then he was thrown out of Sadie's house, door slamming behind him. Josh leaned over the porch railing, trying to catch his breath.

His dad bent next to him. "What is going on? What happened?"

"He's taking her," Josh said.

"Who? What?"

Josh slid down the white siding, landing on hard cement. "He's taking Sadie. She's going back to Montana."

"Without you?"

Josh's head collapsed against the railing. His eyes burned hot as acid. "Help."

CHAPTER 34

"It doesn't make sense," his dad said after Josh explained the situation. "Everything Madsen needs to get a warrant he should be able to do from here. Written testimony. Signature. Dates. All of it. He can get it from Sadie right now."

"Really?" Josh asked.

"Yes." His dad sat next to him on the cold cement. "So why does he need her to go? Why doesn't he need you? I thought you were testifying, too."

"I don't know what's going on. Something feels wrong about the whole thing. Madsen has her so convinced it's the only way to get Guillermo." Josh rubbed his throbbing temples. "Maybe it is. But is it worth it? If she goes alone, she won't come back. I can feel it."

"Okay. So let's think this through," his dad said. "If the prosecutor needs to talk to her, he can do it over the phone. That should be plenty to ask any questions he needs. Madsen will get the warrant. What else is there that she can help with until Guillermo is arrested?" His eyebrows pulled down in serious thought. "I can't think of a single reason he needs her in Montana before the trial."

Josh's head jerked up with a thought so disturbing it shouldn't have been possible. "I can."

His thoughts raced. There was only one reason Madsen needed Sadie in Montana before the formal trial. Josh thought about how Madsen tried to get rid of him earlier because he didn't want Josh knowing his plan. He didn't want Josh going to Montana with Sadie. Why? Because Madsen knew Josh would never in a million years allow his plan. If Madsen's boss didn't even know he was in Tennessee, Josh guessed his boss wouldn't go along with it either.

I can't let him slip through my fingers again. I won't!

Josh felt sicker by the second. "Madsen wouldn't, would he?"

"Wouldn't what?" his dad asked.

"Use Sadie as bait?"

His dad's mouth fell open. "If his job's on the line...if Guillermo goes invisible again...if he thinks it's the only way to bring Guillermo in...he absolutely would."

The anger swelled up inside Josh, hot and fierce. Madsen was going to use Sadie to lure Guillermo in.

He jumped up. "Can you get something from my house?"

He told his dad where to find it, and then he turned and stormed inside. The same two agents were waiting for him.

"You're not allowed in here," the taller one said.

Agent Madsen was off his phone. "Go home, Mr. Young. We'll contact you when we arrive in Montana. Miss Dawson will be back in a few days safe and sound. In the meantime, go home and sleep."

"Do you still plan to use my testimony?" Josh said.

"Yes."

"Then I suggest you let me in. Now!"

Madsen rolled his eyes but waved him in. The two agents fell back.

Josh stormed over to Madsen. "You say you're being upfront and honest? Then answer this: Why doesn't your boss know you're here? What are you planning that he wouldn't approve of?"

Madsen's eyes narrowed. His jaw clenched, but he said nothing.

"Or how about this," Josh said. "Why can't Sadie write her formal charges here? Especially if she has the entire story written out already? What's your straightforward answer on that?"

Madsen's expression hardened. "The prosecutor wants to see her. He wants to know if she's mentally able to handle a trial. With this malicious prosecution lawsuit Guillermo's thrown at us, we have to have every 'I' dotted, every 'T' crossed. There are no mistakes this time."

"Can't all that be done over the phone?"

"No. He needs to see her."

Deputy Croff stepped forward. "A video chat then," she said. "It's been done before."

"The Shetzky case," Harrison said. "It can be done, and you know it."

Madsen's eyes narrowed. "What do you think you're doing, Mr. Young?"

Josh shook his head. Unbelievable. Madsen didn't need her in Montana—at least not for what he said he did. "The question is what are *you* doing, Agent Madsen?"

Sadie came into the front room, carrying her packed bag. She looked back and forth between the two men. "What's going on?"

Josh folded his arms. "I'm waiting for Agent Madsen to answer my question."

Madsen glared at him. "Miss Dawson has to come to Montana to testify eventually. There's nothing you can do to prevent that."

"She already told you she'd come for that. And she will. So will I." Josh gritted his teeth. "I'm sorry your job is on the line, but our *lives* are on the line. I think that takes priority."

"You think I don't know that?" Madsen cried.

"With all due respect, sir," Josh said, "I think your desire for revenge is clouding your judgment."

Madsen's face went red with rage. "Revenge? I want justice, and so should you!"

"I do. Just not at that price."

Josh turned to Sadie. "Do you have your story? The one you wrote for the counselor? I think Agent Madsen will want to take it with him to Montana."

Sadie's brows shot up. "I'm not going? Why?"

"Go ahead, Madsen," Josh said. "Tell Sadie the real reason you need her to go."

Madsen didn't glance her way. His eyes could have burned a hole in Josh's skull. "If Vasquez slips through my fingers again…"

"That's not her problem," Josh said, disgusted. "Do your job, and do it the right way."

Unable to look at the agent another moment, Josh walked over to Sadie. From her expression, she looked as furious as Agent Madsen.

"What did you do, Josh?" she asked.

"There was a door number three Madsen forgot to mention. If you don't mind doing some paperwork from here," Josh said, "maybe a video chat or two, you aren't needed in Montana until the trial."

"*If* there even is a trial!" Madsen snapped.

"Is that true?" Sadie asked, relief clouding her voice. "I can press charges from here?"

When Madsen didn't answer, Deputy Croff did. "Yes."

Sadie dropped her bag.

The front door opened, and Josh's dad walked in and handed a few papers to Josh. Josh glanced over it to make sure he had it all.

Sadie's eyes widened. "Is that what I think it is?"

"Yeah." Josh hadn't told her yet, but he'd written out his version of the story. If he was testifying about all of Sadie's injuries, he needed to know what to say and how to say it. Writing it down had been one long, painful night. "I figured if you could write the whole thing so could I."

He handed his papers to Agent Madsen. "Here's my written testimony. I put in as much detail as I could remember. Kevin has pictures of her eye you can use as well. Let us know what else you *need*."

Madsen snatched the papers. "Prepare yourself, Miss Dawson. You're about to be resurrected from the dead." His furious gaze went back to Josh. "Vasquez won't make another mistake like Chicago again. If he runs, he's gone. Possibly forever."

"Then be smart," Josh said. "He's arrogant. Follow his ego trail. It'll lead you right to him."

"If I lose him, more people will be hurt. It will be on *your* head, Mr. Young."

Josh shuddered but held strong. "Then don't lose him. Now…what do we need to do to make sure you don't miss your flight? I'd hate for your boss to know where you've been."

CHAPTER 35

Sadie stayed in Josh's arms long after Madsen and his entourage left, trying to slow down her heart. She was staying. They were staying. Croff and Harrison were on their phones making plans to move back in. Rocky was scrounging up food in the kitchen, which left Josh and Sadie a few minutes alone.

Sadie knew Josh was mad at her. Furious. His arms were rigid around her, and he hadn't said a word since the blow-up.

"I'm sorry," she whispered into his chest.

"You should be." He tilted her chin up. "Don't ever do that again. I almost spent a night in jail trying to remind you that we're a team. At least…I thought we were."

She couldn't hold his challenging gaze and studied his navy shirt instead. "I couldn't risk you."

"How is it fair that you won't risk me, but you nearly forced me to risk you?"

"Because I love you more." She slid her arms around his waist and pressed her ear to his chest, listening for the soft thud of his heartbeat. It was pounding faster than it should, making her feel even worse.

"Sadie…" he growled.

"Just hold me."

"First, you need to answer something. Are we a team or not? Because if not, that's fine. I just…I need to know."

She went up on tiptoes and kissed him. "We're a team. I'm sorry. We're in this together from here on out. I promise."

His brows rose. "You mean that?"

"With my whole soul. You and I, forever and always."

"Forever and always," he repeated softly.

He studied her a long moment, and then suddenly and completely without warning, his blue eyes started to water.

She jerked back. "Josh?"

He reached up and stroked her cheek like he always did. His finger traced her cheekbone to her jawline with infinite gentleness. Though his eyes still shone, a tiny smile played on his lips. The sudden change in emotion made her even more concerned.

"Marry me," he whispered.

Her breath caught. "What?"

"Marry me, Sarah Augustina Dawson. Please."

Her own eyes liquefied. "What are you doing? You're proposing now? Where did this come from?"

"You said yes to our fourth date."

She couldn't respond. Josh was proposing. Right here, right now.

"Actually," he said, "it's been coming for a while, but it was solidified out on that cold porch. I couldn't imagine the rest of my life—the rest of my forever—without you. I love you, Sadie. Marry me."

"I love you, too, but—"

She stopped because he started to lower himself in front of her. Her pulse pounded in her veins as Josh dropped to one knee. He held her hand and looked up at her with his intense gaze.

"Sarah Augustina Dawson, will you marry me?"

She breathed faster and faster. She wanted to say yes, but the emotions of the moment had her doubting him. He was just stressed. He was just caught up in the fear of losing her.

"Josh, if this is your way to get me to stay, to not leave again, then don't worry. You're not going to lose me. Not now. Not—"

He reached in his coat pocket and pulled out a box. A small, velvet box.

Her hands flew to her mouth.

He grinned an impish grin. "Believe me now?"

"When did you… How did you…? Josh!"

"I picked it up after class today. I never expected to propose like this or so soon, and I promise to do it all fancy later, but…I couldn't wait."

He cracked open the lid. Tears pricked her eyes. Inside was the most exquisite setting she'd ever seen. Perched on the white gold was a square diamond, not too small, not too showy.

"Gregory," she said half laughing, half crying.

"He says 'You're welcome.'"

Josh pulled the dainty ring from the box and held it toward her. The last few inches were hers to cross. She stared at the sparkling diamond, at him and her possible future. She pressed her fingers to her lips to stop them from trembling.

Croff and Harrison stopped their calls to watch them—to watch her.

"Well?" Josh said. "Are you going to torture me? My knee is killing me here."

He was only partially teasing. Part of him looked uncertain as he waited for her answer.

All she could think was, *How did I ever deserve this?* She didn't deserve Josh, not in a million years, but she was done pointing that out to him.

His face started to blur through her tears.

"Okay," she said.

"Okay, as in…yes?"

She nodded. That's all the response she could manage.

His face split into another wide grin. He took her hand, pulled off his mom's ring, and slipped on the new one. He only gave her a second to admire it before he jumped up, swept her off her feet, and twirled her around and around.

Guillermo heard the click of a gun behind his ear. He sighed. Would his problems never cease?

"What took you so long my friend?" he asked without turning.

"Give me one good reason why I shouldn't blow your brains out," Special Agent Stephen Dubois answered.

"Did you enjoy Africa?" Guillermo asked.

"That wasn't it."

Guillermo flinched, waiting for the explosion of pain. After a second—a long second—he realized he might live another moment. He swiveled around in his chair and faced the young agent who no longer looked so young.

"If I do say so, Señor Dubois, you are not looking so good these days. Tell me, what happened to your forehead?"

Dubois raised the gun to Guillermo's nose. "You're under arrest."

"The FBI is in enough trouble as it is," Guillermo said, pushing the gun out of his face. "I suggest you do not make the mistake they did earlier and arrest me without a valid cause. My lawyers already have enough ammunition. If you come here without a valid warrant, it shall be the FBI's undoing."

Dubois held up a paper that suspiciously looked like a warrant.

"Frivolous charges, I am sure," Guillermo said. "What now? Speeding? Jaywalking? Now go away. I am busy."

He twisted back around and started on the Venezuelan report. His contacts down there were having issues converting the supplies to cash, or so they claimed. He had suspicions it was something deeper. He needed to resolve it quickly before his cash flow ran dry.

"I didn't make the last arrest," Dubois said, "because if I had, you wouldn't have survived it."

"Holding a grudge, my friend? Everything went as planned, did it not? When you came to me on New Year's Day, you asked me to improve life for your two daughters. Have I not made them rich?"

"Rich?" Dubois cried. "You think they care about money? Do you know what you've put my family through?"

"You are back in the FBI with no questions asked, and you are back in my office with a fat wallet and no questions asked. Everything worked out as you hoped, has it not? Why are you so angry?"

"I'm here on business, and I said you're under arrest." Dubois rammed the gun to his shoulder. "Get up. Now! Up!"

Guillermo sighed. His head was pounding. He didn't have time for this. "If you are determined to arrest me, you will have to come with a lot more than a flimsy piece of paper. Salvador!" Guillermo motioned to the door. "Get rid of him."

Guillermo saw the movement a moment too late. The butt of the gun slammed into the back of his skull. Metal on bone. Guillermo yelped as he was yanked to his feet. Dubois was half a foot taller than him and held him by the shirt collar, bringing Guillermo to his toes.

"What do you want with me, Vasquez?" Dubois hissed in his face. "Why are you toying with me? I did exactly what you wanted, and you stripped me down, knocked me out, and shoved me in that rat hole in Africa. Is that how you treat your employees? If so, I quit!"

Reaching up, Guillermo felt the back of his tender head. A huge goose egg already. Still, he controlled his temper. "Oh, come now. If you disappeared for my training, Madsen would have never let you return to your post. But now you are a hero. You are the star. You have survived the great Guillermo's wrath and lived to tell about it. You should be thanking me, not shoving that poor excuse for a gun in my face."

Dubois stared him down, chest huffing. After a moment, he dropped him. Guillermo rocked back on his heels and brushed down his suit. If he didn't feel sorry for the guy, he would have killed him on the spot for roughing him up. Nobody touched Guillermo Vasquez. Nobody. But Guillermo knew the whiny FBI agent had received the rough end of their bargain. From what he heard, that prison in Morocco was nasty. The warden was more crooked than Guillermo. But then again, Guillermo lost a pretty penny freeing Dubois. He owed him.

"For a wanted man," Agent Dubois said, looking around, "I'd think you would have found a better place to hide. Madsen sent all available men out twenty minutes ago. Your time is ticking. I'd start running if I were you."

"And why should I hide?" Guillermo picked a piece of dirt from under his nails.

Dubois swore under his breath. "What do you want from me, Vasquez?"

"Tell me why the FBI is arresting me this time."

"The attempted murder of Sarah Augustina Dawson, amid other things."

Guillermo walked around his mahogany desk and sat on the corner. He stared out his full-length window at the ski lifts carrying skiers up the massive mountainside. Things had slowed since the holidays. In more ways than one.

Attempted murder.

"Unbelievable," Guillermo said. "I barely touched Augustina on Christmas. How can Madsen call that attempted murder? He is really stretching it now. If he dares twist her suicide into my fault, my lawyers will rake over the FBI so badly, they will have to disband."

"Actually," Dubois said, "my notes don't mention anything about Christmas. It's referencing January 8th, first in your Mercedes where you assaulted her, and then in some cabin when you tried to burn her alive." He scanned the paper. "Sadie describes it in quite detail. I think they might have you this time."

Guillermo's head turned slowly. "What did you say?"

Dubois smiled a slow, wicked smile. "I thought that might interest you. It appears your precious Augustina didn't die in that cabin after all. In fact, she's been living quite comfortably for some time on the government dime with that new boyfriend of hers. What's his name?"

Guillermo leaped forward to grab the paper. Another click, and the gun was shoved in his face. Guillermo skidded to a halt. Dubois held the gun steady while skimming the last of the warrant.

"What a shame," Dubois said. "If you'd given me the assignment to get rid of her instead of that pathetic, fat assistant, Luis, I would have finished her off. I would have loved to finish her off. But…I guess you get what you pay for, huh?"

"Give it to me!" Guillermo roared.

He snatched the warrant and skimmed down to the official charges. He read it three times before it sunk in. Augustina was alive. He pictured her dark eyes. Dark hair. Perfect smile. Perfect skin. Sarah Augustina Dawson was alive!

Dubois smiled. "For as careful as you are on everything else, I can't believe you actually thought she was dead. My old partner isn't as stupid as I thought. The whole funeral charade was brilliant. And to think, all this time she's been gallivanting around with her new beau, Josh, and you've been completely clueless."

Guillermo could barely think straight enough to read the signatures scribbled below the legal jargon. But there it was. Plain as day.

Informer: Sarah Augustina Dawson

He stared at her immaculately carved signature. It was definitely her handwriting. But what caused the edges of his vision to blur was the signature below it. A man's signature:

Joshua David Young

Guillermo whirled around and kicked his desk, tipping it over. His papers and antique lamp went sailing. "It cannot be. It cannot be!" He tore the warrant into tiny shreds. "Where is she? Where are they!"

"I've been doing some research, but I'm not exactly sure where—"

Guillermo leaped forward. He threw the turncoat agent against the wall. Guillermo had a gun to Dubois' chest before he could blink, and not the little toy gun Dubois threatened him with earlier. This one wouldn't even make a sound.

"You want to rethink that, Stephano?" he hissed.

A thin sheen of sweat broke out on Stephen Dubois' face. "Wait. Wait!"

Dubois tried to squirm free. Guillermo jammed the gun farther into his rib cage, making him wince. "Where. Are. They?" he asked, low and deadly. "You have exactly three seconds. Three...two..."

"I said I wasn't *exactly* sure," Dubois squealed. "But there's a way to find out where Augustina *and* her new boyfriend are. There are records. You might be able to salvage things yet."

Guillermo took two breaths. His vision still clouded with fury, but his mind raced faster and faster.

"How?" he huffed.

"First things first..." Dubois paused with a nervous smile. "How rich are you feeling?"

CHAPTER 36

"Get some sleep, Dubois," Agent Madsen said. "We'll find Vasquez tomorrow."

Dubois didn't even glance over his shoulder. "The longer it goes," he said to his partner, "the less chance we have of finding him. He knows there's a warrant out for his arrest. We can't lose him again." He pounded the desk for dramatic effect. "We can't!"

"Go home and see Katrina. She thinks I'm working you too hard. We got some good leads today. Vasquez was in Kalispell at least twelve hours ago. Hopefully, he'll be cuffed by morning."

Dubois fought the urge to roll his eyes. He had been with Guillermo less than twelve hours ago. After receiving the first payment, he specifically told Guillermo to keep low while he tracked down Sadie and Josh's whereabouts. Payment number two came after he found their location. The third—and biggest—payment came when he brought them in alive. He was starting to think his three weeks in Morocco were worth it.

"I'm just about done," Dubois said. "I'll be right behind you."

Madsen grabbed his briefcase. "Hit the lights on your way out. I'll be here first thing, hopefully with good news."

Dubois puttered around a full ten minutes until he felt it was safe. Then he wandered over to the file cabinet.

Special Agent Bruce Madsen wasn't known for his organizational skills, but when it came to paperwork, he was OCD. Even then, it took Dubois another five minutes to find them. They weren't filed under their legal names, but under their new names:

Josh and Sadie Peterson.

Dubois opened their file and smiled. There were two addresses listed for them. But his smile faded as he saw the city: Olive Branch, Mississippi. According to Guillermo, that location had already been ruled out. It was just a decoy. Dubois read and reread their file, hoping for another clue. Nothing.

Then he had another idea.

He shoved their file back in the cabinet and searched for another name. He wasn't sure why he hadn't thought of it before. Instead of chasing them around the country, why not let them crawl back?

He found the file. Below the name was an address of her new home, a home within five miles of where he stood. And from the records, she was already under FBI protection. It couldn't have been easier if he planned it himself.

Regardless of the late hour, he was buying his wife flowers on the way home.

Josh didn't go to school, and Sadie didn't push him.

Their small group in Tennessee hung around waiting for news. Sadie's mom and brother had supposedly been shipped to a secure location, but no one told them where yet, which stressed Sadie out. When Madsen was here, he said Josh's family should leave Tennessee, but he never followed through, so they hadn't. There hadn't been a single word from Agent Madsen since he left. Sadie could only assume Guillermo was still free and had gone into hiding. And he most likely knew she was alive, which meant he also knew she was pressing charges.

Her nightmares were back with a vengeance.

They played board games, played the piano, watched old Star Trek episodes, and pretended like all was good in the world. Even Croff and Harrison joined in with the family at times. But things were subdued. They all felt the weight of the situation like a ticking time bomb.

As the days wore on, they got more and more antsy and less and less careful. First they ventured to Josh's parent's house for a change of scenery, and then they ventured to church. When there was still no word, Josh called Madsen and got a clipped response.

"We're working on it," Madsen snapped.

Sadie finally convinced Josh to go back to school. It could be months before Guillermo surfaced again. Like they tried to do before, they went back to life as best they could.

The only bright spot was planning a baptism and a wedding. Josh and Sadie wanted to wait to get married until things with Guillermo settled down—if they ever settled down. Plus Sadie wanted everyone to be at their wedding: her mom, Damien, Sam, Kevin, and Trevor. But she didn't want to wait on the baptism. She was ready. And that meant planning. With Croff's permission, they had two last visitors stop by before the big day. And with Sadie's permission, Josh stayed home from school one last time.

"So this is him?" Elder Farron asked, shaking Josh's hand.

Sadie smiled. "Yes. This is my fiancé, Josh." She loved the sound of that word.

"Thanks for teaching her," Josh said. "Sorry I couldn't be here before now."

"No problem."

Elder Farron and his companion took the two oak chairs. Sadie and Josh sat on the couch facing them. His parents, Jake, and Lauren scrunched in everywhere else. They'd sat through the rest of her lessons, something about mission rules and two elders not being able to meet alone with a woman, so it was only fair to let them sit in on her last one.

"Any last questions before tomorrow?" Elder Farron asked.

"Yeah," Sadie said. "How many times can I be baptized?"

Everyone laughed, making Sadie blush heavily. Maybe she should have asked Josh's family to leave before she asked her questions. The more she learned about baptism, the more she loved it, especially the symbolism of being washed clean from all her sins. There were thousands of things she'd done wrong in her life—half in the last month alone. It seemed impossible by any stretch of the imagination that it was about to be washed away. Forgotten. *"I stand all amazed at the love Jesus offers me, confused by the grace that so fully he proffers me."* The lyrics became her constant thought. But try as she may, she knew she wasn't done making mistakes. And then what?

Elder Farron realized she was serious and sobered. "Oh. Sorry. You're only baptized once."

"Oh." She knew it was too good to be true. Except for some reason, Elder Farron was smiling. So was Josh and everyone else.

"What am I missing?" she asked.

"You're missing the good news," Elder Farron said. "The word 'gospel' means good news, and the good news is that there is a way to feel as clean and forgiven each week as you'll feel tomorrow. What do you remember about the sacrament?"

"It's a symbol of Jesus's blood and body."

"Yes. And it's through both that we're forgiven. So when you approach the sacrament with the same reverence and repentant heart as you have now," Elder Farron explained, "you can receive the same forgiveness and peace as you will tomorrow. Every week."

"Every week?" she said. "Sign me up."

Everyone laughed again. "I think we already did," Jake said. "There's no going back now. You're stuck."

"No, you're not," Kathy said. "Don't listen to him."

"I usually don't," Sadie quipped.

Jake pretended to be offended, which made them laugh again.

When she turned back, Elder Farron was watching her with a grave expression. He seemed to look through her like he sometimes did. The guy was younger than her, yet in some ways he was like an old wise grandpa.

She squirmed a little under his direct gaze. "What?"

He looked at his companion. Elder Jensen had only been in Tennessee a week longer than Josh and Sadie. Most the time he looked as clueless as Sadie felt.

"The Atonement was for more than just our sins," Elder Farron said.

"What do you mean?" she asked.

"Christ suffered every pain and sorrow we face," Elder Farron said. "He experienced what we experience. He knows what we're going through because, in a way, He went through it, too. He knows what *you* are going through, Sadie. Right now. Today."

Sadie stared at him. Josh did, too. Elder Farron didn't notice because he was already flipping his scriptures open. Kathy and Peter gave Sadie a look like, *We didn't tell him anything.* So did Jake and Lauren. She knew they hadn't. They'd all been very careful to keep her past vague. Very vague.

"There's a scripture in Alma that talks about this," Elder Farron said. "Can you read chapter seven, verse eleven and twelve?"

She swallowed and turned to the right page.

"And he shall go forth," she read softly, *"suffering pains and afflictions and temptations of every kind; and this that the word might be fulfilled which saith he will take upon him the pains and sicknesses of his people. And he will take upon them their infirmities—"*

"Infirmities," Elder Farron broke in, "is like problems. Our trials. Everything that goes wrong in our life, Jesus Christ takes on himself."

"And he will take upon him their infirmities," she started again. Her eyes skipped ahead and stopped. She swallowed again. *"That..."*

Josh finished for her. *"That his bowels may be filled with mercy, according to the flesh, that he may know according to the flesh how to succor his people according to their infirmities."*

Elder Farron shut his scriptures and leaned forward. "The Atonement is so much more than we can comprehend, Sadie. It involves the Savior experiencing our life. This scripture teaches us that Christ willingly went through everything He did so He would know how to succor His people. Do you know what the word 'succor' means here?"

The tears started to push through. She sniffed them back. "I think so."

"When you study the last part of the Savior's life, you realize how much He went through. The Jewish leaders wanted Him dead, and He constantly went into hiding. Eventually one of His own apostles turned on Him, betrayed Him, and turned Him in. Christ was then stripped, beaten, whipped, and killed in a horribly cruel way. Why?" Elder Farron looked deeply into her eyes. "So He would understand what it's like to be us. And He does, Sadie. I testify of that. That's why He can take care of us when we're down. He understands because He lived it."

Tears streamed down her face. "Why would He do that?"

"Because He loves us—because He loves *you*."

Her chest filled with warmth that pushed more tears from her eyes. They were no longer those of sadness but of overwhelming joy. She wiped her eyes, trying to stop the onslaught. Kathy handed her a fresh tissue. It was another minute before she could find her voice again.

"You guys have to stop doing this to me," she said with a smile. "I'm a mess."

"No," Elder Farron said. "I think you're ready. Do you feel ready?"

"No. Yes. I guess I'm as ready as I'll ever be. Let's do it."

CHAPTER 37

"Earth to Amy. Hello?" Kevin squeezed her hand. "Where are you?"

Amy blinked, realizing the television was off and their show was done. She'd been staring at a black screen for who knew how long. "Sorry. I must be tired."

"You keep saying that." Kevin's brows pulled down. "What's really going on, babe?"

She bit her bottom lip and looked outside. They said they'd be back. What if they didn't find Josh? What if they did? Her eyes stung with bitterness. She'd never forgive herself if they found Josh and Sadie. And yet, if they didn't, then what?

Amy had called in sick to work the last two days and tried to sleep it away. A thousand times she nearly went to the police, but Ivan said he'd be watching. So she avoided Kevin's questions because she couldn't risk him. She wouldn't.

"You haven't eaten," Kevin said. "You're sleeping all the time, and you called in sick to work. That's the first time you've called in sick, and now you've called in twice." Kevin's eyes widened. "Oh…oh…oh, man. Are you pregnant?"

"No." She wished it was something that easy. That happy.

She scanned the room, wondering if they planted a bug somewhere. Sadie's ex-boyfriend planted several listening devices around her apartment.

We have eyes and ears everywhere...

"Babe..." Kevin took her chin and turned it toward him. As she looked at him, she could see the terror in his eyes. He knew she was keeping something from him. Something big.

"I'm fine," she lied loudly. "Let's watch something else."

She grabbed the remote and flipped on the television. Then she pulled Kevin close and whispered in his ear. "They'll kill us if I tell you. They're watching me—us. They want him. They came looking for him. They came, Kevin. They came."

He jerked back, eyes zeroing on the fresh scab on her cheek.

The dam inside her burst. Just when she thought she couldn't cry anymore, she had to cover her mouth to silence her tears. That caused her body to convulse.

Kevin traced the letters of one word on her leg:

Josh.

She nodded.

He whipped around and scanned their small apartment. Then he took her hand and tugged. "Let's go," he mouthed.

She shook her head vigorously. *No!*

He looked at her another moment before he released her. Standing slowly, he crept up to the window. He pulled back the curtain a few inches and peered outside. Amy covered her eyes. She couldn't watch. Two desires warred within her: the desire to run and the desire to keep Kevin alive.

Kevin decided for her.

He crossed the room in huge strides. "We're leaving." He yanked her up, grabbed his keys, and pulled her out the door.

Marcela stopped and straightened. She thought she'd heard a knock.

It wasn't all that late, but she was already in her pajamas, washing her face for the night. She really didn't want to see anyone, but Damien was gone—he left a few minutes earlier to buy gas for the car. She wasn't used to the bathroom sink in the new apartment either. The handles went the wrong way. She turned off the water and listened.

More knocking.

Their new apartment was across town from her old one, but no one was supposed to know where they were. They didn't even have neighbors as far as she knew. She checked the clock. After nine. Why would someone be there so late at night?

Fear leaped in her throat. But then she realized if Guillermo showed up looking for Augustina or them, he wouldn't knock. He'd barge right in.

She dried her face and grabbed her pink bathrobe.

As was her new habit, she checked the peep hole before opening the front door. She relaxed when she saw an FBI agent. Not Agent Madsen, but his younger back-from-the-dead partner. It was a little late for a social visit, which meant more bad news.

Her pulse pounded again.

Calm down, she scolded herself. *It's probably nothing. Augustina is fine.*

She pulled the door open and hid behind it. She wasn't thrilled to have the semi-attractive man see her in pajamas and a pink bathrobe.

"Good evening, Agent Dubois," she said. "Is something wrong?"

"I'm afraid there is." He stormed into her apartment and looked around. "There's been a situation."

Her heart skidded to a stop. "Augustina?"

"She's safe, but your son just sent us a distress call."

"Damien? Is he alright? He's only been gone five minutes."

Dubois continued to search each corner of the room. "He was followed by someone on the way to the gas station. He thinks Guillermo found him."

"No, no, no, no." She crossed herself over and over again.

"Don't worry. Two agents are with your son now. I've come for you. We have to leave now. We're moving you and your son to a new secure location."

"But I'm not dressed."

Dubois whirled around. "There's not time! If Guillermo determined your location, we have to go now! We'll send for your things later."

Pulling her pink robe tight, she ducked her head and followed him outside to his car. February in Montana was still bitterly cold. The cold wind whipped her bathrobe, and the icy sidewalk soaked her slippers through. Luckily his car was already heated.

They drove in silence through the dark streets of Kalispell while she tried to figure out how Guillermo had found her. They'd moved only a few days earlier. They'd been so careful, too. They hadn't talked to anyone or gone anywhere. Damien decided to top off the gas just in case they had to flee further than Kalispell.

Closing her eyes, she said a silent prayer for her two children. They were all that mattered.

When they crossed the railroad tracks, Marcela looked up. The railroad tracks were outside the main part of Kalispell off the main road. They were leaving all residential areas, but they weren't heading for the airport either. They were heading for a dark, old business section that looked like storage units more than anything.

"Where are we going?" she asked.

"Somewhere secure," Dubois said.

"Will Damien meet us there?"

"Probably. If things don't work out, he'll be joining us soon enough."

She hugged herself as they drove past building after square building. They were driving further into a massive complex of warehouses. A few streetlights lit the area. Barely. That late at night, there wasn't a soul in sight.

Questions swirled in her mind. Why would the FBI send her to such a remote place? Why had Agent Dubois come alone? Where was Damien?

Her skin tingled with fear. She could sense something wasn't right, she just wasn't sure what. As the car started to slow in front of a large warehouse, her pulse started to race.

"Where are you taking me?" she asked. "What is really going on?"

Dubois gave her a look that sent a chill down her spine. "Someone wants a word with you, Mrs. Dawson."

"Who?"

"I think you know who."

A name came to mind, but it was so frightening, so horrible, it couldn't be true.

"I want to speak to Agent Madsen," she said.

Dubois smiled. "He's busy."

Terror shot through her veins. Madsen hadn't sent Dubois. Damien probably hadn't even called the FBI. Her pulse pounded so loud in her ears she could barely hear herself think.

"Who are you?" she said, backing up into the door. "Who do you work for?"

Dubois laughed a dark laugh. He stopped in front of a warehouse that didn't have a single window to the outside. He put the car in park and faced her. "You know who I work for, Mrs. Dawson. I can see it in your eyes. Congratulations. You're the first person to figure it out. You should be proud of yourself."

Marcela clung to her seat belt. If she went in that warehouse, she'd never come out. "I'm not going anywhere."

The agent pulled a gun from his belt. "You want to bet?"

With bathrobe and slippers, Marcela walked in front of Agent Dubois toward the dark, cold warehouse.

The inside was much larger than it appeared from the outside. A single light shone from a small office in the corner. Without being told, she walked toward it.

A man at a desk stood as they entered. He had jet-black hair and the most arrogant smile of any human on earth.

Guillermo.

Seeing him brought a whole new level of fear. Marcela dug in her feet. "No!"

Dubois pushed her forward. Her slippers slid on the smooth cement.

Guillermo met them at the office doorway. He smiled warmly as if genuinely pleased to see her. He even reached out to shake her hand. She recoiled, running into Agent Dubois. He shoved her forward again. She still refused to touch the man who tried to kill her daughter.

"Señora Dawson," Guillermo said. "How nice to see you again. I have missed seeing your bright, smiling face. Come in. Come in."

"Stay away from me you…you murderer!"

"Oh, come now. We have too many happy memories for such accusing words," Guillermo said. "I wish to speak to you a moment about your lovely daughter, Augustina." In the flick of an eye, Guillermo's smiled changed from light to dark. "It seems she is not as dead as you made me believe."

"Stay away from her!" Marcela screamed. "Do what you want to me, but you'll never find her. Never!"

Guillermo laughed. "Oh, Señora Dawson. I do not have to find our precious Augustina. She is about to find us. Come. Make yourself comfortable. Let us hope we do not have to wait long."

Sadie's baptism was a quiet affair. There were fourteen people in attendance which was more than Sadie imagined, and yet that was just Josh's family, two missionaries, two bodyguards, and one very supportive, very understanding, very trusting bishop who was still a little wide-eyed after hearing their entire story.

Even from the bathroom, Sadie could hear Lauren playing soft hymns as they finished the last of the preparations. Croff was patrolling the church with Harrison to make sure it was truly empty. That left Sadie a few minutes of solitude.

She stood barefoot on the cold bathroom tile and admired herself in the large mirror. She wore all white, a simple jumper she borrowed from the church. She couldn't remember ever wearing all white. It made her feel clean. Thinking about the next time she'd wear pure white made her smile shamelessly.

Pressing her hands to her stomach, she was surprised by how jittery she felt. Then she grabbed a brush and worked to pull back her dark hair since it would be soaked in a few minutes. She managed to get it into a short ponytail, all except a small lock of hair in the back. It was the first she'd worn a ponytail since Guillermo nearly scalped her. Hopefully no one would notice the small tuft behind her ear. Especially Josh. She didn't want Guillermo ruining this day for any of them.

Once she was done she went back to staring at the mirror. Something was missing. Or rather someone.

The bathroom door opened and Josh's mom walked in. "Oh, Sadie. You look so beautiful. But why the sad face, sweetie?"

Sadie took a deep breath, surprised by how close her emotions were to the surface. "I'm fine. I just wish my mom was here today."

Kathy put her arm around her shoulders. "I'm sure she'd love to be here for this."

"Maybe not. She doesn't even know about any of this religion thing for me. I told her some of what I wanted in the nursing home, but...well...I hope she'll forgive me for abandoning her faith."

"You're not abandoning it," Kathy said. "You're adding to it."

Adding to it. Sadie liked that.

"I think my mom supported my aunt and uncle's decision to become Latter-day Saints several years ago. I think. I hope." Sadie sighed. "I've been thinking about her all day, wishing she was here, wishing I could talk to her. I miss her so much."

Kathy's brown eyes filled with tears. "I'm sure she misses you, too. I wish she could be here for you."

"No. Don't you start. If you get me crying, I'll never stop. I'm a big baby."

"I am, too." Kathy fanned her face. "Whew. Okay. I think I'm ready now. Are you?"

Sadie set her brush on the counter. She looked at herself one last time and smiled. "Yeah."

CHAPTER 38

Sadie shook her head in amazement. Seeing Josh in all white was more unbelievable than seeing herself. Deputy Croff took a few quick pictures of the two of them and then stood guard in the hallway. Everyone else waited for them in the Primary Room as Josh gave Sadie a quick tour of the baptismal font.

"You'll go down those steps there," he said pointing. "I'll already be in the water. I hope it's warm."

"Elder Farron promised it would be," Sadie said. Warmth overcame her that had nothing to do with the temperature. She could hardly believe what she was doing. She'd never pegged herself as the religious type.

"Oh, no," she cried. "Sam!"

Josh gave her a strange look. "What about him?"

"I wish Sam could be here, too. In a way, he was the one who started me on this path at the bonfire. He was the first one to point out that God might love *me* and was watching out for *me*. Sam didn't think it was an accident I found you guys at the cabin. He'll be shocked when he finds out about today."

Josh squeezed her hand. "Actually, I don't think he'll be all that surprised. He could tell you were interested in religion. He got after me for not giving you a chance after New Year's. I think Sam knew this day was coming before any of us."

"Really? Now I miss him even more."

They stood in front of the font in their white clothes and bare feet, taking it all in. Sadie thought about home and her boys from Spokane. She thought about the strange turn of events that led her to where she was. Running from Guillermo. Finding Sam's cabin. Meeting Josh. Falling in love. Running again and nearly dying. As horrible as some parts were, it dawned on her that she wouldn't be standing where she was without them. It was a humbling thought because at that moment, she didn't want to be anywhere else in the world, with anyone else in the world.

Josh kissed her forehead. "Thank you," he said softly.

She tilted her head back. "For what?"

"For giving me another chance. For not giving up on me. For believing."

She hugged him. "Funny. I was about to say the same thing."

Lauren was still playing the piano when Josh and Sadie walked in. After an opening hymn, Jake gave a short talk on baptism and the gift of the Holy Ghost. It took all of Josh's will power to keep from staring at his fiancé through the service. Sadie was light itself.

After Jake's talk, the bishop announced the special musical number. Sadie turned slowly to look at Josh, dark eyes wide in surprise. She had planned the entire program—all except the musical number Josh added at the last moment.

He pulled some papers from under his chair with a shrug. "I stole it this morning. Sorry. I know you can play it ten times better than me, but I thought you should be able to hear your favorite song today. Do you mind?"

She looked too happy to fight him, but she wasn't too happy to tease. "Are you sure you can handle it?"

No. He'd already tried a few times. Cursed flats. He was pretty sure he was about to slaughter her arrangement, but he wanted to do this for her. "I guess we're about to find out."

Wiping his hands on his white pants, he walked over to the piano. He sat, took a deep breath, and started Sadie's arrangement of "I Stand All Amazed."

He knew he was going to make mistakes. He knew his hands were going to shake like mad. What he didn't anticipate was Sadie joining in on the second verse. From her seat, she started softly singing the lyrics. In Spanish. It's a good thing he couldn't understand. It was hard enough to play.

When he finished, Sadie stood and gave him a huge hug. He hoped the tears on her cheeks were from happiness and not from pained ears.

"Thank you," she whispered.

Then the bishop motioned to the door. "Lead the way, Brother Young."

With heart thrumming in his chest, Josh took Sadie's small hand and led everyone down the hallway. On his mission in Scotland, he had baptized three people, plus he baptized Katie after he got home. Yet nothing prepared him for this moment.

Sadie went through her door, and he went through his. His dad and Jake stood next to the font as witnesses.

Josh barely noticed the temperature as he entered the waist-high water. Sadie stood across from him dressed in pure white, looking lovelier than he could ever remember. He crossed the small font, took her hand, and led her down the steps.

As he stood next to her in the water, his emotions rose to his throat. Sadie just looked up at him with those large, beautiful eyes and a smile filled with complete love and trust.

Suddenly he couldn't speak. Everyone waited for him to pull it together. He couldn't. Looking down at the love of his life only made it worse. His heart filled to overflowing. So did his eyes.

Smiling, Sadie reached up and wiped a tear from his cheek.

He took a deep breath. And then another. Then, with a prayer of over-whelming gratitude, he closed his eyes and raised his arm to the square.

"Sarah Augustina Dawson…"

Sadie couldn't move. She'd eaten more than should be humanly possible. She stretched out from under Josh's arm on the couch.

Katie put her hands on her hips. "Sadie. Don't move! You're ruining my picture."

"Sorry." She faced front again. Katie was sketching her portrait as a baptism gift. "Can you see Josh or should I scoot back?"

Katie pulled a face. "Ew. Why would I draw Josh?"

Sadie laughed, but Josh purposely made a grotesque face. "What's wrong with my face, KitKat?"

"You really want to know?" Katie asked.

"No, Katie, don't!" Mike jumped up off the floor and ran to her. "Josh doesn't know about the..." His voice dropped to an unintelligible whisper. Sadie heard something about warts and leprosy, and Katie burst out giggling.

"You think I'm bad now?" Josh chucked a pillow at them. "Just wait until the full moon."

Sadie nodded. "Seriously. I've seen him, and it's...uh...wow. Not pretty."

Josh cupped his mouth and let out a raucous howl, which made Katie giggle again. Sadie snuggled into Josh's side. Life was perfect.

"Hey, guys," Josh said, "have I ever told you about the night of the green snow beast?"

Sadie jerked up, cheeks flushing. "No, don't." She liked Josh's family way too much.

He winked at her. "If there's anyone here you should be afraid of, it's the Giant Green Snow Beast. I saw it one dark and stormy night on the slopes of Deer Basin. I'd just put on my snowboard when suddenly"—his eyes squinted and his hands shielded his face—"I was blinded by this horrible ray of light. When I saw where it came from, I shrank back in horror. It was a girl, only she was unlike any girl I'd ever seen before. Her name was—"

"Sadie," Deputy Croff said, coming into the room.

"Yes!" Josh cried. "Sadie, the Green..." His voice trailed off.

Sadie followed his gaze and noticed Croff's expression. She wasn't laughing. If anything she looked sick. Sadie's smile faded. "What is it?"

"Did Agent Madsen call you?" Croff asked.

"No." Sadie reached for her pockets and remembered there weren't pockets in her church skirt. Her phone was in her purse across the room. "Why?"

Josh pulled out his phone and checked the screen. "Madsen didn't call me either. Why? Did they find Guillermo?"

"No. But…" Croff looked between them. "Are you sure he didn't call?"

Sadie panicked. She scrambled to her feet, jumped over Katie, and shuffled through her purse. She found the phone that was never supposed to leave her side, but like Josh, she hadn't missed any calls.

Croff folded her arms and looked at Harrison. "I thought he would tell them. Why wouldn't he tell them?"

"Because he knows what they'll do," Harrison said. "It's a trap and Madsen knows it."

"What?" Sadie and Josh said together.

Deputy Croff turned to Josh's parents. "You might want to send the younger kids out."

They sent the kids home with Jake and Lauren so the two deputies could explain the situation.

"There was no forcible entry," Deputy Harrison said. "Your brother was only gone a few minutes. When he got back, she was gone."

Sadie felt paralyzed. Her thoughts recreated the scene in Kalispell, and she felt numb.

"Madsen doesn't think he'll hurt your mom," Croff went on. "He knows Guillermo is just using her to lure you in. Guillermo knows you're alive, and he's furious. He's doing this to bring you out of hiding."

"Was there a ransom note?" Peter asked softly.

"No," Harrison said.

"Then it's possible Marcela is missing for another reason," Peter said.

Sadie shook her head. "No." There was no other reason. It was her. Guillermo wanted her.

"I thought the FBI was watching their house!" Josh said.

Croff shrugged. "Marcela and Damien were moved to a new location. They probably had agents checking in on them, but Madsen thought…" She shrugged again. "I'm sorry, Sadie. I figured you deserved to know."

Sadie grabbed the couch, feeling a black hole grow in her chest. Her mom was gone. All the weeks of lies—the funeral, hiding—all of it was useless. Guillermo found her mom anyway.

A new emotion surged inside her. It boiled and churned deep down. Her skin was flushed. Her pulse bordered on dangerous. But it still took a moment to identify.

Rage.

The blood rose in her veins, hot and angry. Guillermo threatened Josh. He almost took Katie. He killed Luis and nearly killed Sadie—twice—and she was done.

She took Josh's hand and waited until he met her eyes. Already his expression twisted with pain, yet she had to say it.

"I have to go, Josh. You know I do."

His jaw clenched.

"I have to," she whispered. Tears threatened to break through the wall of rage. She tensed her muscles, refusing to let them win.

He blinked slowly. "If you go, then I go."

She squeezed his hand, grateful he didn't fight her. They were a team now. Except it gave her something new to worry about: Josh in Montana. How was she going to hide him from Guillermo?

"You never should have told them," Harrison muttered to Croff. "If Madsen didn't tell them, even *he* doesn't think it's safe for her in Montana, which—after everything he pulled—is really saying something."

Sadie stood. "I don't care. I'm going."

Croff sighed. "They need to go to Montana eventually. Maybe it's time. They might be able to help search for her mom. We can't force them to stay."

"How soon can we leave?" Sadie asked.

"I'll check the flights," Croff said. "That is, if you're up for flying."

Sadie's stomach did a flip. Flying. She'd forgotten that little part. She held onto the rage and let it strengthen her resolve. She had to get to her mom and she had to get there fast. "Yes. I want to leave on the next flight."

"Wait!" Josh's mom said. "Can't Agent Madsen find Marcela? He has all the resources. If you two go..." Her voice break broke and her eyes reddened. "Please don't go."

"If Guillermo took Katie," Sadie said gently, "would you stay here and do nothing?"

"No, but..."

Sadie knelt in front of Kathy and took her hands. "I'm sick of running. I'm sick of being scared of him. I'm sick of him hurting everyone I love. This has to stop, and it has to stop now." Instead of feeling drained and frightened, she felt strong. She could do this. "If Guillermo wants me to come to Montana, if that will stop this madness, then it's time."

Josh tugged on her hand, pulling her up beside him. He slid an arm around her waist and held her tight. Though he spoke to his mom, he looked at Sadie.

"Once we're in Montana, we'll work with Agent Madsen to know how we can help," Josh said. "Sadie figured out where Guillermo was hiding last time. Maybe being in Kalispell will spark her memories and she'll find him again. But..." His blue eyes narrowed, "we're going to be overly careful. We won't do anything rash or stupid because we're working together as a team, right?"

It took Sadie a moment to answer. She didn't mind working with Agent Madsen, but she refused to let Josh get as close to the situation as she needed to. But at the same time, she'd promised Josh. Why did she promise?

"Right, Sadie?" he said, voice tight.

"Right," she conceded. "Together."

"There's a flight leaving in an hour," Croff said. "If we leave now, we might be able to make it."

"No. Not yet," Kathy cried. She grabbed Sadie's and Josh's hands and pulled them close. Then she grabbed her husband. "We have to pray first."

They formed a small circle. Croff and Harrison stood awkwardly behind them until Sadie motioned them over. "Come on. We need all the help we can get."

As the four of them entered the airport and Sadie saw the masses of people, her muscles started to seize up. She breathed slowly through her nose, but that made her ribs hurt. She couldn't afford to freak out. They didn't have time. Her mom couldn't wait. They had to fly.

She lowered her gaze to the white floor, clutched her fake passport, and tried to numb her thoughts as she filed behind the others.

Josh squeezed her hand. "Are you okay?"

Sadie took another slow breath. *Think about flowers. Think about pretty mountains. Montana Mountains. Guillermo.* "Yes. I'm fine."

"She has to be," Harrison said, shepherding them toward the back of the line. "If not, we'll buy her a few drinks for the flight."

Josh stopped mid-stride. The man behind them almost ran into him.

"He was kidding," Sadie said. "You were kidding, right?"

"Right," Harrison said. "I was just trying to lighten the mood."

Josh glared at his bodyguard.

Sadie nudged him. "Relax. Both of you. I'll be fine. Really. I brought a book and the music Lauren gave me." She even thought about bringing ropes so Josh could tie her to the seat. "I'm fine," she lied again.

Instead of flowers and mountains, she thought about Whitefish Lake, her place of serenity. She could do this.

"Did you end up calling Agent Madsen?" Deputy Croff asked.

"No," Josh said. "We figured if we don't ask, he can't tell us not to come—or what to do once we're there."

"That's probably wise," Croff said. "He's not going to be happy."

Once seated on the plane, Sadie kept her eyes closed. She never looked over her shoulder. She didn't even crack her book. She told herself she needed to sleep so she could be awake and aware once they arrived, and that's what she did. She woke up as they touched down in Denver. As they moved through another airport, she reminded herself it was Croff's job to keep her safe, it was Harrison's job to keep Josh safe, and it was her job to find her mom.

The only time she opened her eyes was as they descended into Kalispell so she could to see her gorgeous Montana mountains. They were close enough now, she dropped the blockade in her mind and used the mountains to spark her memories, thinking through every place Guillermo ever mentioned. His office at the ski lodge. His office in town. His place in Los Angeles. His apartment in Miami. But she couldn't think of anywhere Madsen didn't already know about. Still, her mom was in one of those places and Guillermo expected Sadie to know which.

Once they landed, the four of them drove straight to the FBI office. The roads were snowy and wet, but Harrison pressed the envelope, getting them there in record time.

The last time Sadie had been in the FBI office was during the middle of the day to identify the redhead. This time, it was dark, late, and silent. Croff and Harrison got them through the security gates. Then Sadie took over.

She walked right through the back doors and down the long hallway. She no longer needed crutches and she no longer limped. The others struggled to keep up with her.

As they burst into the offices, she stopped. The room was full of people working well after normal working hours, but that's not why she stopped. The first person she saw wasn't Agent Madsen. It was Agent Dubois. He was hunched over a desk, talking to someone. It was one thing to know Agent Dubois was alive. It was another to see him in person, alive and healthy. It was like erasing a thousand nightmares.

The entire room came to a standstill. From the shocked looks on every-one's face, Sadie figured they knew exactly who she was.

Agent Dubois noticed the strained silence and looked up. An ugly gash on his forehead shot up when he saw her and Josh. He jumped to his feet and approached them.

"Miss Dawson," Agent Dubois said, "what an unexpected surprise. I didn't know you were coming to Montana."

Dubois held his hand out to shake hers. No anger. No malice. He didn't blame her for leaving him to die because it hadn't happened. He was safe, and she was ready.

"No one did," she said. "Where's Agent Madsen?"

CHAPTER 39

Madsen was furious. It took him ten full minutes to stop yelling. After that he kept dropping snide remarks to Josh.

"When *I* want her to come to Montana," Madsen fumed, "you refuse and accuse me of being self-serving. But when I *don't* want her to come, you barge right in and demand to take over. Do you have any respect for the badge I wear, Mr. Young?"

For the most part, Josh ignored him. It's not that Josh wanted Sadie in Montana. His nerves were already fried. He just knew Sadie was going with or without him. Better with. Someone had to keep her head on straight. There was a determination in her eyes that scared the living daylights out of him.

"What places have you checked so far?" Sadie said. "How long has my mom been gone?"

"Just over twenty-eight hours," Madsen said. "We know Guillermo Vasquez was in the Kalispell area earlier that morning."

"Technically," Agent Dubois said, "we don't know he took her. It could have been anyone."

"Guillermo has her," Sadie said. "There's no doubt in my mind."

"Then I'm guessing he has her on the run," Dubois said. "They could be anywhere. As you're aware, Miss Dawson, he has the ability to disappear. I doubt he'll be as careless as he was the last time. I wouldn't be surprised if they aren't even in the country right now."

Sadie glared over at him, a chilling sight when used full force. "No. They're either in Kalispell or Whitefish. I'm sure of it. Guillermo wants me to find her. I know he does."

Dubois glared right back. "And how are you suddenly the expert?"

"Because I found him the last time. He thinks I can find him again, so I just have to think. Where is he?"

Josh shoved his hands in his pockets to keep from punching the wall. He wanted to argue but couldn't. Sadie was right. Guillermo set a trap so she'd come. But she was so disturbingly accepting about the whole thing, it was driving him mad. He was sick thinking about what was coming—what insanity was running through Sadie's mind. She was ready to throw herself to the wolves—to the wolf—if needed. Josh couldn't let her. There had to be a rational way to find Marcela.

"What places can you remember of his?" Agent Madsen asked.

She scanned the map of Kalispell. "Nothing that's not on the list. You've already checked them thoroughly?"

"Yes!" Dubois snapped. "Several times. Try harder. Think!"

"Why don't you?" she shot back. "You're the one who's been investigating him for six months. I only dated him for three."

Josh shifted forward to block Sadie from Dubois' view. It was late, and with tempers mounting, they wouldn't accomplish anything. Rash behavior led to rash decisions. There could be none of that. "Sadie has the list memorized, Agent Dubois," Josh said calmly. "If she remembers anywhere new, you'll be the first to know."

Dubois threw down his pencil. "That's not good enough. Time is ticking."

As if they didn't know that already. Josh had never met Agent Dubois before tonight, but he'd seen him on the ski slopes New Year's Day—the skier in gray. Dubois seemed headstrong and arrogant, almost like Guillermo. But what disturbed Josh was how often he glanced at Sadie.

Even when she wasn't speaking, Dubois constantly watched her. She was an attractive woman, but his expression wasn't one of admiration. It was one of deep and immense hatred, as if he blamed her for Morocco. Josh kept shifting positions to keep her out of Dubois' line of sight.

"Where are they?" someone said from the hall. "Where's Sadie?"

As one, their small group turned. Sadie's older brother, Damien, burst into the room. His eyes were frantic as he searched for Sadie. He looked awful, like he'd been hit by a bus.

"Damien?" Sadie ran across the room and into his arms.

Sadie's brother engulfed her. "You're here. Why are you here?"

"We just got here," Sadie said. "We had to come."

Damien buried his head in her hair as his shoulders began to shake. "I'm so sorry. So, so sorry." He hugged her long and hard.

"Hey, stranger," another voice said behind Josh.

Josh turned and saw a tall, lanky guy. "Kevin?" Josh cried in surprise. "What are you doing here?

Kevin sighed a heavy sigh. "Oh, we kind of live here now."

"We?"

Kevin shifted so Josh could see behind him. Amy stood in the hallway with tears streaming down her face as she watched Sadie and Damien's reunion.

Josh's stomach dropped. "Oh, no. Not you, too."

Their small group sat around a small table swapping horror stories. The longer Josh listened, the angrier he became. Amy could barely look up as she spoke, which wasn't like her at all—although it explained how Guillermo had found Josh's family. Amy apologized over and over, but Sadie kept telling her not to and assured her she wasn't the first to fall for Guillermo's traps. Still, Amy was an emotional wreck.

"How did you guys escape if they were watching your house?" Josh asked.

"When I didn't see anyone outside," Kevin said, "I hoped it was just a threat to keep Amy quiet. It sounds like we got lucky. We went straight to the police, and they brought us here. We've been here ever since."

Sadie glanced at Josh, looking like he felt. Marcela. Kevin and Amy. Luis. Katie. Where did it stop? Or did it?

Agent Madsen came back into the room, and Josh jumped up. "Did you get a hold of Sam and Trevor?"

"Yes," Madsen said. "They're heading to their local police stations until we have a better handle on the situation. I'm hoping now that Vasquez has Mrs. Dawson, he'll leave everyone else alone. But we can't be too careful."

Sadie flinched. Madsen didn't even realize how calloused his words sounded. But in a way it was true. Sam and Trevor were safe, so that was good. But who were they forgetting? Would Marcela appease Guillermo's desire for revenge?

Josh's stomach turned with fury. Marcela was the sweetest, gentlest woman he knew. If Guillermo harmed a single hair on her head…

His fists clenched and unclenched. He begged himself to stay calm and rational. Level-headed.

"My agents are due back in ten minutes," Madsen said. "Their searches should be completed. Hopefully, we'll have something useful then."

Dubois strode forward into the room. "Croff and Harrison," he said, "the U.S. Marshal Administrative officer just showed up. He wants a word with the two of you."

Harrison and Croff stood and left the room to get a report from their branch of the government.

Josh watched Sadie as she quietly talked to her brother. She looked exhausted, reminding Josh of the late hour. It was almost one in the morning in Montana, which meant it was nearly 3 AM Tennessee time. He didn't know how she was functioning.

Then he turned slightly. Like Josh, Agent Dubois was watching Sadie, only the muscles were tight in the agent's neck. Dubois spotted Josh and quickly went back to his laptop, but Josh didn't like the situation. If the FBI agent blamed Sadie for his kidnapping, there was bound to be fallout. They couldn't risk any mistakes now. While Sadie caught up with her brother, Josh decided to do something about it.

He wandered over to the far corner. "Agent Dubois, can I talk to you for a second?"

"No." Dubois went back to his computer without looking up. Josh stood over him, arms folded. After another minute, Dubois realized Josh wasn't going away. He sighed.

"Let me finish this email and we can talk, Mr. Young. But you need to give me some space. I'd appreciate if you'd back up. In spite of what you think, this is still a classified investigation."

While Sadie and the others waited for the latest report, the room grew quiet and tense. Sadie's thoughts strayed to her mom, wondering what Guillermo had done to her. Threats. Violence.

Sadie took Damien's hand. "Was Mom okay before all this?"

"Yeah. She missed you a ton, but she was doing fine. She wasn't too happy about moving to the new place, but we didn't have a choice." Damien's voice grew tight. "How did they find us?" His chin dropped. "Why did I leave her alone?"

"Guillermo won't hurt her, right?" Kevin said to Sadie. "I mean, I know he's crazy, but there's no reason to hurt your mom."

Sadie thought about the Guillermo in the dark Mercedes and the way he'd expertly flicked his knife around as if it gave him a thrill. She thought about Luis' missing fingers and bullet to the head. She shuddered. "Who knows."

Damien nudged her. "You're not going after him, right? You can't. That guy is a freak. You can't give him what he wants. You have to let the authorities deal with this."

In her mind, she knew she shouldn't go looking for Guillermo, but her heart struggled to agree.

"Sadie?" Damien said.

"Have you been talking to Josh? You sound just like him." She sighed. "No. I'm not going to do anything stupid."

"Speaking of Josh…" Kevin reached across the table and picked up her left hand. "What's this, Ice Woman? That's a pretty sparkly ring you got there. It doesn't look very fake to me."

In the midst of everything, Sadie managed a genuine smile. Josh and Agent Dubois were talking in the hallway, so she lifted her hand to show them. "I forgot to tell you. Josh and I are engaged. Surprise."

Damien's eyes popped open. "What?"

"Congratulations," Amy said with her first smile. "That's exciting. Josh is a great guy. You're very lucky. So is he."

Sadie was taken back, but she returned the smile. "Thanks. We're excited."

Kevin shook his head. "That sly dog. I knew once you gave him a chance, he wouldn't wait long. Man, I'm going to razz him so bad. By the way, I'm totally taking credit for the two of you."

She laughed. "Taking credit might be pushing it a little, don't you think, Kev?"

"Oh, please. It was all me."

"So when's the big day? Next week?" Damien asked with a mischievous grin.

She elbowed him. "Come on, I'm not totally crazy."

"Josh is," Kevin said. "Once he knows what he wants, he doesn't let up. You better watch yourself, girl."

Sadie laughed again. She'd missed Kevin. She'd missed all of them.

"Whenever it is," Kevin said, "we're coming. None of this *Agent Madsen says you can't come* garbage. We're going whether you invite us or not."

"Don't worry. We haven't set a date yet, but we'll find a time you all can come once all this settles down." She thought about her mom and the heaviness crept back in. "If it ever settles down."

The room grew silent. Only a few lights were on, creating an atmosphere that felt as lonely as it did cold. Sadie glanced up at the clock. Agent Madsen's team should be back with their reports any second. Until then, there was little she could do. If they came back with nothing new, she didn't know where to start. Guillermo wanted her back in Montana, but if he wanted to see her, he needed to let her know where she was supposed to go.

"Is Josh's family alright?" Amy said softly. "I...I..." She blinked quickly. "I can't believe that I—"

"They're fine," Sadie cut in quickly. "You can't blame yourself, Amy. They're safe, you're safe, and we weren't in Mississippi. I'm just glad you weren't hurt more than you were."

Kevin's blank expression returned again. It was disturbing to see the jokester that way. He pulled his wife close and kissed her forehead. "Me, too," he whispered.

Amy dissolved into tears. "I'm such a coward. I never should have told them. But when they, when he, when I..."

Sadie reached across the table and took her hand. "Don't. I'm serious, Amy. Don't let them get in your head. It's not worth it. Trusting those guys means you aren't evil like they are. You never dreamed what their intentions were. None of us did. And that's okay. Seriously." Sadie waited until Amy looked up. "Don't give them the power. They don't deserve it."

Though it took a minute, Amy nodded.

Agent Dubois walked back into the room. Sadie wasn't sure what Dubois and Josh discussed—Josh probably grilled Dubois on keeping Sadie from doing anything stupid—but Agent Dubois looked stiffer than ever.

"Where's Josh?" she asked.

"He's in the other room with Madsen," Agent Dubois said. "The other agents are back and—"

Sadie knocked over her chair jumping up. "Did they find anything? My mom? Clues? Anything?"

"I'm not sure, but Agent Madsen wants you there for the report."

Sadie didn't have to be told twice. "Show me where they are."

She followed Agent Dubois down the hallway. They turned a corner and headed down another, then he pulled the last door open for her. "After you," he said.

As she entered, she found herself in a semi-dark room. No agents. No Josh. Not even lights. It was a large office with dark shapes of furniture. She tried to turn back, but Agent Dubois pulled the door shut behind them. Her heart jolted.

"What's going on?" she asked. "Where are the others?"

She could barely make out the edges of his smile, but the hair on her arms stood on end. The air pricked with electricity.

"You and I need to talk, Miss Dawson."

CHAPTER 40

Something wasn't right. Sadie was alone in a dark room with the agent who had glared at her for half the night. "Why do you want to talk to me?" she asked.

Dubois stood in front of the door, blocking it. "Because I need to know what you want to do."

"About what?"

"The note," he said.

"What note?" she snapped. Her pulse pounded wildly in her ears. She could barely see his face. Her instinct to run was overpowering to the point of insanity, though she had no reason to. But something felt wrong, horribly wrong.

"This one." Dubois reached in his suit and pulled something out. He handed it to her. Without more light, she couldn't make out anything more than a simple paper folded in half. "Madsen didn't tell you about it because he doesn't want you to know. But Guillermo left this note in your mom's apartment."

"Turn on the light," she said. She couldn't think without a blasted light.

Dubois flipped on the switch behind him. She was momentarily blinded but breathed a little easier.

"Guillermo left me a note," she said, catching up. Of course he had.

It took all of a second to realize what would be in it. She'd known this was coming from the moment she heard her mom was missing.

She clutched it a moment before finding the strength to read it. Guillermo's perfectly formed handwriting lay before her.

Hermosa,

The beautiful Marcela is simply a way for me to find you. Nothing more. You must believe I bear her no ill will. I simply wish to see you. She has not been harmed and will not be if you come to the place we first met. 3 AM. Come alone or you will never see her again. Do not test me on that. It is non-negotiable. If Madsen or anyone else comes within a mile, she dies on the spot.

I look forward to seeing your lovely dark eyes.

~ G

A shiver racked Sadie's body. Guillermo used to leave her notes with roses all the time: to ask her to dinner, to say he'd be away for the day. He loved notes. Now he sent a note inviting her to her death.

Hermosa.

"Why didn't Madsen tell me?" she whispered.

"Because he doesn't have the capability to pull it off," Dubois said. "He won't risk you. You can't press charges if you're dead. You can't testify against Vasquez if you're dead."

Her skin crawled as she pictured the scene Guillermo envisioned at 3 AM. Her walking straight into his arms without a fight.

Your lovely dark eyes.

She looked up at Dubois. "You think otherwise?"

"Guillermo wants a quiet trade. You for your mom. But I think I can pull off a ruse. If you can tell me where you first met, we can scope out the place and see if I can get some agents in there to cover things without being seen. We might be able to get your mom *and* arrest Guillermo without compromising you."

"But he said—"

"I know what he said! I've been studying that note for an hour. But I'm telling you, I can pull it off."

"I don't know." Sadie hugged herself, feeling horribly chilled in the small room. "I need to talk to Josh about it."

Dubois' expression darkened. "You already know he won't risk you. Your boyfriend doesn't trust the FBI, Guillermo, or you."

"Fiancé," she corrected softly.

His brows shot up. He glanced down at her left hand. "Interesting. All the more reason. He'll never risk you."

"Is that what you talked to him about?" she asked.

"Indirectly, yes. I was feeling the situation out while he was chewing me out."

She shook her head. *Josh.*

"Your fiancé is beyond reason," Dubois said. "He's beyond overprotective, as if he doesn't trust you to take care of yourself. He guards you like a watch dog. It's creepy."

Her temper flared. "If you'd been through what we have—"

"I have," Dubois cut in dryly. "I suppose it would have been nice having someone guarding me."

Morocco.

She stared at her hands. She'd wanted an opportunity like this since she heard he was alive. "I haven't had the chance to apologize for what happened to you at Guillermo's cabin. I feel like your disappearance was partly my fault."

"It wasn't," he said flippantly, but there was something off in his tone. He didn't sound convinced. His eyes narrowed down at her. "Do you wish you'd listened to me on Christmas Day?"

"Yes," she said. "I was naïve and stupid. And frightened. It was hard to admit who Guillermo truly was. I only saw what I wanted to see. But a lot of people have paid for my blindness, so I'm sorry. I should have listened to you and Madsen."

"Wow. You've done some maturing, Miss Dawson. Nice to see you admit we were right."

His arrogance was maddening. "What about you?" she fought back. "Do you regret planting the listening device in my purse? That bug almost got me killed. Agent Madsen told me you did it against his direct order."

"Madsen, Madsen, Madsen." Dubois smiled a tight smile. "He's married to his rules, which is why we can't let him ruin this opportunity. Time is running out, Miss Dawson. Your fiancé and Agent Madsen are waiting for us. If you want to make the trade tonight, I need to know now so I can plan and we can sneak you out. Where did you first meet Guillermo?"

She clutched the note, remembering.

The ski lodge. The dining room. She'd been the in-house pianist hoping to catch a break. Guillermo was part-owner of the ski lodge, and he frequented the dining room every day. For some reason, he took an interest in her. At first, he requested a song or two for her to play, and then he stayed longer and longer at the piano asking more about her. After a year of casual flirtations, Guillermo finally asked if he could buy her a drink after her shift. Within a week of their first date, he approached her with an offer to be food service manager, a job that would pay her bills so she could do what she really wanted on the side—compose.

She glanced down and studied his note with a sinking thought. Guillermo didn't want to meet her in the dining hall because that's where they met. He wanted to meet her there because that was the same piano where she'd fallen in love with Josh. Guillermo read her journal. He knew what happened.

That's why he would kill her there.

She bit her bottom lip. Two years of working at the lodge, and she knew the layout inside and out. She struggled to believe Dubois could get anyone into *Guillermo's* lodge without being seen. The place was too restricted and watched. Plus, she promised Josh they were doing things together.

But her mom...

And Josh...

She reread the note. If she went along with Guillermo's plan, Josh wouldn't be involved. Guillermo hadn't asked for Josh to come. Just her. Maybe he didn't know Josh was in Montana, too. Josh would be safe. Her mom would be saved. Guillermo would get what he wanted and leave Josh and everyone else alone.

Her heart sank. She knew she was lying to herself. Guillermo might get her tonight, but he wouldn't stop hunting Josh until he was dead. She knew that with her whole soul. If she went along with this plan, not only could she possibly disappear forever—which would devastate Josh—but he would still be running. She couldn't do that to him. She promised she wouldn't.

Sadie faced Dubois. "If you can reassure us that tonight will go smoothly and we can get my mom without any incident, I'm sure Josh and Agent Madsen will agree to your plan. But I can't do this behind Josh's back. I can't. I owe him too much."

Dubois' expression hardened. "You never do things the easy way, do you? First Christmas, then New Year's. And now you're doing it again. Although, maybe I should be thanking you."

"What do you mean?"

"If it wasn't for your obstinacy, I wouldn't have gone looking for a new boss and a new job." He gave her a bone-chilling smile. "And guess what, I've quadrupled my salary. So thank you, Augustina."

She froze. New job. New salary. But that's not the reason her skin crawled. Only two people in the world called her Augustina.

Her mom.

And Guillermo.

She backed up. Dubois matched her steps, towering over her. "We can't get Agent Madsen and Josh involved in this," he said. "They just complicate things. Plus, by some turn of fate, they're wonderfully preoccupied right now. I'd hate to disturb them. So it's just you and me. Oh, and one other person. He's eager to see you."

Sadie backed into a desk. Her hands felt behind for something she could use—a weapon. She felt papers, papers, and more papers. Her heart pounded. Dubois had murder in his eyes.

"Stay away from me," she said.

"I don't think so. Give me your phone."

Her phone! She reached in her pocket and started punching buttons. "Why?" she stalled.

"To see if Madsen's trying to call you."

She fumbled in her pocket, trying to find the #1 key. Speed dial. Madsen. "Why would Madsen call me?"

"Give it to me now!" Dubois yelled.

"Over my dead body." Her thumbs punched key after key. She couldn't see what she was doing, but she tried every button, hoping to get—

Dubois whipped out his gun and leveled it at her face. "You sure?"

Her hands flew up. She couldn't help it. Dubois was a traitor. Dubois worked for Guillermo. She stared at the end of the black gun, putting the last pieces of the puzzle together. Luis' location had been compromised. Her mom's location had been compromised. She was staring into the eyes of the reason why.

Dubois took her mom. Dubois killed Luis. And at 3 AM, Dubois would turn her over to Guillermo. He wouldn't sneak agents in. There would be no one besides her and Dubois. He would convince her to leave Josh and Deputy Croff and walk right into the hands of Guillermo. No fighting. No struggle. She would walk blindsided into the trap.

Keeping the gun trained on her, Dubois stepped forward and reached in her pocket. He quickly checked her phone and saw what she did. The screen was black. No call had been placed. Madsen wasn't coming.

She was dead.

Dubois smiled, realizing the same thing. "It's time to go now, Miss Dawson. We can't have Madsen or your bodyguard looking for you. This isn't how things were supposed to happen, but this will have to do. I'll never get you alone again. So"—he waved the gun toward the window—"move."

She dug in her heels. "No."

"I said move! And if you make a peep or try to fight me, I'll make sure it's not just your chest filled with lead. I'll kill your mom, brother, fiancé, his cute little family, and every other person in that room back there as well. You or them? Your choice."

The betrayal sliced deep. Dubois had separated her and Josh on purpose. He probably sent Josh to Madsen early so he wouldn't follow her. And, she realized, the U.S. Marshal Administrator to distract Croff and Harrison. She wondered how long before anyone noticed she was gone, especially with one of their own feeding them lies.

Too long.

Her heart shattered. She would never see Josh again.

"The whole time," she whispered. "It's always been you. You weren't patrolling Guillermo's cabin the night of the shots, you were showing up for work."

"Enough talk." Dubois pushed her toward the window. "Open it nice and slow. Don't try anything stupid either. It's a bit of a drop. I'd hate for you to break another leg."

The anger burned hot inside her as she opened the locks. "What's the going rate for stabbing people in the back?" she asked bitterly. "Or how about shooting people through the head?"

Dubois smiled. "You're lucky Madsen was more careful with your file, or I would have found you, too. But I think this worked out better. You came crawling back to Montana just like he predicted. He's so anxious to see you."

Tears pricked her eyes. She refused to let them fall. She would meet Guillermo with her chin held high. She ground her teeth so hard they should have cracked. "I hope it's worth selling your soul to the devil."

"I'd work for free if it meant never hearing your voice again. Now move!"

She opened the window slowly, calculating. There were bushes a few feet down. If she dropped right, she could make a run for it. But then what? What would happen to her mom or Josh if she ran?

Her only hope was in Guillermo holding true to his promise and making the trade. Her for her mom. As devastating as it was, all of her hope rested on the oath of a murderer.

She climbed out the window and lowered herself obediently down. The second her foot touched ground, someone grabbed her from behind. She screamed. One hand clamped over her mouth, cutting off her sound. The other went around her waist and cinched her close.

"Señorita Dawson," a voice hissed in her ear. "How wonderful to see you alive. I did not expect you so soon."

She didn't need to see the face to know who it was.

Salvador. Guillermo's right-hand man.

Agent Dubois waved from the upper window. "I'll be out after I finish things in here," he said. "I just have to make sure they don't come looking for her."

CHAPTER 41

"Give me your hands."

Agent Dubois sat with Sadie in the backseat as Salvador drove. She held her hands out without a fight. She already knew the drill. Instead of using duct tape, though, the agent cuffed her with government-issued metal handcuffs.

"Are you going to gag me, too?" she asked.

"I don't know. What do you think Salvador? Should I gag her?" Dubois said.

Salvador looked in the rearview mirror. "I do not see the point. She cannot be heard where we are going. I think you should leave her be. He shall wish to hear her speak."

Insides shaking, Sadie faced forward, readying herself for the moment she would see Guillermo. Would he drag it out and make her pay for turning against him, or would he just kill her quickly? More importantly, would he let her mom go?

That's where she focused. No matter what else happened, she had to get her mom free.

"I enjoyed your funeral, Señorita Dawson," Salvador said. "It was a lovely affair. And if I might say"—his eyes lifted to the mirror again—"time has not marred your outstanding beauty. It is a great pleasure to see you again. Guillermo will be thrilled."

"Can you gag *him*?" Sadie said angrily.

Dubois laughed. "Aren't you the spicy one tonight? This is going to be fun."

She glared at him. "While you're at it, gag yourself, too."

The men chuckled but thankfully stopped talking.

Sadie risked a glance over her shoulder. No cars followed them. She didn't know what Dubois said back in the FBI offices to Josh or Agent Madsen, but whatever it was, Dubois hadn't glanced over his shoulder even once. He wasn't concerned they were being followed. He confidently kept the gun pointed her direction without the slightest tremor.

Her eyes started to burn. *This is it.* She stared out her side window. She couldn't fathom Josh's reaction when he found out. And after everything they'd been through. She closed her eyes, refusing to imagine it.

Madsen!

Her pulse started racing. Madsen knew about the note. If Agent Madsen could figure out where she and Guillermo first met, he could find her— maybe in time.

The only thing is, Sadie never told Madsen where she and Guillermo met. For the life of her, she couldn't remember if she told Josh either. She didn't like talking about Guillermo. Neither did Josh. But then she remembered something even better. The counselor made her write down every part of her relationship with Guillermo, including where they met. Madsen just had to read it.

Oh please, she begged. *Figure it out.*

Fast!

She watched out the dark window, waiting. Her mountains loomed in the distance. Only instead of growing as they should have, they were shrinking. Salvador was driving the wrong way for the ski lodge. Maybe he was double-checking to make sure they weren't being followed. If that was the case, Madsen and Josh might have time after all.

She worked on stall tactics with Guillermo. He said he wanted to talk. She could talk. She could talk all night if it meant living.

Salvador turned onto a road, taking them further and further from town. She glanced over her shoulder again. Still no cars. As they crossed some railroad tracks and wound off the beaten path, her stomach clenched.

"Where are we going?" she asked. "This isn't the way to the ski lodge."

Dubois gave her a strange look. "Why would we go to the ski lodge? Oh, wait. The note?" He chuckled. "I have a little confession. I told a white lie back there. There wasn't a note—at least not at your mom's apartment. When you showed up unexpectedly, I sent Guillermo a message. He scrawled the note for me and sent it via email so I could give it to you. No. Even if you'd agreed to the 3 AM plan, we wouldn't have gone to the ski lodge. It's much too public a place for what needs to happen. I would have escorted you to the same place I am now."

Sadie stared at him, feeling her world slow to a stop.

No ski lodge. No note.

No Madsen or Josh.

She was dead.

Dubois smiled. She twisted her hands in the metal handcuffs, trying to gauge the space. There wasn't much. Dubois had cinched them tight.

They reached a group of large rectangular buildings. Warehouses. Salvador pushed a button on his visor and a large door opened, like a garage door only three times as big. Once they pulled inside, the door shut behind them. Salvador shut off the lights of the car, casting the whole warehouse into complete darkness.

Salvador got out and flipped on a switch. The immediate area around the car lit up with overhead fluorescence. The rest of the warehouse was pitch black.

Salvador walked around and opened the door for her like he had hundreds of times before. "Come, Señorita Dawson."

She didn't move. She couldn't.

Dubois pushed her out the door. "Go, or you won't see your mom."

"My mom? You mean I can see her?" She scanned her surroundings. What she could see of the warehouse was vast open spaces and high ceilings. "Where is she?"

Salvador grabbed her arm and yanked her up. "She is not expecting you. No one expected you this early. But I am afraid my employer is occupied at the moment, so we must wait. While we do, I shall be compassionate and give you a few minutes to say goodbye to your mother—*if* you do not fight me."

Guillermo wasn't there. He wasn't there yet because he wasn't ready for her. A change of plans. And she was about to see her mom.

There had to be a way out.

As Salvador led the way, Sadie checked every wall of the huge warehouse. She couldn't see a single window or door besides the one they'd come in, but there had to be others somewhere.

Discreetly, she twisted her hands, trying to slip out of the cuffs. They cut into her skin. With a miracle, she'd squeeze out, grab her mom, and run.

They turned a corner and ended up in a hallway with more fluorescent lights. Two huge dark-haired men sat outside of a door at the end of the hallway. As soon as they saw Sadie with Salvador and Dubois, they shot to their feet.

"Let Señor Vasquez know we had a slight change in plans," Salvador said. "Señorita Dawson is here ahead of schedule."

The two men nodded and walked toward them. Both locked eyes with Sadie as they passed, sending a chill down her spine. Her time was ticking. Guillermo wasn't there, but her mom was.

She could do this.

Salvador opened the last door and stepped out of her way so she could enter. The office was dark like most of the warehouse. With the light from the hallway, Sadie could barely make out a mound on a small cot.

"Mamá?" she called softly. Until that moment, she hadn't fully considered that her mom had been hurt. Guillermo said she wasn't, but he lied about everything else. "Mamá?" she called more loudly.

"Augustina?" Her mom rolled over and pushed herself up on the cot. "Augustina is that you?"

"Mamá!"

Sadie tried to leap into the room. Dubois yanked her back.

"Let me go!" she shouted. "Let me see her!"

He pulled out some keys and unlocked her handcuffs. "There," he said, shoving her into the room.

Sadie's bad ankle gave out, tripping her. She landed on her hands and knees.

"Enjoy it while you can," Dubois said, flipping on the light in the small office. "You only have a few minutes."

Sadie's mom grabbed her. They hadn't seen each other since the night before the funeral. Sadie quickly scanned her mom head to toe for any injury, which was difficult to do with how tightly her mom hugged her.

"Are you hurt?" Sadie asked. "Did he hurt you, Mom?"

"No. No, I am fine. Are *you* okay? I can hardly believe my eyes. You are here."

"I'm fine. They didn't hurt me." *Yet.*

Her mom stroked her face. "Oh, *querida*, why did you come? I begged the heavens that you would not come for me. It is a trap. That monster knew you would come."

"I had to, Mamá. When I heard…" Sadie shook her head. There wasn't time. Hugging her mom again, she quickly took in the small room. Desk with a small lamp, a chair, a cot, and a decorative plant in the corner. Nothing else. Not even a file cabinet. Dubois and Salvador stayed by the open door watching them, standing guard where the other two men had. That complicated things.

Sadie pulled her mom close. "We have to find a way out of here," she whispered. "We only have a few minutes. Any ideas?"

"I have been here the whole time, but I have not seen anything. I have checked every corner and there is nothing. That extra door is sealed. There's not even a handle on this side."

Sadie whipped around. She hadn't noticed another door. It blended in with the wall. No handle. No lock. Nothing. Just flat metal shaped like a door. Maybe if they pried it open.

She checked the chair legs. Too fat to fit in the cracks. She needed something thin and strong.

"The door is sealed, Miss Dawson," Dubois said. "Save your breath and spend your last minutes with your mom."

She ignored him. Maybe one door was sealed, but the other was wide open. She quickly took in the size of the two men. Salvador was built like Guillermo, slim and maybe 5'7. But Dubois was a problem. He was close to Josh's height and had a body made for combat. Each of them carried at least one gun, possibly more. And the door was narrow enough to block any chance of escape. She felt her hopes sinking.

There had to be a way.

She heard male voices in the hallway. She froze, listening. It didn't sound like Guillermo, but more men were coming. Or the two men were back. They'd told Guillermo. Whoever it was, time was running out.

She turned her back on Dubois and Salvador. "Did they give you any supplies?" she whispered to her mom. "Anything at all. Think! We need something strong." Sadie eyed the small lamp. If needed, it could be a weapon.

Her mom shook her head. "This is it. There is nothing in the desk. Not even a pencil."

Sadie kept her in a tight embrace. "It's okay. It's going to be okay. Just give me a minute to think."

She didn't even get a second.

"Time's up," Agent Dubois called. He entered the small room. "Follow me."

"No!" Marcela cried. "You will not take my daughter!"

"You're right," Dubois said. "She's staying. You're leaving, Mrs. Dawson. Time to say goodbye."

He grabbed her arm and yanked her to the door. Sadie's stomach dropped at the same time her mom's eyes bulged with terror.

Marcela squirmed and kicked to break free. "NO! I will not leave her! Let go of me!"

Sadie sprang into action. She leaped forward and grabbed her mom by the waist. She tugged and pulled with all her might, hoping their combined body weights could pull Dubois' arms from their sockets.

"Let her go!" Sadie yelled.

"Believe me," Dubois growled, "you don't want her here for this. I'm doing you both a favor."

Sadie stopped cold. Dubois knew what was coming. He was right. Sadie didn't want her mom to witness it.

Her hands opened, letting her mom slip through her fingers. With tears streaming down her face, Sadie watched Dubois drag her mom kicking and screaming toward the door.

"I love you, Mamá!"

Her mom couldn't hear through the tumult. She thrashed around, trying to kick Dubois and whatever else she could find. "Let go of me, you two-faced liar!"

"Mom!" Sadie yelled. "You have to go!"

"NO!!!" It was the growl of a lioness. She thrust out and caught hold of the door jamb. Her legs clamped around the molding, halting Dubois in his tracks.

In a flash, Dubois whipped out his gun and jammed it in Marcela's ribs, making her yelp in pain. "Let go!"

"No!" Sadie screamed. "Don't hurt her!"

"Kill me if you have to," Marcela said through clenched teeth, "but I'm not going! Not without my daughter!"

"Fine! You want to watch her die?" Dubois yanked her back up and into the room. He didn't let go of her. Breathing heavily, he grasped her arm but kept his body between them, separating mother and daughter. His gun stayed by Marcela's cheek. "You make one sound, even one, and I'll put a bullet through your brain so fast you won't know what hit you. Not one word, do you understand, Mrs. Dawson?"

Sadie's mom nodded, mouth clamped shut. Her eyes found Sadie, tears leaking down her reddened cheeks. Sadie heard the words she couldn't speak. *I love you.*

Sadie's heart pounded so loudly in her ears she couldn't speak either. *I love you, too.*

With her mom silent, the hallway fell frighteningly quiet, too. And empty. Salvador had disappeared. The other men's voices stopped as well. Sadie couldn't see anything out there but white walls, yet she could feel it coming.

When would it hit?

When would he come?

What would he do?

Why did her mom have to watch?

She felt a sudden presence behind her. She whirled around. Nothing but a desk and a wall. And then she saw something that caused her blood to run cold. The sealed door was no longer sealed. It was opened a crack.

She spun around again. No one but Dubois. Even her mom was blocked from view. But she could feel him in the room.

Guillermo.

"Where are you?" she breathed.

Dubois laughed. "Oh, this is payback."

Sadie hugged herself, waiting for the ball to drop. Though nothing changed, the room felt ten degrees colder.

She heard a movement and whirled again. Her fists swung wide and hit nothing but air. Her claws were ready.

"Where are you?" she screamed.

Dubois motioned behind her.

She turned too late.

Someone grabbed her by the waist. Not hard. Not sudden. More like a snake slithering its coils around its victim.

She froze as the chest of a man pressed up against her back. The man was short and his arm forceful around her waist. She felt his smooth business suit and smelled his familiar cologne. Only one person in the world wore a business suit and cologne at two in the morning.

Guillermo pressed his face into her short hair. He inhaled slowly, taking in her scent as well. Then he whispered one word in her ear and one word only. A word she'd run from in her dreams. A word she never wanted to hear again. Though it was barely a breath against her skin, it shook her entire body.

"*Hermosa.*"

CHAPTER 42

Sadie didn't wait.

She thrust her head backward. She judged wrong and only grazed the side of Guillermo's face.

His arm cinched around her waist, sucking the air from her tender lungs. Her ribs weren't totally healed and she cried out as he crushed them. His other hand ran up her arm, over her shoulder, and to her throat. It didn't clamp around it, though. Slowly and softly, his fingers stroked the skin of her neck, leaving a trail of fire in its wake.

"You look well, *hermosa,*" he whispered.

"Don't call me that! Get away from me!"

She clawed his arm, trying to break free. When it did nothing, she raised her leg to ram her heel in his shin.

"Dubois!" Guillermo shouted.

Dubois' gun rose to her mom's eye. Seeing a gun that close to her mom took the last of Sadie's breath. She went completely limp in Guillermo's arms.

"Stop!" she cried. "Stop. I won't fight. Don't hurt her, please!"

Guillermo nodded at Dubois, who lowered the gun. He didn't put it away, though. He kept it low. Her mom was crying softly though her lips were tight and determined to remain silent.

Slowly, Guillermo's grip loosened on Sadie's waist as if testing to see if she'd bolt. When she didn't, he turned her toward him.

"Ah, that is more like it," he said with a smile.

Suddenly she was face to face with the man who had haunted every day of her life since that dark night in the Mercedes—both for her and her loved ones. His eyes, black as ever, slowly took in every inch of her.

"Hermosa, my beautiful one," he whispered. "How I have missed you. Your short hair suits you well."

"Is that why you cut it?" she said bitterly. "Or were your knife skills so poor you missed my throat?"

His hand whipped out so fast, she didn't have time to flinch. Metal flashed, he lunged, and his knife was at her throat. "You tell me."

Marcela jumped. "You touch one hair of her—"

Dubois whirled and punched Marcela in the jaw. Marcela yelped and went down. "I said not a peep!" he yelled over her.

Sadie's mom doubled over, crying and holding her head. Sadie didn't flinch for fear of the blade millimeters from her throat. Her breathing turned painful as she looked at Guillermo again. He didn't give Dubois or her mom a single glance. His gaze never left her.

"My knife skills are as good as ever, *mi amor.* But it seems your inner fight has improved some. I like that." He smiled a smile that sent a shudder through her entire body. "I like that a lot."

"You're sick," she whispered. She meant to yell it in his face, to scream at him for everything he'd done to her and her mom. To Josh, his family, Kevin and Amy. It all deserved to be screamed in his face, but she couldn't get the air into her lungs. A whisper would have to be good enough.

"Are you okay, Mom?" she asked, turning her head slowly to face her.

Her mom stayed hunched over, but her chin lifted slightly. Though her face was red and puffy, she nodded.

Sadie's eyes burned with hatred. "Don't touch her again."

"She was warned," Dubois said.

Sadie looked into the black eyes inches from her own. "This is between you and me, Guillermo. Leave my mom out of it. Tell Dubois to leave her alone. You promised. Tell him to back off."

Guillermo took this in a moment before he dropped the knife and slid it into his suit coat. "Agent Dubois has earned my utmost respect recently. He found the two people no one else could. He has proven himself well, which is why I am making him a junior partner."

Dubois looked up in surprise. "Really?"

"It was a test," Sadie whispered. "Luis said that night was a test, but it wasn't for me, was it? You were testing *him.* You sent him to Morocco to see if he'd come crawling back to you." She felt sick. "And he did."

Guillermo smiled. "Brilliant strategy, no? But it was a test for both of you, and it panned out perfectly. I needed to test your loyalty to me." He paused, jaw clenching a moment. "And Dubois needed to prove his loyalty without alerting Agent Madsen. You have seen tonight how valuable it will be to have him on the inside. My life will be so much easier now."

The anger grew inside her like a hurricane. "I hope you both die a long and painful death. And I hope that day is today."

"Now, now." Guillermo stroked her cheek. "A little venom is attractive—seductive even. But do not let it grow to the point of poison."

She jerked back. "Don't touch me!"

"Fair enough." He took a step back and clasped his hands in front of him. "I am here to talk, *hermosa.* We have much to say to one another. Life has been cruel to both of us. We should not be here like this."

"You're right," she spat. "You should be in prison."

He shook his head with a long sigh. "Cruel indeed. After we talk, you will see. We belong together."

Sadie stared at him. He was insane. Certifiably so. "If you want to talk, then let my mom go. Now. You promised if I came, she wouldn't be hurt."

"You are right. To show you I only mean well…" Guillermo motioned to Dubois.

The agent sprang into action.

Sadie squeezed her eyes shut, but try as she may, she couldn't block out her mother's cries as she was dragged from the room.

The door closed behind them, and after a second, Sadie couldn't hear her mom anymore. Still, tears leaked from her eyes. She hated her tears and quickly blinked them away. Guillermo didn't deserve them.

"There," he said. "Now, let us speak amiably to one another."

"Not yet," Sadie said. "You have to promise that not a single cell of her is harmed ever again."

"Done."

"Everyone else, too. Your hunting days are over. I don't want to hear of another person harmed again. You're through." She didn't know what she was asking, or why she thought an insane crime-lord would agree with her ridiculous requests, but he nodded.

"Agreed," Guillermo said. "No more hunting. You have my word."

Josh. His family. His friends. She was desperate enough to believe him.

"Now…relax, *amor*. Please."

He took his own advice and leaned against the small desk. Now that the door was closed, the room seemed to shrink around them.

"I have missed you, *hermosa*. I mourned for you deeply. Do not forget, I believed you dead until yesterday." He smiled sadly. "Grief can change a man."

Bile churned in her stomach. His peaceful demeanor frightened her more than his wrath.

His black brows lifted. "You do not believe me?"

"Not for a second," she hissed.

"Hmmm." He motioned to her ankle. "Tell me, what did you do to your leg? You favor it quite heavily."

She had the sudden urge to scratch out both of his eyes. "You'll find out in court."

"Ah, yes. Court. I saw your name on the paperwork." He folded his arms. "It seems my friend, Señor Madsen, has sunk his lies deep into your head. Tell me you do not believe him."

"*You* tried to kill me in the car," she shouted. "You did. Not Madsen. *You* tried to burn me alive—not Madsen! And *you've* tried to kill little girls and wives of my friends since then. People you don't even know. Where are the lies in that?"

"Misunderstandings," he said, picking a piece of lint from his black suit. "Nothing more."

Words escaped her. Guillermo's reality was more bizarre than her nightmares. His world was so upside-down and delusional, she could do nothing but gape at him.

He pushed away from the desk and approached her again. He reached up as if to stroke her cheek, but she swatted his hand away.

"I said don't touch me!"

He looked genuinely pained. "Why? We belong together."

"What kind of dream world are you living in?"

"The kind that ends up with you and I together. The kind that finds your mother safe, happy, and very wealthy. You would like to see her again, no? You would like to see your brother as well? Damien is a fine, young fellow. I imagine you would like for him to have a long, happy life. I imagine you also want your own life back, no?"

She didn't answer. She couldn't. She could barely even breathe.

He took another step closer. "Everything could go back to how it was, *hermosa,*" he whispered. "In fact, it could be better. I am more powerful than ever. After the FBI botched Dubois' death, I have people flocking to me. Mayor Calstop has joined my ranks. Judge Grimmel. As you can see, I even have FBI Agents on my side. I am running half of Montana, and soon, it will be more. We can live wherever you chose, however you chose. Can you not see that?" He reached up again and somehow found skin. His fingers brushed her jawline the way they used to, causing fire to burn through her soul. His black eyes locked on hers, pleading. "You would never have to run again. You would never have to be scared again. We belong together."

She felt like throwing up. Nothing made sense. Why try to kill her—twice—if he supposedly loved her? She couldn't find any logic in it. Guillermo had never acted so crazy before. She wanted to close her eyes to block him out but didn't dare. Instead, she found the strength to push him away.

"I said don't—"

He caught her hand mid-air. His eyes widened. "What is this?"

She followed his gaze and froze. A large, square diamond sparkled in the lamplight.

His jaw tightened and the veins in his forehead bulged. His eyes lifted to hers with sudden vengeance.

"What is this?" he hissed in her face.

She lifted her chin. "I'm getting married."

She waited for him to strike her. She braced herself for the imminent blow. It didn't come. He just heaved deep breaths. In. Out. In. Out.

"Little mousy got brave, did he?" he seethed. "He wants you for his own now, does he?"

She winced as his grip tightened on her wrist, strong enough to snap bones.

"And you said yes?" he spat.

"Wholeheartedly."

Again, she flinched in anticipation. She'd felt his fist before and for much less defiance. Maybe this time she would duck the right direction. Instead, Guillermo lifted her hand closer.

"You left me for this?" Humor suddenly colored his tone. "For this?" He turned her ring so she could see it—as if she hadn't memorized it already. "What rags have you reduced yourself to? You want to be the wife of some…peasant?"

She yanked her hand free. "Josh is everything you are not. He's generous, honest, and—"

He swung fast. She saw skin before pain exploded on her cheek as the backside of his hand slapped her. The sting blindsided her. She resisted the urge to cradle her cheek and found the strength to stand tall.

Squaring her shoulders, she said, "I love Josh. He is mine. And you...are nothing."

Guillermo's black eyes turned to small slits. "Careful, beautiful one. Those are strong words with strong consequences. I am offering you a life—a perfect life. Do not force us down another path."

"There is no us!" she yelled. "There never will be. That ended the second you tried to kill me!"

Guillermo's chest heaved in and out. "Give me the ring."

She closed her hand in a fist. "No."

"Take it off!" he screamed.

"I hate you."

The knife she'd forgotten whipped out. He lunged and pressed it to her neck. "Give me the ring. Now!"

She winced as her skin stung with pain, but she stood her ground. "What are you going to do, try to kill me again? Really? Because that's getting old."

The blade pressed into her skin. Pain burned, not unbearable, but enough to bring tears to her eyes. "This new Augustina talks too much," he hissed in her face.

"My name is Sadie."

"I am done negotiating! You have two choices: live a life of luxury with me and your mother, or die."

She was ready to say die and nearly did. It was on her lips, but something else leaped in her mind. It explained why Guillermo hadn't killed her yet. Why he supposedly wanted her back. But more than anything, it explained why he was acting completely insane.

"You're scared of me," she whispered.

He jerked back. "What?"

"You're scared of me," she said again, awed by the realization. "You tried to kill me twice, and I escaped both times. For all you know, I'll escape again. As soon as I do, you know I'll throw your psychotic self into prison. I'm ready to tell the whole world and every one of your precious little contacts exactly who the real Guillermo Vasquez is. A coward who's scared of little Sadie Dawson." She started to smile. "You're scared of me."

Something flashed in his eyes. Validation, perhaps. She didn't wait to find out.

She bolted.

Ducking, she ran to the left. She made it to the desk and nearly had the lamp when he caught hold of her.

She jerked back. Her skull collided with his cheek bone. He cried out. Her head spun with pain of her own, but she whirled around, grabbed the lamp, and ripped it from the wall. She swung wide and missed.

Guillermo rammed into her. Grabbing her, he threw her against the wall. The lamp crashed to the floor. Air rushed from her tender lungs. He grabbed both wrists and pinned her to the wall as she gasped for air.

"You added steel to those delicate bones," he whispered in her face. "I like it. But you will be tamed. Tamed or broken. Makes no difference to me."

Tears leaked from her eyes. She tried to knee him. He was leaned too far forward. "Stay away from me!" she wheezed. Then she spat.

He dodged in time.

Her fingers curled around his hands and scratched any skin she could reach. He put more pressure on her wrists until she couldn't feel her fingers anymore.

"It has come to this, my precious, feisty Augustina," he said, breathing heavily. "Either you come with me willingly, or you take your last breath right here, right now."

"Or none of the above!"

She squirmed. Pain shot down her arms. In another second, he'd shatter her wrists. "I'm done letting you decide my fate," she said. "I don't know how, but I'll get out of here, and I will take you down."

"Are you certain?" he said.

Was she? Guillermo had a huge organization with thugs, mayors, and judges backing him up. Plus an endless supply of cash. She was nothing in comparison. And yet, she was something, and he couldn't take that away from her. He never would again.

"I could die right now," she said, "and that's fine." Tears streamed down her cheeks, contradicting her bold words, but she didn't care. She found a resolve she hadn't felt before. God loved her. Her mom knew she loved her. And Josh knew she loved him more than life itself. It had to be enough. "You can't do anything to me you haven't done already, so get on with it, because I'll never change my mind."

His murderous gaze bore into her. She didn't blink, refusing to back down. Refusing to cower another minute to Guillermo Vasquez.

Suddenly, he shouted over his shoulder. "Salvador! Bring him in."

Him.

The word unhitched something inside of her. A blinding panic. Her head whipped back and forth, trying to see around Guillermo. He kept her pinned against the wall as the door opened.

With a grunt, Salvador dropped something heavy inside. A mound.

A body.

It hit the floor with a loud thud.

Her heart jumped into her throat as she saw the mass of dark hair. She knew that hair anywhere.

Josh.

Guillermo broke into a wicked smile. "I think you shall change your mind now."

CHAPTER 43

"Josh!" Sadie yelled.

Josh didn't move. He was tied at the wrists and ankles like she had been once. His mouth was taped to keep him from speaking. Not that it mattered. His eyes hadn't opened.

She writhed and kicked to break free of Guillermo's grasp. She was pinned to the wall, and Josh wasn't moving.

"Josh!" she screamed.

How did Guillermo have Josh? Josh was meeting with Madsen. He was getting the reports. He was safe! Yet his face was pale and silent. He looked dead already.

Her breaths came in short bursts. "What did you do to him?"

But before Guillermo answered, she suddenly remembered. The last time she'd seen Josh, he was talking to Agent Dubois. Josh never met with Madsen. He never made it that far.

And Guillermo had been late getting to her. He was late because he was dealing with something—or rather, someone.

Josh.

Her world collapsed. So did her voice.

"What did you do to him?" she cried, voice hoarse. "Josh!"

Guillermo didn't release the pressure on her wrists as he glanced over his shoulder. "Oh, your man and I had a little talk. Actually, he does not deserve the title of man. A boy. An insignificant mouse, perhaps. One little punch from me, and he dropped like a rock. Even you lasted longer than that." Guillermo chuckled. "It is a shame he did not feel the rest of his 'talking to.' It is a bigger shame you arrived early. I had big plans for Señor Young. I was truly enjoying our time together."

"Josh!" she cried again.

Still nothing.

She searched every part of his body for injuries. He was faced away from her too far to tell. She had no idea how beaten he was. How broken he was. She couldn't even tell if he was breathing. For all she knew, his injuries were internal. Fatal.

She felt herself sliding down the wall. Her legs couldn't hold her up any longer. Guillermo pressed harder on her wrists to keep her from falling.

"That will be all," he said to Salvador. "Keep watch outside the door. Make sure we are undisturbed."

Salvador nodded and left the room. Left Josh on the floor. Motionless.

Sadie couldn't make out Josh's shape anymore. The tears flowed freely. Everything was a huge blur of pain. "What did you do to him?" she tried again.

"Oh, he is alive. For the moment. He just needs—"

Guillermo turned and that was his mistake. Sadie kicked. Hard. She found shin.

He grunted and loosened his grasp. It was enough.

She jerked left and broke free.

Dropping, she scrambled on the floor and found the lamp. Guillermo grabbed her leg and yanked back. She swung around. The metal base caught his shoulder. He cried out but only for a moment. Then he was scrambling after her.

She ran for the sealed door that was no longer sealed. Ten feet. Eight feet. Just a little—

Guillermo leaped and caught her shirt. The corner ripped off. With a loud growl, she saw a flash of metal. Black metal.

A gun.

She dropped, rolled, and rammed the lamp up again, not knowing where he was, but trying anyway. She hit nothing. The momentum sent her sprawling. She fell flat on the floor.

Guillermo leaped up and rolled her over. He straddled her stomach, pinning her wrists to the floor. His expression was something animal, heaving in deep gulps of breath over her.

"Are you done fighting?" he asked.

"Nev—"

The pain cut off her words as his weight squeezed the air from her lungs. She squirmed and kicked and struggled to maneuver. She managed to kick his back. It did nothing but anger him further. He shoved the gun to her cheek.

"Enough!" he yelled. "You will yield, or I will—"

Suddenly Guillermo was flying. He was flying and then falling. He slammed onto the floor next to Sadie.

She scrambled backward, trying to get free. Trying to figure out what happened.

Then she saw.

Josh jumped on Guillermo. He rammed his knee in Guillermo's back. One hand held Guillermo's arm behind his back, the other held his head to the ground.

Sadie couldn't think straight. She watched it all like a dream. Josh was shouting at Guillermo, but someone was shouting through the door. Salvador.

Something rammed into the first door. The door was locked. It didn't budge, but it snapped her out of her stupor.

She jumped up. "Josh, are you okay?"

"Get the gun!" he shouted.

She spun around, searching. Guillermo's gun lay on the floor behind her. Somehow, Josh knocked it from his hands. She scrambled over, grabbed it, and ran it back to Josh. Josh put more weight on Guillermo's back, pressing his knee into his spine. Guillermo grunted in pain.

Sadie struggled to hand over the gun. Her hands were shaking like mad. "How are you okay?"

Josh pressed the gun to Guillermo's side. "I was playing dead, waiting for my chance to break free. He's an idiot to believe me, just like he was an idiot to believe you were dead. But it doesn't matter. He's done. You're done!" Josh shouted at Guillermo.

"You cannot shoot me," Guillermo said, cheek pressed into the floor. "You probably do not even know how to use a gun."

Josh shoved the gun into his ribs, making Guillermo yelp. "My dad's a cop. I grew up doing target practice. You should know that, or didn't your research on my family turn that up?"

Sadie saw something animal in Josh's eye, too. It frightened her beyond anything else.

"Josh, stop!" she cried.

"I heard every word you said to her," Josh said without looking up. "Your guy, Salvador, was listening in, and so was I, you sick jerk. You're never going to hurt her again. You're never going to touch her again. Ever, you hear me?"

"Josh!" she cried, grabbing his arm. "Stop!"

She tugged hard. He looked up at her and blinked hard, as if coming back to reality. As if realizing he was seconds from killing Guillermo. Pushing himself up, he stood next to her, never letting the gun leave Guillermo's line of sight.

"Let the authorities deal with him," Sadie said, holding Josh around the waist. "They'll take care of him."

He nodded, breathing heavily. He wiped his cheek. His hand came away red.

Sadie gasped. "You're bleeding!"

The upper part of Josh's cheek had a nasty red gash. His left eye was swollen, and blood dripped down the side of his face onto his shirt. That's when she noticed his shoulder. His left shoulder hung lower than the right, like it was dislocated.

A wave of nausea hit her, remembering how Guillermo talked of beating up Josh after he 'passed out.'

"What happened?" she asked, checking for more injuries. "What did he do to you?"

"I'm fine." Josh's eyes flickered to her briefly. "Are you okay? I was working on the duct tape, trying to get it off without alerting him, so I heard everything. And I thought... I thought he might..." His hand tightened on the trigger. "Call Madsen before I do something I'll regret."

She nodded. But then she remembered. "Dubois took my phone."

"He took mine, too."

They both looked around the room. No phones on the desk.

Salvador shouted through the door, pounding it, reminding them he was there.

"I locked it when I jumped up," Josh said, "but the door's not going to hold for long. He's going to break through any second."

"There's another door," Sadie said. "Guillermo came in—"

"Salvador! Now!" Guillermo yelled.

Something rammed into the door. It wasn't human. It was metal on metal. Something huge.

"Get behind there!" Josh shouted at Sadie.

Sadie ran behind the desk as Josh, keeping the gun steady, shoved all his weight against the door.

Salvador rammed the door over and over again. Josh was taller and heavier set than Salvador, but the door jumped with every slam. It took all Josh's weight to keep it shut. And with his bad shoulder, he had to work sideways.

Salvador shouted through the door, something incoherent and furious. Sadie was more concerned about Guillermo. He was starting to slide sideways. Toward her.

She grabbed the lamp from the floor. "Don't move!"

Josh turned and saw Guillermo moving. He raised the gun. "Not another inch!"

Guillermo froze, face down, hands sprawled outward. "I'll stop, but first..." In an instant, he switched to rapid Spanish, knowing Josh would never understand. "Shoot through the door!" he ordered. "He is behind the door. Now! Now! Now!"

"Josh!" Sadie screamed.

He'd already moved. He rolled to the side as a blast of fire hit the door. The bullet whizzed past and slammed into the back wall. Another shot sounded, and Sadie crouched behind the desk, hands over her ears.

Another shot.

Josh slid along the wall and dropped into a crouch next to her.

"Stay down!" he shouted. She wasn't sure if he shouted it at her or Guillermo. Probably both. She curled in a tight ball under the desk as another shot sounded, this time with a high metallic screech.

The lock.

Suddenly the door burst open. Salvador leaped into the room.

"Drop it!" he yelled at Josh. "Drop the gun! Now!"

CHAPTER 44

The gun fell to the floor with a thud.

"Now kick it toward me," Salvador said.

As soon as Josh did, Guillermo jumped up and grabbed it. Suddenly Sadie and Josh had two guns pointed at them, one from each side of the desk.

Josh pulled Sadie close, both of them crouched low against the wall. He didn't look at either man, but he stared deeply in her eyes. "I'm sorry. I'm so sorry. I love you."

"Silence!" Guillermo shouted.

Sadie didn't. She tried to smile at Josh. "It's okay. It's going to be okay." Even if it wasn't, it was. Josh was with her. No matter what happened next, it was okay. "I love you more than anything."

"I said silence!" Guillermo kicked the chair, sending it flying. It slammed into the wall, making them both jerk up.

"Now stand," Guillermo said. "Both of you. Slowly."

Josh held Sadie's hand and pulled her up. Her legs shook beneath her, but she kept her chin high. If she was going to die, she was dying with dignity. She interlocked fingers with Josh and squeezed his hand with all her might, trying to reiterate the message.

I love you. I love you. I love you.

Josh took a step sideways, pulling her with him. Guillermo smoothed down his business suit which had gone askew from his face plant. Josh took another tiny step sideways—another step toward Guillermo. Only not quite. He was moving them diagonally away from the door and Salvador. Sadie didn't know what Josh was doing, but she kept sliding with him. Guillermo brushed the dust and dirt from the front of his suit before he looked up.

"That's close enough," Guillermo said, waving his gun.

Another tiny step forward.

The gun rose to Josh's chest. "Back away from her now, little mouse. Nice and slow."

In a flash, Josh yanked Sadie behind him, throwing her off balance. Before she could right herself, she was shoved behind his body and pressed into the corner of the room, shielded from the onslaught of shouting that erupted.

"I said back away!" Guillermo yelled. "Now!"

"Not a chance!" Josh said.

"I will shoot you, little mouse! I have been waiting to for some time. And now I have the perfect shot."

"NO!" Sadie yelled. She tried to get around Josh. Both of his hands grabbed her, trapping her behind him in the corner of the room. Then he leaned back, ramming her so far in the corner she could barely breathe. She couldn't see a thing. She couldn't move if she tried.

"Josh, no!" she cried into his back.

He ignored her. "You missed your chance," he said to Guillermo. "You won't shoot me, and we both know it because if you shoot me, you'll shoot her, too. The bullet will go through both of us. She'll go down with me."

Sadie realized he was right. If he died, she died.

She grabbed his hands and pressed her cheek to his back, waiting for it.

Guillermo laughed a horribly disturbing laugh. "Why should that matter to me now? You turned her against me."

"Believe me," Josh said, "that was all your own doing. So do what you must. If you kill us, we die together. We still win."

Sadie squeezed his hands. Josh squeezed back.

"I will do it!" Guillermo screamed. "I will shoot both of you if you do not back away from her right now."

"No, you won't," a new voice said. "Drop the gun."

Sadie heard shuffling around the room. She peeked out from around Josh. Agent Madsen stood behind Guillermo and Salvador as the room flooded with a dozen men in black.

"I said drop it!" Madsen shouted. "Now!"

Salvador dropped his gun immediately. It clanked to the floor. But Guillermo held strong. His nostril's flared as he glared at Josh and Sadie shoved in the corner. Sadie wrapped her arms around Josh's waist and closed her eyes, bracing for Guillermo's last stand. A last shot.

"Now!" Madsen yelled.

She heard metal hit cement and looked up. Guillermo's black eyes bored into her as he dropped his gun.

"Now hands in the air," Madsen said. "Do it!"

Guillermo's hands rose slowly.

The SWAT team swarmed the two men. Half grabbed Salvador. The other jumped Guillermo. Both men were patted down and checked for more weapons.

"He has a knife," Josh said. "Inside his suit coat."

Sadie watched it all in a haze, unable to do anything else. Josh didn't move either. He kept her in the corner as if both of them were unable to budge. But then Sadie started to shake. From her stomach outward, her entire body started to tremble.

Guillermo's eyes never left her as he was handcuffed.

"You're done," she said to him. She wasn't able to shout it. It was barely more than a whisper in the room, but he understood perfectly. He blinked in response.

She was done, too. Done looking at the face that would no longer ruin her life. She buried her head in Josh's shoulder as more of her started to shake. Her legs. Her arms. She breathed as slowly as she could to convince herself it was over.

Guillermo was done.

Suddenly, she was enveloped in a hug so fierce, it nearly choked her. Josh grabbed her, and she melted into his chest.

"We did it," she said. "We beat him."

He kissed the top of her head. "*You* beat him."

Someone ran over to them. A tall and terribly frightened-looking Deputy Croff. "Are you okay? I can't believe you're here. What happened?"

"Dubois took us—" Sadic started to say. Then her stomach dropped. "Oh, no! My mom!" She grabbed Croff's hand. "Agent Dubois has my mom. He's working for Guillermo, and he has my mom somewhere."

Croff laid a hand on her shoulder. "The former FBI Agent, Stephen Dubois, was taken into custody moments ago. Your mom is out front in a squad car, safe and unharmed."

"You got Dubois?" Sadie asked, struggling to breathe, to think.

"Yes," Croff said. "You should probably show her you're alive as soon as possible. I don't think she'll believe it until she sees it for herself."

"I'm not sure I believe it."

"Me, neither." Josh hugged her to him with his good arm, reminding her of his injuries. Now that the adrenaline was dying down, she realized what bad shape he was in. She wiped the blood from his cheek with her sleeve. The gash below his eye was hideous, and his left eye was swelling shut. Then there was his shoulder. It hung at a sickening angle.

"You need help," she said. "Josh needs help."

"I'll go get someone," Croff said.

"No, I'm fine," Josh said.

Only he wasn't. Sadie blotted his cheek with her sleeve. It kept coming back bright red.

"Where else are you hurt?" she asked. Guillermo could have inflicted all sorts of injuries on him while he was playing dead.

"I'm fine. We're fine," he said. "I just need to hold you for a minute."

He pulled her in again, and they leaned on each other. Sadie's limbs shook less and less as she hugged him with all her might to keep both of them upright.

After a minute, Madsen wandered over. "Good to see you two again. Alive. Dubois told us you two took off to find your mom."

"How?" Sadie said.

Madsen gave her a strange look. "How what?"

She worked to slow her breathing and racing thoughts enough she could speak coherently. "How did you find us? Here?"

"We had a little help." Madsen turned slightly, revealing a man in the doorway. He wasn't dressed in black like the SWAT team. But neither was he dressed in a suit like Agent Madsen. He was just a simple young man with black hair and tired eyes.

"Manuel," she breathed.

Guillermo's little brother didn't hear her. He was too busy watching the scene unfold. Already Salvador had been escorted from the room, but Deputy Harrison was in the middle of reading Guillermo his rights. Guillermo was faced away. He still hadn't seen his little brother. But Sadie had.

She took Josh's hand and led him through the mess. Manuel's eyes widened as he saw her approach.

"You're alive," he said.

Her eyes burned with gratitude. "You brought them?"

"I'm sorry it took so long," Manuel said. "I had to shake a guy. And then I had to find Agent Madsen because I just…" His chin dropped. "I couldn't let you die again."

Guillermo's head spun around at the sound of his brother's voice. The rest of him tried to turn as well, but Harrison had him in a tight grip, arms bent behind his back.

"Manuel!" Guillermo screamed. "What have you done?"

"What I should have done years ago. Excuse me," Manuel said to Sadie. Then he walked straight up to Agent Madsen. "Everything you need is in

Guillermo's office down the hall. All of his business records, his drug income, plus his contacts in the States and back in Venezuela. It's all listed in the brown file in the lock box. The code for the box is 83—"

Guillermo turned red with rage. "Don't you dare! Do not say another word!"

"—4032961," Manuel finished tiredly. "Whatever isn't in there, I can help you find."

"You are dead!" Guillermo thrashed around, and two more agents jumped in to help Harrison. Guillermo wasn't going anywhere, but he tried anyway. "Do not believe when they say they will hide you," he ranted. "I found Luis, I found Augustina, and I will find you. And when I do, you are dead. Dead, *hermanito*!"

Agent Madsen nodded to Deputy Harrison. "Get him out of here."

Sadie forced herself to watch Guillermo go. She wanted it to be a lasting image in her mind. Justice. So she did. But the second he was gone, a weight lifted from her shoulders.

Josh pulled her close again and pressed his lips to her forehead. "It's over."

She hugged him. If a list of Guillermo's contacts were down the hallway, then it really was over. Guillermo's organization would unravel faster than he could build it. Without his contacts, he was friendless. And if the FBI seized his assets—which was bound to happen if his business files were there, too—he was powerless to buy more friends. Manuel said it. Everything they needed was here in the warehouse.

"Guillermo should have taken me to the ski lodge," Sadie said with a sudden smile.

Josh gave her a strange look. "What?"

"Never mind. Just hold me."

"That I can do." His chin rested on her head. "Just don't expect me to let go of you anytime soon."

EPILOGUE

Four counts of first-degree murder. Two counts of insurance fraud. Three counts of aggravated assault and two counts of attempted murder. Add to it the mounting drug and conspiracy charges, and Guillermo had more years in prison than he could possibly live.

Yet Sadie and Josh weren't flying back to Montana for sentencing day.

"Are you okay?" Josh asked.

Sadie squeezed his hand. "I think so. You?"

"Yeah. I think."

She laid her head on his shoulder. She never tired of flying in over her mountains, even after a year of flying back and forth. But this time was different. Croff and Harrison weren't escorting them. That was in part because this trip wasn't trial related. But also, the threat from Guillermo had dwindled to nothing. With Manuel exposing the inner workings of Guillermo's close knit society, those not arrested weren't coming within a mile of Guillermo Vasquez. Even those outside the United States. That left only Salvador on Guillermo's side, but Salvador had a conviction list nearly as long.

Sadie almost felt sorry for Guillermo. Almost. With each new trial, Guillermo seemed to lose more weight and his shoulders sunk a little lower.

Rumor had it that he'd tried to take his life once behind bars. Tried and failed.

Even with the long, drawn out and, at times, emotionally-draining trial, things settled into a quiet rhythm for Josh and Sadie in Tennessee. School. Work. Married life.

They chose to stay in the small house on the hill outside of Knoxville. By some miracle, Josh graduated from UT-Knoxville. He immediately started his MBA. Marcela moved in with them for a time, but only briefly until she found a practical 'Grandma' house. She had high hopes for becoming a grandma and started dropping hints the second Josh and Sadie were married in the summer. So Marcela moved into Josh's little house down the street.

Sadie glanced out the small airplane window and caught the familiar sight of Glacier National Park, now blanketed with a fresh coat of snow. Regardless of how long she and Josh stayed in Tennessee, Montana would always feel like home.

They rented a car and drove through the snow-lined streets of Kalispell, winding toward the familiar road to Whitefish. The closer they got to the mountain, the one that started it all, the more Sadie's stomach fluttered with apprehension. It was the first time she'd been back.

She twisted her wedding ring around and around. "Do you think it will look the same?"

"I don't know. I hope." Josh glanced sideways. "Are you sure you're up for this?"

No. But she nodded anyway.

For their honeymoon, she'd taken Josh to her beloved Whitefish Lake. They spent a week swimming in the glacier-fed water and enjoying the crisp Montana air. Whitefish Lake was now *their* lake, and yet they passed it without a second glance as they headed straight for the mountains.

The snow was stacked two feet high, but the roads were dry and clear. Still, Josh slowed to a crawl as they neared the massive ski lodge that was no longer owned by Guillermo Vasquez.

A thousand memories hit Sadie. Surprisingly, not all were bad. In fact, some of her favorite moments happened at that ski lodge. Playing the piano with Josh. Skiing with the boys. Lunch at the Blue Moose. Even exploring the mountains with her brother, Damien, long before the days of Josh or Guillermo. Like her counselor counseled her to do, she let the good overshadow the bad and not the other way around. She even found herself smiling, hardly believing it had been a year.

"Do you want to go in?" Josh asked.

"No. Maybe later this week we can come back so I can visit my old coworkers. Right now, I just want to get there. I'm anxious to see everyone, and"—she took a quick breath—"it."

They climbed the last few miles in silence. Sam sent Josh a few pictures during construction, but Sadie purposely hadn't looked at them. She wanted her first view to be in person.

Two more bends, and they cleared the last turn.

She saw the roof first: a bright, shiny green roof. Not blackened ashes. Then the rest of the Jackson's cabin came into sight. Logs stacked on thick, pine logs. Massive, framed-in windows surrounding a stone chimney that scaled the two-story cabin. The property was void of trees nearest to the cabin, but since everything was covered in deep snow, no one but Sadie probably noticed anything amiss.

Sam's cabin looked exactly as it once had. Perfect.

Hot tears sprung to her eyes. She blinked rapidly. She was *not* going to cry. She promised as much before leaving Tennessee. This was a happy time. This is exactly what she wanted: a perfectly-restored cabin, four friends restored, and a Christmas Break tradition continued. Tears were uncalled for and most unwelcome.

Besides, Trevor would kick her out if she got all weepy.

Josh pulled to a stop on the road. He leaned forward, straining to see the cabin from the driver's side, giving Sadie time to get her emotions under control.

"It looks the same," she said. "It looks great. Wow. I can't believe…"

Once again, she was overcome. Her eyes started to leak. Stupid hormones. She wasn't sure if it was better or worse that the cabin looked the same as before the fire. At the moment, worse. Trevor would seriously freak if she ruined his ski trip with a lot of blabbering tears. He wouldn't hesitate to uninvite her from here on out. She quickly wiped her cheeks, grateful Josh was distracted.

"Yeah," Josh said. "They did a great job, didn't they? Sister Jackson used the same floor plan. I think the only thing she changed was adding an extra room in the loft. You can't even tell the fireplace was burned."

Sadie's eyes widened. "That's the same chimney? The same rocks?"

"Yeah. They were able to salvage it. It looks great, doesn't it?"

A hundred more memories slammed into her. Like before, not all were bad, but her nose began to drip as well. Trevor was definitely kicking her out. She sniffed quietly and, with a few deep breaths, worked to get in control.

Sam's F-150 was in the driveway, bright chrome grill glittering in the sun. People were waiting for them. A few more breaths and she was able to smile. "Are you ready?" she asked.

When Josh didn't answer, she looked at him. Only then did she realize how tensed his neck muscles were. He was nervous, too. She wasn't the only one with dark memories.

She leaned over and kissed his cheek. "Come on. They're waiting."

They didn't knock. They hadn't called ahead since they couldn't. Even with all that happened, Sam's mom insisted on no technology at her family cabin. Maybe Josh and Sadie should have found a way to warn everyone, because when they entered, the cabin was silent.

Except a galloping black lab.

Rocky bounded across the two-story great room and jumped up on Josh.

"Hey, boy!" Josh said, rubbing the spot behind his ear. "We missed you. How've you been? Where is everyone?"

Rocky's tail wagged like mad.

"I think I hear people," Sadie said. "They must be in the back room."

"Hello?" Josh called. "Hey, we're—"

She grabbed his hand. "Wait. Let's look around a second." She wanted to get her bearings before they were bombarded.

He dropped their bags by the front door, and they wandered into the great room. The carpet was slightly different, but the kitchen looked the same. The countertops and pine cupboards, too.

Sadie pointed with a laugh. "Look, Sister Jackson bought the same uncomfortable couches. I love those couches."

A fire even roared in the stone fireplace.

The only thing noticeably different about the cabin was the picture above the mantle. The Jackson family portrait had been replaced with a new one. Sam's parents sat in the center still, surrounded by their five children and spouses, all with matching outfits—apparently some things would never change. But there were new faces, new babies, and more wrinkles on the adults. More importantly, Sam no longer stood alone.

"Hey," Sadie said, "they let Elizabeth in the picture."

"Probably a safe bet since they're getting married next week."

Sadie smiled sadly. "I wish I could be there for their sealing."

"Don't worry," Josh said. "Once they're done, I'll come out and get you."

"I know. It would just be nice to see a sealing before our own. I'm not sure what to expect."

"Well…it's amazing, and…" Josh slid an arm around her waist. "Like nothing else. And it's not that far away, Mrs. Young."

Exactly one year from the day she was baptized. "I know. And then you're stuck with me forever."

He kissed her nose. "Sounds heavenly."

Sadie studied the portrait another moment. Josh looked up as well, probably wondering why it held her interest. She didn't even totally understand the picture's significance. All she knew is the time she spent staring at Sam's family, she saw the possibility of something better that existed out there somewhere. She just had to find it.

And she had.

Peace I leave with you, my peace I give unto you.

Josh pulled her down to sit by her on the hearth. The rocks were warm, almost hot from the roaring fire. "You know I fell in love with you right here," he said. "Right on this very rock."

"That rock? That one right there?" Her brows rose. "You're awfully sure of yourself."

"Hey, a guy doesn't forget a moment like that." He stroked her cheek from ear to chin, bringing the warmth of the fire to her skin. "I knew then I'd never be able to keep up with you."

"And that's a good thing?"

"That's a great thing. I love you, Sarah Augustina Dawson Young. I will always love you. Thank you for saying yes."

She kissed him softly. "And thank you for—"

A back door opened, and an onslaught of people rushed in. Kevin and Amy. Sam and Elizabeth. Trevor waved with a cute brunette girl Sadie had never met and probably wouldn't see again.

Josh's friends called out warm hellos, but Sadie couldn't answer. Beyond them were other people, two faces from the portrait above the mantle. Sam's parents were there. It was their cabin, so it shouldn't have surprised her, but...

Sadie saw someone more shocking. An eleven-year-old blonde ran out from behind them.

"Sadie! Josh!" Katie said. "You're here! You're here!" She nearly knocked over Sadie in a giant hug.

"KitKat?" Sadie cried. "What are you doing here? I haven't seen you in—" Sadie stopped as Josh's entire family emerged from the hallway. "Kathy. Peter," she whispered. All of them.

The stupid hormones won out. She started to cry.

In an instant, she and Josh were swarmed with friends and family, most of whom Sadie hadn't expected to see. The girls cooed over Sadie's stomach that barely bulged with her new pregnancy, making her glad she had worn the form-fitting sweater—Josh's request—to highlight her condition.

"Have you picked names yet?" Katie asked.

Josh ruffled her hair. "It's way too early. We don't even know if it's a boy or a girl yet." He winked at Sadie. "Although I have a pretty good hunch."

Sadie shook her head. He was definitely sure of himself these days.

Josh's mom grabbed Sadie next and pulled her in for a hug. "I hope it's okay we barged in on your week. We're only staying a day or two, and then we promise to get out of your hair. We just had to see you."

"Not at all," Sadie said. "This is great! We've missed you so much!"

Kevin emerged from behind Josh's mom and gave Sadie a quick hug. "Hey, Ice Woman. How is it to be back?"

Sadie thought about the Jackson's cabin, now full of her favorite people in the world. "Perfect. Absolutely perfect. Where's Amy?"

"Right here." Amy gave Sadie a sideways hug. "You look great, girl."

Sadie smiled. "So do you." They couldn't hug straight on because of Amy's protruding stomach. Amy only had a month left, but she still looked amazing. Sadie hoped she'd be as lucky. "How are you feeling?"

Kevin answered before Amy could. "All she does these days is sleep. Sleep, sleep, sleep." He winked at Sadie. "Sounds like someone I remember."

Amy poked him. "Hey. No teasing the pregnant ladies."

Sam hugged Sadie next and introduced her to his cute fiancée, Elizabeth. From what Sadie knew, Elizabeth seemed like the perfect match for Sam, a little on the shy side but very sweet.

"Did you happen to bring your wedding album?" Elizabeth asked.

"Yeah." Sadie pointed. "It's over there on top of our bags."

"Thanks. I want to show Sam's mom how you added the flowers to the girl's headpieces. Oh, and how you pulled your hair back in that low bun with a few curls. It was so gorgeous." Elizabeth grabbed Sam's hand. "Come look with me."

"But…" Sam started. Sadie could tell he hadn't come on this trip to talk wedding plans—especially girly hair stuff. He wanted to ski.

Kevin slapped Sam on the back. "Just go. You should know by now that when she speaks, you don't question. You just obey."

Josh nodded vigorously. "Rule number one."

Sadie rolled her eyes at both of them. Then she added with a smirk, "By the way, Kev, you should probably go over there, too. Elizabeth has some specific pictures in mind for the wedding. There's one shot of the back of my wedding dress she wants you to copy."

"Oh, yes!" Elizabeth cried excitedly, waving them over. "And the one of Sadie with Josh's brothers in their tuxes. Come look with us, Kevin."

Kevin glared at Sadie as he left. She laughed.

Josh squeezed her hand. "Nice work."

One of her brows rose. "I speak. You obey?"

He grinned. "Something like that."

"Sadie!" Trevor called. He pushed through the group to give her a hug, but at the last second he glanced down. He jumped back like she'd electrocuted him. "Oh, you gotta be kiddin' me. Not you, too!" Trevor held her at a distance, eyeing her pregnant shape. "You did this on purpose!"

"The timing is a little suspicious," Josh said.

"A little? It couldn't be worse!" Trevor shook a finger at Sadie and her stomach. "Don't think this gets you out of snowboarding."

She laughed. "Oh, it does. It most definitely does. I'm spending all week by that bonfire, and there's nothing you can do about it."

"No way. What's your doctor's number? I'm calling to find out what's allowed."

Knowing Trevor, he probably would. But Sadie was saved from answering as Katie tugged on her hand. Katie pulled Sadie and Josh to the center of the group, and everyone quieted down. Even those by the wedding album grew quiet.

"We have one more surprise," Katie said, bouncing with excitement. "Are you ready?"

"I'm not sure I can take any more surprises," Sadie said.

Damien walked out of the back room. "Hey, sis."

"Damien?" Though Sadie had seen her mom every day since things settled down, Damien went back to San Diego to work, which meant she hadn't seen him other than briefly at their wedding.

Damien crossed the room and swept her up in a giant hug. "How's Mom?"

"She's fine. She's great," Sadie said. "What are you doing here?"

Trevor slapped Damien on the back. "Damien got bragging at your wedding about how he could tear it up on the slopes. I couldn't let a challenge like that go, so we decided to let him in on our Christmas Break tradition. You don't mind, do you?"

A week with Damien. A week with her boys. A week with everyone apparently.

"This is…" Sadie's throat burned with pending emotions. She closed her eyes briefly before managing a smile. "This is perfect. Thank you."

Josh's mom clapped her hands over the noise. "Alright everyone. Dinner is about done. Kids, go finish setting the table."

As people headed for the kitchen, Sadie pulled Josh off to the side. She slid her arms around him and laid against his chest. "Thank you," she whispered.

"Hey, I can't take credit for anything," Josh said. "I'm as surprised as you are."

"That's not what I meant. A year ago today I ended up here. And now…" The memories enveloped her. Her eyes lifted to the Jackson's family portrait again. "It's hard to believe how far I've come."

"What is it about that picture?" he asked. "You've loved it since you first came."

"I think it's because I knew they had something, something in their eyes I couldn't put a finger on. But I finally figured out what it is."

"And what's that?"

"Peace. That's what makes them smile the way they do. That's what was missing in my life. But I finally found it." She went up on tiptoes and kissed him. "Because of you. Thank you."

"You're not the only one who found it," Josh said. "Thank *you,* Mrs. Young."

She straightened with a sudden thought. "What do you think of the name Jackson?"

"I like it—for our second kid."

She shook her head with a smile. Josh was convinced their first baby was a girl. From day one, she couldn't convince him otherwise.

"Deal," she said, and she sealed it with another kiss.

THE END

NOTE FROM THE AUTHOR

Thank you for reading *Augustina*! I loved telling this story,
and exploring beautiful places like Montana and Tennessee.
Sadie is a character who has been whispering thoughts to me
for quite some time. I hope you've enjoyed her story!
Explore more on my website about the story, characters,
and music, including the song I arranged called "Still Be My Vision,"
inspired by this story—a medley of "Be Thou My Vision"
and "I Stand All Amazed."

If you enjoyed *Augustina*, please help me spread the word
by leaving a review and telling your friends.
Thanks!

CITIZENS OF LOGAN POND

The economy crashed, the country is floundering, and Carrie Ashworth struggles to keep her siblings alive. She has two jobs in her newly formed, newly outlawed clan: grow crops to feed thirty-six people, and maintain contact with Oliver Simmons, their local patrolman. Carrie's life is almost content when Greg Pierce shows up. A man with the ambition to help them survive. A man determined to hate her. CITIZENS OF LOGAN POND (*Life, Liberty, The Pursuit*) is the bestselling dystopian romance set in the not-too-distant future.

> *"A powerful, realistic story about life and love and the resilience of the human spirit."* - Readers' Favorite
> *"A piece that should be required reading for young and old alike."*
> In D'tale Magazine

NEW FROM REBECCA BELLISTON

Princess Gisela of Steinland was born without color. Albino. When her betrothal to Prince Jerrik of Kronga ends in his death, it starts a ten-year-war her father is determined to win, even if it means bringing her out of hiding to do it. Now the savage Krongon war commander, Bloodless Kristoff, seeks the hearts of the entire royal family, especially Gisela's. Desperate, her father agrees to another alliance that will marry her off to an old brute of a king. Unwilling to be the sacrificial lamb, Gisela goes on the run. Thrown into a battle between three kingdoms, she must fight for her life and the right to be truly loved. Can the girl who started the war find a way to end it?

"This book is a masterpiece! One of my top reads of the year!"
– Min Reads and Reviews

"5 enthusiastic stars . . . An epic story with adventure, romance, deception, and memorable characters. Highly recommend! - Heidi Reads"

ABOUT THE AUTHOR

Rebecca Lund Belliston loves books and music. Even more, she loves to write both. As an author, she writes clean romances with heart-pounding suspense. She also composes religious and classical-style piano and vocal music. When she's not writing, she loves to play tennis, make sarcastic comments, or cuddle up with a good book—usually not at the same time. She and her husband have five children and live in the beautiful state of Michigan, which she loves for eight months of the year (she's a baby about cold weather). Visit her website for characters, maps, music, and other freebies.

CONNECT :
Facebook: @rebeccalundbelliston
Twitter: @rlbelliston
Pinterest: @rlbelliston
Instagram: @rebeccabelliston
YouTube: @rebeccabelliston

SUBSCRIBE: